Copyright © 2023 by Stevie Sparks All rights reserved. No part of this publication may be reproduced, distributed, or transmitted in any form or by any means, including photocopying, recording, or other electronic or mechanical methods, without the prior written permission of the publisher.

ISBN: 979-8-377592-334

This book is a work of fiction. Any names, characters, places, and incidents are either a product of the author's imagination or are used fictitiously. Any resemblance to actual people living or dead is entirely coincidental.

Cover design: Holly at Swoonies Romance Art

Contents

Language	V
Trigger Warnings	VI
1. Annabelle	1
2. Kit	13
3. Annabelle	27
4. Annabelle	38
Sixteen Years Later	46
5. Annabelle	47
6. Kit	54
7. Annabelle	64
8. Kit	68
9. Annabelle	74
10. Kit	89
11. Annabelle	101
12. Kit	110
13. Annabelle	120
14. Annabelle	132
15. Kit	150
16. Kit	171
17. Annabelle	187
18. Kit	199

19. Annabelle	203
Also By Stevie Sparks	213
Emmeline	215
Michael	237
About the Author	246

Language

Please note that this book is written by an English author about British characters. It's therefore written in UK English, which differs slightly from US English. Examples of their differences are:

Realize is Realise
Organize is Organise
Behavior is Behaviour
Spelled can be Spelt
Dreamed can be Dreamt
Jewelry is Jewellery
Anemia is Anaemia
Traveled is Travelled
License can be Licence
Whiskey is Whisky

There are obviously too many examples to catalogue (that's another one) them all here, but just to make you aware ahead of time.

Trigger Warnings

<u>What triggers are **not** in the book?</u>

There is no mention or appearance of rape, attempted rape, child abuse, on-page animal death, dub-con, fatphobia, homophobia, incest, misgendering, needles, paedophilia, racism, self-harm, sexual abuse, sexual harassment, slavery, stalking, suicide, terminal illness, torture, or transphobia.

MAJOR SPOILERS BELOW

∞

<u>What triggers **are** in the book?</u>

Despising the Duke heavily features a storyline that either involves **or** mentions abortion, maternal death after a backstreet abortion, infertility, pregnancy, childbirth, stillbirth, miscarriage, and baby loss. This is in part based on personal experience, and I would like to highlight the vital work that the *Tommy's* charity does in helping people similarly affected.

Additionally, alcoholism, avalanches, drug use, prostitution, physical violence, and war are all mentioned or appear in *Despising the Duke*. There is mention of a deceased cat, but the cat is neither seen nor described.

1

Annabelle

It was just her luck to miss her own bloody coming out ball.

Annabelle could see the funny side, sat there on the outskirts of the bustling dancefloor, her arm in a sling and a crutch at her side, watching the endless dancers swirl around the room.

Mama, however, was *devastated* for her. "Endless opportunities gone down the drain," she whispered, tight-lipped and strained.

"I can still talk to people," Annabelle countered, itching to pick up the *Femina* magazine on the table at which she sat, the intricate faux bois design polished to perfection. Thirty seconds of watching the dancers was all it had taken to bore her. "Perhaps you should go and dance, Mama."

"Perhaps you should think of the consequences before riding an unfamiliar horse at break-neck speeds through Hyde Park!" Mama hissed.

That was fair. It was also nothing she hadn't heard before. Had she been riding Olympia, her beloved mare, Annabelle would have made the jump with ease.

Unfortunately, she had been riding the skittish Phoebus, and he'd skidded to a halt before a fallen log instead of jumping over it, sending Annabelle flying through the air.

"Mama," a deep, familiar voice said, filling Annabelle with relief; an ally. "Lady Dunbeck is asking for you. She's with the Princess of Wales in the orangery."

With a stern look at Annabelle, Mama got to her feet. "Please don't add to your collection of injuries whilst I'm gone, darling girl."

"I'll do my best," she replied, smiling.

Mama bent to kiss Annabelle's cheek. "I just wanted this to be perfect for you. You're the daughter of the Duke of Fox—" Mama caught herself and gestured to

Theo instead. "You're the *sister* of the new Duke of Foxcotte; you could have any husband you wanted."

"Even if I wanted a footman?" she answered slyly, nodding at young Vernon over in the corner, his impressive stature prompting a few double-takes from the nearby guests.

Those tight lips returned with a vengeance.

Annabelle quickly held up her hand in lieu of a white flag. "I'm joking, but I am sorry. I didn't mean for all of your hard work to go to waste."

Nodding, Mama slipped away, holding her head high—as she'd always done, looking every inch the widowed Countess of Foxcotte, still dressed in the black of mourning more than two years after the death of Annabelle's father.

"Are you trying to give her an apoplexy?" Theo muttered, idly perusing through *Femina's* pages. "Or me, for that matter."

Annabelle knew he wasn't talking about Vernon, but about Phoebus throwing her off. Theo had witnessed the entire thing, and she had never seen him as terrified as he had been in those first few moments after her accident, white-faced and trembling, clutching her in his arms as though she had but moments to live.

It was a side of him she'd never seen. The eldest of the four Foxcotte children, he had always very much been the elder statesman. Strict and dutiful. Never putting a foot wrong.

"I wasn't *trying* to be thrown off the horse, you know. It was an accident." An accident that she'd ridden headfirst into, but an accident nonetheless.

Theo's eyebrow tilted up. "Was it? I wouldn't be surprised if it had all been some ploy to avoid marrying Lord Moordale."

Smiling, Annabelle shifted her sling. "You would never make me marry Lord Moordale."

The shadow of a smirk crossed his face. "No, I wouldn't. For his sake. He'd have no hope of controlling you."

Her mouth fell open in outrage. "*Controlling* me?"

"Well someone has to keep you out of trouble," he said, his voice rising above the orchestra's crescendo. "If we married you off to Moordale, you'd have blown up the Houses of Parliament in a fortnight, and we'd all be burning effigies of you on bonfires for the rest of our lives."

She snorted, not caring to mimic a ladylike giggle. "Good, I should like an annual tribute, thank you very much."

"Yes, I'm sure you would." Theo surreptitiously pointed at a passer-by, his voice lowering again. "You see Lord Blackhall? His sister plays the *piano*." He shook his head in mock disgust. "I mean, can you imagine what other men have to put up with?"

Annabelle played along. "Lady Maria over there actually embroiders, can you believe it?" She gave the girl a brief wave upon catching her eye; so far, Lady Maria was the only friend Annabelle had made during her first season.

Theo shot her a grin that would have floored any debutante it was directed at. "No matter how much trouble you are, I'm glad that you're my sister."

"And I'm glad I have a brother that wouldn't dare marry me off to Lord Moordale."

"Only because I'd live in fear of assassination attempts for the rest of my life."

"Attempts?" she asked him seriously, leaning back against the chair. The scarlet fabric depressed beneath her. "You really think it would take me more than one try?"

He chuckled, running his fingers through his black hair—the same shade as her own. "But marrying… It would mean you'd be mistress of your own estate, Annabelle. It needn't be the death sentence you seem to think it is."

Here we go. "Marriage would mean I'm subject to a man's whims—mind and body, need I remind you."

Theo's fingers tapped the table in short, rhythmic bursts. "They're not all like Moordale."

"And what about my involvement with the Women's Social and Political Movement? Do you think I'd find a husband that would approve of my support for women's suffrage?" She shifted her sling once more, quickly becoming irritated at it digging into her neck. Lowering her voice, she leant across the table. "What about you coming to bail me out when I was arrested during the Women's Parliament? I can't imagine a husband being too pleased about that."

Theo looked around quickly, ensuring that they were out of earshot of the surrounding partygoers in the packed Fraser House ballroom. "The older ones? Probably not, but I wouldn't want you to marry an older man anyway."

Her eyebrow twitched. "I don't know. Find me one on his deathbed and I'll be on my back before you can say *think of England*."

Theo turned bright red. He choked, emitting an oddly high-pitched noise for a man so broad. *Michael would have laughed.* He had always been the brother she was closest to. The brother who understood her.

"That's what marriage is, is it not?" she carried on. "You forget that I am the one whose body will be… *invaded*. I know you've attended your friend Aylesbourne's parties, the ones on that floating brothel he calls a yacht. Michael has told me all about them. I know you've—" Annabelle lowered her voice to a whisper "—*bedded* women there, so you cannot turn around and say you're ignorant of the process."

Looking as though he was praying to the heavens for mercy, Theo stood. "I'm going to get some fresh air. Excuse me."

The fight left her as she watched him leave, cutting a ducal figure across the vast ballroom. Already regretting her words, Annabelle sighed. She shouldn't have scared away her only ally in London.

Michael would have understood.

But Michael was also in the army, and was currently on a ship heading to Ceylon as part of his first deployment. The two of them had always been close, with a mutual desire to challenge the rules and bypass boundaries.

Annabelle missed him with an almost palpable ache. She loved Theo, but they didn't have the easy rapport that she and Michael had. And Effie, her only sister, was but four years of age. She was exceedingly sweet, with her bouncing blonde curls and mischievous giggles.

"Have you seen anyone you like?"

A voice pulled her out of her reverie, and Annabelle looked up to find Lady Maria standing in front of her. "I'm sorry?"

Lady Maria took Theo's recently vacated seat. "The eligible lords. Have any of them caught your fancy?"

"Oh." She had met Lady Maria at Queen Charlotte's Ball; a fellow debutante standing in line, nervously awaiting her chance to bow to King Edward and Queen Alexandra. "I haven't looked, to be honest."

Lady Maria did not share Annabelle's hesitancy about marriage. In fact, it seemed to be the girl's sole aim in life, like most of their peers. "Both Lord Stockley and Lord Ravenwood have asked me to dance already," she grinned excitedly, wringing her hands together.

"Congratulations," Annabelle replied, feigning some semblance of excitement. "Were they... interesting?"

"Dull as ditchwater, but what does that matter? My mother tells me Lord Ravenwood's estate is the largest in Cornwall. *And* he's discreet with his affairs."

Annabelle's smile must have been as tight as her mother's had been earlier. "What a catch."

"Truly," Lady Maria leant across the table. "But he's not the big fish of tonight."

Worry crept in for a moment. Lord Ravenwood was a marquess—the only fish larger was a duke, and the only duke here tonight was her brother. "Do tell."

For the love of god, she did not want Lady Maria as a sister-in-law.

"The Duke of Aylesbourne has just walked in," Lady Maria said, clasping her hands together and holding them to her lips.

Just stopping her eyes from rolling back in her head, Annabelle faked a smile. "I thought he was on that expedition to... wherever it is he's supposed to be going." She'd heard Theo on the phone to Aylesbourne the other day, discussing some mysterious expedition. London's courtesans would no doubt be panicking at the upcoming loss of their biggest milch cow.

"The Shackleton one?" Lady Maria gasped. "Good lord, is he? It's not leaving for a few weeks yet though." Lady Maria tapped the empty space on her ring finger. "Just enough time for banns to be read."

"In that case," Annabelle gestured to the dancefloor with her uninjured arm, "happy fishing." *Please leave me alone.* Lady Maria was nice, but they had little as far as common interests, and it was not in Annabelle's nature to be chatty.

Thankfully, Lady Maria took the hint, floating away with a look of glee on her face, shoving past an older gentleman who looked daggers at her, his impressive handlebar moustache twitching.

Annabelle didn't share Lady Maria's happiness, shaking her head almost imperceptibly. "God strewth," she muttered. How could anyone be so happy to marry a man they barely knew? Some of her fellow members of the Women's Social and Political Movement had shared their marital woes with her, and they were *horrifying*.

She had tried to explain to Lady Maria, but the girl would have none of it.

Marriage meant giving a man free reign to one's body. And she couldn't refuse him—after all, she had said "I do" at the altar. That apparently sufficed as consent in perpetuity.

A member of the movement had told of how her husband had used her as a brood mare, despite childbirth nearly taking her life twice over, despite the doctors warning her how a third pregnancy would be a death sentence for her, the husband insisted on getting his precious *heir*. Only the husband's untimely death saved the woman's life.

It was not what Annabelle wanted for her future.

She didn't quite know what she *did* want, but she knew it wasn't that.

It was the first time she was seeing the Fraser House ballroom on show like this. Before coming out, she would have been relegated to the upstairs whilst the ball spilled into the early hours, the house full of women in the kind of clothes Annabelle could only dream of wearing.

Now she was here, Annabelle found it overwhelmingly lacklustre. The run-up to the ball far exceeded the night itself, if anything. Choosing a dress had been wonderful, seeing her vision come to life with the help of Madame Renaud.

But the ball itself?

Even if she was able to dance, the patriarchal undertones of the ball suddenly shone as bright as the gleaming chandeliers above their heads. The London season was nothing but an extended livestock auction for naïve young ladies.

The realisation soured the night.

Annabelle carefully scanned the ballroom for any sign of Mama or Theo. No, she could see Lady Maria dancing with a gentleman easily thrice her age, but neither her mother nor her brother were anywhere to be found. Getting to her feet, she surreptitiously picked up her cane and limped towards the side door that would take her to her father's rose garden.

The cool night air was invigorating after so many hours sat inside watching people dance. To her left, she could see the electric light overflowing from the orangery into the gardens, accompanied by the distant voices of her guests.

Few would know of the rose garden at the side of the house—and fewer still would get there in the dark.

Annabelle was glad. This had been her father's place, and she didn't want it sullied. A slate path to floral paradise, brimming with stone benches and a pavilion drenched in climbing roses. It was his oasis nestled within the bustling streets of Belgravia. She would forever remember him taking his breakfast at the little table and chairs in the corner, surrounded by the buzzing of the bumblebees he was always fascinated by. He had even made a friend of one of the robins, with the rotund bird comfortable enough to take crumbs out of his hand.

She wondered if the robin missed him as much as she did.

Had there been a morning when the robin zoomed over, waiting for Phillip Fraser to come out and start his morning? How long had it taken for the robin to realise he wouldn't be coming?

And why did the thought of that little bird, waiting alone on an empty table, nearly have her in tears?

Before her first tear had fallen, her injured foot caught on a plant pot, sending a shard of pain through her ankle. Annabelle let out a shriek as she fell, bracing for an unforgiving impact.

But it didn't come.

Strong, capable arms caught her, and for a brief, utterly insane moment, Annabelle thought it might have been her father.

"Are you bloody mad, woman?" her rescuer asked, briskly shoving her back on her unsteady feet.

Maybe not, then.

In the dim moonlight, Annabelle drew herself up to her fullest height, catching a hint of her rescuer's irritatingly attractive features. Her handsome rescuer looked to be older than her, but not by much. A head taller, with overlong black hair, a straight nose, and narrowed eyes.

He pointed towards the door she had just come through, his arm thick with muscle. "Go back inside before you break your other arm."

"Thank you for your assistance," she said sweetly, biting back the snide reply she wanted to make. She was alone in the dark with a strange man, and her friends in the Women's Social and Political Movement held far too many horror stories for her to ignore the risk inherent in her situation. "But I'd rather sit outside for a moment."

He rolled his dark eyes. "I'm sure you would."

Now it was Annabelle's turn to frown. "What's that supposed to mean?"

"It means if your mother or sister or whoever is going to come outside, *discover* the two of us sitting alone together in the darkened garden, and cry scandal in an attempt to force me to propose, your scheme is going to fail."

Annabelle's guffaw of disbelief carried through the night. She took a seat on the stone bench at the edge of the garden, taking care to look down her nose at the interloper. "For your information, this is my *father's* garden. I am perfectly entitled to be here, but you are not, *sir,*" she spat.

The animosity fled his features almost instantly. "You're Annabelle."

"*Lady* Annabelle," she amended coldly.

"Thank god for that." A grin curved his lips. Bloody Norah, he was attractive. Her chest fluttered at the very sight, as much as she wanted to hate him. "My apologies," he sat down on the stone bench next to her, lazily leaning his broad shoulders against the brickwork behind them. "I've been accosted by young ladies and their mothers since walking through the door. I was afraid you were going to start undressing as part of some marriage scheme."

Annabelle tilted her head, looking him up and down. "Not for you I wouldn't."

He seemed to take offence at that. "What's wrong with me?"

"Marriage as an institution is inherently patriarchal, and benefits men almost exclusively. If I were to enter into a marriage contract, I would want my husband to be exceptional." Annabelle held his gaze with a slow blink, letting the insult land.

The intruder smiled at that. "You're Lady Annabelle, all right. What would this *exceptional* husband of yours need then?"

"To look upon women as equals, and to apply the principles of equity to his everyday life." Sadly, she reached out to touch one of the roses growing in the plant pot next to her; a vivid peachy blossom that was as smooth as silk. "And Westminster Abbey."

"You want your husband to own Westminster Abbey?" he said sarcastically.

Ignoring his remark, Annabelle took the chance to talk about her father. Nowadays, the opportunities were coming fewer and far between, and it kept him alive a little longer. At least in her memories. "My first memory is of my father at Westminster Abbey. He was receiving the Order of the Bath for his service during the Boer War, and he told me that, barring Scarlett Castle, it was his favourite building in the world. And I promised him that one day I would be married there, so he had the opportunity to visit again."

It was silly. A young girl trying to please the father she adored—and who adored her in turn. But she'd never forgotten her promise.

The stranger's expression softened. "You shall have a wedding fit for a queen, in that case. I say, the title rather suits you."

"The title?"

"Yes, there's something distinctly queenly about you. From what Theo and Michael have told me over the years, little queen, you are rather… aloof. Is that not how queens are supposed to be? An ideal, elevated above the masses."

"Little queen?" she asked, attempting to dodge the compliment.

His smile was adoringly crooked. "Well, you are quite small."

"Only compared to you." Annabelle elbowed him in the ribs with her good arm, disconcerted at how muscular his torso was. "Although your ability to catch falling women is appreciated, your assumption that any woman would be clambering to marry you does reek of priggishness."

For a moment, Annabelle thought his face would contort into outrage, but instead he laughed. "It's like you've known me all my life. Truly remarkable." He pulled a hip flask from his pocket and took a swig before offering it to Annabelle.

"My mother would scold me," she smirked, taking a hefty gulp and savouring the whisky's burn.

"I have it on good authority that you've been sneaking sips of whisky and port since you were a girl, little queen."

She blinked, almost forgetting about her sling digging into her neck. "You really do know Michael then."

"I really do know Michael. And Theo." Although she was surprised Michael had told him of her sneaking sips of alcohol.

"My mother would die if she knew the great Sir Prig knew of my unladylike behaviour."

"The great Sir Prig even gave Theo a lift down to bail you out of jail after the Mud March."

Annabelle leant back in surprise. "I'm amazed he told you about that. Theo stressed that only he and I could ever know or else my prospects would be ruined."

Sir Prig waved a lazy hand, looking up at the sky. "Your prospects are safe with me, Lady Annabelle." He pointed upwards with a sigh. "Do you see that light in the sky? The bright yellow-orange one?"

She lifted her chin. There it was, a little ball of light in an ocean of twinkling stars. "I do."

"That's Jupiter."

Annabelle tore herself away from the stars to shoot him a doubtful look. "How could you possibly know that?"

"How does anyone know anything?" Sir Prig shifted closer on the stone bench, until she could feel his thigh pressing against hers. "I was taught." He looked skywards once more, bending closer to point her in the right direction. "And that smaller one over there. Do you see?"

His darkly alluring scent filled her lungs. She nodded, chancing another glance at him.

"That's Saturn," he murmured, looking like a man in his element. "You can usually only see it when the sky is darkest."

Annabelle found another one. A white one, this time. "What about that? Is that Venus? It can't be Mars, it looks far too pale."

"*That*, Lady Annabelle, is the North Star. The saviour of many a sailor."

"How so?"

"The North Star points towards true north. If sailors have lost their way, all they need to do is use the North Star to orient themselves once more. To sail towards home."

Hardly a foolproof plan, in Annabelle's opinion. "And if they pick the wrong star?"

Sir Prig lifted his arm in the air. "Do you see that constellation there? The Plough."

"Of course. Everyone knows the Plough."

"Well, if you're in England you use the edge of the Plough and draw a straight line up from it; the next star you come to will be the North Star. And there it will always be. Even Shakespeare wrote of it. '*I am as constant as the northern star.*' Whereas the Greeks called the constellation to which it belongs the Dog's Tail. No matter how far back humankind stretches, we have always looked to the stars and wondered."

Annabelle didn't find Sir Prig to be quite so priggish anymore. "And have you always looked to the stars?"

"Ever since I was a boy." He rested against the wall behind them once more with a nostalgic expression. "My uncle is a bit of a scholar; he taught me everything. Astronomy, zoology, evolution, botany. He's a remarkable man. I'm lucky to have him."

"And your father?" she frowned.

"Both of my parents died when I was a boy. Russian Flu. But my uncle loved me as his own, for which I'm grateful." He let his head loll to the side. "I know your father passed the year before last. I'm terribly sorry. He was a good man."

The tears threatened to return then, as though they'd simply been waiting for the right opportunity to escape. The first year without him had been the hardest. Christmas. His birthday. Their annual hunting trip up at Aviemore. The grief had been ever present then, but now it liked to sneak up on her. "This was his rose garden," Annabelle bit down on her bottom lip to stop its downturn. "He adored spending time here."

"I'm sorry," he cleared his throat and stood. "I didn't know. I shouldn't have intr—"

She grabbed his hand, pulling him back towards her and ignoring the sudden pounding in her chest at his touch. "Don't leave. I don't find your company all that awful, Sir Prig. And I enjoy your teachings of the stars."

"I shall write to you of them, if you like."

Annabelle laughed softly. "Are you going to give me nightly explanations of what is above my head?"

"If that is what you wish, little queen." Teeth flashing in a smile, Sir Prig continued. "My uncle has a garden dedicated to my aunt, and I know he finds comfort spending time there, breakfasting amongst the bluebells. He's rather devoted to them, actually."

"My mother is the same with the rose—" The sound of the door grating along the slate stopped her in her tracks.

"Annabelle?" Her mother's worried voice came. "Annabelle, darling?"

Speak of the devil.

She motioned to Sir Prig to hide, and he quickly disappeared behind a bustling trellis of climbing roses. "I'm here, Mama."

"Oh thank *heavens*, I was so worried." The bottom of Mama's black mourning gown whisked across the stone as she came into view, light pouring from the open door behind her. "I half expected to find you in a heap somewhere, broken and bruised."

"I'm fine, I just…" Annabelle trailed off, knowing Sir Prig could hear every word, but then decided to tell the truth. "I wanted to sit in Papa's rose garden tonight," she said sombrely.

Mama took a long, trembling breath. "I so wished he could have danced with you to open the ball."

Annabelle gestured to her cane as she stood. "Perhaps it was better this way, with my ankle and all. There was no way anyone could take his place."

Her mother slipped her arm around her waist, slowly guiding her towards the back door. "Well… that's one way to look at it. I'd still prefer if you weren't injured, though."

Sighing, she lay her head on her mother's shoulder. "I suppose."

Just as she was about to close the door behind her, Annabelle couldn't resist the urge to glance back.

There stood Lord Prig, half hidden in the shadows. His smile was compassionate, but his wink restarted that unfamiliar fluttering in her chest.

And Annabelle thought of nothing else for the rest of the night.

2

Kit

The door of the dusty bedroom Kit had claimed as his own flew open, wafting a fresh coating of sparkling dust motes through the air and into his lungs. Emerging from the choking layer, Kit glanced up to see his cousin Anthony brandishing a letter with a familiar hand inscribing *Sir Prig* on its face.

Little queen.

She was late. Her first letter of the day should have arrived hours ago. The footmen had been over twice to collect it, only to return empty-handed. They were up to three letters a day now, bandying them back and forth across Berkeley Square.

Kit bit back his smile. She was everything Theo and Michael had said she was—and so much more. Feisty and fearless, with endless passion for her beliefs.

"Dare I ask why you and Foxcotte have been squirrelling letters back and forth for the past couple of months?" Anthony tapped the envelope with a smug grin. "Although I do approve of the new moniker." He looked around with his nose scrunched up. "Not so much of the new bedroom."

Kit snatched it out of Anthony's paint-smudged hand before his cousin rested against the windowsill, peering out at Berkeley Square. "I can see the stars," he pointed at the impressive skylight above their heads. "Why would I not want to move to this room?"

Plus, it allowed him to remain true to his word; every night, he wrote to Annabelle of what he could see, telling her of the constellations and the planets.

Anthony pulled a second letter from his jacket. "I saw Shackleton at White's. He wanted me to give you this. Please tell me you're still not thinking about that blasted expedition."

"I'm debating it," Kit took it, his gaze flicking from letter to letter. What he was *debating* was not whether or not he was going on the expedition, but how to break the news of his upcoming departure to Anthony and Uncle Eric. "How is your painting going?"

"I'm not quite there yet," Anthony sighed. He'd been working on a landscape painting of the gardens at Campbell House as part of his final project at the Central School of Art and Design. "I've painted myself into a pickle with the colours."

"I wish I could offer some assistance but—"

"Thanks but no thanks?" Anthony suggested.

"*Quite.*"

"You know," Anthony said, chucking his thumb towards the window, "you can just go and speak to him. Their London house is right *there*. Or has Lady Foxcotte finally banned you after you vomited in the middle of her ball last year?"

Embarrassment scrunched his face up. "God, I hope Uncle Eric didn't record that in his journal."

"My father records *everything* in his journal."

"I know," Kit groaned, carefully placing the letter next to the book he was reading. It was one of Annabelle's favourites, apparently. *A novel every feminist should read,* she had said. "But no, I haven't been banned." Nor was he writing to Theo, but he didn't correct Anthony's assumption.

"Then go and talk to the man. The footmen have been running back and forth like pigeon post. My father's valet says they're sick of it."

"Da Silva is a troublemaker."

Anthony sat on an old trunk, wiping his finger across the layer of dust accumulating on its surface and pouting in distaste. As though he wasn't covered in oil paint. "Oh, no doubt. The man is the biggest fop in London."

Kit smirked. "I don't know about that. Have you seen the King lately? I bet he's got his entire funeral planned out, with flags and bunting—made only by Poole & Co, of course."

Another ugly grimace. "In which case, God save the King."

"Don't turn into a monarchist on me now, Anthony," Kit leant back, his chair balancing on two legs.

"If Princess Mary heard you say that, she'd be *furious* with you."

"She's my godmother," Kit waved his dismissal. "She's contractually obliged to forgive me. Plus I don't think she's particularly fond of her father-in-law's frivolous expenses anyway."

Anthony snorted. "Is anyone?"

"Don't let your father hear you say that."

Anthony pointed a stern finger at him. "Don't rat me out again."

Kit threw his hands up in outrage. It had been perhaps the sole point of contention between him and Anthony during their shared childhood: Anthony had scratched a tea caddy owned and used by Nelson on HMS Victory during the Battle of Trafalgar. "That was one time! Mrs Crawford threatened to have me sent up in front of Bell."

"Bell was harmless and we both know it. We literally watched him nursing injured fledglings back to health every single year."

"We were also told that Bell would come and take us away if we were naughty," Kit scoffed, as he had done every time Anthony had presented his argument. "Based on the knowledge we had at the time, you would have ratted me out as well."

"I would have held my tongue."

"Not against Mrs Crawford you wouldn't. She literally marched me down to the line of pet graves." It had been terrifying, to be told that the pet graves weren't actually pets at all, but the graves of naughty little boys that Bell had *dealt with* over the past fifty years.

This was where Anthony's argument faltered, as it always did. Rather than admit it, however, he changed the subject. "Awful woman."

"At least it got her fired." Mrs Crawford's strategy to extract information had worked, but she hadn't counted on Kit being traumatised enough to go crying to Uncle Eric. Their housekeeper had been gone by the end of the day, being frog-marched down the driveway and dumped at the nearest bus stop.

"I bet she'll haunt Eilean Rìgh the first chance she gets."

Kit narrowed his eyes, although the thought of Mrs Crawford haunting their ancestral home did make him feel slightly ill. "Don't bring that evil upon us." He paused. "Is she even still alive? She might already be dead."

"No," Anthony said conclusively. "People that awful always live forever. In which case, the new Lady Poynton will be joining her."

That surprised him. Poynton was a Casanova if ever there was one. "I didn't know he was getting married."

"Neither did he," Anthony bit out.

Kit finally stopped teetering on the chair and let its front legs fall to the floor with a *thump*. "I don't understand."

"Do you remember young Miss Perry?"

The name did ring a bell. "Wasn't that the one who pulled you into a cupboard at Lady Foxcotte's ball last year?"

"The very same. Well, turns out she had an end goal in mind: to have her mother catch her and cry scandal."

"Ah."

Anthony's eyebrow perked up. "Exactly. Poynton was hauled in in the same net."

"I mean…" Kit looked at it from another perspective. "He took the bait. He was attempting to seduce the daughter of a viscount. What did he expect? Playing with fire from the beginning. You were simply lucky you weren't burnt."

"My father has warned me about it," Anthony replied seriously. "His friend's son was ambushed by a young woman as well."

Kit pushed the book he'd been reading towards his cousin. "You should read this, it's enlightening."

Anthony's eyes nearly popped out of his head when he read the title—and the author's name, along with the Foxcotte coat of arms stamped in the inner sleeve. "God al-bloody-mighty, has Foxcotte's radical of a sister infected him and now it's spreading through his group of friends like wildfire?"

"She's hardly a radical," Kit said, prickling with annoyance.

"She was arrested at a suffragette march and force-fed."

"She was only held until Foxcotte got there. I was with him the entire time. It was less than three hours after the Mud March. She was barely there long enough to get peckish, let alone starved and force-fed."

"I'm not talking about the Mud March. She's been arrested before." Anthony picked up the book with a sceptical expression, slowly flicking through the well-thumbed copy. "And as far as I know, Foxcotte was never told."

Kit couldn't help glancing through the window—through which Foxcotte House was easily visible. "When was this?"

"Last year. Da Silva knows the detective inspector who oversaw her release."

"Da Silva knowing anyone who doesn't work in *haute couture* is unbelievable on its own," Kit responded tartly. "Let alone someone who works in a prison."

"Prison isn't the same thing as a jail," Anthony replied.

"A minor technicality."

"Regardless, at some point last year she was held at the comfort of His Majesty's Justice and force-fed. They only released her because one of the prison officers was told by another suffragette that she was the daughter of a duke. At which point they presumably shat themselves and shoved her out the door."

"To be honest, I still don't believe anything past the fact that Da Silva knows someone who works in a prison."

Anthony seemed to take personal offence at that. "It's Da Silva's son, if you must know."

Kit's mouth fell open far enough to catch flies. "He has a *son*?"

"Is that so outlandish?"

Kit paused. "I don't know how to put it kindly, but I always thought of him as, well, an invert."

"An invert?" Anthony asked innocently.

"An... unusual sort?"

"A what?"

For god's sake, was his cousin as thick as a plank? "He... enjoys a bit of fruit cake."

The snort that ripped from Anthony's throat must have been painful, but the booming laughter that came next had Kit feeling like a fool. "I'm sorry," Anthony said, wiping tears from his eyes. "He enjoys a bit of fruit cake," he said, giggling between the words. "Fruit cake." The snorts renewed themselves.

Kit couldn't help the reluctant grin that tugged at his lips. "You're such a twat."

"I wanted to see where you'd run out of ideas," his cousin replied, tackling residual giggles as they arrived. "But no. Da Silva has a son. The son is in the Met. The son knows that Foxcotte's sister was force-fed. She's a radical, no question, with the force-feeding to prove it."

"So it seems," he said, pursing his lips. "You *should* read this though. Darwin was once thought to be a radical, was he not?"

"As was Francis Burdett, now I think on it," Anthony sighed reasonably, picking at his sleeves. "Without him, working class men wouldn't have a vote at all."

"History progresses, and so must the people that live through it."

"Albeit reluctantly. Some more reluctantly than others, mind." Anthony shared a long-suffering glance with Kit. "If you hear the things Lord Curzon spews out over Parliament, it makes *me* look like the radical. Man's a menace. I pity his wife. If he has one."

"Now imagine how much of a menace *you'd* be if your views were neither heard nor respected."

"If I was a woman, I would listen to my husband."

Now it was Kit's turn to snort. "No, you wouldn't."

"No, I wouldn't," Anthony grinned. "Can you imagine? I'd be the *ugliest* wife in history."

"*Boys!*" Uncle Eric's voice boomed from downstairs. "We need to leave in an hour."

They looked at each other, with Kit feeling the anticipation rising in his stomach just as Anthony rolled his eyes.

Tonight, little queen.

⸻

Lord Linwood's ball truly was a sight to behold, and from where Kit sat, he had the best view of all. Through the rosy haze of cigar smoke, wall to ceiling windows allowed the occupants of the upstairs smoking room to overlook the ballroom below, casting judgement upon the guests.

Lord Poynton and his new wife were in attendance, although neither looked particularly pleased to be there. So too were Lord and Lady Knaresborough, their Berkeley Square neighbours.

It was not them that Kit was eagerly looking for, however.

"I've heard Shackleton has nearly gained the funding he needs to launch his expedition to reach the South Pole," Sir Humphrey Hodge piped up, yanking Kit's concentration away from the windows. He glanced down at the cards in his hand, resting his elbows on the table's green baize top, having long since lost track of the game. "Bound to end in disaster. They've little-to-no experience—highlighted by Shackleton's choice of ship. The damn thing is a dinghy compared to Scott's ship, and don't get me started on the men."

"Aye," the man sitting next to Uncle Eric nodded, throwing a meaningful look at Kit. "I've also heard that a certain duke has signed up to go along."

Fuck.

Uncle Eric laughed, a deep boom across the table. "You've been paying heed to the idle gossip of young ladies, no doubt."

"As a matter of fact," the man replied, affront in his voice, "I overheard Shackleton himself discussing it. I am not one to pay attention to the chattering of women, Lord Eric."

The air seemed to still as Uncle Eric's alarmed gaze locked onto Kit, his bald head flashing in the electric lights. "That's not true, is it, Kit?"

This had not been how he'd wanted to break the news to Uncle Eric. He was bound to be mad, but what an opportunity—Kit would be one of the very first men to reach the South Pole. He was young. He was fit. He was an excellent navigator. He'd always had a taste for adventure.

"It's true. This is my chance to be part of history, uncle."

Uncle Eric's face fell in shock, his eyes owlishly round. "My boy, do you know how many men have died trying to make history?"

"I'll be fine. How often have I gone hiking across the Highlands for days and weeks at a time?"

"In Scotland!" Uncle Eric threw his cards down. "This is dangerous, Kit. Too dangerous *by far*. I forbid it."

The judgement of the men in earshot pressed down on his shoulders, but Kit stood firm. He was an adult. "In what world does a lord tell a duke what to do?"

The moment he said the words, he regretted them.

Uncle Eric jolted back, as though the words brought with them a physical impact. Kit said nothing as his uncle stood and made his way over to the door, laying his hand on Kit's shoulder as he passed.

The same hands that had wiped his tears when he'd had nightmares as a boy. The same hands that Kit had clutched with terror on the day he first started at Eton. The same hands that had stroked his forehead when he was sick. The hands that carried with them nothing but safety and kindness and love.

Kit itched to move, but he forced himself to stay in his seat for the next hand, feeling the judgement of the other men all the while. It hadn't been the ideal place for Uncle Eric to discover he would be going on Shackleton's expedition, but at least it was out in the open now.

The corner of his vision promised a long-awaited diversion from the smoking room and the low murmuring of masculine conversation.

Lady Annabelle Fraser had just crossed over to the tables heaving with canapés, wearing a long, sleek dress that looked as though it had been spun from liquid silver.

Kit threw his cards down on the table, ignoring the protests of the other players, and headed for the door without a word.

Lord Linwood's London home was a maze of glaring familial portraits and antique oddities, including a suit of armour that Linwood swore one of his ancestors had worn at both the Battle of Stamford Bridge and the Battle of Hastings.

Theo was obsessed with the thing, and even Kit could admit it was mildly interesting, but his quarry lay two floors beneath it.

By the time Kit reached the ground floor, Lady Annabelle was nowhere to be found. Her mother, Lady Foxcotte, stood at the edge of the dancefloor in a deep purple dress that was almost black. To Kit, she looked strange without her husband beside her. The couple had always been inseparable whenever he'd seen them—usually at rugby games at Eton or Cambridge, in which both he and their second son, Michael Fraser, would play.

It was madness, he knew. She was Theo and Michael's *sister*, and entirely off-limits, but he had spent the past few weeks thinking of little else. His friends had mentioned her in passing over the years; he knew she was a passionate feminist who wasn't afraid to fight for her beliefs. Michael had shared a little more, giving him enough snippets to have collected a reasonable measure of her personality, but now he viewed them all in a different light, combing through his memories to gather any information he might have missed the first time around.

Taller than most men, Kit's gaze shone straight across the crowd, finally finding who he was looking for: Theo.

Slicing a path through the ballroom, Kit made a beeline for his friend—and exerted a burst of speed when he realised that his hopes hadn't been for nought.

In conversation with Theo, Lady Annabelle surveyed the ballroom with a raised chin, as though she had assessed everything around her and found it wanting. She held a glass of champagne between both hands, her cast having been removed since the last time he'd seen her, although Kit could see a walking stick leant against the wall next to her.

Theo met his eyes as he approached, and Kit nodded. "Foxcotte." And then *she* finally saw him. "Lady Annabelle."

"Sir Prig," she said, mischief rising in her eyes. "I'm surprised they let *you* in here."

Kit barked out a short laugh. No one spoke to him like this. *No one*. Not even Anthony. "I'm quite good at getting into places I'm not supposed to be."

Theo cleared his throat, his suspicious eyes darting between Lady Annabelle and Kit. "Sir Prig?"

"The first time Lady Annabelle and I met I may have mistakenly assumed she was attempting to trap me into marriage," he explained, "unaware that she is more averse to matrimony than myself."

"Albeit for completely different reasons," Lady Annabelle interjected.

"I wasn't aware that the two of you had met."

"It was only brief," Kit eyed the walking stick propped against the wall. "Are you able to dance, Lady Annabelle?"

Lady Annabelle opened her mouth to respond, but Theo got there first. "Absolutely not," he decreed. "You're barely back on your feet as it is."

Her eyebrow hitched up, as though amazed her brother would dare speak over her. "A walk in the garden then. Lord Linwood has an extensive path running through it. It's quite level." She pursed her lips. "Perhaps you can teach me more about the stars, Sir Prig."

"I would love to." Kit pulled out his silver pocket watch inscribed with the Campbell coat of arms; a gift from his uncle. "It's early enough that we might be able to see Mars and Venus tonight."

Lady Annabelle thrust her champagne glass into Theo's hand and sauntered towards Kit, taking his proffered arm. "What a treat."

Just as he began to walk, Theo pressed a hand to Kit's chest, halting him in his tracks. "Look after my sister," he said quietly, the threat evident.

"I will," Kit said sincerely. He didn't speak again until they'd bypassed the swarming dancefloor, until the swell of the cool night air rolled over them in a refreshing, invigorating wave.

Lady Annabelle had been right about Linwood's garden; lights illustrated the carefully landscaped collection of flora blooming before them. Water lilies and roses and poppies abounded, painting the night with a plethora of reds and whites, sprinkled with the last of the daylight as the sun sank below the horizon.

They were not the only couple traversing the paths, attempting to escape from the sweltering heat of Linwood's Eaton Square townhouse.

Whilst the scene was a pretty one, the gas lights made it difficult to see the stars.

"Are you able to go this way?" Kit asked, pointing to a sloping path off to the side, past a swaying willow tree. Gentle music filled the night, drifting up from the illuminated bandstand at the base of the path. "Or is it too steep?"

"It's a bit steep for me at the moment, I'm afraid." Annabelle smirked. "Sir Prig, are you trying to separate us from the other partygoers?"

Instead, he steered them down a dimly-lit path that would lead deep into the garden's bowels. Kit's eyes slid over to hers, the implications of her question hitting him. "A lady should not be thinking of such things."

"A lady should *always* be thinking of such things, because not all men are as honourable as my brothers." Despite her protests, she let Kit lead her down the deserted path. "A man may act as he wishes, but the moment the slightest doubt is cast upon a young woman's virtue, her prospects are ruined."

He glanced back, ensuring that Theo wasn't tailing them. "Then why are you coming with me?"

"Perhaps I wan—" Lady Annabelle cut herself off as Lord Linwood himself emerged from the darkness at the end of the path, a short, thick man with fiery red hair.

Linwood inclined his head to them as he passed. "Aylesbourne. Lady Annabelle."

Pausing beneath the cover of an enormous oak, Kit responded in kind. "Linwood."

But Annabelle remained frozen until Linwood strode out of earshot. "Aylesbourne?" she whispered, looking at him as though he'd transformed into some hideous creature.

"What? Did you think Sir Prig was my real name?"

"I thought you were…" Lady Annabelle hissed, before the words exploded out of her, "*decent.*"

He was confused. "Why am I suddenly not decent?"

"Because Michael has told me everything that occurs on your *yacht*! Which, by the way, sounds more like a floating brothel than anything else. Forgive me if I mistook you for a star-gazing academic."

Kit sincerely hoped that Michael hadn't told her *everything*, or else his dignity would be in shreds by the end of the night. In fact, he was slightly annoyed Michael had told her anything at all. "I may have academic interests but how I spend my time outside of Cambridge is my own business."

An unladylike snort raced through the garden. "How you spend your time is the business of every gossip in London. I have heard that you stuff your yacht so full of prostitutes that it's a wonder it hasn't sunk. I have heard how your room at Cambridge nearly went up in flames. I have heard how you deflowered a debutante last year on her father's piano, so forgive me if my impression of you has hit rock bottom."

"I did not deflower anyone on their father's piano," he hissed back.

Lady Annabelle rolled her eyes. "Debauched, then." She waited for his response, but there was none he could give. "You can't even deny it, can you? Do you have any idea of the damage you did to her? Her prospects went up in flames that night. You *ruined* her life, and yet you're still welcomed to balls with open arms, and where is she?"

"In a cottage in the Lake District, *exactly* where she wants to be." He pulled Lady Annabelle closer, holding her arm. "And if you knew anything other than gossip, you would know that Lady Phyllis was about to be married to a man she despised. The piano *debauchery*, as you so elegantly described it, was her idea. Her fiancé walking in on me with my head between her legs? Her idea."

Lady Annabelle's plump lips formed a perfect *o*.

"Yes, I may throw ill-advised parties, but I am young. I am rich. I am a duke. I am perfectly entitled to live my life how I please. The women at my parties are all consenting, well paid adults." Kit couldn't help the grin that stretched his lips. "And I can assure you they leave well pleasured indeed."

But the naïve young lady in front of him was clearly only focused on one thing. "Your head between her legs?"

Kit's frustration morphed into something else as they stared at each other, until the heat inside him bubbled to the surface. Lady Annabelle was no less affected, refusing to break their connection, even as her chest heaved.

She spoke first. "What.. what exactly were you doing there?"

"Licking." His tongue brushed over his lips involuntarily, his eyes raking her body. "Sucking," he rasped. "Drinking."

With any other deb, Kit would have expected a short, horrified retreat, followed by a shouting match with her father. But she only drew closer. "What does that feel like?"

Fucking hell. His cockstand was surely about to burst through his trousers. Kit dragged his fingers from Lady Annabelle's wrist to her neck, only stopping when he reached her bottom lip. "Have you ever touched yourself, little queen?"

Once again, another deb would have fled, but not Lady Annabelle; she simply stared, like a disappointed queen glaring at her subject. "Many times."

Kit broke, turning away lest her stare burn him.

"Last night I thought of you."

His head shot up again, finding her gaze had never left him. "You what?" he whispered.

"When I touched myself last night, I closed my eyes and pretended it was you touching me." Her hand pressed against his chest, meandering upwards. "I thought of your fingers, your face." Lady Annabelle pulled his head down, until her lips were at his ear. "Your cock."

That was it. Kit manhandled her backwards, pushing her up against the thick trunk of the oak tree sheltering them and grabbing her cheeks with both hands. "I thought of you too."

He descended, his lips seizing hers with a casual arrogance, but her enthusiasm surprised him. Instead of the gentle sighs he'd encountered elsewhere, Annabelle bit back, warring with him for control. His lips journeyed down her neck, leaving a hot, wet trail of possession.

Even then, Annabelle wasn't placid, she gripped his hair with one hand and explored his shoulders with the other, running her hands over his frame as though she couldn't get enough of him.

"Theo and Michael would kill me for this," Kit said, his lips against her neck. Her hands went to the buttons of his trousers, caressing his length through the fabric. Groaning with pleasure, he halted her hand in his larger one. "What are you doing?"

That eyebrow flicked up again. "If you're allowed to sow your wild oats, then why can I not do the same?"

"Because your body does not produce *oats*."

Her rolled eyes suggested she was disappointed with his answer. "Fine. If you can fuck anything that moves, why can't I?"

Kit almost choked at such language coming from a gently bred young lady. "And yet you judged me for precisely that." He paused when the realisation struck him, a laugh clipping the back of his throat. "You're not being judgemental at all, are you? You're *jealous*."

"I am no such thing," she spat.

But then his own jealousy crept in. "Does that mean you've slept with men already?"

"No."

There was brief relief followed by a sobering realisation. "You mean… you want *me* to take your virginity? Now? Against a tree at the bottom of Linwood's garden?"

Annabelle's jaw shifted to the side. "I won't apologise for wanting sex, Aylesbourne. I have no intention of marrying."

"Call me Kit," he said softly, letting the back of his knuckles trace her high cheekbones. "If you want to give me your virginity, I think you've earned the right to call me by my name." He hated himself for what he was about to say, but it had to be done. Even he wasn't enough of a scoundrel to take her up on her offer. "I can't take your virginity tonight, Annabelle."

She hardened as quickly as his cock had at her touch. "I don't believe I've given you leave to refer to me without my title."

His heart pulsed; she'd gotten underneath his skin far too quickly, but he was helpless to stop it. "Mark my words, however, I *will* take it."

"When?" she whispered, her words throaty with desire.

"When I can give you more than just a quick fuck," he said against her lips in a brief kiss. *When I can give you everything I have.*

"That is *not* an answer, Aylesbourne."

"I said to call me—"

Annabelle's nostrils flared as she shot him a saucy grin. "The first time I call you Kit will be when I'm moaning your name in pleasure."

Just the image of it had his cock leaking with arousal. "In which case I will endeavour to plan quickly." Even more quickly than he'd already intended to anyway.

"Good," she bit her lip, giving his cock a quick squeeze. "Because I won't wait forever."

His commitment to the expedition came back to bite him a second time around. "I have a month left on British soil." Although Annabelle was making him question that obligation, but then she had no intention of marrying. Upon returning from his expedition, perhaps she would feel differently.

Because with every letter they wrote, with every interaction they shared, Kit found he was increasingly questioning his aversion to marriage.

Lady Annabelle tilted her head. "The expedition you mentioned in your letters."

Kit nodded. "I wish to go down in history. Like Francis Drake was to circumnavigation or Livingstone was to Africa. This is the last unknown; the last great wilderness." He took her hand. "I shall see the stars as no man ever has before. Did you know there is even talk of a southern aurora?"

Her lips pursed in a smile. "It does sound splendid."

"Give me the month, little queen."

"Very well, Sir Prig. The month is yours." She pulled him down into a captivating kiss. "But on your own head be it."

The longer Kit thought on it, the more precariously attached that head seemed to be. Not only had he kissed the younger sister of his oldest friends, he planned to deflower her into the bargain.

If Theo or Michael ever found out, they'd have his head on a spike.

3

Annabelle

The yacht's speed whipped the crisp sea breeze through her hair as seagulls screeched in the distance. Theo had a firm grip on her elbow whilst she stood at the *North Star's* bow, relishing the light misting of salt water on her skin.

A particularly large wave brought a squeal of glee from her lungs, and her shriek of laughter mirrored those of the distant gulls. "This is amazing!" she cried.

Theo's disagreement was whipped away with the wind. "This is insanity."

But Annabelle didn't care. She had never felt more alive than she had sprinting across the waves, occasionally glancing back to Kit steering in the wheelhouse, smiling from ear to ear.

They were returning to Southampton, where the *North Star* was currently being moored.

Because today had been organised by Sir Prig. It had been enjoyable, to be sure. Standing at the helm of a boat flying across the sea had Annabelle wanting to explore further, to truly see how far it went, to reach that ever-distant horizon.

Throwing a glance back at Kit, she smirked. How could anyone not love this? It was simply wondrous.

Even if the joyous day had been nothing but a cover for what Annabelle hoped was an equally joyous night.

When they finally slowed, Theo spoke quietly in her ear. "Can I ask you something?"

Annabelle looked up at her eldest brother, just as port came into view. He had always been there for her, perhaps not in the same way that Michael had been—as a comrade-in-mischief. Theo was a protector. As the Duke of Foxcotte, he was head of the family, whether he liked it or not.

The ducal burden was one that Theo seemed to shoulder with ease, meeting it head on after their father's illness and subsequent death.

For the first time, Annabelle realised that it may not have been a burden he wanted. "Only if I can ask you something."

Theo's smile was more of an apprehensive grimace. "Is it something that your governess would faint to hear you say?"

"Amazingly, no."

"That makes a change."

Annabelle swatted him. "What is your question?"

Theo gave her a long, hard look. "Are you sure of Aylesbourne?"

"Why do I need to be sure of him?"

He frowned, somehow looking more like Papa than ever. "Courtships end one of two ways, Annabelle."

"I don't believe a courtship has ever been mentioned." She almost rolled her eyes. "Can we not simply have fun together?"

"So you haven't committed to anything?" Theo leant against the railing, eyeing the shoreline.

"Of course not," she scoffed, speaking with far more certainty than she felt.

Perhaps because it was expected of her. Perhaps because she didn't want to appear weak in front of her family. For years, Annabelle had eschewed the concept of marriage, declaring it to be no better than a charnel house for women's freedom, talent, and individuality.

And yet…

Every time she looked at Kit, her chest wanted to burst with happiness. She had expected to hate the man, but she'd never expected him to be like *this*. Every night, he sent her letters telling her of the sky above her. When Parliament was in session, he had even asked her for advice on the Women's Enfranchisement Bill—and had *spoken in Parliament* accordingly. In the Houses of Parliament, in front of hundreds of MPs, in front of hundreds of other men.

Annabelle had truly believed that she would never find a man who would meet her standards, and yet Kit was exceeding them in every way.

A small part of her wanted him to be terrible in bed. There had to be *something* wrong with him, surely. Something that would pull her away from this madness.

"No," Theo said softly, touching her with a warm glance. "You're far too much of a free spirit to do that." He pulled her close with a proud grin, kissing the top of her head in a brotherly embrace.

So why did it feel as though she'd let her pride get the best of her?

It wasn't until they docked that either of them spoke again.

"I forgot," Theo said. "What was your question?"

Annabelle took a step back to look him in the eye. "What would you do if you weren't a duke?"

"If I could be anything I chose?"

"Anything."

He broke their gaze, his eyes meeting the horizon. "Once, I would have said a historian, or an archaeologist, perhaps."

"And now?"

"More and more I seek simplicity. The loss of grandeur and pomp." His smile was almost sad. "A simple life—with a simple wife. That is what I want now."

Annabelle closed her hotel room as quietly as humanly possible, hoping against hope that the sound wouldn't reach Theo in the room next door. Feeling ever so slightly like a thief, she crept along the seaside hotel's long central corridor. Its furnishings were clean, with an ever-present smell of fresh paint pervading through the building.

A burst of excitement hit when she saw Kit come into view at the end of the corridor, looking devilishly casual in a simple white shirt, the sleeves rolled to the elbows.

Eyeing her like he wanted to eat her for supper, he held out his hand. "Come," he whispered, standing next to an old daguerreotype photograph of the hotel. A caption dated the image as June 1842, as if the restrained dresses and narrowed bonnets worn by the women within the image wouldn't have given it away.

Annabelle found a perverse pleasure in the knowledge that those stuffy old women would have keeled over in horror at her plans for tonight. Her eyebrow jumped. "I intend to."

"Oh you'll be the death of me, little queen." He tugged her along with him, leaving the corridor—and her sleeping brother—behind.

The hotel was deserted at this hour, with no one but a snoozing young gentleman manning the desk, a copy of some penny dreadful resting on his chest.

Blindly trusting Sir Prig himself, Annabelle followed him out into the night.

Nerves turned into excitement at the first breath of sea air, the acrid scent of new paint falling away behind her. The hotel's front door's deposited them on the seafront—as Kit had conveniently arranged, but Theo had taken far longer to go to bed than expected, with Annabelle chomping at the bit to rid herself of her virginity.

Specifically, at the hands of the duke at her side.

Well, hopefully not his hands. She had something else in mind for that.

The walk to the marina was a short one, and Annabelle recognised the *North Star* as they crossed the road and stepped onto the unsteady pontoons, with the sea lapping at the boats moored around them. Kit quickened his pace, clearly eager to get her on board.

"Last chance to change your mind," he said, pausing before she took that final step.

She held his chin between her thumb and forefinger. "Ye have little faith, Sir Prig." Shoving him to the side, she hopped aboard, turning around to curl her fingers at him in a *come-hither* motion.

Kit shook his head and followed. "You truly are one-of-a-kind. Come on," he grabbed her hand, pulling her towards the wheelhouse, only letting go of her to get them underway.

"We're leaving port?"

He nodded. "Sound travels over water," he began, moving about the wheelhouse so competently that it was almost alluring. "I want to be far enough away that no one hears you scream."

Annabelle's nose creased in a grimace. "You do realise how murderous that sounds?"

Kit froze, both hands on the wheel. "Screams of pleasure—I would like to clarify. Your brothers are going to be the ones with murderous intentions if they ever found out about this."

"They'd have to follow you to the Antarctic to act on them because I'm certainly not going to say anything."

Their speed steadily increased, leaving the shoreline far behind. "Are you not going to boast of my prowess?"

Annabelle stepped forward, coming between Kit and the smooth handles of the wooden steering wheel. "Your prowess is yet to be determined, Sir Prig."

Kit's gaze darkened. "Is it now?"

"Your queen will not wait any longer. Take me below decks before I have to drag you there myself." She pressed her palm flat against his chest, drunk on her own arousal.

"Fuck, you're beautiful." His words were a whispered curse as he seized her lips, holding her face in his hands to keep her steady. Instead of taking her below decks, however, Kit dragged her towards the bow, their lips never parting.

It wasn't until his kiss transferred to her neck that she saw his destination; a huddle of pillows and fur blankets at the very tip of the boat. "Here?"

"Mmm," he groaned against her neck. "Beneath the stars."

It was an intriguing thought; the two of them together, surrounded by the inky black ocean. By now, shore was nothing but a line of glittering lights in the distance. "This is truly scandalous, Sir Prig."

Kit cocked his head. "Have you changed your mind?"

"Oh no," Annabelle replied, hooking her arm around the back of his neck. "Now I'll settle for nothing less than a million stars above me."

He grinned before manoeuvring them both against the furs. "A million stars... and *me*."

The furs were silky soft to the touch as she fell back against them. Her hands flew to his buttons, rapidly undoing them. "I want to see you."

"Demanding little minx, aren't you?" he smirked, shouldering out of his undone shirt to reveal a tanned chest. Dark hair was scattered across his torso, and Annabelle bit her lip, tracking the muscular lines sending her gaze downwards.

"I know what I want, and I'm not going to apologise for it."

He gave her perhaps three seconds to ogle him before jumping into action. "My turn," he rasped.

Whilst Annabelle had had an entire shirt full of buttons to contend with, he had but three. She'd picked out her dress specifically for disrobing, and she waited for his reactio—

Aylesbourne almost choked. "You're not wearing any underclothes."

Reclining on the lustrous fur, she gave him a crooked smile. "They seemed superfluous to our endeavour."

Sir Prig looked as though all of his Christmases had come early. He peeled the dress off her in slow increments, kissing every inch of skin he unwrapped.

Discoveries abounded; Annabelle had never imagined her collarbone to be as sensitive as it was, nor the valley between her breasts, and when he finally pulled the fabric over her tightly-budded nipples—

Annabelle's moan was a corporeal mass of surprise and pleasure both. She trembled, wholly unprepared for the bliss this would bring. The scrape of his stubbled jaw over the delicate underside of her breast. The flick of his tongue over her nipple. The rapture that came with every hollowing of his cheeks.

Aylesbourne rumbled out a laugh as he sucked, the dark flames of his eyes rapt with attention, capturing every reaction his touch evoked.

"More," she whispered, pushing his head towards her other breast.

He went willingly.

Annabelle clenched her thighs together, feeling the slickness between them. She let her head fall backwards, absorbing the colours of the twinkling stars above them, the endless ripple of the ocean against the yacht—and most of all, Aylesbourne's groans of satisfaction.

Now she was here, she couldn't imagine losing her virginity any other way.

She was nearly at breaking point when he finally moved away from her breasts, her arousal stretched so tightly it was near to snapping. Panting up at him, she felt a certain satisfaction to see him as out of breath as she was. He placed a hand over the rigid outline of his cock in his trousers as they sat low on his hips, repositioning himself.

"Would you like some assistance?" she asked, rounding her eyes with undeserved innocence.

The hidden section of the library at Scarlett Castle—the one with filthy, filthy books and tantalising photographs—had assisted her in preparing for this moment. She had read about it enough, wondering what it would be like to finally touch a man *there*, to feel him pulse beneath her fingers.

Annabelle held out her hand. "Let me ease you."

Aylesbourne seized her gaze as he undid his trouser buttons, stringing out her anticipation until the final moment.

A sigh escaped her when he finally revealed his cock. He gripped it in his fist, his breathing heavy. The tip was a bright, burgundy red, weeping with every pass of his hand. "Do you like what you see?"

Her dress pulled down far enough to expose her breasts, Annabelle sat up. "Do you?"

"I'm so fucking hard I feel like I'm about to explode. *Yes*, little queen. I like what I see." Aylesbourne shoved his trousers off, moving closer to her head in the process.

When he was distracted, she struck.

Annabelle mimicked his movements, fisting his cock in a soft slide. She'd expected it to be hard, but his slick heat surprised her.

"Oh fuck," Aylesbourne whispered, stilling in the act of throwing his trousers off the furs. He fell forwards, his knees on one side of her head and his hands resting on the other.

The drips of arousal leaking from his tip soon drenched the skin between her forefinger and thumb, but Annabelle's mind had moved into territories that were filthier still. "Come closer," she murmured, her voice throaty with arousal. "I want to taste you."

"I have one condition." Kit's bottom lip was a dark red, as though he'd been biting into it whilst she was otherwise occupied.

"Namely?"

"Lift your hips so I can take off your dress—and taste you in turn."

Annabelle was all too willing to comply, watching his expression with a keen eye.

"Oh fuck," he said again, those wolfish eyes burning bright with arousal as he unwrapped her fully. Aylesbourne threw her dress to the side, gazing at her naked body adoringly. "Hold my eyes as you take my cock in your mouth."

For once, she obeyed, teasing the tip with her tongue before closing her lips around his length, moaning at his salty taste.

Teeth gritted, Aylesbourne murmured words in a language she'd never heard before. "Just like that, *mo chridhe*. You're so perfect."

Annabelle neither knew nor cared what *mo chridhe* meant, sucking him deep into her mouth, drunk on power and lust in equal measure.

She'd expected him to keep watching her with those dark eyes of his, but his hands traversed her body, paying her breasts a brief visit before delving lower. Annabelle moaned around his cock when he reached between her legs, exposing the slick mess waiting for him.

The lustful creature that descended between her thighs couldn't have been the same man who talked to her of the stars in the rose garden. No, *this* Aylesbourne was a tower of dominance and sin, fiercely splitting her with a lick and teasing her clitoris until her eyes rolled back in her head.

When she thought of losing her virginity, Annabelle had never imagined a scenario such as *this*. They attempted to outpace each other, losing themselves utterly. It was pleasure beyond anything she'd expected, wanting to come and make him come in equal measure.

Her climax charged down on her, clamping her legs around his head. Her entrance tightened in rhythmic movements, pulsating with bliss. Annabelle cried out around his erection, sucking him hard, but Aylesbourne didn't so much as pause, riding her orgasm with her until the last.

When she couldn't take anymore, she pulled away from his cock. "Stop," she gasped.

Panting hard, Kit laid out on his back, his erection wet with her saliva. "Bloody hell, Annabelle."

"I still haven't given you leave to refer to me without my title." Quickly recovering from her climax, she lifted herself into a sitting position, taking the time to absorb the defined lines of his impressive stature.

"Does licking your cunt count for nothing?" he asked, his tone self-satisfied. He watched her like a predator, tracking every movement she made.

Smirking, Annabelle straddled him, wanting to take him by surprise.

Aylesbourne's lips curled into an almost disbelieving smile. He fisted his cock with one hand and gripped her hips with the other. "Sit on your throne, little queen."

"That's more like it," she whispered, lifting herself above his cock, until she could feel the head at her entrance. Her lips parted at such a foreign sensation, but every instinct told her to bore down on him.

"Whenever you're ready." Aylesbourne held his length steady for her as she sank down on the first inch.

"Oh god," she whimpered, letting her head hang between her shoulders.

"That's it," Kit's encouraging nod came. "There's no rush. And if you need to stop, then we'll stop."

Her eyebrow twitched. *Well that's not bloody likely, is it?*

Buoyed on by his talk of quitting, Annabelle felt herself mould around his cock in a slow slide that nearly took her breath away. There was none of the pain she'd been expecting, only pure, unadulterated bliss. Her sigh of relief split the night, and his wasn't far behind.

"Kit," she gasped, taking him to the hilt. Struggling to get used to the feeling, she took a deep breath. "Oh god, it's so big."

Kit's smirk was comprised entirely of masculine smugness.

Annabelle rocked her hips, eager to take it away—and with pleasing results.

"You're such a tease," he laughed through heavy-lidded eyes, the bump in his throat jumping. "Do that again, *mo chridhe*."

She did, finding her years of horse-riding coming in handy. Annabelle began to ride him hard, her slow, tentative rhythm soon becoming a purposeful race to the finish. Kit moved beneath her, meeting her with thrusts of his own that had them both crying out.

Even so, her hips began to tire, her movements becoming slower and slower. She would certainly need to build up some stamina for future meetings, then.

For now, Kit simply flipped them in a single, effortless movement. Whilst her hips were burning with exertion, his had no such trouble, driving into her in slow, rolling thrusts. Annabelle moaned, feeling his torso undulating beneath her touch.

"Harder," she begged, another climax approaching fast and hard. "I need you."

Without pausing his rhythm, Kit claimed a savage kiss from her, his lips passing over hers in a chorus of moans and cries.

"Yes," Annabelle gasped, every exhale accompanied by a mewl of desire. "There, there, there. Oh god, this is madness."

Sweat rolled off his forehead, strands of black hair clinging to him, but Kit took no notice of it. "Then go mad with me, little queen."

Annabelle detonated, her screams of pleasure echoing across the water in short bursts, corresponding to her body clenching around his. Kit shook above her, bellowing out his own pulsating release into her kiss.

He collapsed beside her, pulling her close, as though he never wanted to let her go, and Annabelle couldn't help thinking the feeling was mutual. Their bodies tangled together, but she tried to get closer still, burrowing beneath his chin. The silence that fell between them wasn't an uncomfortable one; in fact, it was perhaps the most comfortable silence she had ever been a part of.

The world was at peace, and so was she.

But Annabelle was the first to break it, with reality intruding upon her thoughts. "When are you leaving for the expedition?"

He let out a long sigh, clutching her tighter. "The expedition leaves in the first week of August, but I'll be travelling up to the Highlands in a few days to put the dukedom in order before I leave. The next time I travel south will be for the expedition."

"That soon?"

Nodding, Kit frowned. He propped himself up on his elbow, looming over her. "I never thought I'd meet someone like you."

"Someone like me?"

There was a hard edge to his smile, but those dark eyes of his were as soft as could be. "Someone to make me reconsider my entire attitude to life."

Annabelle's heart thumped beneath her breast, and she bit down on the corner of her lips to hide her grin. "I'm glad I'm not alone in my predicament," she admitted.

"You're not alone." Kit palmed her cheek, his hand soft against her skin. "If I could stay, I would."

Disappointment caved in on her. With the high standards set by her brothers and father, Annabelle had never hoped to find a man who could live up to their decency. Let alone someone like Kit, who accepted everything she threw at him—and gave it back to her in equal measure.

"I understand."

"No," he shook his head, a wry look on his face. "You don't." Looking out over the water, Kit paused for a moment. "Wait for me."

"Wait for you?" Surely he wasn't asking what she thought he was. "As in… marriage?"

But he didn't shy away from it. "Neither of us had any plans to marry, Annabelle. You've said it yourself. I'll be gone for several years in Antarctica. Wait for me. Write to me." His hand came up to her cheek, holding her gaze his way. "And if I return, I'll be that exceptional husband you always wanted."

Bending his head, Kit pressed a chaste kiss against her lips, teasing her shock away. "Promise me you'll wait for me, little queen."

"I promise," she replied, cursing her face's inability to stop a maudlin grin from spreading across it. "I promise I'll wait for you."

Kit's next kiss was fierce as he positioned himself atop her. "I have another request."

"You're getting greedy."

"When you're around, I can't help it."

Annabelle laughed. "What's your second request?"

Kit's intense eyes pinned her to the furs. "Can you take me again?"

Widening her legs, her breath hitched when he rolled between them. "Why don't you come and find out?"

4
Annabelle

With a deep breath, Annabelle stood over the bed she had just vacated and peeled back the heavy duck down covers.

The white sheets were as damning as the blade of a guillotine.

She swallowed down her rising panic.

Well, she had given Kit the month. It seemed like he'd left her something in return. Her hand went to her navel, unable to believe that it could be true, that she was carrying a life within her.

Papa would have hit the roof.

Annabelle shook the thought away, throwing on the dress she'd picked out yesterday, not bothering to wait for her ladies' maid to arrive. Now was not the time for hysterics and worry; now was the time for action, and she had a letter to send.

She had written it out last night in anticipation of this very moment, somehow never expecting it to arrive. Annabelle snatched it up off her bedside table and dashed out into the bedroom corridor, taking a left at the fork that would take her to the Grand Staircase.

The heart of the Foxcotte dukedom was the glittering jewel that was Scarlett Castle, a maroon behemoth that had sat on this very spot for centuries, overlooking the Hampshire countryside. And at the heart of Scarlett Castle was its Atrium, a hollow centre topped by a glass dome that gave them round-the-clock access to the sky above them.

Kit would love it here.

Annabelle's fashionable but sensible heels clipped a quick pace across the Atrium's marble floor, her steps shadowed beneath her. She departed not through the castle's main entrance, a monstrously heavy iron giant guarding the Foxcotte family, but through a side door that would take her straight to where she needed to go: the stables.

Amongst the homely haze of horses, Olympia was waiting for her expectantly. Annabelle ran her hand up her treasured mare's snout. "Are we ready to go, pretty girl?"

Olympia pressed her jet black head against Annabelle, allowing herself to be saddled and bridled with the kind of grace even Queen Alexandra would struggle to achieve.

Leading Olympia out of the stable, Annabelle looked up at the castle. Her baby sister, Effie, waved down at her from the nursery window, as she so often did when Annabelle took her morning rides. Effecting a cheery wave back, Annabelle led Olympia alongside the familiar tree stump on the edge of the courtyard. She stepped up onto it, the stump's rings having long since disappeared beneath its blackened hue.

With the stump's leverage, Annabelle leapt atop Olympia and gave the mare her head.

Olympia snorted, launching into a rapid gallop down the road. Her family would think nothing of her journey, all too used to her morning rides, but never had she ridden with such urgency. Even Olympia seemed to sense it, egged on by Annabelle's movements, running faster than her usual breakneck speed.

They reached the village in what seemed like seconds. Few people were about at this hour, but the brimming milk bottles sitting on the doorsteps of the houses they passed told Annabelle that the milkman had been through here recently.

She reined Olympia in outside the Post Office, sliding off her back slightly earlier than was sensible. The bell tinkled as she pushed open the door, finding the postmaster sitting in his usual seat behind the counter. A wall of notices met her as she walked in; people advertising puppies for sale or job openings, but she rushed past, arriving at the counter just as the postmaster looked up.

"I need to send a lett—"

"The morning post has already left, I'm afraid," the gruff postmaster replied.

"That doesn't matter. I need it by special messenger. The quickest boy you have. The messenger will need to wait to bring back their reply. It's urgent." With worry knotting her gut, she gave the letter one final read-through.

The Duke of Aylesbourne
Campbell House
Berkeley Square Gardens
London

Wednesday, 7th August 1907

Kit,
I am desperately sorry to have to send this, but I have no other option. I'm pregnant with your child, Kit. I have waited for as long as I could in the hope that my courses would arrive, but they have not.
I beg of you. Do not leave on your expedition this afternoon. You MUST stay—to give our child a name, if nothing else.

Urgently awaiting your reply by return special messenger,
Little queen

Annabelle's hands shook as she held Kit's reply, waiting in Theo's office.

Her heart felt like it had been torn out. She'd *trusted* him. She'd overlooked tales of debauchery and carnality. Aylesbourne was friends with her brothers—he would have never thrown her aside, for fear of brotherly retribution, if nothing else.

Promise me you'll wait for me, little queen.

Through the window, Annabelle watched Theo walk up the driveway, amiably chatting with Chambers, their butler, her patience running thinner and thinner with every step.

Just when Theo had entered the castle, his steps echoing across the Atrium, another delay had arrived.

"Have you brought more cake back from the tearoom again?" Mama was saying.

"So I like cake," Theo retorted playfully, his voice carrying across the Atrium's marble floor. "Shoot me."

It was a relief when he finally opened his office door—and even more of a relief to see their mother's retreating back behind him. Surprise flashed on Theo's face when he saw her, but whatever he saw in her expression had him quickly closing the door behind him.

"Annabelle?" Theo's eyes slid down to the letter she held in her trembling hands. He placed the wicker basket he'd been carrying on his desk before approaching her, clasping her hands to finally hold them steady. "What's happened? What's wrong?"

She let him take the letter from her hands, closing her eyes as he opened it.

"*I will be continuing on the expedition,*" he read aloud, his dark brows pulling together. "*You have my sympathies regarding your situation. The Duke of Aylesbourne.*"

Not Kit. Not even Sir Prig. The Duke of Aylesbourne. As though he was a stranger. As though the promises made during their night together meant nothing to him.

"What situation?" Theo asked slowly.

Annabelle lifted her chin. She wouldn't be ashamed. "I'm carrying his child."

As much as it pained her to admit it, Theo was her last resort. Had Michael been here, she would have gone to him for help. She didn't fear judgement from Michael, but Theo was so… honourable. He held himself to such a high standard, so how could he not hold his siblings to it as well?

But it was not judgement she saw raging in Theo's eyes; a foreign, violent undercurrent vibrated through the air with such prominence she took a step back in fear, but his hand shot out to grab her wrist. His other hand came up to enfold her cheek. "Did he force you?" he whispered frantically, his eyes darting over her body, as though scanning for bruises.

She shook her head.

Theo slumped forward in relief, all hint of violence vanishing. As though it had never been there at all. He crushed her in a tight hug, kissing the top of her head. "Thank god."

"He's been your friend for years," she said, her voice muffled by his shirt. "Do you really believe him to be capable of such a thing?"

Theo pulled back. "Five minutes ago, I wouldn't have said Aylesbourne would be capable of abandoning a woman carrying his child." He shot a hateful glare down at Aylesbourne's letter, sitting unassumingly on the desk. "If he can be guilty of *this*, then he could be guilty of anything."

Silence stretched for a few moments, the cold reality of her situation finally setting in once Theo's initial fury at Aylesbourne receded, merging into a dull, hardened acceptance. All at once, Theo sparked into action, pulling out the battered pocket watch that had belonged to their father. "You have options," he told her. "But two of them require a decision to be made quickly."

The knot in her stomach eased somewhat now that she had shared her secret with him. There was no judgement or shame in his gaze, only the stern, capable look he always had. She should have known better than to worry; Theo always had a plan, and he always looked after her. Suddenly, Annabelle looked on Theo so fondly she wanted to hug him and never let go. "Two of them?"

"Aylesbourne leaves on the British Antarctic Expedition in six hours, Annabelle. I spoke to him yesterday; he left the Highlands last night on the *North Star*, stopping in London before going down to Southampton. I know *exactly* where he is. You only need to say the word and I'll intercept his departure and drag him back here by his coattails. We can have him up at an altar as soon as I can obtain a marriage licence."

She straightened, having not considered holding Aylesbourne against his will. A brief spurt of hatred urged her to take the opportunity presented to her, to ruin Aylesbourne's plans, but hurt quickly overwhelmed it. "I do not want a husband that has to be dragged to the altar, Theo. He'll resent me and the child both."

Theo opened up the brown packaging in his wicker basket to unveil a selection of cakes from Mrs Simpkin's Tearoom in the village. "Here," he said, pushing a slice of strawberry tart towards her. "Eat. You barely ate anything at dinner last night."

Annabelle took it. He wasn't wrong; last night she'd been so worried about her courses that she couldn't have digested anything for love nor money.

"Aylesbourne never has to see the child, Annabelle," Theo continued, rubbing his chin. "But they would not be born out of wedlock. It would give them a name—and a title."

"And a father who despised them." Annabelle shook her head once more, thinking of their father, who had never had a sharp word to say to anyone. "I suppose that is the disadvantage of having a wonderful father like Papa."

Theo sat on the edge of the desk—just like their father had always done, looking every inch the duke he was born to be. "Namely?"

"I want my children to be as lucky as we were."

A half smile settled on Theo's face. "As do I." He took her hand in his, squeezing. "So no to Aylesbourne?"

"No," she replied, the finality of her decision weighing heavy in her shattered chest.

"Very well."

"And your second time-sensitive option?"

Theo took a deep breath, his lips tightening. "My second question is to ask you whether you want to keep the child."

She looked away, her gaze coming to rest on the window opening out onto the long, sweeping driveway. "One of my suffragette friends attempted to terminate her pregnancy."

"Attempted?"

"She died during the procedure. The doctor had been struck off for negligence, her husband discovered later." Annabelle remembered news of her death arriving in a black-rimmed envelope—mourning stationery. A sight to strike fear into one's heart, knowing that such letters carried death with them. "As much as I do not want a child, Theo, I cannot risk it."

He nodded. "I cannot risk you either. But pregnancy comes with its own set of risks."

"Where does that leave me?" Annabelle leant against the desk, helping herself to another strawberry tart. Out of the window, she saw Mama and their nanny enjoying a morning walk, little Effie toddling between them. "I'm to have a child out of wedlock."

The prospect was daunting. She was going to bring scandal upon the house, upon the dukedom.

This was not how she saw her first season going. She wanted to spend her time going to fashion shows, perhaps sketching the designs she liked, and absorbing every ounce of knowledge about the industry.

Theo's response was so quiet she almost missed it. "Not necessarily."

"Excuse me?"

His hand slipped out of hers as he stood, indecision marring his features. "It won't be out of wedlock if you marry before the child arrives."

Annabelle went cold. "I swear to god, Theo, if you suggest marrying me off to Lord Moordale I shall gouge your eyes out."

A laugh burst from him, breaking the heavy tension that had fallen over the room. "I don't believe the situation is as dire as all that."

Wasn't it? "Who, pray tell, are you suggesting I marry?"

Theo shot her a hard, hesitant look. "Let me make a call."

Lord Buckford could barely meet her gaze, instead electing to arrange his toy horseman on their mock battlefield whilst he listened to Theo's low murmur next to him. An army of miniature, one-dimensional figures were laid out on Lord Buckford's enormous dining table, presumably in the middle of some sort of campaign. The Battle of the Pyramids, judging from the mock-pyramids on the edge of the battlefield.

The dinner service, conversely, was displayed in a dusty glass cabinet against the wall.

"This is Meissen Porcelain," Mama said to her, idly glancing over the floral plates, platters, and tureens. "They were the first company to develop genuine porcelain outside of Asia. Did you know?"

Obviously not. Had Mama forgotten who she was talking to? "I didn't," Annabelle said mildly, using the time to observe her potential husband instead of his dinner plates.

Lord Buckford was... unusual.

He never attended any parties or dinners. He was never seen during the London season. In fact, he never left his house at all, judging by Theo's comments on the matter, instead preferring to send his valet in his stead.

Mary tsked. "Such a waste."

"Lord Buckford?"

"His porcelain, darling." With a sigh, her mother edged closer, and Annabelle braced herself for yet another round of questions. "Are you sure about this?"

"Yes, Mama."

"You've never even met him before," Mary said, coming round to block Annabelle's continued observation of Lord Buckford. Annabelle refocused her gaze. "And he's older than I am! You... you would tell me if you were in trouble, wouldn't you?"

Annabelle's placating smile stretched tight across her face. "Of course, Mama," she lied, resisting the urge to place a protective hand over the life growing inside her. "Lord Buckford has been kind. Theo and I drew up the wedding contract ourselves. I'll have all the freedoms I enjoy now. I'll be able to spend more time with the suffragettes—Lord Buckford has given over an entire wing of the house to me, meaning I can host events for them," Annabelle disclosed, hoping her faux excitement covered her nerves. "My allowance will be more than generous."

And he's agreed to raise the bastard son of the Duke of Aylesbourne because he's in dire need of an heir.

"I wasn't ready to lose you quite so soon," Mama's brow was a mess of creases, but she nodded sadly. "If you're sure."

Her new fiancée finally looked up to meet her gaze, offering her a shy smile before going back to his models.

She was. Because she had to be.

Sixteen Years Later

5

Annabelle

"The first ball of our first season!" Effie exclaimed excitedly, her hand jumping to the doorhandle before the chauffeur had stopped the car. Lord Linwood's Eaton Square townhouse loomed before them, his red-and-black liveried footmen jumping into action when yet another car arrived to drop off fidgety guests eager to start their night.

The family's ward, Caroline, was just as thrilled. The two girls had spent so long choosing their costumes for Lord Linwood's masquerade ball that even Annabelle thought it was excessive. Their dressmaker, Madame Renaud, had the patience of a saint. The girls had taken weeks to choose what they were going as, eventually settling on birds.

Annabelle had been relieved.

And then she'd nearly screamed when they began to debate *what* birds to go as.

Was this how Theo had felt when chaperoning Annabelle through her first season? He must have been miserable, because Annabelle couldn't wait for this to be over.

Effie leapt out of the car first, her swan-white costume bristling with every step. Caroline wasn't far behind, ruffling her peacock feathers as she did so.

"Matching," Effie had said to Madam Renaud. "But not so matching that we cannot express our individual personalities."

Once, Annabelle would have been right there with them, choosing fabrics and designs, coordinating each individual piece of jewellery until she was a walking masterpiece.

"Come on, little birds," she said, ushering them towards Lord Linwood's open front door. "We're blocking the way for the next guests."

Annabelle didn't bother to hold up her mask as they walked in, choosing instead to swipe a glass of dark amber liquid from a passing footman. Whisky, she hoped. One well-satisfied sip later, she followed Effie and Caroline, choosing to let them go where they wished.

She was their chaperone, true, but two more innocent young ladies she had never met.

Annabelle had never been like that, had she? At their age, she'd seen the inside of a jail cell more than once—not that her mother knew that. She'd lost one of her closest friends at the hands of a negligent doctor. She'd even ridden one of Michael's motorcycles. Or had that been the following year?

It had all been so long ago. A lifetime.

It was bittersweet to return to Lord Linwood's ball. Because it was in Lord Linwood's renowned gardens that she and Aylesbourne had planned their ill-fated tryst. But there were good memories here, too. Theo had danced with her here. She could still see him in her mind's eye, promising her only a single dance for the night after her Phoebus-related injuries. She had been so excited for the evening back then, just as Effie and Caroline were now.

Annabelle tilted her head up, her breaths stuttered with memories.

"Annabelle?" Effie said, her voice full of worry. Of course darling Effie would notice. "What's wrong?"

She swallowed, taking a sip of whisky to buy her enough time to ensure her voice wouldn't crack. "Theo would be so proud if he could see you now."

Effie made no effort to cover up her emotions, letting the tears pool before blinking them free. Her smile was sad. "I miss him."

"We all do, darling," Annabelle assured her baby sister, who had been eleven when Theo was killed. She thought back to Lord Linwood's ball all those years ago. So many of those men had shared Theo's fate: death at the hands of the Great War.

But for Effie, Theo had been the only father figure she'd ever known. Michael had played the role of her mischievous uncle; a role that fit him like a glove.

Although Michael was a father of four these days, and that role seemed to fit him like a glove as well—albeit with a mischievous streak a mile wide. Only the other day she had gone down into the kitchen to find Michael and his two girls sneaking cakes from Mrs Kirkpatrick just after breakfast.

"But Mama and Michael will be here for your coming out ball," she reminded Effie. "After their holiday."

Effie shared a conspiratorial little smile. "As much fun as sailing around the south coast sounds, I'd much rather be here."

Sailing around the south coast… on the *North Star.*

Not that she had ever told anyone of its significance. It was easier to leave the past be. Because back then she had been a foolish girl, all too easily swayed by the meaningless words of a cad. Like so many foolish girls before her.

A pang of grief tolled in her heart, but she kept it there.

"Me too," she said truthfully, patting Effie's arm and giving Caroline an encouraging look. Behind her two little birds, Annabelle sighted a couple of waiting gentlemen. One was dressed as Macbeth—skull in hand—whilst the other had made virtually no effort in his costume beyond holding a masquerade mask, just as Annabelle herself had done. "I shall leave you to your admirers, girls."

She observed the girls for a while, watching a seemingly endless series of young men come and go. The prickling sensation along her spine, however, told Annabelle that she was being watched. Her eyes traced the room coyly, knowing he was there somewhere.

Good. She needed to feel something good. It had been far too long, and she needed the relief that came only from secret gasps and pulsing ecstasy and hushed moans. The kind of relief that could only be found in another's touch.

"Uncle Robert always hated coming here."

Pink-cheeked, Annabelle turned to find Eva Allenby approaching her. A relation of her husband, the late Lord Buckford. "Considering he didn't leave the house once in the four years we were married," Annabelle entwined her arm through Eva's, "I'll have to take your word for it. Did he hate it any more than everywhere else?"

"Oh yes," Eva nodded seriously, a tiara of opulent jewelled violets sitting on her head, although heaven knew what the rest of her floral-inspired costume was meant to be. "He hated Lord Linwood's home even more. I remember my step-mother telling me Lord Linwood's father was rather unkind to Uncle Robert when he was a boy. Apparently Uncle Robert was friends with the old Lord Linwood's son—now the current Lord Linwood—and Linwood senior caught Uncle Robert skulking around a suit of armour in the middle of the night," Eva narrowed her eyes, as though she had slightly lost track of her bearings. "Or something."

"You said Linwood so many times in that sentence I'm no longer sure it's a real word."

Eva snorted. "But yes. Uncle Robert hated the house's master, so he hated the house."

"No Lady Kingswood tonight?"

Shooting Annabelle a knowing glance, Eva took a glass of champagne offered by a footman making his rounds. "Why? Are you that eager to get your hands on my husband?"

"Would it be uncouth if I said yes?"

"Oh sweetheart," Eva flapped her hand dismissively. "You're no more uncouth than I am. And to tell you the truth, I'm glad. Cornelius has been restless lately. It'll do him some good to expend some energy."

"Speaking of your purported uncouthness, where's your *amie* this evening?"

"On chaperone duty," Eva nodded over to the other side of the ballroom, not far from where Caroline danced with a young gentleman. The devastatingly beautiful Lady Kingswood laughed with a young girl Annabelle knew by sight, if not by name. "Same as you."

But then Annabelle saw the quarry she sought. "I don't suppose I could ask Lady Kingswood to take over for the evening in regards to Lady Caroline and Lady Effie?"

Sans costume, Cornelius Allenby casually strolled across the ballroom, looking as dapper as ever. "My darling," he said, kissing his wife amicably on the cheek, his golden hair immaculately styled, before turning his eyes to Annabelle. "Lady Buckford."

Annabelle lifted her chin. "Mr Allenby."

"Cornelius, sweetheart," Eva grinned. "Why don't you take Lady Buckford out for a walk in the gardens? She's been simply *dying* to hear about your trip to America."

With a final smirk at her husband, Eva sauntered away in the direction of Lady Kingswood before either of them could say another word.

Cornelius leant in close, lowering his voice. "You look as desperate as I feel."

"Then hurry up and do something about it."

Annabelle kept up with Cornelius's quick pace with ease, almost bulldozing some ancient widow in their haste. Lord Linwood's gardens had bloomed since she'd been here with Aylesbourne, fit to burst with flowers that looked far too exotic to have come from British shores.

But Cornelius abandoned the well-lit paths for a section of the garden steeped in darkness. Rather than being level, their path was filled with stairs and steep slopes, ending in a distant but—most importantly—unused bandstand that was almost invisible in the gloom. Looking up, they had a prime view of the vast balcony surrounding the rear of Linwood's house, meaning they would be able to spot any unwanted guests far before they arrived.

Perfect.

Cornelius descended on her like a hurricane, whirling her around until her back slammed hard into the bandstand's wooden pillar. Her breath whooshed out, quickly replaced by arousal. They'd been lovers long enough for him to know she liked it rough. And for her to know exactly what he liked in return.

Summoning all her strength, she slapped him.

Her hand stung like it had been swarmed by a thousand bees, but his face must have hurt ten times as much. Cornelius's icy blue gaze only darkened in his arousal, as she'd known it would.

Cornelius advanced, but she held up her still-stinging hand. "If you mess up my hair or rouge, the next blow won't be part of our little game."

He held her proffered hand, pressing a kiss to the centre of her palm before trailing it higher. "Well, now you make it sound tempting," he murmured against her neck.

Her hands beginning to wander, Annabelle bit her lip when she finally found the hard length in his trousers. "Judging by *this*," she squeezed, eliciting a familiar groan from him, "you're tempted enough."

"Too right I am," he snarled in return, bending her so far over the bandstand's wide wooden balcony her feet left the floor. "Dress up or off?"

"Up," she panted, keeping her legs firmly together whilst he all but peeled it over her hips. The mermaid dress was tight over her thighs, but once he'd exposed the bottom of her lacy chemise, she was free to spread them.

Cornelius yanked her chemise up with such urgency that it was in danger of tearing.

"That's by *Doeuillet*, Allenby," she hissed, the cool chill of the summer evening creeping up her exposed legs. "If you rip that, you're replacing it!"

There was a pause before his touch returned—presumably whilst Cornelius freed his erection—but when it did it was exactly where she wanted it.

Their soft, simultaneous moan was one of relief, but the softness didn't last. Cornelius soon set his usual pace; a quick, hard fuck.

They never made love, the two of them. There was no passion or adoration. Cornelius was not even her type, nor was she his. There was friendship, true enough, but that was all. Friendship and a shared desire to have their needs met.

Their activities had never included anything but pure, old fashioned sex. The idea of sucking his cock seemed too intimate; he was her friend's husband, after all. Such tenderness was for lovers brought together by adoration, not for the two of them; driven by animalistic need and little else.

Cornelius grunted with the force of every thrust, until Annabelle was biting down on her own arm to try and keep quiet. They were a distance away from the balcony, but they could hear the numerous partygoers milling around on the cold stone slabs, taking a refreshing break from the heat of the ballroom.

"Fuck, you feel so good," Cornelius groaned, bracing one hand around the nearest pillar.

Annabelle hardly heard him, lost in her own pleasure. The rapid, powerful thrusts had her mouth hanging open, an inaudible cry of need threatening to break free. "There!" she whispered, needing something *more*, attempting to tilt her hips to meet his thrusts.

"Like this?" he asked, aligning himself so that he hit *exactly* where she needed him.

Her broken, garbled sob was intended to be a yes.

Cornelius clearly took it as one, maintaining his rhythm, his knuckles turning white as he gripped the pillar.

Every thrust brought her closer to release, until she could barely keep in the ecstasy threatening to break loose. She began to rock her hips backwards to meet Cornelius's movements, reduced to nothing but a cat in heat, until finally the tension within her snapped like a chain. The sudden rush of pleasure nearly drowned her, clenchin—

A myriad spotlights suddenly illuminated the bandstand, attracting the attention of the dozens of guests on the vast balcony.

Mid-orgasm, Annabelle's eyes widened in panic. She flopped herself off the bandstand's wooden balcony like a startled fish, hiding beneath its low wall. Cornelius stumbled backwards, swearing as the audience gasped above them.

Oh shit.

She was ruined.

6

Kit

Here he was again. Lord Linwood's fucking ball.

"Please behave tonight, Kit," Uncle Eric muttered beneath his thick grey moustache, his dark eyes betraying the difficult night he'd had. Kit's own were doubtless any better. "And if you need to leave, we'll leave. All you need to do is say the word."

Anthony and his wife Daisy, on the other hand, were bright-eyed and bushy tailed. Their bedroom was two floors down from Kit's, far enough away to be out of earshot of his night terrors. He was glad of that. Daisy was a new addition to their family, and Kit didn't want her opinion of him falling any further than it already had. His ragged screams in the night would certainly do the job.

Even thinking of them had Kit looking upwards. The glittering chandelier above his head glared back at him, like a thousands stalactites threatening to break free over the ballroom. He swallowed. The ceiling here had stood for some hundred years; it wasn't about to crush down over his head, squeezing the air from his lungs and leaving him buried alive next to—

The icy condensation of a glass being shoved into his hand snapped him back from the brink.

"Drink." Uncle Eric's frown deepened in disapproval as he watched Kit down it in one. "Better?"

"It would have been better if it was feni instead of gin," Kit conceded, but it cleared his head somewhat. Eyes flicking up to the ceiling, he caught the shared look of uncertainty between Anthony and Daisy.

Perhaps he wasn't hiding this as well as he'd hoped.

"Is there anything you'd like to add to the refurbishment plans, Kit?" Daisy's sweet voice piped up, and she tucked a loose strand of her red-orange hair behind her ear. "The drawing room and morning room are finished, but we'd really like to start on your office."

"The ducal office?" he asked, frowning. No one had told him *his* rooms were being refurbished as well. Or perhaps they had, and he'd been too drunk to recall.

Daisy's nodding response was almost hidden beneath her shock of vivid red hair. Combined with her fiery Boudica costume, passers-by would be forgiven for thinking she had been set aflame.

The ducal office was currently cluttered with expedition-related equipment and photographs, covered with layers upon layers of maps and plans for a third attempt at scaling Everest. Brigadier-General Charles Bruce, the leader of their previous expedition, was talking of having their next meeting in just a few weeks. "Does it have to be done now? We're in the middle of planning."

"It's the last room on the lower ground floor," Anthony answered decisively, giving his wife a gentle look. "It needs to be done, Kit. I've already completed all the oil paintings. What Daisy is trying to say is where would you like the room's contents to be stored?"

"It's inconvenient. We're holding the meetings for next year's expedition there," he replied, ignoring Uncle Eric's disapproving look.

"Why don't you meet at Major MacGillivray's set at Albany?" Daisy proposed kindly. "It's empty now."

The air seethed from Kit's lungs. He choked, furiously trying to suck air back in, but he felt as though he was back on Everest. The air was too thin, the oxygen too scant. He could even hear echoes of Brigadier-General Bruce's Valleys accent in his ear, pulling him from the snow. *Not here. Not here.*

Uncle Eric's mouth moved, but Kit couldn't hear him over the rush of blood in his ears. He had to get outside. He couldn't be in this room, with the ceiling threatening to crush him at any moment. He shoved through the crowd of people with a singular, desperate purpose.

He didn't remember crossing the ballroom. All Kit focused on was the crispness of the night breeze on Linwood's balcony. A choked gasp of relief left him when there was nothing above him but air. On and on it went, for thousands of miles.

Mutters surrounded him when he bent over, his hands on his knees, his messy hair hanging freely around his ears. He took deep lungfuls of air, as though it was the most precious thing on earth. A sprinkling of their whispered insults reached his ears, souring his relief.

Drunkard. Shameless. Lowlife.

Kit tilted his head up, recognising one of the voices. Lord Morton's aged sneer hit him, his lips twisted in revulsion. "What was that, Morton?" Kit spat, standing to his full height.

Lord Morton shook his head. "I went to Cambridge with your uncle. A more honourable man there has never been. And look at what he raised. I hear the first place you scarpered to after stepping back on British soil was a brothel."

The accusation hit true. Kit couldn't deny it. Spending months in Darjeeling after failing to reach Everest's summit had made him desperate for a woman's touch. And *Chéries* was his establishment of choice. "The ladies at *Chéries* prefer the term courtesan," Kit slurred, "if you'd be so kind."

Morton scoffed in disgust. "Lord Eric must be so ashamed of you, Aylesbourne. I know I would be."

Kit never made a conscious choice to advance. One moment he was standing three feet away from the man, and in the next he was shoving Morton against the house's stone exterior by his throat, ignoring the horrified whispers of the people surrounding them. "Shove your judgement up your arse."

"Everyone is thinking it, *boy*," Morton hissed, his throat attempting to swallow beneath Kit's increasingly tight grip. Anger swelled within him, with emotion trailing behind, until it was all he could do not to smash Morton's skull against the brick behind him.

Suddenly appearing at the edge of his vision, Anthony jumped in, shoving him away from Morton before he could do something he'd regret. "Lord Morton," his cousin exclaimed, horrified. "Good lord, I'm so sorry. Are you all right?"

Morton's choking, gasping answer only enraged Kit more. He staggered away from the fray, shoving through the crowd of busybodies who had been attracted to the chaos like flies to shit.

Kit walked without aim, following whatever path he'd lurched onto. That was one of the sole advantages of where he was; Linwood's extensive gardens allowed him to hide from whatever fracas he'd created.

He found himself on the steep slope to the side of Linwood's property, on some tiled rectangular platform with piles of stacked chairs shoved in the corner.

Uncaring of his suit, he sat on the cold ground, defeated and miserable, leaning his head against the thigh-high brick wall surrounding the platform, dodging a large brass lever that would have dug into his spine.

It had been a mistake to come here. It had been a mistake to think he could behave like a normal human being again. Morton was right, he admitted to himself. Uncle Eric… It didn't take a genius to recognise his disappointment when he had to pull Kit out of his nightmares yet *again*.

He was a 37-year-old man who couldn't sleep through the fucking night.

Anyone would be embarrassed of him. He was embarrassed of himself.

He should have died on Everest. Major Charles Bruce should have dug for John MacGillivray first, not Kit. It would have been better for everyone. The thought of Anthony and Daisy as Duke and Duchess of Aylesbourne. His stomach lurched. The picture was perfect. He knew they were trying for a baby, a little cherry on top of their flawless lives.

The sound of a sharp, ringing slap pulled Kit from his self-pity. Allowing his vision to adjust to the darkness, Kit peered around him. For the first time in years, something rose in his chest other than anger or pain or regret. Something wonderful.

Little queen.

A woman he hadn't seen for sixteen years. A woman he *craved* like the oxygen he breathed. A woman he hated to love with every fibre of his being.

His lips parted when he realised what he was seeing: Annabelle in the bandstand below, embracing another woman's husband. None other than Cornelius fucking Allenby, an old schoolmate of Kit's.

There was that anger again, and jealousy fierce enough to tear him asunder. But something else bubbled beneath as she watched Annabelle cup Allenby's groin, something that had his own cock growing in response.

Kit watched in silence as Allenby kissed her neck, honing in on Annabelle's pleasured expression.

When Allenby bent her over the wide balustrade surrounding the bandstand—*facing* him—Kit couldn't help himself. He was, presumably, on the viewing platform for the bandstand, but tonight she was only performing for him.

He unbuttoned his trousers and took out his cock, stroking himself as he watched Annabelle's expression, her mouth hanging open, attempting to keep her moans in. Moans he would have killed to hear again.

"Come on, little queen," he whispered, timing his strokes with Allenby's thrusts. If he thought hard enough, he could almost *feel* her cunt around him.

Kit didn't last as long as she did. He gritted his teeth as he came, letting his seed splatter onto the unfortunate bush to his right. She gave a little choke as he did, prolonging his pleasure. God, what he wouldn't give to feel her again.

The regret crashed into him seconds later.

What the fuck had he just done?

Disgusted with himself, he went to stand up. Bracing an elbow on the stone wall, his hand knocked against the large brass lever he'd noticed when he first sat down.

Only this time he saw the words *Bandstand lights* engraved in the metal.

He glanced back down to the bandstand, where Annabelle looked to be on the edge of her orgasm… alongside a married man. Disgust pricked his skin—in himself and in them.

Not far above him, a crowd still lingered on the balcony at the back of the house. With the lights on, Annabelle and Allenby would be on centre stage.

Fuck it. It was no more than they deserved.

With a hand on the lever, Kit bided his time, watching Annabelle like a hawk. He knew what she looked like when she was on the edge. All he had to do was wait.

When he heard the tantalising little noise that signalled the start of her orgasm, he viciously pulled the lever.

Stage lights flashed on around the bandstand to rival Blackpool Illuminations. The momentarily blinded Annabelle cried out, although Kit couldn't be sure if it was shock or pleasure that caused it.

He savoured it either way.

He also savoured the cries of outrage from above him, on the balcony proper. He *definitely* heard Linwood's voice, in addition to Morton's. Was that Uncle Eric too? He couldn't be sure. All he knew was that the crowd gathered on the balcony had grown exponentially, with a commensurate rise in its volume.

Their clothes still ruffled and their faces still red, Annabelle and Allenby had no choice but to follow the long, humiliating path up to the main balcony. Kit hoped they suffered, knowing that the crowd above them had seen them in their most intimate, scandalous moments.

He had been friends with both of them, once upon a time.

Perhaps that was why Kit stayed sat on the viewing platform's brick wall, his smirk equal parts smug and hateful. He knew both Annabelle and Allenby would have to follow the only path back up out of the garden. Perhaps he just wanted to be close to her again, to look her in the eyes.

His heart pounded with trepidation as they rounded the corner that would bring them past the viewing platform. After sixteen years, he was moments away from finally seeing her again.

Annabelle's shamed walk came to a standstill when she finally saw him, her eyes widening further than he had ever seen.

I promise I'll wait for you.

"You look like you've seen a ghost," Kit observed dryly.

It was Allenby who spoke, however. "What the fuck are you doing here?" he spat, holding out an arm across Annabelle's torso. Was that supposed to be protective?

Kit's lip twitched in disgust. "I thought I'd brighten your day," he remarked, effecting an exhausted sigh and tapping the lever next to him.

Allenby's jaw ticked. "You fucking prick."

"A fucking prick," Kit nodded in agreement, before gesturing to Annabelle with a strained smile. "And a fucking whore."

Annabelle shoved past Allenby, a look of such hatred on her face he was surprised it didn't burn. He saw the slap coming from a mile away.

And yet he did nothing to stop it.

His head whipped to the side, his cheek aflame with a piercing sting. Annabelle drew her hand back for another round, but Kit pounced, clutching her and spinning her around, his front to her back, pinning her arms to the side.

"Careful," he murmured in her ear, drawing great gulps of her scent into his lungs. "Or Allenby will be bending you over again before you can say hussy."

She kicked out at him, the narrow heel of her shoe striking him square in the shin. Wary of the bruise he'd be waking up with—and of the fact that her next target may very well be his cock—he let her twist from his grasp.

Annabelle turned her nose up at him, a revolted grimace twisting her regal features. "I admit my expectations of you were low, but to see you in person…" she trailed off, shaking her head. "Even society's dregs would cast you out now."

He bit out a cool, ironic laugh. "And yet those plump red lips of yours have been stretched round my cock."

The fist that seized hold of Kit's front belonged to a furious Allenby. "Enough," he hissed.

"By the looks of that chattering crowd up on that balcony," Kit remarked, "I think you're just getting started. Is that the delightful Mrs Allenby up there?"

Allenby's head twisted, his face dissolving into shock. That was indeed Mrs Allenby up there. "God above."

"I remember attending your wedding," Kit goaded him. "She looked *so* very happy. And yet you've shoved your cock in the first tart to spread her legs for you. How on earth is your wife going to show her face in society again?"

Like Annabelle's slap, Kit saw Allenby's fist swinging.

And like before, he did nothing to stop it.

In fact, he *revelled* in it. He needed the pain. He needed to feel something other than grief and regret.

Kit spat out the blood pooling in his mouth and returned fire. If his fist hurt, he didn't feel it, but the sound of his punches crunching against Allenby's face were music to his ears. Adrenaline lit a fire in his blood, urging him on like a devil on his shoulder.

As though from far away, he heard screams from up on the balcony, but they didn't stop him. He blinked blood from his eyes, dimly aware that one of Allenby's punches must have split the skin on his temple.

Allenby had just landed another punch when someone kicked his knee in from behind, their sharp stiletto almost puncturing his calf. Too drunk to right himself, he toppled to the ground like a collapsed marionette, his head hitting the stone tiles with a sickening crunch.

The next time he opened his eyes, he was being dragged to his feet by unknown hands. There were so many voices he couldn't differentiate between them. Shouts of outrage and excited whispers. A woman's cries could be heard somewhere in between. Pressed against his face was a slightly scratchy red-and-black livery; he was still at Linwood's ball, then.

"I'm so sorry, Lady Buckford," Anthony was saying sincerely, whilst Daisy's voice murmured beside him. "And Lord Linwood—"

"Just get him out of my sight."

Kit was about to let unconsciousness lull him closer when he recognised Uncle Eric's sombre tones. "I cannot apologise enough for his behaviour."

There was a scoff. "He's not the only one whose despicable behaviour necessitates an apology. That such a vile display of infidelity should happen under my roof is more of an insult than anything else."

Kit groaned in pain as he was suddenly hefted against something. Was that leather he felt? One inhale told him exactly where he was. He recognised the sharp, acrid smell of the beeswax leather conditioner their chauffeur used to maintain the seats in the motor.

Linwood's servants had thrown him in the back of his car.

Somewhere in his mind, he felt the car sink as someone climbed aboard. "Back home, m'lord?"

"Home," came Uncle Eric's distant answer. "I need to stay here to sort out this mess. Return after you've dropped him off at Campbell House."

The rumble of the engine shook Kit's cheek where it pressed against the leather, and he let himself be lulled to sleep by the car's twists and turns.

It was barely a ten-minute drive to Berkeley Square, but somewhere along the way Kit grasped consciousness, rather than the vague in between he'd been hovering in.

They were trundling along Hill Street when Kit finally sat up, the tall buildings gently passing them by. His chauffeur's plump figure loomed in the driver's seat, the man's usual patchy blond comb-over on show. "Ogden?" he rasped.

Ogden jumped in fright, the car veering off course. "Your Grace! I didn't realise you were awake."

"Take me to *Chéries*."

Ogden shot Kit a side glance, his eyes quickly refocusing on the road. "But Your Grace, His Lordship said to take you straight home."

"Take me to fucking *Chéries*, Ogden," Kit slurred, leaning his head against the back seat, letting it loll around as Ogden turned them around. "Good man," he said, his eyes closing once more.

A sharp prod in his side pulled him back to the land of the living.

"Your Grace?"

Kit grunted, annoyed at being woken.

"We're at *Chéries*."

Well that was certainly worth opening his eyes for.

Everything remained out of focus when he finally pulled himself up and—with Ogden's valiant assistance—dragged himself from the motor.

The delightfully familiar Madame Arceneaux stood at *Chéries'* bright white front door, smiling coquettishly, although he noticed her gaze dart up to his temple. Was he still covered in blood? "I was beginning to think you had deserted us, Your Grace."

He grunted again, grasping onto the railings as he climbed the steps to paradise. He didn't bother with the pleasantries. Kit only wanted to know one thing. "Is she here?"

"She is, Your Grace. And she will be most pleased to see you." Madame Arceneaux clicked her fingers at some unseen employee as they passed through the entrance hall. In some regards, it resembled an art gallery, lined by Renaissance-era oil paintings. Kit had been here enough to realise that they typically depicted gods of some sort or another. Always nude. Usually debauched.

Venus was the most frequently featured goddess—and in one painting engaged in sexual acts with another woman.

Kit was particularly fond of that one.

By the time he'd made his way across the black-and-gold marbled entrance hall, he had his wits about him. And just in time too.

"Your Grace," the black-haired temptress standing before him said, angling her head. As with all of Madame Arceneaux's darlings, she was dressed in a simple satin robe—white, of course. She took his hand, threading their fingers together.

"Not tonight I'm not."

"Come on then," she pulled, leading him to her room. It was something he'd always liked about *Chéries*. Each girl had their own room, which they could decorate according to their own choosing. It somehow made it more… personal. "Lay on the bed."

He did as she asked, watching her saunter over to the sink in the corner. She returned with a bowl of warm water and a flannel, beginning to dab at his forehead.

"What trouble have you gotten yourself in tonight, Your Grace?" she asked, the barest hint of an accent layered somewhere in her pronunciation. Eastern European, he would have guessed.

Kit traced the underside of her wrist. "Don't call me that. Not in here."

"Kit, then," she relented, looking slightly guilty when she said it—as she always did.

She was almost as good as the real thing. *Almost.* The black hair and the plump cupid's bow lips. She didn't quite have the high-handedness or the haughty demeanour necessary to complete the look, but it was as good as he was going to get.

"I saw you tonight."

Surprised sparked in her features before her lips pressed together. "Judging by your injuries," she rinsed the flannel in the increasingly pink water, "it was not a happy reunion."

"No." When she was done, he patted the bed beside him. "Lie with me."

Putting the bowl aside, she stretched out next to him, pushing back strands of damp hair to inspect the wound on his head, but Kit slipped a hand over her hip and yanked her closer, until her face was inches from his. "I've missed you, little queen."

She smiled at him then. "I'm here now."

The incoming hush of sleep made his movements clumsy, but he managed to palm her cheek before he closed his eyes for the final time. "Annabelle," he whispered.

He could pretend again. Just for a little while.

7
Annabelle

"What in the name of all things holy were you *thinking*?"

Annabelle didn't immediately react to her mother's anger, choosing instead to direct her attention to the cedar trees lining the gardens of Scarlett Castle, steadfastly ignoring the pile of fresh letters they'd received today—all wanting to know more about Annabelle's affair with Cornelius. Or condemning her for it. Or uninviting the family from the rest of the London Season.

Home. She was home.

And yet she had never felt more out of place.

"I am at perfect liberty to do as I please, Mama."

In the corner of her eye, Annabelle saw her mother take a seat on one of the well-cushioned armchairs opposite her; one of many dotting the morning room. "I understand, Annabelle. *Believe me*, I understand. As widows, we can become… lonely. But there is a difference between taking discreet comfort from another in your widowhood and carrying on with another woman's husband! And to do so in public…" Mama trailed off, her face screwing up in disgust.

"It's not what you think," Annabelle said, picking idly at the macramé creation draped over the armchair's sleeve. Her mother's words had rankled her. She could deal with accusations of stupidity, loose behaviour, and downright recklessness, but she was not a homewrecker. "Not entirely, at least."

"Is it not?" Mama had never looked so disappointed in her. "Eva Allenby was your *friend*, for heaven's sake, and to sleep with her husband—"

"Eva Allenby," she interrupted, "is like Aunt Leonora."

A pause. "Aunt Leonora? As in…"

Annabelle nodded. Her father's sister had always seemed unusual, from Annabelle's perspective. It was she who had encouraged Annabelle's support of the Women's Institute and the National Union of Women Suffrage Societies. Indeed, Aunt Leonora's companion, Miss Florence, had taken Annabelle to her first suffrage meeting, back before they were called suffragettes.

Lord Loughborough, Annabelle's uncle, even allowed Miss Florence to live in the room connected to Aunt Leonora's, which she had found strange. Until she connected the dots and realised their marriage was more of a business arrangement than anything else.

A business arrangement that had produced Cousin George, second in line to the Loughborough earldom, and so Annabelle declared it a success.

She was relieved to see the look of revulsion had disappeared from her mother's face. "Did Mrs Allenby know?"

"Yes."

"Did she consent?"

Annabelle nodded. "She has Lady Kingswood, and Mr Allenby…"

"Has you."

"Had." Annabelle clocked her jaw to the side.

"Oh, darling." Her mother's shoulders drew inwards on a sigh. Pity had replaced the disappointment in her gaze. "Did you love him?"

She shook her head. "Cornelius and I were friends, but nothing more. Either way, he's broken things off and they've retreated to their estate to wait things out."

"I suspect he will be forgiven far quicker than you. Women always bear the brunt of things like this, I'm afraid." A knock at the door stole Mary's focus. "Come in."

Effie entered, and guilt punched through Annabelle at her teary, reddened eyes. "I've received another letter."

Mama crossed the room to her youngest daughter. "From whom?"

Shooting Annabelle a look overflowing with venom, Effie croaked, "The Court of St James's."

"A representative on behalf of the Court of St James's, darling," Mary said, her eyes flicking across the page, line by line. "The royal court is more concerned with matters of an ambassadorial nature than individual debutantes."

"The message remains the same," Effie's voice broke on the last word. "I am not welcome at Queen Charlotte's Ball due to *recent events associated with my family*. I am not welcome anywhere, it seems."

Annabelle stood, moving towards her sister. "Effie, I'm so—"

"No!" Effie's blonde ringlets and bumblebee earrings shook as she pointed a menacing finger in Annabelle's direction. "You do *not* get to be sorry. You've ruined my first season. You've ruined Caroline's first season. You've ruined things I've worked towards for *years*. We trusted you to chaperone us and all this time you were off cavorting with your friend's husband in broad daylight."

It had been nighttime, but Annabelle said nothing. She had never heard Effie so much as raise her voice before; her younger sister was sweet, Scarlett Castle's resident cherub.

"You thought of no one but yourself." Effie stepped forward, slamming the letter against Annabelle's chest. "And I am ashamed to call you my sister. It would be better for all of us if you just disappeared."

Annabelle's hand came up to hold Effie's letter as her sister turned on her heel and stormed out of the morning room.

"Effie, darling," Mama said, giving Annabelle an almost apologetic look before rushing after her.

She listened to the combined footsteps of her mother and sister racing up the stairs, in addition to the distant cries of a baby. One of Michael and Emmeline's twin sons, she presumed. It didn't sound like either of their older girls.

Annabelle swore under her breath, leaning against the back of the armchair.

She had made a pig's ear of things.

Effie was right.

A throat cleared over by the door. "Your Ladyship."

Annabelle's head shot up, finding Scarlett Castle's butler, Granville, standing there.

"There's a Miss Rose Youd on the telephone for you."

Youd? "I don't believe I know anyone by that name, Granville. Did she say what she wants?"

Granville hesitated. That was never a good sign. "She says she's calling from the *Illustrated London News* about their Lady's Letter column."

God, not that utter drivel. Her cursing this time was mental—not wanting to offend Granville's delicate sensibilities. At this time of year, the Lady's Letter column dealt primarily with gossip from the London Season.

"Tell them I'm not here," Annabelle requested. "I'm taking an extended leave of absence."

Granville's usual habit of keeping his personal opinions secret was no match for his surprise. "I see."

Her actions had put them all under a spotlight, and the letters and calls would keep coming whilst she remained here. If journalists had managed to get the bit between their gaping maws, the furore was only just beginning.

Annabelle sighed. She didn't want to go, but there was nothing else for it. "Tell Enid to pack a suitcase for me." Enid, her lady's maid, would have to remain here on account of her son attending the village school, but Annabelle had a job for her. "And tell her to respond to these letters. The same for each one; I'm at Foxcotte Moor, and all correspondence on this matter should be sent there."

Hopefully identical responses would cease the influx of letters.

Granville nodded, his bowed head briefly showing off the sharpness of his side parting.

Foxcotte Moor would be empty this time of year, except for the skeleton staff in charge of maintaining the castle.

Scotland. Annabelle had fond memories of her time there as a child, and it would be better for her family if the source of outrage vanished for the time being.

She had already caused them enough grief.

8
Kit

He was dying. This was how it was going to end. Kit tried to breathe normally, to ration the oxygen that remained to him, but his lungs wouldn't comply. Buried under the snow, his adrenaline levels had spiked, but he couldn't move a muscle.

Sound was all around him, the great rumble of the earth as thousands upon thousands of tonnes of snow moved above his head. He was pinned in the position he'd fallen in, rendered immobile by the might of nature.

He was going to die. Was anyone else trapped in here with him? Major MacGillivray hadn't been far away when the avalanche hit them, but there was no way of differentiating up from down in his current position, let alone finding his friend.

Panic swarmed him, his heart racing. Kit screamed for help, bellowing until his throat was raw. He frantically tried to move his arms and legs, but he was pinned. The snow compressed his limbs, squeezing until he felt his heart almost give ou—

The burning in his right shoulder yanked him from his nightmare faster than Uncle Eric ever had.

Kicking his way out of the bedcovers, Kit swore at the red embers creeping their way across his mattress.

"Fucking hell," he mumbled, furiously slapping at them. How the fuck had he managed to set his bed alight?

The ashtray on his mattress—surrounded by crisp, blackened fabric—was the likely culprit.

Stumbling to his feet, Kit swiped one of the empty bottles of feni littering the floor before filling it up in his en suite and dumping it back onto the bed. Plus another round for good measure.

After putting out the almost-fire, Kit collapsed onto one of the boxes of paperwork he was supposed to be sorting out, his head in his hands.

This was not his finest moment.

And he'd had so many of those of late.

Huffing out his shame, Kit glanced up at the skylight above him. It was the only place in the entire house he felt calm. The sky was overcast, signalling the start of another dull, grey London day. Shrugging on a dressing gown, he started the long journey downstairs to what was simultaneously his least favourite and most favourite place in the house: the cellar.

Did feni need to be stored in a cellar? The delivery men would do just as well delivering it directly to his bedroom. Well, the old loft office turned bedroom. The ducal bedroom was on the second floor, but Kit had little interest in suffocating under five storeys of brick.

Besides, he'd wake up every man and his dog down there.

On the ground floor, Kit almost ran head-first into a red-haired sprite leaving the ducal office. "Daisy." He cleared his throat, conscious of the fact that he was dressed in nothing but residual soot and his dressing gown. "Morning."

"Kit!" His poor sister-in-law nearly jumped out of her skin, clutching her heart. "Good morning. I, erm," Daisy's gaze trailed down his open dressing gown before whipping back up to his face. "I didn't expect to see you up so early."

He tightened it around his large frame, conscious of the fact it was slightly too small for him. "I needed to fetch something."

"Right," she clapped her hands awkwardly. She had been like this since his performance at Linwood's ball last week, barely able to look him in the eye. "Actually, on your way back upstairs, would you mind taking one of these old correspondence boxes to the loft? They're awfully heavy."

He grunted his agreement, quickly moving down the corridor before she asked him to do anything else.

By the time he'd reemerged from the cellar, a bottle of feni in hand, Daisy had disappeared somewhere within the belly of the townhouse. As agreed, however, he collected the dusty box of letters, plus a tray that lay on top with a note declaring it to be *morning post*.

Right then.

Today he'd tackle a glass of feni, the morning post, and the box of old correspondence. In that order.

By the time he got to the morning post, he was more than a little tipsy. One glass of feni had become two, which had become three, and before he knew it Da Silva, his uncle's judgemental valet, was bringing up luncheon and another box of old letters—complete with the look of disapproval he reserved solely for Kit.

The morning post, as it turned out, was nothing of consequence. Invitations to events throughout the Season, all of which would go unanswered. He snorted, remembering that Annabelle had been forced back to Scarlett Castle by the uproar after Linwood's ball. He hoped she was miserable. Even so, he had no intention of doing anything other than planning for his third attempt to scale Everest. Brigadier-General Bruce was counting on him, both as part of the team and for financing.

Great Britain had lost the race to both the North and South Poles, but the third pole, Everest, would be theirs. After their failure last year, and the death of John MacGillivray, Brigadier-General Bruce was more determined than ever to make the first ascent.

And so was Kit.

He gritted his teeth, clumsily reaching for the bottle of feni.

Only to knock over the dusty box of letters that Da Silva had haphazardly placed on the edge of the desk—probably out of spite. Its contents scattered to the floor; letters, old expedition maps, telegrams, even an old uncashed cheque.

"Christ's sake," he muttered unhappily, half tempted to let the mess live there. Bending down, he shoved handfuls of paper back into the box, freezing when he recognised the elegant scrawl of an achingly familiar lady.

Little queen.

Kit picked it up, rasping his thumb over the written indentation. *The Duke of Aylesbourne.*

He shouldn't open it. He should have done what Pandora ought to have done; leave the fucking box alone.

But his willpower was shot, so he slid the letter out of the opened envelope.

The Duke of Aylesbourne
Campbell House

Berkeley Square Gardens
London

Wednesday, 7th August 1907

Kit,

I am desperately sorry to have to send this, but I have no other option. I'm pregnant with your child, Kit. I have waited for as long as I could in the hope that my courses would arrive, but they have not.
I beg of you. Do not leave on your expedition this afternoon. You MUST stay—to give our child a name, if nothing else.

Urgently awaiting your reply by return special messenger,
Little queen

Kit's eyes moved quicker than his drunken brain could process, reading the letter several times over to ensure he had not misunderstood Annabelle's message. *I'm pregnant with your child, Kit.* There was no misunderstanding that.

He was going to be sick.
Barely making it to the toilet, he retched until he wasn't sure whether the tears rolling down his face were from his physical woes or their mental counterparts.
Jesus fucking Christ.
This explained everything.

Everything he had struggled to understand, everything that had ripped his heart to shreds. He had been in Australia when he'd received the news of Annabelle's marriage to Buckford, a stranger thrice her age.

But then...

Where was the child? *Their* child. God, no wonder she'd hated him so. She'd had to raise their child with a stranger. How old would they be now? Fifteen? Sixteen? On their way to being an adult. Was their son at Eton at this very minute? Or did they have a daughter being raised in secrecy at Scarlett Castle?

He finally understood Theo's anger, when he'd returned from the Nimrod expedition and gone to Scarlett Castle with a thousand questions.

Leaping to his feet, Kit washed his mouth out before thundering downstairs, feeling more sober than he had in years. It was time to go to Scarlett Castle and finally get his answers.

∞

Michael Fraser, the Duke of Foxcotte, was greyer than the last time Kit had seen him. He was also considerably angrier. "How dare you fucking come here?" Michael whisper-snarled, presumably because his horde of children played in the library behind him.

"I need to see her," Kit pleaded. At first glance, he had wondered if one of them was his and Annabelle's child. Two dark-haired boys, chubby with infancy and wobbly on their feet. The two young girls were older, battling it out over a chess board, one with long black hair and Theo's sapphire blue eyes, the other with curly blonde ringlets. All of them, however, were far too young to be his and Annabelle's.

Michael shook his head, hatred in his grey eyes. "You're lucky I haven't broken your nose after what you did at Linwood's ball. Leave."

Even in his fervent panic, that made him laugh. "Theo already beat you to it."

The mention of his dead brother threw Michael. "What?"

"Theo," Kit explained, his words tinged with a bittersweet edge. "He broke my nose the last time I was here."

Michael fisted the front of Kit's crumpled shirt, attempting to tug him towards the door. "If *Theo* broke your nose, then you bloody well deserved it."

"I've just found out why." Kit slapped the letter against his old friend's chest. "From his perspective," he admitted, "yes, I did."

It only took Michael a moment to read the aged letter, his face slackening with shock. "This is Annabelle's writing." Those haunting grey eyes pinned him, storm clouds of anger unfurling within them.

Kit's desperation intercepted his fury. "I read this for the first time *today*, Michael. So I ask you again—*where* is she?"

9
Annabelle

The stag watched her, just as she watched him. Its harem of females lurked behind, spread out along the glen's sloped side. Moss-covered boulders dotted the landscape, as though some giant game of marbles had been played long ago.

"*Boo!*" she said suddenly, lazily watching the small stampede of hooved feet, feeling the vibrations through the picnic blanket on which she sat.

If it was hunting season, she'd have done worse. The deer were lucky she wasn't in the mood for venison tonight. She eyed the loaded stalking rifle propped up against a log over to her right.

There was no point in picking it up. As it was, she was stocked up for several days. The bothy did not have the luxury of electricity, but the cook at Foxcotte Moor had packed an icebox for her. The river running through the base of the glen like a silky blue ribbon provided the water, although she boiled it before it ever touched her lips—as her father had taught her. A few hundred yards away, the river opened into Loch Domhainn, which provided the fish.

The trip had been a nostalgic one. Once upon a time, her father, Phillip Fraser, had taken his three children on hiking trips to this very bothy. He was, first and foremost, a soldier, and believed that all of his children should know how to fell a tree, hunt their dinner, and light a fire.

Effie hadn't even been born when they'd taken their last hunting trip before his death, Annabelle realised sadly. Did she know how to do any of those things?

It had been far too long since Annabelle had put that knowledge to use. Since her father was alive, in fact.

"Bothies," Phillip Fraser had once said, "have long since been a source of shelter in the Highlands. They're typically simple huts or cottages located in remote areas that are available for anyone to use, free of charge."

"So they're houses?" she had asked.

"Not in the normal sense of the word," Phillip answered, tending to the fire around which they sat. "They're usually nothing more than a roof over your head and a hearth in which to cook your dinner. Sometimes previous visitors will have left some supplies, cooking instruments and the like. Sometimes there's nothing at all."

Annabelle looked back at the bothy in which they were staying. "And what happens if someone wants to come in the bothy you're staying in?"

Phillip had grinned. "Then you'll have company for the night."

"But it's on Foxcotte land. *Our* land," ten-year-old Annabelle had protested.

"And the Foxcotte dukedom allocated it as a bothy some two hundred years ago. It used to be a farmer's cottage, I believe, but I see no reason to change its status."

She sighed, watching the retreating deer and thinking of her father. How long had it been since she'd thought of him? *Too long.* At Scarlett Castle, there were photographs of him dotted around the house, and even painted portraits, but she hadn't truly thought of the time they'd spent together.

For the first time in years, she missed him.

Annabelle pressed her pencil back to the sketching pad, returning to the half-finished dress she'd been drawing. It typified the *la garçonne* look she adored, half because of the comfort it offered and half because of the outrage it drew.

A few weeks ago, she would have thrived on the latter.

When it was her family in the line of fire, however, the threat of outrage spo—

The cracking of a twig lifted her head. She had heard something similar this morning, along with a disembodied *mew*. Adrenaline flooded her system when she saw that the individual responsible was not a lowly cat, but a dishevelled, frantic-looking Aylesbourne. His hair was mussed, with a leaf caught in his jaw-length black strands. Combined with the wet soil on his trousers—as though he'd taken a hard fall—and the agitation in his expression, his appearance immediately set off alarm bells.

God strewth. He'd completely lost his mind.

Annabelle's focus flicked down to the stalking rifle propped against the log, perhaps ten yards away. It was closer to her than him, but only just.

Aylesbourne followed her gaze, his eyes widening.

Both of them moved simultaneously. Her panic flung her sketching equipment in all directions, but Annabelle's only aim was to grab the rifle before Aylesbourne reached it. In his current state, there was no telling what he'd do if he reached it first.

She was miles from Foxcotte Moor, their Scottish baronial castle, which had been incorporated into the Foxcotte dukedom from one ancestor or another. Nowadays, it was primarily let out for the hunting season, but her father had taken the family here every year during her childhood.

Annabelle knew these lands well. Which meant she also knew she was entirely alone out here.

She was quick in her attempt to reach the rifle, but so was Aylesbourne, barrelling over an old animal trough that lay in his way. After her mad dash, half walking and half crawling, she landed so forcefully her fingers carved grooves into the soil, ramming it beneath her freshly-painted fingernails.

Her hands had just clasped the smooth, cold metal barrel when Aylesbourne hit her like a freight train, shoving the rifle from her grip and pinning her to the floor. The back of her head slammed against the soil, but Aylesbourne straddled her, clearly not convinced he'd eliminated the threat.

"Are you bloody mad, woman?" he panted, gripping both of her arms in one hand and pinning them above her head.

Annabelle was about to spit in his face, but his question sent a shiver down her spine. *Are you bloody mad, woman?*

Those were the first words he'd ever said to her.

He seemed to realise a moment later, his face draining of colour. With his free hand, he traced her cheekbone, ignoring her attempts to flick him off. "How I wish we could start again from that moment."

Quickly recovering, Annabelle tried to kick him, but his weight over her hips rendered her legs useless. "Stick your wish up your hole, Aylesbourne." Ignoring his grin, she spoke again. "Why are you here?"

"I…" Aylesbourne opened and closed his mouth, like the fish she'd caught that morning—moments before she'd ended its life with a well-aimed blow of her priest. Well, the priest she'd borrowed from Foxcotte Moor's ghillie. "I read your letter."

"I didn't send you a letter."

With one hand, Aylesbourne took out a letter from his breast pocket, briefly struggling to remove it from the envelope. Finally, he shook it open, and Annabelle was struck dumb at the sight of the words she'd written so long ago.

I beg of you. Do not leave on your expedition this afternoon. You MUST stay—to give our child a name, if nothing else.

Annabelle cringed at her own words. *I beg of you.* She looked down her nose at him; the man who was responsible for so much of her misery. She would never beg anyone for anything again. "What of it? Did you fancy a trip down memory lane? I must admit, I would have picked a more cheerful subject matter."

"I read this for the first time *yesterday*," he whispered. "I would never have forsaken you, *mo chridhe*. I would sooner forsake my very soul."

Blood pounded in her ears at the sound of that affectionate little endearment, but her lips warped into an ugly grimace. "I don't believe you."

Aylesbourne's head bowed, a great huff shaking his shoulders. "I have no proof otherwise, Annabelle. But I swear to you, on everyone I hold dear, that I had never read this letter before. I swear to you that I didn't know about the baby. About our child, about what you had to go through." Cautiously, he let go of her hands for the first time since he'd pinned her down. "I was in Australia when I heard you had married Buckford. I thought you'd thrown me over. I thought everything between us was a lie. Fuck, I buried my only photograph of you at the South Pole because I couldn't bear to have it on my person. I couldn't bear to think everything we'd shared meant nothing to you."

When he climbed off her, Annabelle sat up. She was silent, preferring to listen to his explanation. It had been something her father had once taught her; if one remained silent, people tend to overexplain to compensate, and in doing so reveal far more than they had originally intended.

She was alone with a man who looked like he'd been dragged through a hedge backwards. She was no shrinking violet, but she also didn't have a death wish.

Her heart jumped into her throat when he reached for the gun, but he merely unloaded it, handing her the rifle and throwing the bullets over his shoulder. "I loved you, little queen. That night on the boat…" He shook his head. "I knew I wanted to marry you then. I knew you were the love of my life. But you deserved an exceptional husband, a husband you could be proud of. One that had earned the right to stand by your side. And so the trip to the South Pole…"

Annabelle's focus slid down to the letter in his hands, and Kit seemed to follow her line of thinking. "Had I read this letter," he said, holding it up between them, "I would never have left. Christ, I would have married you on the spot."

Kit laid it on the ground between them. "The fact that you had to go through everything alone… I've thought of little else since yesterday morning. It *burns* at my soul that you had another man at your side when we should have raised our child together, as we were meant to. Husband and wife."

The image burned her too, but not in the way he would have expected. "Kit…"

He smiled. "I could listen to you say my name until the stars die out."

Annabelle simply came right out with it. He may have broken her heart, but the hope on his face was too much for her to bear. "I lost the child, Kit."

Kit flinched, as though her words brought a physical blow. "What?"

The memory of the blood on her bed at Buckford Hall haunted her. She had woken up to a massacre. Lord Buckford had responded to her pained cries, ringing for a doctor, but there had been no stopping it. And then the delivery itself… "It was perhaps three months after we'd married." Annabelle took a deep breath, dipping her toe into memories she'd avoided for years. "I'd felt the baby for the first time the night before. A strange flutter in my stomach."

Kit was by her side in an instant, far closer than she wanted him. "*Mo chridhe…*"

She swallowed her emotions down, as she was so used to doing. She had long since grieved for her child. "It is in the past," she said, getting to her feet and stepping away from him. "It matters not."

"It may be in the past," he mimicked her actions, standing tall behind her. "But I am only just learning of it. Oh god, Annabelle. The things you had to go through alone are a knife in my gut."

The things she'd endured alone made her the person she was today, and the person she was today had been built upon a fortress of isolation and strength. She crossed her arms. "Is that why you're here, Aylesbourne? To discuss the letter?"

"I'm here for you," he said simply, as if that explained everything.

And I would prefer you were not.

Her emotions roiled so violently they constricted her gut. Annabelle closed her eyes, taking a deep breath to steady herself. "Leave."

"Excuse me?"

"What did you think was going to happen? You were going to reappear in my life with news of your supposed discovery of the letter, and I would jump back into your arms?" His silence spoke volumes. "Did you forget that it was only a few days ago that you *humiliated* me in front of a crowd of people? Why do you think I'm here instead of enjoying myself in the season?"

Her anger grew the more she spoke, letting out more emotion than she had in years. "The results of your actions have sent shockwaves through *so* many people's lives. Me. My family. Effie. God, do you know what kind of state she is in? Cornelius has been painted as an adulterer. Eva has been humiliated. Lord Linwood has been marred by association. And I am now looked upon as a harlot. All because of your spiteful decision. And you come here a week later with an ancient letter expecting everything to have changed? It doesn't change the fact that I grieved our child alone, whilst you were off seeking personal glory. I don't care that you're here for me, Aylesbourne. My answer remains the same: stick your wish up your fucking hole."

Aylesbourne had somehow grown smaller and smaller through her tirade. "I'm sorry," he whispered.

Annabelle's laugh was cruel, and she revelled in it. Finally, an outlet for her frustration. "I told you of the child because I believe you're entitled to the knowledge, but an apology doesn't fix what you've done. Go and deal with the consequences of your actions somewhere I'm not reminded of the curse of your continued existence."

∞

The dark wood of the aged rafters was the first thing to greet her the next morning. Followed by a cursory glance at the whitewashed walls. Despite the shoddy paintwork, Annabelle smiled at it—because it had been Theo and Michael who'd painted it. She had been the self-appointed manager of the project, barking instructions as her older brothers worked.

The rest of the bothy was simple. It comprised a single room, with exposed floorboards covered in dust and soil, courtesy of the many muddied boots that passed through here on their travels. Annabelle didn't mind roughing it, and certainly not here. True, she was most at home choosing fabrics and watching shows held by fashion designers. Indeed, she had not long returned from Paris, attending a show on the rue Cambon by Coco Chanel.

And now look where she was. Annabelle didn't even know what day it was.

Still, the sloppily painted walls were a fond friend to her, with all the memories they brought with them. And then she blinked at one particular spot, her head tilting to the side. Was that a phallus drawn into th—?

Someone snored outside.

Her good mood slipped away like bird mess sliding down a window.

Annabelle leapt to her feet, storming over to the front door and throwing it open, ready to spit venom. Daylight spilled into the dimly-lit bothy. Aylesbourne was fast asleep next to the blackened fire pit, his head resting on a log.

She took a deep breath. And then another. What was the punishment for murdering a duke in his sleep?

God, it would be worth it.

Instead, she gave a malevolent smirk, and picked up her empty water bucket. He wanted to stay here, did he? Well he bloody well wasn't going to enjoy it.

The trip down to the river was pleasant, and one she made every morning. The glen in which the bothy was located was bordered on either side by rocky crags reaching up into the sky. Patches of lilac heather provided splotches of colour on the green landscape, whilst the river's crystal clear water rushed over the smooth stones below, burbling merrily.

Annabelle looked back at the bothy. No, perhaps the accommodation wasn't as luxurious as she had grown to expect, but everything else about this place was paradise.

Boots crunching over the pebbles at the side of the river, Annabelle bent to fill her bucket. To the side of her foot lay a wide, flat stone the size of a half crown coin. *Perfect.*

She stood, aiming for one of the quieter parts of the river. Her father had tried to teach her how to skip stones when she was a girl, but she had never quite got the hang of it.

Flicking her wrist, Annabelle let the stone fly.

It sunk on its first so-called skip.

Bugger.

Down but not out, Annabelle lifted the water bucket. The water inside it slopped to the side as she walked, leaving a damp trail to mark her route.

Aylesbourne was where she'd left him, still sleeping soundly. *Not for long if I have anything to say about it.*

Feeling a cruel satisfaction, Annabelle crept towards him, her shadow falling over his sleeping form. She hoisted the bucket upwards, aiming for his head. Tilting it forw—

"*Mew.*"

She froze, lowering her weapon. Carefully, she put the bucket back down. Had that sound come from *Aylesbourne?*

Movement shifted under his jacket, but Aylesbourne himself remained still. Lying on his back, he'd crossed his arms in his sleep, creating a large ruffle in the fabric.

A ruffle in which something appeared to have taken up residence.

Annabelle bent down to peel the ruffle back, her jaw falling open.

Three tiny tabby kittens were huddled on his chest, their paws tucked under their bodies. Whilst two of them slept, one did not. Was this the sentry, perhaps? The awake kitten glanced up at Annabelle, its bright blue eyes judging her, letting out the most adorable hiss she'd ever heard. It rose to its feet, walking towards her to swipe.

She almost laughed when the movement pulled the kitten off balance, watching it stumble. One of its tiny, curled ears twitched at the noise, and she smiled when it hissed at her once more. "Oh my goodness," she whispered. "You're the sweetest thing I've ever seen."

The kitten swiped again, with a hiss for good measure.

This time Annabelle couldn't hold her snort back.

"Annabelle?" Aylesbourne croaked, opening eyes heavily shadowed by dark circles. He went to shift, but she slapped a hand over his collarbone.

"Don't move," she snarled, before a look at the kittens changed her tone. "You made some friends in the night."

"*Mew*," the ferocious little kitten squeaked, coming up to brush its head on the underside of Aylesbourne's chin.

He grinned, scrunching up his face when it began to lick his cheek. "Where did these come from?"

"You tell me. I came out of the bothy to find, firstly, *you* sleeping here and, secondly, a litter of kittens on your chest."

Aylesbourne broke her gaze, focusing on the two kittens still curled up together. With all the noise, one of the two was awakening, stretching its teensy claws out. "I wasn't just going to lea—"

Annabelle frowned as he cut himself off and reached towards the third kitten, which remained asleep. "What's wrong?"

"I think this one might be dead." He scooped up the first two, handing them over to a concerned Annabelle and sitting up, cradling the third one in his hands. The first kitten pounced out of her grip, clumsily making its way back over to Aylesbourne and crawling into his lap. The second, however, meowed up at her before starting to lick the palm of her hand.

She held in a breath as he checked over the limp kitten in his arms. "What's wrong with it?"

"I'm not sure." A tiny noise left the kitten's throat, something less than a meow, and the two of them sighed in relief. "But they're thin, all of them. I think they're hungry. Do you have any milk with you?"

Annabelle shook her head, focusing on the limp kitten. Its fur was ragged, and its eyes crusted over. "I have fish in the ice box." Cats liked fish, didn't they?

"I don't know if they'll be able to eat it." He caught the fiery kitten, which—to Annabelle's surprise—let him peer into its mouth. "Their teeth look like they're only just coming in."

"I could mash it up for them?" she suggested. "With some water."

Aylesbourne nodded. "I think that's our best bet."

Quickly grabbing what she needed from the bothy, Annabelle lit a fire using a match and some kindling. Luckily, she'd filleted the fish she'd caught yesterday, meaning she only needed to cut it up before putting it into the pan.

The fiery little kitten, however, had other plans in mind. She'd barely cut the first piece before it pounced, shoving its tiny teeth into the raw chunk of meat. Annabelle attempted to take it back, but the kitten growled furiously.

Conceding defeat, Annabelle returned to chopping the rest of the fish, keeping an eye on the little troublemaker all the same.

After the fish was cooked, she poured a healthy amount of water onto the pan and used a fork to mash the mixture into a paste. There was a veritable choir of meows by the time she slopped it onto a plate for the mobile kittens, who immediately dived in.

Aylesbourne scooped up a clump with his finger, holding it out to the limp kitten in his hand.

To her relief, it opened a single eye to lick the clumpy mixture. A moment later, however, it stopped, resting its head against Aylesbourne's palm. "Is that one the runt?"

He nodded, running his hand down its back before inspecting its leg. He stilled when the kitten gave a sharp *mew*, inhaling sympathetically. "Oh you poor little thing," he murmured, looking up at her. "There's a wound on its leg that's crusted over. Do you have anything that I could—?"

Annabelle looked towards the bothy. "I don't have any steamed bandages," she said, remembering her time as an auxiliary nurse in the war, "but I do have a clean petticoat."

She expected him to make some sly comment, but he merely nodded, his attention entirely on the injured kitten.

It had been some time since she'd revisited her medical training as a voluntary aid detachment nurse during the Great War. If she was honest, she didn't thrive in the role like her sister-in-law, Emmeline, had. She'd simply enrolled because it was the right thing to do.

The soldiers who were sent to Yateley Military Hospital—the hospital in which she'd worked—all had families desperately hoping their boys would survive the war. She'd done the same with her brothers and cousin. Theo, Michael, and George had all spent at least a few days in the cottage hospital during the war, albeit to varying degrees. Michael had been her most frequent patient, given that Theo was an aide-de-camp to Douglas Haig and George was a medical officer. Michael, on the other hand, was in the trenches for the entire war.

Her family members were doing their part for the war effort, so she did too. In doing so, she wanted to care for all the soldiers to the same standard that she wanted her family cared for. She'd had no problem with the medical side of things; she was neither squeamish nor unintelligent, but she did struggle with her bedside manner. After Emmeline had trained, they often worked as a team, and her sister-in-law compensated for Annabelle's brusque personality.

"Good," Kit answered, his focus entirely on the poorly kitten in his hand. "Any clean fabric will do. I'm not the best at bandaging, but—"

"I'll do it," she offered, running into the bothy to grab her petticoat. "Tear it into strips about half an inch thick," she told him, taking the kitten from his grip and delicately cleaning the wound with the fresh water in the bucket. "I was a nurse during the war. I've bandaged more limbs than I can count."

"I know," he said softly, grimacing at the kitten's pitiful little squeaks.

"You do?"

Aylesbourne turned to his task, carefully ripping her petticoat into strips. She frowned, noticing his hands shaking. It was a chilly morning, but it wasn't freezing cold by any means. "I was effectively stranded in Antarctica during the Great War. Did you know?"

"No."

He almost flinched. "The last contact we had with the outside world was in 1914. We didn't learn that war had broken out until the beginning of 1917. It was only two or three months later we arrived on British shores. Most of us signed up immediately, of course, but I had a friend who had spent some time in the hospital near Scarlett Castle. He told me of you." Aylesbourne passed her one of the strips he'd made.

She took it, crafting a comfortable bandage for the poor animal. The kitten gave a distressed whine. "I'm sorry," she whispered. "You'll feel better afterwards, I promise."

"Animals suffering…" Aylesbourne shook his head. "Makes my gut turn."

"You took dogs with you on the expeditions, did you not?"

Was that another flinch? "We did." The feisty little kitten chose to interrupt then, and Annabelle had the sense that its interruption was a welcome one. "These cats may be quite rare, in fact."

"Rare?" Annabelle blinked. "Are they not just… cats?"

"These?" The first hint of a real laugh illuminated his face. "They might be Highland tigers, them."

"A rare subspecies of their Siberian cousins?" she snorted.

"Not quite. They look a bit like Highland wildcats. They could be proper wild animals."

"Oh," Annabelle said, taking another look at the injured kitten in her hand, partially hidden in a cloud of bandages. "I didn't know there were any *wild* cats. I thought they were all just feral or stray."

"Not at all. They're rare, I'll give you that. But these could be just as wild as foxes or badgers."

"Should we be feeding them then? If they're wild, surely their mother is going to be quite angry with us." Annabelle aimed a look at the feisty kitten, currently purring in Aylesbourne's lap. If their mother was anything like *that* one, she didn't want to meet her.

"With how thin these little ones are, I'm thinking their mother is long gone." He held the second kitten, the sweet one, up to his face and gave it a kiss. "But it's all right, I'll take care of you."

Annabelle gritted her teeth. It was hard to hate a man when he was cuddling a kitten.

Annabelle pressed her hand to her lips, watching the ball of purring kittens. The backdrop of the crackling fire and raindrops on the roof?

Perfection.

Truly, there could be no greater sounds against which to live one's life. Her lip quirked, sorrow edging its way into her mood. They had left fish out on the doorstep, but so far no mother cat had visited.

Well, fish and Aylesbourne himself.

When it became clear that he would be remaining here, Annabelle had decreed that he wouldn't step one foot over the bothy's threshold.

That had been after he'd moved the disused animal trough into it, of course. She couldn't lift that thing by herself, and she wanted to contain the kittens. Otherwise, there was nothing stopping them from getting too close to the fire in the hearth.

Annabelle didn't think they were that stupid, but she didn't want to test that theory.

Cupping a hand around her face to dim her reflection, she peered out of the window, attempting to ignore the plucking of her heartstrings. The hate she carried for Aylesbourne fought valiantly against it, but in the end, what she saw was plain.

Beyond the reflection of her knee-length nightgown, Aylesbourne lay in the same spot she'd found him in this morning, albeit now huddled into a shivering ball rather than reclining on his back. The rain had extinguished his fire, and he'd given his jacket to the kittens to sleep on. If they'd found it comforting this morning, he'd told her, then they had more need of it than him.

It was early May, and nights in the Scottish Highlands were not that far above freezing.

She muttered a curse brimming with frustration and opened the door. "Aylesbourne?" she called softly, not wanting to wake the kittens.

He uncurled, glancing over his shoulder, dark hair splattered across his forehead. "Is s-something the matter?"

"Get in here."

Annabelle stopped him when he reached the doorway, using the firelight to get a closer look at him. She laid her hand against his cheek to pull his face towards her, feeling his stubble score her palm. His skin was as cold as ice. "Your lips are blue!" she exclaimed, shoving him inside and closing the door behind him. "Why didn't you say anything?"

"I've slept in w-worse conditions than this," he stuttered.

Rolling her eyes, she directed him to a spot in front of the fire. She swallowed, eyeing the firm set of his shoulders. He'd filled out from when she'd last seen him like this, his muscles honed by years of pushing himself to the limit.

He looked almost pitiful as he stood, shivering all the while. Mud had plastered itself to his shoulders, but the rest of his white dress shirt was transparent, revealing parts of him she never wanted to see again.

One thing that hadn't changed over the years was her reaction to him.

There was no way his clothes were going to dry whilst he was wearing them. "These need to come off," she heard herself say.

She watched his unsuccessful attempt to undo his buttons for an entire minute before she took pity on his frozen, shaking fingers.

Aylesbourne merely stood there, shivering drops of water all over the wooden floor, but his eyes never left her face.

She could feel his gaze as she battled to undo the buttons, the fabric logged with water and difficult to manoeuvre. When she'd finally finished, she peeled the shirt off his skin…

Only to be met with two obstacles hitting her at once; his bare chest, and the buttons on his trousers.

Damn him, but she *yearned* to touch his skin, to run her fingers over him and discover the changes the years had wrought. She swallowed again, remembering what he'd done to her just recently. He'd *ruined* her. He'd *ruined* Effie's first season. He'd brought so much scandal upon her through a simple action.

Annabelle despised him.

And yet she'd never wanted anyone more.

She swallowed again, trying to shove those feelings down to her gut. Hanging the soaked shirt up on the washing line strung across the ceiling, she turned back to her task.

Aylesbourne simply stared at her, his rich, dark eyes giving nothing away. His shoulders were another story, heaving as she neared. He flinched as she touched the buttons on his black trousers, finally breaking the silence that had grown between them.

"Little queen…" he whispered hoarsely, a residual shiver shaking his shoulders.

"Shut up and stand still."

Once she'd undone the buttons, she turned away. No longer distracted by the line of hair disappearing into his shorts. No longer thinking of the way the water droplets clung to his skin, like she'd once done.

He could manage the rest by himself. "Here," she said abruptly, handing him the blanket she'd been using and turning away. "Take off the rest of your clothes and cover yourself with this."

The sounds of wet clothes being slapped against the floor filled the room, and she closed her eyes against it.

"You can turn around now."

Reluctantly, she did. His chest remained bare as he clutched the blanket around his waist, styling it like a kilt. Well, she supposed. He *was* Scottish. Silver scars were little nicks across his chest, but she couldn't help but notice he hadn't fastened the blanket particularly well, a small sliver of leg showing from hip to ankle.

Annabelle pulled herself away, her nightgown swishing around her thighs. "You can sleep on the floor."

"As I expected," he rumbled, his deep, low voice barely louder than the crackling fire.

Well she wasn't going to invite him into her bed now, was she? Scoffing, she turned away and climbed onto the mattress, cursing him all the while.

It was his own fault he was here. She shouldn't take sympathy on him.

Before long, Aylesbourne's shaky breaths calmed, turning into long, soothing inhales. Staring at the darkened rafters above, Annabelle hated him. She hated that he was here. She hated having to look at his face. She hated that he'd brought with him memories of giving birth to their deceased child.

The firelight illuminated his features in the darkness. She also hated the way the soft light danced across his cheeks, and the way his hair was just long enough to curl around his ears. She especially hated the fact that he'd moved in his sleep, revealing the dark thatch of hair just below his navel.

And then she began to hate something different.

She sat up, forgetting that she was attempting to sleep, because his breathing had become shaky again. Shaky enough for him to make a small whimper in his sleep, his face contorting into agony. And another. Mumbled words quickly followed, louder and louder, but they were too unclear to make out.

Other than one.

"*Annabelle,*" he pleaded desperately.

10

Kit

The feel of Annabelle's cold, lifeless body stuck with him under the snow would haunt him forevermore. He choked in air, immediately looking skywards. "The ceiling," he whispered, his eyes darting around, expecting it to cave in on him at any moment.

Strangely, it was Annabelle herself who answered. "What about it?"

He froze, like he should have done all those months ago, but then he pounced. Still half asleep, Kit grabbed her and shoved her beneath him. "Just stay still," he whispered, positioning his body over hers, bracing his shoulders in anticipation of the heavy wooden rafters landing on them.

Annabelle tried to open her mouth, but he put his hand over her lips. "You don't have to worry," he told her softly. "I'll protect you."

Her narrowed eyes softened at that, as did her nails, which had been digging into his forearm like claws.

The seconds passed, with him expecting death to be imminent and her shaking in his embrace. Slowly but surely, fear receded, quickly replaced by logic. Until he realised that it hadn't been her shaking at all. It had been him.

Relief almost drowned him when he realised it had all been another nightmare. "Annabelle," he gasped, half apologetic, half reassured.

She didn't look away, Annabelle. No, his little queen held his gaze, but there was no hatred in it now.

"You were dead in my nightmare," he eventually offered. What other explanation could he give? He was broken, and the only thing that would absolve him of his sins was the ascent of Everest itself. To finish what he and MacGillivray started.

"I'm here," she whispered. "I'm alive."

He almost shuddered in relief. "My soul has been tethered to you for so long. If you were to leave this earth…" Kit left the sentence unfinished, the idea too awful to comprehend.

Annabelle said nothing, her hair splayed out on the floorboards behind her. He could feel the embroidery of her nightgown against his skin—his *bare* skin.

Fuck. She'd woken him up from a nightmare and he'd tackled her like some savage beast. It was a miracle she hadn't screamed. In fact, he'd slapped his hand over her mouth, hadn't he? That was probably why. In that case, it was a miracle she hadn't kneed him in the groin and gone for the rifle in the corner.

Drowning in a sea of self-loathing, he was suddenly thrown a lifeline. Her hand came to rest against his cheek, and he leant into it. God, in his weakest moments he'd paid a black-haired, high-cheekboned courtesan for such attentions, but those touches were *nothing* compared to the real thing.

"Annabelle," he rasped, daring to touch her back. This time he wasn't callously silencing her in a fit of terror, but marvelling at the softness of her skin. Those tiny, almost invisible hairs on her cheeks were velvety against his palm; a stark contrast to the hard floorboards he'd pinned her against.

She sucked in a breath when he carried his touch downwards, sensitising her neck with the rough callouses of his hand.

The wide neckline of her dress presented a wealth of opportunity. With one quick tug, he could have her breasts bared. Indeed, the fabric was so thin he could already see the outline of their dusky tips.

Instead, he bowed his head until his lips landed over her heart. He savoured everything; the feel of her skin, the scent of her body—and the touch of her hands as they slid into his hair, holding him against her chest.

And then her gentle touch turned into a rough yank, tearing his face back up to eye level. "I despise you," she hissed, her eyes flicking down to his lips as she sharply pulled on his hair once more.

Kit wasn't proud of the lustful noise that left him. His cock hardened, trapped between the two of them. "You have no idea what I want to do to you when you talk like that."

Her brow arched, but even she couldn't hide that bite of her lip. "Tell me."

"I want to hold you down and fuck those words right out of your mouth," he smirked, running his thumb across her bottom lip. He bent down, until his own lips brushed against her ear. "Do you remember what my cock tastes like? Because I remember *exactly* what you taste like."

Annabelle gasped, clutching him closer. "Go fuck yourself, Aylesbourne."

The sound of his own name coming from her lips almost had him combusting there and then. "I'd rather fuck you." He remembered what he'd seen her do with Allenby. "Or do you need to slap me first to put you in the mood?"

"Don't make offers you can't fulfil."

Couldn't fulfil? If she wanted a servant, he'd fucking give her one.

Kit pushed himself off her and rested back on his haunches. He didn't bother to cover his painfully hard erection, letting her look her fill. "If you need me to kneel before you, Annabelle, I'm only too happy to oblige."

As she rose, Annabelle's flagrant judgement of his manhood only made him harder. She stood over him, glancing down at the strength in his spread knees—and what lay between them. She held out the palm of her hand expectantly. "Kiss it."

So she liked to be in control, did she? Two could play at that game.

Nevertheless, he was obedient. He laid his lips against the centre of her hand.

"Beg me to hit you."

He held her gaze. "Hit me, little queen." Fuck, he was so hard it hurt. "I beg of you."

And then he watched as she pulled her hand back and whipped it against his cheek.

Kit grunted, wholly unprepared for the rush of arousal and pain that coursed through him. He gripped his cock, pleading with it not to unman him in front of her.

"I don't remember giving you permission to touch yourself."

Obediently, he pulled his hand away.

He knew of brothels and courtesans that catered to men who liked to be dominated. Kit had never thought much of them. He'd certainly never envisioned himself as a man who shared their appetites. Quite the opposite, in fact; his tastes were of the rougher variety.

It seemed he'd learnt something new about himself today.

Licking his lip, he grinned up at her. "Are you wet?" He got to his feet, sliding his hand into her hair and tightening. "Answer me."

Her nostrils flared as she panted. "I'd like to slap you again."

Did she now? He laughed as an idea struck him. "If you're in the mood to dole out punishment, how about you suffocate me instead?"

"Suffocate you?"

Kit walked her backwards towards the bed, still gripping her hair tight. "It's quite simple really. You put a part of your body over my mouth."

Understanding filled her eyes.

"Did you do that with Allenby?"

He loosened his grip on her hair just enough to allow her to shake her head.

A frown. "Have you done that with anyone at all?"

She shook her head again.

It was primitive, but that pleased him more than he could say. When her legs hit the bed, he let go of her hair. "Do your worst. Make me suffer."

The challenge seemed to light a fire in her. "Lay down," she bit out, glancing around the room for god-knows-what.

When he saw that wicked smile on her face, he knew he was fucked.

Nevertheless, he followed her instruction, his eyes widening when he saw her unhooking a length of rope from a hook on the wall. "What are you doing?"

Annabelle walked up to the bed holding the rope as though it was the most normal thing in the world. "Put your hands above your head and hold the slats on the headboard."

Swallowing the seed of doubt in his mind, he once again obeyed. The frayed rope was like sandpaper against his skin, but she gave him no mercy, tightening the knots until he was well and truly bound.

She turned away then, digging around in her suitcase until she returned—with a silken sash in her hand.

Kit panted. He'd never been tied up before, but he had to admit this was doing… things to him. Back when he was younger, he'd certainly played with courtesans who enjoyed bondage, but he'd never realised being tied up would make his cock harder than an iron rod.

"You wanted to be punished, did you not?" She laid the sash across his eyes, cutting off his vision entirely. The mattress dipped to his right, as though she'd knelt on it, momentarily putting him off balance, but evened out when he felt an equal depression on his left.

"Fuck," he grunted, feeling her spread her thighs over his chest. The heat of her cunt was directly above his thundering heart. "Annabelle—"

Before he could say anything else, she moved again. The bed dipped once more, but this time around his head, her feathery soft thighs inserting themselves between his bound arms and his head. "Be quiet and take your punishment," she said from above him, her voice low with arousal.

And then she enveloped him, and he let out a hoarse groan into her blazing hot wetness. The restraints and blindfold alone were driving him out of his mind with lust, but this was beyond his wildest fantasies.

Kit parted her with a lick, feeling her rock with his movements. *Just like that.* He savoured her taste, exploring her satiny curls with his tongue and swallowing her honey. He attempted to dive his tongue down to her entrance, lowering his head—

Only for Annabelle to grip his hair and put him where she wanted him.

A groan against her clitoris was his first reaction, and the beginnings of his seed steadily leaking from his aching cock was the second. He moaned against her when she began to rock again, riding his tongue and letting out those carnal, *wonderful* noises he'd needed for sixteen years.

Her thighs muffled his hearing, but he found that her honey down his throat more than made up for it.

Flicking his tongue against her, Kit was rewarded with another pull of his hair, and another, until she was using it as reins to guide his tongue where she needed it.

He loved this. The sobs of pleasure he could only just make out. The searing pain on his skull. The rough chafing at his wrists. The complete darkness she'd plunged him into. The mouth-watering taste of her on his tongue. The way her scent completely and utterly cloaked him. The fact that he was just a vessel for her pleasure.

He knew in that moment that he'd never get enough of this—of *her.* Her thighs began to shake, and he ached to hold her up, to spread her to his heart's content. *Give me your orgasm, little queen.*

Was that his name she'd just moaned? Animalistic need pumped in his veins, where pain had become synonymous with pleasure, and he was about to explode every time she pulled his hair. His hips pumped with a mind of their own, touching only air, wanting her attention most of all.

Thoughts of his own desperation were driven from his mind when he heard a choked gasp from above him, joined by the hardest pull on his hair yet.

Annabelle's rhythm broke as she came on his tongue, but he picked it up for her, licking her needy clitoris. She bucked against his mouth, finally letting in a stream of sound filled with hoarse gasps and broken cries and the delight of his name.

When she'd finally had enough, she lifted off of him without a word, coming to rest on his chest. He mourned the fact that his eyes were covered, desperate to see what she looked like flushed with pleasure and slick with sweat.

The loss he felt when she clambered off the bed was palpable. He could hear her moving around, but when she finally tore his blindfold off, she stood innocently in her nightgown, trying her hardest to look down her nose at him. For the most part, she was succeeding—with the exception of those pink slashes across her cheeks.

He almost laughed. She wanted to pretend this had never happened, did she?

Kit waited like a crouched predator, watching her come forth to untie him. He calmed the rapid rise and fall of his chest, effecting a polite, casual mien.

When she'd finally ridden him of his bondage, he struck.

He gripped her waist, slamming her against the bed and sliding atop her. "Do not think that you can ride my tongue and pretend it never happened," he snarled into her ear, biting at her lobe. "Do you not remember my threat to fuck those words right out of your mouth?"

"I have neither my pessary nor a French letter to hand," Annabelle panted, her cheeks still deliciously flushed from her climax. "You are not coming near me."

Kit's laugh was a mocking one. "Did you think I meant that I would fuck your cunt, pretty queen?" His thumb once again traced her bottom lip. "I had something entirely different in mind."

Her mouth fell open in shock—a rare occurrence, he assumed, but he took advantage of it anyway.

He pressed a finger between her lips, repeating the filthy motion. "I mean to fuck those words from your lips, Annabelle. Quite literally."

Sharp little teeth bit down on his finger, a warning.

It curved his lip in amusement. "My vicious queen."

High-pitched cries stole their attention, pulling Kit's head to the side. The sounds came from the trough; desperate little *mews* that pulled on his heartstrings. He climbed off Annabelle, swiping up the forgotten blanket and his belt and tying them around his waist in a vain attempt to cover his raging erection. It wasn't long enough to function as a *breacan an fhéilidh*—a great kilt, which he often wore at home—but it did the job.

"Hello, little ones," he murmured to the kittens, two of whom were wandering about the trough, pawing at its sides. "Did we wake you up?"

The little kitten mewed, whatever that meant.

"Or is it food you're after?"

Another *mew*, louder this time.

Kit gave Annabelle a glance on the way to the icebox, putting out the pan of mashed fish. Thankfully, the more he walked about, the more his erection flagged. On his way back, he found her pulling the kittens out of the trough, cradling the weak one against her chest.

Between the two of them, they ensured that all three kittens were sufficiently fed. Even the runt had taken a few bites, he was relieved to see. The food energised the tiny cats. Accompanied by the rise of the sun above the bluffs, Kit knew there was no chance of them getting back to sleep tonight.

∞

"I think I found the kitten's mother," he announced as he entered the bothy with his freshly filleted salmon. His mouth was set in a grim line.

Annabelle looked up, mindlessly stroking the male kitten in her arms. Kit didn't need to ask which one it was. They were easy to tell apart. The two girls were the lively ones, whereas their sick little boy stuck to Annabelle like a burr—although he had eaten thrice today, and taken some shaky steps as he tried to follow his sisters around. "Has she eaten from the food we left out?"

Kit shook his head sadly, scratching the chins of the two girls as they greeted him. "She's dead."

Her stroking of the little male ceased. "What happened to her?"

"There's a wound on her side, but that might have been caused by scavengers after her death. Either way," he scooped up the orphaned girls, their fur silky soft, "these little ones are our responsibility now."

"Did you not say they were wild animals?"

"I said they *may* be wild animals." Although the longer he spent around them, the more unconvinced he was. He remembered the ghillie at Eilean Rìgh once saying pure wildcats had no white fur, and all three of their little charges had white patches. "Either way, they're in no state to fend off attacks from foxes. They wouldn't even be able to feed themselves." The feisty little girl swiped her face against his chin. "I can't abandon them. Not when I know what it is to be abandoned."

And then there were the dogs on the *Endurance* expedition…

Kit swallowed; that was a memory he'd rather never revisit. Like all bad memories though, it was permanently branded into his brain, no matter how much he tried to forget.

"When have you been abandoned?"

He frowned, incredulous. "*You*."

Annabelle's nostrils flared as she stared into the hearth. The little male that had been snoozing on her lap stretched, clumsily wandering over to their water bowl.

"I understand why you did what you did, little queen," he sat down next to her. It was encouraging she didn't try and push him away, at least. "I don't blame you, and, *Christ*, I know it must have been ten times worse from your perspective. But I did nothing wrong."

Her choked laugh was a warning alarm. "*Nothing wrong*? You disgraced me in front of everyone I know the moment you turned on those lights at Lord Linwood's ball."

Kit didn't run away from that fact, wincing at his actions that night. He had been drunk on feni, jealousy, and rage. Seeing her again had stirred up the emotional sediment he'd kept buried for years. But that was no excuse. "I did," he accepted, meeting her narrowed eyes. "I'm sorry. If you need me to get on my knees and apologise every day for the rest of my life, then that's what I'll do. The consequences of what I did cannot be ignored. Not to mention the damage done to Lady Effie's first season. You have every right to be angry, Annabelle. You have every right to despise me."

God knew he despised himself.

"If there's anything I can do to rectify the situation," he took her hand with a shaky grip, rubbing his thumb over her knuckles, "all you have to do is let me know."

Alcohol withdrawal. That's what it was. The inability to sleep. The endless shaking. It was nothing he hadn't gone through before. It would pass, he knew, but he'd be miserable in the time being.

A hint of a smile played about her lips. "Don't play the gentleman, Aylesbourne. It doesn't suit you."

Something eased in his chest, something that had been locked up tight for years. Like glass turning back into molten sand. "No," he grinned, letting his eyes leisurely roam her figure. It was fuller than it had been when they were young, purely through the passing of time, and he appreciated every curve. "It does not. You like me rough and untamed, don't you?"

The quirk in her eyebrow was all the proof he needed.

Annabelle could try and resist him, but her body betrayed her.

"You certainly liked the way I bathed in your cunt last night."

Shock flared her eyes. He wasn't surprised. Annabelle had mentioned nothing of their intimacy throughout the day, as though she was pretending it had never occurred, but he'd had enough of ignoring it.

"You can pretend you're immune to me," he brought his hand up to her chest, sliding it around her throat. "But we both know differently. I know how you taste when you're crying out my name. I've swallowed your honey down. I know exactly how you like to ride my tongue."

Her throat moved against his grip. "You flatter yourself."

Kit pulled her forwards, until their lips were less than an inch apart. "Can you honestly tell me that Allenby ever made you climax as hard as I did last night?"

"Allenby was different."

"It wasn't based on passion," he supplied helpfully, filling in the gaps of the few details he'd discovered about their arrangement. "Or desire."

"Exactly."

His smug grin was victorious. "So you admit that we have passion and desire both."

"You're insufferable."

"I am," he whispered, his other hand coming up to cradle her face. "But fuck it."

Kit captured her tightly held lips in a seething embrace of hunger. A victorious groan shuddered through him when Annabelle's lips softened, kissing him back so quickly it was a wonder she'd ever tried to resist this at all. Her hatred should have tasted bitter, but it was *divine*.

"I hate you," she moaned, letting pleasure close her eyes when he moved down her neck.

A half-laugh clipped the back of his throat. "But you don't, do you? You hate the idea of me, but the reality is something quite different. I'm innocent of the crime you accuse me of. I always have been."

"You may be innocent of abandoning me when I was carrying your child," she considered, the words leaving her slowly, as though she found it hard to let them go. "But you are guilty of the rest."

"I am guilty of behaving abominably at Linwood's ball."

"Is that all you think you're guilty of?" she asked quietly.

Fuck. He was falling into a trap here, he knew it. "What are my other charges?"

Annabelle pulled away from him, a sheet of ice sliding over her demeanour. "I have heard of the *parties* you throw when you are back on British soil, Aylesbourne. The term *orgy* would be more appropriate."

He leant back against the wall, letting his head bump against its flaking white paint. It was true. It was his habit to throw a party before departing from an expedition; a party full of alcohol and women and narcotics. And another upon his return. "During every expedition I have been on, Annabelle, I have faced death more than once. I almost went through the ice multiple times during the *Nimrod* expedition, nearly starved on the *Endurance*, was stabbed during the Eddington experiment in Brazil, fell through a crevasse on my first Everest expedition and was buried alive by an avalanche next to the corpse of my closest friend during the second, so apologies if I feel the need to drown my sorrows once in a while."

Before he went on an expedition was different. He did *that* because it might be his last time experiencing the softness that only a woman's touch could provide.

The accusatory creasing of Annabelle's forehead vanished as he spoke, either at his words or the crack in his voice. Her whispered response was a long time coming. "What was your friend's name?"

"John," he breathed. "John MacGillivray."

Her sudden inhale suggested the name meant something to her, but MacGillivray would surely have told him if he knew Annabelle. The man had known everything about his and Annabelle's relationship—or what Kit had thought was everything. "Did you know him?"

"Not personally. He married a girl I came out with. Lady Maria. We still send each other the occasional letter," Annabelle replied. "I know she loved him very much."

Kit's clenched teeth ticked his jaw. "She did." And he had been the one to write to her to tell her of her husband's death. The death of the father of her children. He blinked away the moisture attempting to pool in his eyes. "She still does. A love like that... it'll never leave a person."

He stared at her. Not intentionally, at first, but he found he couldn't look away.

As much as he'd tried to fuck, drink, or narcotise it away, his love for Annabelle had never ceased. He'd attempted to extract it as though it was a parasite, feeding on his life itself.

But here it was, as corporeal as the night they'd met, stargazing in her father's rose garden.

"No," Annabelle admitted finally. The hard lines of her judgement had faded to nothing, as though their barriers had been lifted. "It won't."

Kit choked out a noise of relief and reached for her—just as she reached for him. He pulled her atop him, splitting her legs over his thighs. Their kiss was a desperate mass of grasping hands and hungry moans. He licked into her mouth, savouring her taste and immediately returning for more.

"I never stopped wanting you," he revealed, getting to his feet with his little queen wrapped around his waist. "I never stopped stroking my cock thinking of you, of you coming around me."

Annabelle laughed when he deposited her on the bed, yanking her clothes off. "Some women expect poems from their lovers."

"I know," he panted, pulling his shirt over his head. Here she was, laughing in bed with him. How often had he fantasised about this moment? "But you get my tongue on your cunt instead. I'd say that's a fair trade."

She blinked, her eyes scanning his bare chest. "Where were you stabbed?"

Slowly, Kit's hands went to unbutton his trousers. He watched her bite her lip, unveiling his cock for her.

"You were stabbed on your cock?" she asked uncertainly, rising to sit with her legs dangling off the side of the bed.

"Thankfully not." Kit let his trousers fall to the floor, stepping out of them as he did so. He waited for her to lean back to avoid his cock, but she did no such thing. Always up for a challenge, his little queen. He outlined the scar an inch or two beneath his navel, hidden in the dark trail of hair. "I was stabbed here."

Annabelle leant in so close her breath brushed against his cock, but he didn't miss the way her thighs squeezed together. She was doing this on purpose. She had to be. "Why did someone stab you?"

He made sure to look unaffected. "Word about my title reached the locals. Three of them attempted to rob me."

"Did they make off with any of your money?" she sighed, glancing up at him so innocently he'd have thought butter wouldn't melt.

"Annabelle?"

"Mmm?"

"Open your fucking mouth."

11

Annabelle

Annabelle nearly moaned in relief, obeying Kit's instruction. His hands moved, one palming his rigid cock, the other cupping the back of her head, bringing her to his tip. Her lips closed over the thick head of his manhood, and she eagerly lapped up the droplets of salty lust spilling forth.

Harsh moans in a tongue she didn't understand came from Kit's lips. Words she'd never heard him use before, except two: *mo chridhe*.

What she lacked in experience, she attempted to make up for in enthusiasm. Her hands latched on to his hips, encouraging his thrusts into her welcoming heat. Her cheeks hollowed as she sucked, her arousal lighting a fire in her blood that only he could quench.

"Are you wet?"

Her answer was an affirmative moan around his throbbing length.

"You look so fucking good sucking my cock," he half moaned, half laughed. "I'll have to consider wearing my *breacan an fhéilidh* more in the future, just so I can squirrel you away and shove myself down your throat whenever I want."

Once she'd found a proper rhythm, Kit's grip on the back of her head changed from authoritative to reverent. He spoke in hushed curses, enthusiastic groans, and unfamiliar tongues.

This was something she'd never explored with anyone else. Her marriage to Robert Buckford had never been consummated, whereas her arrangement with Cornelius Allenby was purely physical. But with Kit… it was everything and more.

The taste of his seed began to increase in its intensity as Kit approached his climax. Her eyes were hooded with arousal, drunk on the power this gave her. Kit was at her mercy like this, and she *loved* it.

The thought had only just crossed her mind when he withdrew. "Give me a minute," he panted, the shadow of a grin playing at the corner of his mouth.

"Not a chance," she slapped his hand away, attempting to pull him back towards her by his cock.

"Annabelle, I'm not going to spend in your mouth."

"Why not?"

Surprise flashed in his eyes. "Because you're a lady."

"I thought I was your queen," she whispered, anger lifting her tone. Annabelle took his cock in her hand once more, pleased when he accepted her touch with a hiss of pleasure. "And if I say I want you to spend in my mouth, then you spend in my fucking mouth."

Her lips stretched around him once more. His hushed curses and enthusiastic groans were music to her ears, and they propelled her towards her aim. This time, she was faster, pushing him to the brink.

Her every touch was a wordless act of acceptance. *I want you. I need you. Against every instinct, I'm desperate for you.* Aylesbourne's hips jerked forward rhythmically, and she met them with a rhythm of her own, sucking his taste deeper and deeper into her mouth.

"Fuck," he whispered from above her, one hand cradling the back of her head and the other reaching down between her shoulders. "Fuck, fuck, fuck. *Oh* fuck!"

Hot pulses of seed filled her mouth, and she moaned with pleasure at his taste, swallowing fiercely. In a strangely intimate movement, he curled around her in his ecstasy. His touch was almost tender, a strange juxtaposition to their deliciously filthy actions.

This time, Annabelle let him withdraw from her mouth without complaint. A trickle of warm liquid slipped from her lips as he left, and she collected it on her thumb before bringing it to her tongue.

"Fucking hell, little queen," he heaved, shaking his head as he watched her.

She crossed her legs with a smile worthy of a siren. "Don't tell me I've shocked you, *Your Grace*."

Within a few breaths, Kit's demeanour changed from pleasure-wrung exhaustion to something darker and more sensual. "You think you've shocked me, do you?"

Unease began to creep in, but she didn't show it. She and Cornelius Allenby had shared a bed for some years, but their encounters had all followed the same pattern. There was a hidden collection of illicit books at Scarlett Castle, which she had perused—some of them quite thoroughly—but her real-world experience remained limited.

Kit tumbled them both back across the bed, propping himself up on one elbow. His other hand traversed her naked body, following the dip in her waist. "Did you know, for instance, that although I cannot fuck you *here*—" Annabelle sucked in a breath as his finger circled her entrance "—without risk, there is somewhere else you're able to accept me."

Did he mean what she thought he meant? "Where?"

An undignified noise came from her throat when he travelled downwards, to the puckered skin below. "Here."

She swallowed thickly, relieved when his hand moved away. "I have read of such things."

"And what did you think?"

"I fail to see what is in it for me," she bit back. "From my perspective, there would be no pleasure for the woman at all. It seems like an excuse for men to insert themselves somewhere they don't belong. As usual."

Kit smirked. "With proper preparation, it can be pleasurable. It isn't unheard of for a woman to climax during such activities."

"Is that what you want to do tonight?"

"No," he answered calmly, loosening the knot of worry that had settled around her chest. He closed the gap between them without another word, taking her lips in a sweet, almost chaste kiss. Each pass of his lips over hers lulled her into another sigh of pleasure. "Tonight, I want to watch you."

Whilst his kiss was sweet, his touch was anything but. The tips of his fingers teased her breasts into peaks, plucking and pinching until she gasped. "If you don't do something else, I swear to god I'm going to slap you."

"Oh no," he replied humorously, the edges of his lips tipping up as he kissed his way down to her breasts. "What ever will I do?"

She moaned when he sucked her nipple into his mouth, followed by a sharp cry when he raked his teeth over it. "*Kit!*" Before her cry had even finished, his tongue was soothing the sting, lapping at her sensitive skin in a wet apology.

When he switched over to her other nipple, she knew what was coming. This time, her thighs clenched together in anticipation. Her eyes rolled back at the raking of his teeth, and her moans brimmed with full-throated bliss.

Then one of his large hands moved, spread wide as though it wanted to soak up every inch of her exposed skin. When he finally reached the slick flesh between her thighs, Annabelle let out a sigh of relief.

As always, Kit toyed with her. His touch was almost a massage, stroking up and down each side of her clitoris, but never straying too close. Annabelle rolled her hips, trying to entice him closer, but he simply loomed over her on one elbow, watching her struggle with a smug expression.

"*Kit!*" she finally growled, genuinely considering her previous threat of violence. His touch was ecstasy and agony both, teasing her until she felt she would explode with a single touch.

He slid down her wet, needy flesh, close enough to her entrance to have her clenching around nothing. Instead of entering her, however, he merely coated himself in her wetness and brought his fingers to his mouth, groaning in satisfaction. "I've missed your taste."

A devious idea occurred. She pulled him down to meet her lips, taking control of a low, slow kiss.

And slipped her free hand down between her legs, almost shuddering in the relief that her touch promi—

Kit slammed both of her hands above her head, bending over the side of the bed and emerging with his belt. "You," he snarled, winding the leather around the bed's slats before immobilising her, "are a deceitful vixen."

The feelings evoked by the bondage were… unexpected. Something forbidden and *oh so* enticing. She struggled against them, strangely excited by the fact that she was truly helpless. She was truly at his mercy.

It was something she had never expected to enjoy.

In her life, she had always favoured control. Control over situations and people, but control over herself most of all. She had few friends, preferring instead to remain aloof, to look down her nose at everyone.

She even liked control during intimacy. Cornelius had enjoyed some aspects of being controlled, and so she had gotten to explore her fantasies. She had never been under someone's control like this. Foxcotte Moor was miles away; here, she truly was at Kit's mercy.

"You drove me to desperation," she replied, letting her legs fall open for him once more. *Touch me. Please.*

"That was my intention. I *want* to have you desperate. I *want* to have you needy. I *want* to drive you out of your mind." Kit knelt between her legs, his thumbs spreading her wide. Between them, his cock swayed, once again erect and dusky. "I also want to be inside you so badly it hurts." The sudden panic in her eyes had him holding up a hand. "I wouldn't risk it. But it doesn't stop me *wanting.*"

Unexpectedly, his fingers penetrated her, eliciting a long moan of relief from her chest. She was so wet he sunk in deep. "Do you like the feeling of me inside you?"

Her affirmative answer was garbled by pleasure.

Well, if he expected a clear, calm response, he wouldn't be pumping his fingers inside her, nor rolling the heel of his palm against her clitoris.

From beneath lowered eyelashes, she saw him lean forwards, bending over her until they were nearly chest-to-chest. His hot, hard cock throbbed against her opening for a split second before he readjusted, laying it over her stomach.

Kit inserted another finger inside her, and her back arched at the stretch. Her thighs opened wider, almost of their own accord. Her orgasm hovered just out of reach, with Kit easing it closer and closer until she was crawling out of her skin with need.

"Please," she begged. "Please."

Those dark, intense eyes stared down at her, absorbing every minute change in her face. "When you touch yourself, who do you think of?"

Annabelle was so far past pride it was almost laughable. "You," she sobbed, rolling her hips. The prickle of heat built inside her; her release was so close she could almost taste it.

There was a hard edge to his grin. "And I think of you, little queen."

The climax that rolled over her was so strong she screamed at its force. Her spine arched, almost leaving the bed entirely, freezing her for long, agonisingly pleasurable moments. Black threatened to crowd her vision, but she couldn't have cared less, more concerned with gulping in air through the strongest orgasm she'd ever had in her life.

Finally, she sagged to the bed, her legs falling open and her eyes closing. Kit nuzzled against her neck, rolling her head to the side slightly. She had nothing left in her; his teasing touches had sapped away her restraint until she comprised *need* alone.

Without it, she was exhausted.

He nuzzled against her again, chuffing when he received no response.

An odd clank had her opening her eyes. It had been the belt landing on the wooden floor. Was she so exhausted she hadn't realised he'd undone her restraints?

Annabelle was aware enough to know that he had pulled her into his arms, and she sank into his embrace. A small smile came to her face unbidden, but she was thankful her cheek was squashed against his chest—where he wouldn't see it.

God knows he had seen enough of her intimate moments today.

Despite her exhaustion, she didn't fall asleep. Her position allowed her a view of one of the bothy's two windows. Instead, she watched the full moon drift across the window, overtaken by the occasional cloud.

Perhaps she did sleep, because his deep, sorrowful voice snapped her eyes open. When had she closed them?

"Do you ever think of what our child would have been like?"

The tentative question tore open wounds that had long since turned into scars. She wasn't used to answering questions about their child; the only people who knew had been Theo and Robert. Both of whom had been dead for years.

Since Theo's death, she had grieved her child alone. It was a queer feeling to realise that was no longer true.

Annabelle sat up, wrapping the blanket around herself like armour. "He was perfect," she whispered, her voice barely audible above the gentle purring of the sleeping kittens.

"He?" Kit croaked, his eyes widening with shock. "How do you know?"

Memories of the worst day of her life struck her. The endless blood. The rush of the doctor. The pain of the contractions. The midwife's frantic instructions to push. And the knowledge in the back of her mind that it was far too soon—that, despite everything, her baby wouldn't survive.

Medicine had advanced far beyond blood-letting and humours, but it wasn't magic.

Although her face remained passive, her heart was ravaged. "Because I gave birth to him."

Horror struck Kit. "I thought you said you had a miscarriage."

Annabelle glanced down, picking at a loose thread in the blanket. "Not quite," she murmured. Clearly he didn't understand the difference. "A miscarriage is before a certain point in the pregnancy. There is no birth, as such. A miscarriage is too early for that."

Kit crept closer to her, cloaking her in his comforting scent. "But you gave birth to our child? To our... our *son*?"

Her nod was slight, grief blurring her vision. "And he was perfect, Kit. So very, very perfect, and so very, very still. Ten tiny fingers. Ten tiny toes."

A sob left Kit then, and he embraced her.

"Theo was with me." He had been her champion, ensuring Annabelle was kept abreast of the doctor stampeding through each step of the birth, bleating that there was nothing that could be done. "He took care of me. Of us."

"Admirably so, I imagine."

She tucked her head under his chin, now fully awake. "Even now, I wonder who he would have been. His favourite colour." A thought almost made her laugh. "Whether he would have gotten your sense of adventure, or your sense of humour."

Annabelle heard an exhale pass through his chest. "Did you have any names picked out?"

She felt almost embarrassed admitting it in front of him. "I... I named him Oscar. Oscar Phillip Fraser. Oscar after you, and Phillip after my father. I wanted to give him a small connection to his real father."

Kit pulled back, tears running down into his stubble. Oscar. His middle name. "Even when you thought I'd abandoned you both?"

"Even then." Annabelle shrugged. She had almost done it as an act of rebellion, in a way. Kit may have shirked his responsibility—or so she thought—but she would be damned if there was no record of their son's parentage.

Kit didn't bother to wipe his tears away, a small smile distorting their path. "Thank you," he managed. "Thank you for that." A gruff noise left him. "Buckford didn't want you to name the child after him?"

"No. Robert needed an heir, but I don't think he particularly wanted to be a father."

He opened his mouth, but hesitated.

"What?" she asked, worried.

"I may have shown Michael the letter you wrote me. The one where you told me of your pregnancy."

Annabelle shot up, her eyes widening. The fact that Michael, of all people, had read those words… "Why would you do that."

Kit coaxed her back down. "I didn't know he didn't know. I'm sorry. He wanted to come here with me, but I made him stay." His brow creased into a sympathetic line. "Did any of your family know? Other than Theo?"

"No, only Theo. He's the one I went to for help. He sorted out my marriage to Robert. They had written to one another previously, apparently."

He stroked her hair, as though trying to soothe her. "Why didn't you tell your family of your pregnancy? You were married. There would have been no scandal there."

"I needed to wait a couple of months before announcing it to ensure it looked genuine. I'd actually already written the letter to my mother," she said, exhaling old pain. "I was intending to post it, but I woke up in a bed of blood the next morning and…" Annabelle trailed off. "And then there was no pregnancy to tell of."

Kit hugged her closer, his dark chest hairs against her cheek. "I'm sorry, little queen. I'm sorry I wasn't there."

"Me too." She thought back to how frantic she'd been whilst writing the letter, and how her heart had been ripped in two by the reply—

Annabelle shot up. How had she been so stupid to not have remembered it before? "The reply," she croaked.

"Reply?"

"When I sent you that letter telling you of my pregnancy, I received a reply."

"You *what*?" he raged. Emotions crashed across his face in a swirling mix, but he remained dangerously still. "What did it say?"

The words were burned into her brain like a brand. "*I will be continuing on the expedition,*" she recited, though she hadn't laid eyes on it in sixteen years. "*You have my sympathies regarding your situation. The Duke of Aylesbourne.*"

His nose crinkled in rage. In one rapid movement, he shoved himself from the bed, grabbing his clothes from the drying rack with a savage urgency. "We're leaving," he snarled.

"Excuse me?"

"Someone kept this from me!" he thundered, shoving his legs into his partially dry trousers. "The letter I found from you—*fuck*. I was so focused on its contents I didn't think to consider the envelope it came in. It had been opened."

He strode over to the window and peered out into the night. "I can make it back to Foxcotte Moor in an hour or two on foot." Awakened by his movements, the kittens began to mew.

The pang of disappointment in her chest wasn't unexpected. "And then?"

Kit bent to give the kittens some fuss, his mind clearly on other things. "And then I'll be back. When I arrived, I had a ghillie drop me off in his wagon, perhaps a quarter of a mile away. I'll call on him again. Pack everything up here. I want to reach Eilean Rìgh as soon as possible."

"Eilean Rìgh?" she said, stumbling over the pronunciation.

His voice softened. "My estate." There was an odd look in his eye, but he shook it away. "I'll bring a basket of sorts for the kittens. We're not leaving them here."

"Why are you going to your estate?"

"*We* are going to my estate. Eilean Rìgh. Say it."

"Don't tell me what to do." She smiled down at the little male kitten, who was ambling over to her. Pulling him into her arms, Annabelle laughed at his scraggly *mew*. "Are you feeling better this afternoon? You certainly look better. And why exactly are we going to your estate?" He had skipped over that entirely.

"There are…" Kit paused, "daily *records* kept, and they may mention who was handling the post that day. I don't know whether the records would be at Eilean Rìgh or Campbell House in Berkeley Square. I need to know exactly who was responsible for the cover-up of your pregnancy. Of our *son*." They shared a sad glance, eternally tethered by their loss. "Of Oscar."

Annabelle stilled. No one had used his name since Theo had died. "And then?"

"If we find nothing at Eilean Rìgh, then we sail to London."

"*Sail*?"

"The *North Star* is moored at Inverness. I think it's time we paid her a visit."

12

Kit

Eilean Rìgh was like an old friend welcoming him home. A sigh eased the tension in his shoulders the moment they'd passed beneath the ancient barbican, the setting sun disappearing behind the walls. Their stone had been worn by both age and the harsh sea air whipping in across Lake Torridon. On their approach, the high curtain wall and accompanying battlements blocked most of their view of the castle, but Kit turned to Annabelle as they entered the bailey proper, eager to see her reaction to his ancestral home.

Her lips parted as she took it in, her eyes darting to the vast central keep. Eilean Rìgh sprawled in all directions, from the chapel to the south, the kitchens to the east, the stables to the west, and the keep to the north.

Unlike most castles further south, this was not merely a fortified home to its ruling family; it was a fortress, and centuries ago functioned as a small town in its own right.

"What do you think?" he asked.

A coldness had returned to her when they'd left the bothy, as though she wanted to keep the world at arm's length. "Do you want my opinion, or do you just want me to compliment your home?"

Kit gave the driver a half-glance. As strange as it was, he liked her coldness—because he got to see her fire when they were alone. "I want to know what you think."

"For you, I feel it would be unpleasant."

"How so?"

"You always wanted to explore, did you not? Being cooped up like this..." Annabelle shrugged. "I suppose it must have been unpleasant."

His answer was halted by a footman opening the door, and Kit grinned at the sight of his butler waiting a few feet behind. "Munday," he exclaimed, holding the kittens' wicker basket under one arm. The kittens themselves had done well on the journey, with only a few uncertain *meows* after they'd set off.

Munday's white blonde hair appeared to have greyed significantly since Kit had seen him last. "Your Grace. Foxcotte Moor rang to let us know that you were on your way. We've prepared your rooms, but we did not expect—"

"This is Lady Buckford, Munday. Put her things in the *Banrìgh* room."

The only evidence of Munday's surprise was the slight flicker of his eyelashes. "Of course, Your Grace. Will you be wanting dinner now or later?"

Annabelle's stomach had been rumbling in the car. "Now," he replied. He was keen to get upstairs. "Have it brought to my sitting room. We'll also need food for these kittens. Herring and goats milk, perhaps? I doubt squashed fish alone is the best diet for them."

Carrying the snoozing kittens in the wicker basket, Kit led the two of them down the ornate cloisters stretching over the walkway into the keep. Above them, the painted ceiling was organised in square tiles, each tile representing a different battle fought in Scottish history—albeit up to 1683, when the paintings were first installed.

They passed by the banquet hall, candelabras hanging low from the ceiling. Up on the first floor, Annabelle could have gotten glimpses of the view he wanted to show her—if she had known where to look. Thankfully, her attention was stolen by the strange mesh of modern and ancient that the castle had become.

True, there were candelabras instead of chandeliers, but there were also photographs that Kit had taken on Everest—including a photo of Kit with Brigadier-General Bruce—and a gramophone in the entrance hall.

Annabelle paused just as they were about to climb their final set of stairs. "Is that a painting of a motorcycle?"

He nodded, looking through the open door into Anthony's apartments. He could just about make out an easel in one of the rooms. "It is. Anthony painted it—he's a fan of Fabrique Nationale. Although I think he prefers portraits nowadays. Those are his living quarters when he's here."

"Anthony?"

"My cousin. I don't know if you've ever met him, actually."

They began to climb the smooth stone stairs; dips had been worn in the middle of the stone, a sign of their heavy use over centuries. "Are they here often?"

"No. Uncle Eric and Anthony prefer to live at Campbell House. Anthony went to art school in London, so I think they've gotten used to living there. Anthony also has a wife now—Daisy."

That was one reason why this trip home would only be short. Discomfort weighed him down. He knew what he was here for, but going into Uncle Eric's apartments would be a betrayal of trust, regardless of his potential justifications.

"And these," he said as they crested the final set of stairs, opening the closed door guarding the ducal space, "are my apartments."

Most of the furnishings here had been inherited. Sleek dark wood and polished gold glittered around the central room, with the walls showcasing family portraits, but he had added a photograph taken from high up on Everest, and another at the South Pole. *That* was something no other duke could have done.

The doors to the connecting rooms were open. "My bedroom," he gestured, putting the basket down on the floor and opening it up. Predictably, the little girls were keen to explore, immediately wandering around their new space. The boy, on the other hand, was reluctant to exit the safety of the basket. Kit left it open for him, so he could leave when he was ready. "Bathroom. Sitting room. Office. Smoking room. And the *Banrìgh* room."

"What does *Banrìgh* mean? You mentioned it downstairs."

"It means queen. Because the *Banrìgh* room belongs to the Duchess of Aylesbourne."

Annabelle's head jerked around. He couldn't help but notice that she retreated slightly. "You're putting me in the room that's supposed to belong to your *wife*?"

Kit stalked forward, closing the distance that she'd put between them. He'd expected her to continue retreating, but was pleased to see she stood her ground with her chin in the air. "We have danced around the subject for days now. So let's be clear. Had that letter reached me, I would have never left British soil. I would have married you in a heartbeat." Fuck, he still would. "You would have been my duchess, Annabelle, as you were meant to be. So yes, I'm putting you in the room that is intended for my wife, my duchess, my *banrìgh*. It is *yours*, little queen. And it always has been."

Her eyes were as round as saucers. "Kit…"

His shrug was unapologetic. "I know what I want. And I think you do too."

"A fortnight ago I would have gladly gone after you with a pitchfork, you can't expect—"

A throat cleared behind them, and Kit turned to find Samuel, one of the footmen, holding a tray laden with serving dishes and staring worriedly at Annabelle.

He almost laughed, but directed Samuel to his sitting room. "Come in here," he told Annabelle, glancing back to see all three kittens following them. Or, more precisely, following the smell of food. It seemed the little male had gained his courage after all.

He hadn't expected to clash with Annabelle so soon. Indeed, he had taken her straight to his bedroom with a single purpose in mind.

When Samuel had closed the door to the ducal apartments behind him, Kit pulled Annabelle over to the window and opened the curtains.

Before them, Lake Torridon bathed in the golden light of the setting sun. The mountains rose high on either side, a barrier to the outside world. In this weather, they were tipped with the barest hint of snow. The lake was a mill pond below, reflecting the stunning sunset and mountains both.

"This is beautiful," she sighed, her hand resting on her chest. "Why did you ever want to leave when you had this view?"

Sometimes he asked himself that. "Foolish boyhood dreams of making history."

"You've changed your tune."

MacGillivray's death had done that to him. The terror of suffocating with—

Kit blinked, suddenly realising that such thoughts had not troubled him in days. Except for his nightmare, he had slept peacefully at the bothy… with Annabelle. When was the last time he had slept through the night?

Before last year's expedition, that was certain.

Even his waking thoughts had not troubled him as much. He'd been shaky to start with given his lack of alcohol, but it hadn't been the first time his body had gone through the withdrawal symptoms. When attempting to scale Everest, one thing that was left at the bottom was alcohol. Brigadier-General Bruce had decreed that all unnecessary weight was left behind, including luxuries like feni.

Kit's smile was bright enough to rival the sun setting across the lake. "Come," he said, pressing a kiss against her neck. "Eat. You'll need your energy."

Because tonight she would finally be his.

༄

The *snick* of the door closing behind him was marked by betrayal. Kit had never been in Uncle Eric's office without his uncle being present. The characteristic scent of old books seemed to be imbued in the dust motes dancing around him.

He had told Annabelle he was going downstairs to organise tomorrow's jaunt on the *North Star*. Instead, he was snooping around his uncle's office, desperately hoping that he wouldn't find what he was looking for.

Like many people, Uncle Eric kept a journal detailing his daily life. The time he woke, what he had for lunch, the people he spoke to, the letters he wrote, what he put in them, and on and on and on. *Like Queen Victoria herself,* Uncle Eric once said. Kit had never understood the need to keep a journal *every* day. He had journalled during the expeditions, but the inanities of everyday life? Who would want to read about that?

Over the years, Kit had seen snippets of Uncle Eric's journals, particularly as a boy. He remembered helping his uncle detail the story of Kit's first rugby game at Eton, minute by minute, play by play. Kit remembered wanting his uncle to document every detail.

The memory made him smile.

Fuck.

And now he had to snoop through Uncle Eric's journals to discover whether he had been in charge of covering up Annabelle's pregnancy.

The row of leather-bound books on a shelf behind the desk were all embossed with the years they documented; 1900, 1901, 1902, 1903, all the way up to 1910. Gritting his teeth, Kit pulled down the 1907 edition, feeling the supple leather slide beneath his touch.

He let the journal fall open, catching sight of his and Anthony's names on the page. Regardless, he flicked to the 6th and 7th August. He didn't want to infringe on his uncle's privacy any more than he already had.

Holding his breath, he scanned the entry, bypassing the details of his uncle's breakfast, until he found the relevant section.

> *The source of my sleepless night was, of course, Kit's departure to Antarctica. I waved him off from Southampton with my heart in my throat, wondering if this was to be the last time I would see my dear boy. Already there is a pile of post for him, which I have sorted through and been instructed to forward on to the South Orkney Islands, before a post base is later established, I am told. They shall need a second* Nimrod *just to transport all the well-wishes he has. The number of letters he received from ladies did make me smile, and their words indicate they shall miss him just as much as I.*

Kit closed the journal, not wanting it to be true. He'd always trusted his uncle—implicitly so. He had no reason not to. Uncle Eric was the only parent Kit had ever known.

As if conjured by his thoughts, Kit suddenly realised what he had been mindlessly staring at; a framed daguerreotype of himself, his mother, and Aunt Edna—Uncle Eric's late wife—at what must have been Kit's christening. Kit was dressed in the long christening gown that, according to Uncle Eric, had been passed down from the 4th Duchess of Aylesbourne more than two hundred years ago.

It was something that Kit and Annabelle's child would have worn if they'd lived.

He barely noticed where his feet were carrying him until he found himself back up in the ducal apartments, journal in hand, leaning against the door to the smoking room.

The smoking room—which had apparently turned into a cosmetics factory in his absence.

Cosmetics were scattered across the green expanse of the billiards table. With her back to him, Annabelle's skirts swished as she circled her collection, intently focused on her task. But when she bent over to reach across the table...

Once again, his feet moved before his brain could catch up. He slammed into her, grinding his groin against her rear and pressing her body flat to the coarse baize lining the table. "What," he snarled into her ear, "have you done to my billiards table?"

After her initial gasp of surprise, Annabelle let out a tinkling laugh. "I've put it to better use, *Your Grace*."

Kit had a better one in mind.

He roughly shoved his fist in her hair and pulled her up, bending her spine submissively. Something halfway between a cry and a moan left her. "I hope you're wet, little queen. Because I'm not going to stop."

Letting her go, he shoved up the skirts of her dress, bringing them up over her hips when a cruel thought occurred to him.

"This baize," he growled, fisting her hair and dragging her cheek across it. "It's rough, isn't it?"

"Yes," she panted, her voice dripping with arousal.

"Does it hurt your skin?"

"A little."

"Good," he answered, pulling both her dress and her chemise over her head. It left her standing in nothing but her fashionable little heels, but he was more concentrated on shoving her back down until her front met the rough fabric. "Because I'm going to fuck you with your nipples against the baize the entire time. I want you fucking *raw* by the time I'm done with you."

Freeing his erection, Kit slid a tin of condoms out of his pocket and rolled one over his length. He swiped it between her legs, grunting when he saw how soaked she was. Teasing the head of his cock over her entrance, he smirked at her needy hips rolling back.

She was going to get what she wanted, whether she enjoyed it or not.

"Hands behind your back," he said roughly, shoving her arms behind her. "You're entirely at my mercy—" Annabelle cried out once more when he yanked her up by her hair, the only thing now supporting her weight "—and you're drenched anyway."

And then he did exactly what he wanted, and sunk into her.

Their moans intertwined somewhere in the air, just as connected as their bodies. The feeling of sliding home was incomparable, even after all these years, even after all that had happened. They would always have *this* ecstasy between them. Her warm honey bathed his cock, and he couldn't resist reaching down to feel her spread tight around his length.

"Kit," she whispered, attempting to rock her hips against his grasp. "Please. Move. *Please.*"

A cold laugh left him. Despite the relentless need to thrust until he filled her with his seed, he also grappled with the need to savour what this felt like. Kit slipped his free hand round to her breast, seeking to torment her a little further. "Does this hurt? Your nipple resting against the baize?"

Annabelle attempted to nod, inhibited by his firm grip on her hair.

"Good. Because it's only going to get worse. You may present yourself like a lady, Annabelle. Out there, you can live on your high horse, looking down your nose at everyone. But in here, we both know the truth; *I'm* in charge."

And then Kit began to thrust in earnest, slamming his hips against her with every ounce of his strength. The billiards table shook with his movements, the cosmetics Annabelle had piled up toppling over and rolling about. He groaned with every thrust, accompanied by Annabelle's piercing moans fuelling his strength.

"You feel so good," he snarled, leaning over her and biting her neck hard enough to mark. Desire was a raging beast inside of him, urging him on. "I want everyone to see what I've done to you. What I've reduced you to."

Annabelle's cries reached a crescendo, and he groaned as she tightened around him in pulses of bliss.

"That's it. Come for me. Come for my cock. Soak me. Soak me while I worship you, because I never want to leave your cunt again. Because no matter what I do to you, what I reduce *us* to, it will never be enough. I'll never have enough of you. Because this is a fucking privilege to have you like this. Because you're my *queen*, Annabelle."

The more he spoke, the harder she came, until her legs were shaking and her moan had turned into a blissful sigh.

He picked up the slack for her, roaring as he exploded. His sac was drawn up tight underneath him, furiously pumping his seed into her. Exactly where he wanted it to be. Exactly where he had *always* wanted it to be.

By the end of his climax, Kit was no longer holding Annabelle up by her hair. Instead, both of them had collapsed onto the billiards table, breathing hard. A sheen of sweat covered him, and he pressed his forehead to her back—directly beneath the bite mark he'd given her.

"Never leave me again," he pleaded against her skin, drawing her scent into his lungs before kissing a path up to her ear. "I'll hunt you across the seven seas, if I must."

Annabelle attempted to rise, and Kit lifted his weight to allow her to do so. His cock slipped out of her, and he grabbed it to remove the condom. She turned, twining her arms around his neck. "I'd outwit you, Aylesbourne. And we both know it."

"Mmm," he hummed against her lips. "But what a chase you'd give me."

Binning the condom, he pulled her into the ducal bedroom. The kittens momentarily froze as they entered, apparently in the middle of chasing each other around the room, before resuming their game. Kit grinned at the little male getting the best of the feisty little girl. "You know we're going to have to give them names at some point."

"One, two, and three?" Annabelle suggested, reclining onto the bed. Kit's eyes swept over her appreciatively, and his nostrils flared when she widened her legs to give him a better view.

"Look at what I've done to you," he crooned, kittens forgotten. "Are you sore?"

"Wonderfully so."

He rid himself of his clothes and followed her into bed, sighing with contentment at the fact that she was finally here. "This is where you were always supposed to be."

A flicker of doubt crossed her brow. "You can't know that."

"But I do. I have always wanted you with a strength that terrified me. *Always*. When we first met and I discovered you were Theo and Michael's sister, I should have left you well enough alone. I didn't. I *couldn't*." He swallowed. "Without you... I have been a husk, living without my heart for sixteen years. Because it has always remained with you. Even when I clung to the side of a freezing mountain or stared into the black heart of the sea, half of me always remained here—with you. Where I was meant to be. There are immovable constants in the world, little queen, and you are mine. My life. My love. My soul. They are all irrevocably yours."

The corner of Annabelle's lips began to flicker downwards as he spoke, and she rapidly blinked away the sheen of moisture in her eyes.

Kit tilted her chin up to him. "I never abandoned you, Annabelle. I never could. I would sooner forsake my very soul."

"You can't say things like that," she choked out a laugh, pressing the side of her hand up to catch the tears in her eyes.

"Why not? They are true."

"Because they make me want to forgive you for ruining me. And I am trying so very hard to hate you."

He chuckled, resting their foreheads together. He was still working on the *how* of that. "Do not forgive me. Do not forgive me until I have *earned* your forgiveness."

"And if it takes a decade?"

Kit tucked them into bed, pulling her close. "Then it shall be a decade well spent. Because it will be with you."

13

Annabelle

Annabelle snapped open the pewter clasp on her clutch bag, digging around for her lipstick and monogrammed compact. "Do you know," she said, "I would have preferred to use my Kissproof lipstick."

The bastard had the gall to smirk, extending his hand along the back of the car's leather seat. "Is that the one that's now a smear across the billiards table?"

She gave him a bad-tempered murmur, twisting the Tangee lipstick out of its container. "It is. Brand new as well. I hadn't even used it yet."

"I'll replace it."

She pierced him with a glare. "You're damn right you will."

The lipstick was less than an inch from her lips when Kit's hand reached out to stop her applying it. "You're going to wear *that* colour?!"

Annabelle eyed the bright orange lipstick, playing the fool. "What's wrong with this colour?"

"I mean… it's hideous, Annabelle." Kit held up his hand. "I admit I'm no expert in fashion—"

"You don't say," she scoffed.

"—but you'll look like you've lost a fight with a pumpkin."

"As if I would ever lose a fight."

"Fine," he conceded, letting his hands dance across the back of her neck possessively, brushing the tender bite mark he'd left last night. "You'll look like you've put up a valiant fight against a pumpkin."

Her grin was smug as she applied the bright orange Tangee lipstick. "Watch and learn." The lipstick was lighter than most, and it was her go-to everyday look. Annabelle delicately traced her cupid's bow before clipping the lid back on the tube, enjoying Kit's confused expression.

"But… where did the colour go?"

"It's a colour-changing lipstick," she explained, ensuring her tone was heavy with elements of snobbishness. "It changes to a light blush after it comes into contact with the wearer's body heat."

Kit took the lipstick, holding it up to inspect. "How ingenious."

Annabelle stuffed her compact back in her bag and glanced out of the car's window. They sat in Inverness's port. Well, in the car park next to Inverness's port, where the air was rich with salt and petrol both. Kit's spur of the moment decision to sail down to London had meant that, despite the two-and-a-half hour drive from Eilean Rìgh to Inverness, the yacht still wasn't ready by the time they arrived.

Her thoughts of Eilean Rìgh were interrupted by the sounds of an unhappy *mew*. Annabelle smiled down at the little male in the wicker basket. "I know," she agreed, far more comfortable with taking them from their home now that one of Eilean Rìgh's ghillies had taken a look at them and declared them to be domestic cats with a mere smidge of Scottish wildcat in their blood. "We'll feed you when we get on the boat, sweet boy."

"We're always in need of more mousekeepers here," the ghillie had said, his hoarse voice indicative of a lifelong smoking habit. "But we've no nursing mothers at present. These three will need a caring hand if they're to survive. Heat. Regular feedings—goats milk with eggs, fish, or bone meal would be best."

Annabelle had nodded along. She had become really quite attached to the little things, telling Kit in no uncertain terms that the kittens were coming with them.

She had waited until the ghillie was out of earshot before asking Kit the question that had been burning in her mind. "What the bloody hell is a mousekeeper?"

"Ah," Kit had chuckled, rubbing his thumb with his jaw. "That's the official job title of the cats at Eilean Rìgh. To keep the estate clear of vermin. There was a large infestation a few years ago, but the servants' quarters was spared from it by the presence of the housekeeper's three cats. The housekeeper suggested we increase their numbers, and she'd ensure they were all looked after, give them a weekly pennyroyal bath to stave off their fleas and what not. I remember one day a week we'd have a load of angry, soggy cats. We thus have a housekeeper, and her little army of mousekeepers."

"Ah." Back in the Inverness car park, Kit shot up in his seat at the sight of a black-haired man advancing towards them, pulling Annabelle away from her mental images of a convoy of cats in tiny aprons.

"The *North Star* is ready to sail, Your Grace," he said, his voice drifting through the open window.

With Kit carrying the wicker basket, the two of them followed. They left the tarmac behind to journey through the maze of pontoons criss-crossing the port. Annabelle was always unnerved at the way they moved beneath her, and she grabbed Kit's elbow for support.

"Don't read into this. I merely don't want to go arse over tit into the harbour." Annabelle didn't want him to think she needed him. She didn't even want to think it herself.

The *North Star* came into view along the next row of pontoons, a vast steam yacht standing proudly. Its dark wood absorbed the little sunlight provided by the day, ready to glide across the ocean before it.

It *was* a pretty boat, loathe as she was to admit it. She came to a stop in front of the ramp that would grant her entry. "I sailed on it last year."

Kit squeezed her hand. "Uncle Eric told me."

Standing in front of the yacht itself, Annabelle suddenly froze. "About being on here last year," she said, with the air of someone about to confess to a crime.

He turned to her. "What about it?"

"I... *may* have indulged in some mischief."

She could almost feel the disappointment in his glare. "Tell me that wasn't you."

Her nod was an odd combination of frantic and shameful. "I'm afraid it was."

The week on the yacht had been miserable—as miserable as it was possible to be on a luxury yacht. Michael and Emmeline were dancing around each other, the former endlessly in love with the latter. Annabelle had spent the time wisely: drinking and amusing herself.

She'd poured fish oil on all of Kit's clothing.

She'd glued the pages of Kit's favourite books together.

There had been a writing desk in the owner's cabin, with a ceruleite encrusted inkwell set on top. She'd glued the lids shut on all of those. She'd also glued the cap onto the pen, and the pen to the table, drunkenly giggling all the while.

Kit swore under his breath, pinching the bridge of his nose. "You ruined thousands of pounds worth of alcohol."

God, she'd forgotten about that. Near the end of the trip, she'd opened all of the bottles of alcohol, drank her fill, and filled the rest up with fish oil. Other than the one she knew her brother liked; that one had been spared. She was capable of mercy in certain circumstances.

"And made tens of thousands of pounds of damage to the oil paintings onboard. Anthony was cataclysmically furious. I've genuinely never seen him so angry."

Oh. Yes, she'd done that after she'd drank all of the alcohol: carving tiny penises onto every bit of artwork she could find. At first, she did it subtly, but there was a photograph of Kit at the South Pole that broke that rule entirely. Perhaps that alteration had been the first to be discovered, because she'd carved the not-so-tiny penis into his forehead.

That one was the least destructive, given that the photograph could be duplicated very easily, but it was by far the most satisfying.

"In my defence," she began slowly, "I was *very* drunk."

Kit was not amused. "Is that the only reason?"

She pursed her lips apologetically, her shoulders rising up. "I thought it was deserved." She'd also had to consider the fact that her brother and sister-in-law would be staying on the ship for another week, and she didn't want to inconvenience them.

"For god's sake," he grumbled, but there was a hint of mirth in his eyes. "Get on the damn yacht before I shove you in the sea."

Annabelle grabbed onto his tie and pulled him closer. "If I'm going in, I'll take you with me, *Aylesbourne*."

His voice was a snarl. "Fuck, I hope so."

The vessel was much as it had been last year. Its smooth teak bow stretched forward, as though it was eager to cut through the waves. Three masts stretched to the heavens above them. At the base of the first, a canopied lounge area had been placed. It was where Annabelle had spent her time last year, plotting on the cushioned lounges beneath the deftly arranged canopy.

Even she had to admit it had been perfectly designed; thick enough to block out the brightest of the sun's rays, but thin enough to allow her to read her magazines with ease.

Belowdecks was much the same too. A surprised Captain Sutton was there to greet her, along with several other members of the crew. Kit swept her past them, across the plush beige carpet and into the owner's cabin.

Annabelle caught a brief glimpse of walls clothed in panels of white and silken bedcovers that matched the sea outside before Kit pounced. His rough kiss stole the very breath from her lungs, just like his free hand stole any sense of relaxation from her skin. A gruff noise of pleasure erupted from his lungs when she began to respond, angling her head and squeezing his shoulders until they were both panting with want.

"Last night..." Kit's shoulders heaved with need as he put the wicker basket on the floor and freed the kittens. "I was too rough with you."

Oh please. She almost rolled her eyes. "I liked it."

"I could tell." He cupped her between her legs, grinning at her gasp. "Our first time in sixteen years should not have been in anger though, and for that I'm sorry."

"Was I the subject of your ire?"

A chuckle. "No."

"That makes a change."

"Speaking of which, you are going to have to apologise to Anthony."

Annabelle leant against the writing desk, mildly amused to see the pen still glued to the dark wood. "Why? For corrupting his beloved cousin?"

"No, for making all of his holiday clothes reek of fish."

The realisation almost forced a laugh out of her. "Those weren't your clothes I doused in fish oil."

"No, but I did enjoy the cock you drew on my forehead in my photo with Sir Ernest Shackleton. That was a nice touch."

"What can I say? Some artists use a signature. I use a penis."

He laughed, backing her onto the writing desk. "It was Queen Mary who discovered it."

Annabelle froze with alarm. "What?"

"Queen Mary. She stayed on the yacht after you and Michael."

Whoops. Annabelle hoped she wasn't going to be beheaded for her crimes. "I didn't realise you were so acquainted with royalty." Annabelle had met the King and Queen numerous times, most recently during a visit to Kew during the early days of the season. Before the man before her had forced her to tuck tail and run.

"Queen Mary is my godmother. Thankfully, she's duty-bound to forgive my indiscretions."

"Of which there are *many*."

"Mmm," he hummed. The two of them paused briefly as a pair of stewards knocked on the door, bringing in the suitcases they had brought with them and—most importantly—food for the kittens.

Amongst a hailstorm of *meows,* Annabelle took the bowl of milky fish mush and placed it on the floor. The kittens were ravenous, and she couldn't help but smile every time she looked at them. Their little boy was growing more confident by the day, barging his feistier sister out of the way. The second girl, the sweet one, chose a more sensible approach; going around to the other side of the bowl where she could eat in peace.

When the stewards were gone, Kit spoke again, his gritted teeth and hushed tone instantly setting her on edge. "I need to talk to you about my uncle."

Annabelle frowned. "What about him?"

"Last night, when I went to order the motor for our journey here, I also had a look at those records we discussed."

Suspicion prickled an irritated path down her spine. "I thought you said you couldn't find them."

The guilty look on his face told her everything she needed to know. "I may have fibbed." Kit turned, unlocking the suitcase that had been placed on the floor next to the bed. After a few moments of digging, he emerged with a blue book with *1907* splashed across the spine. "They're not records, either. They're my uncle's journals."

Annabelle glared at the journal hatefully, realising what Kit was about to say. "And?"

Kit's gaze fell, landing on the floor between them with a sad, faraway glaze. "It was my uncle who never sent your letter on to me."

"And sent me a reply telling me to sling my hook," she scoffed. "So we're not going to Campbell House to conduct an impromptu search; we're going there to confront him."

A task he clearly didn't relish the idea of. "Effectively. But you mentioned you still had the letter from my uncle pretending to be me. I'd like to stop off at Scarlett Castle to collect it first, and then we can confront my uncle with every piece of the puzzle."

Nodding, Annabelle's hatred grew like a wave, bubbling beneath her until it threatened to sweep her away. "Is that why you were so angry last night?"

He nodded. "I found out that the man who raised me as his own turned away the woman I loved, and my unborn child with her. My *son*. My heir."

Her heart flickered traitorously. "The woman you loved?"

Kit smiled. "I've always loved you, Annabelle. You must be daft not to see it."

For the first time, she really considered how she felt. There was a layer of anger there, but in recent days it had turned into more of a veneer. A thin sheet of rage to cover the burgeoning feelings below the surface. "And your uncle?" she asked, deflecting.

"I wouldn't have believed him capable of something like this. I loved you then as I love you now. He knew of my feelings."

That veneer of anger became perilously thin. "He did?"

Another nod. "But I chose—erroneously—to wait. I wanted to give you a man worthy of your hand in marriage. I wanted to give you an exceptional husband that had achieved something more than his birthright. I just… I don't know why he'd do it."

Annabelle did. "Maybe he wanted the dukedom to himself." She spoke over Kit's noises of dismissal. "Think about it. Think of what he would stand to gain. You were off to the South Pole; a perilous place at the best of times. There was a chance you were never going to come back."

"Uncle Eric has never wanted the dukedom. He's told me that himself—more than once."

That was a possibility, true. But Lord Eric wasn't the only man in line to inherit. "People do things for their children that they would never do for themselves," she said softly, thinking of baby Oscar and her marriage to Lord Buckford. "Your uncle is currently next in line, true, but after his death…"

"Anthony would inherit," Kit finished for her.

"Exactly."

He froze for a moment, and Annabelle realised how tired he looked. How utterly exhausted. The lines marring his brow were deep, and his mouth pressed into a firm line. He approached her, and she welcomed his body heat, eagerly lapping it up.

"Are you still sore from last night?" he murmured against her temple.

Annabelle tilted her head up. "Yes."

"Can you take me again? I can't promise to be gentle."

The smirk that curved her face was filthy. She let her hand roam his hips, squeezing his hardening cock through the fabric of his trousers. "Oh, I don't want you to be gentle."

∞

Annabelle exhaled softly, her eyes rolling back into her head beneath the blindfold. With her vision cut off, every sensation was heightened. His teasing caresses. The brief warmth of his kisses on her bare skin.

"Kit," she whispered, her mouth opening in a silent cry as he plucked her nipples.

"Do you not like it when it's my turn?" he asked, a moment before raking his teeth across the pink tip of her breast.

Her cry wasn't silent this time, erupting from her in a mixture of pain and pleasure. Anticipation rose when he moved to her other nipple to repeat the motion, and she basked in the feeling, balancing on the knife edge of agony and ecstasy.

Kit had all but ravaged her after she'd gripped his cock, pinning her to the bed and ripping her clothes from her body.

Annabelle had never been blindfolded before. Her previous sexual partners had been simple men with simple needs, with the exception of Cornelius Allenby. His tastes touched on being dominated, and Annabelle had discovered that she had an appetite for it.

But to be on the receiving end...

She threw her head against the pillow when Kit caught her legs, bending them back to spread her open. The cool air rushed over her needy flesh, and the simple act of exposure almost made her moan.

Kit's hands rushed down her thighs to spread her folds wider, exposing her completely. "Do you have any idea of how vulnerable you are right now?"

"Don't toy with me, Aylesbourne."

There was a hard pinch at her nipple. "*Don't* call me Aylesbourne."

"*Oh!*" she gasped. It had been as painful as it was pleasurable.

And then his touch was everywhere; her shoulders, her stomach, her thighs, even her feet, but never where she needed it most. Kit mapped her body possessively, until she was gyrating her hips with need.

"Touch me," she commanded. It came out more like a beg.

"You're not in charge tonight, little queen. I'm going to worship you as I want to. As I've *needed* to for sixteen years. Do you know why?" He began to tease her, running on either side of her slick pink flesh but never delving between it.

She stifled a desperate plea. "Why?"

He moved, bending over her until his voice was at her ear and his cock prodded against her entrance. "Because we belong together, Annabelle. Because the broken pieces of our souls fit together so perfectly it ought to be a miracle. Neither of us work alone, do we?"

Annabelle didn't want to think about it. "Just touch me."

There was a hard laugh against her neck. "You can't shy away from it. You can't outrun this. God knows I've tried. Tell me the truth; have you ever gone a single day without thinking of me?"

Her only answer was a damning silence.

Because he was right. Even when she hated him, she craved his touch. Her casual encounters with men like Allenby had been sans strings—which she preferred, because it allowed her to fantasise about the man she really wanted.

Annabelle had remained separate, even from her family. She'd always been aloof, but after Kit's apparent betrayal she had grown inwards. The loss of their son had only compounded the issue. She had never let another person get too close. Never allowed herself to become attached.

She'd already had one love, and no other could compare.

"No," she finally admitted, flinching as her blindfold was ripped off. The sudden brightness made her squint, but Kit blocked the light out for her.

The barest hint of a smile was visible on his face. "Sometimes I'd look up at the sky and wonder if you were watching the stars too."

A shiver passed through her. "I looked up at the stars. Just like you taught me."

Kit laughed again, joy lighting his face like the very stars they discussed. "I'll never stop loving you, Annabelle." He kissed her, clearly not expecting a reply. "I'll never stop wanting you."

She arched backwards as his lips caressed her neck, and gasped when they reached her breasts, teasing and tugging at her nipples until she writhed endlessly. His erection prodded at her, and she lifted her hips to meet him.

"Not yet," he murmured, crawling down to exactly where she wanted him to be.

He spread her with an achingly slow lick that turned into an open-mouthed kiss to her clitoris, his tongue following the smooth lines of her folds up before flickering over it in light strokes that had her gasping.

Kit's tongue plunged in and out of her entrance, simultaneously giving her what she wanted and increasing her need all the more.

An *oh* of surprise left her when he unexpectedly dove down lower, spreading her far beyond her comfort zone. "Kit!"

"Has anyone else touched you here before, little queen?"

"No!"

"Good." His thumb circled the puckered skin, lubricated by her copious wetness. "Because this is all mine." Tonguing her clitoris once more, he spoke in between those all-consuming kisses. "How many other men have had you?"

They were having this discussion *now?* Annabelle could barely keep her head on straight. Having a man explore her so completely—and with his tongue, no less—was sending her straight to the stars. "F-four," she stammered, finishing in a moan as Kit plunged two fingers inside her.

"And how many of them made you come?"

"Two."

"You're dripping down my hand." Kit withdrew his wet fingers, much to her chagrin. She bit her lip as he licked a drop that had indeed began to make its way down towards his elbow, darkening the inky hairs on his arm. Instead of dipping them inside her once more, however, he held them up to her lips. "Taste."

Holding his intense gaze, Annabelle sucked on his fingers, tasting the metallic tang of her own body.

He thrust them back inside her, licking and sucking all the while. Annabelle rocked her hips to meet his movements, until her inner thighs were soaking and every vulgar sucking sound pushed her closer to her climax.

"I'm going to come," she gasped, resting her feet on his muscled shoulders. "Kit, Kit, *Kit!*"

His response was to groan into her.

The vibrations of his gravelly voice sent her over the edge.

The crew be damned, Annabelle's ecstatic moan would no doubt have been heard all over the yacht. She thrashed around on the bed, unable to open her eyes for sheer pleasure. It barrelled down on her unforgivingly, arching her spine and curling her toes. She had never experienced pleasure like it, so complete that it eliminated the world around it. Breaths choked out of her in cries and whimpers, until she'd lost track of how long it had gone on for.

When she could finally breathe freely, Annabelle let her exhausted body rest. An orgasm had never taken it out of her like that before.

And so when Kit stalked up her body, sliding a condom onto his cock, she could only wait to receive it.

"Have I broken you?"

The sole noise she could make was an exhausted sigh of acquiescence.

"Good," he grunted, burying himself to the hilt in a single move. "I tried to forget you, you know. Over and over again I tried."

His thrusts were urgent, slamming into her wet, sensitive flesh.

"But you're unforgettable." *Thrust.* "Incomparable." *Thrust.* "Utterly perfect. And fucking you, being with you like this, is nothing more or less than a privilege. Because I have existed in the dark without you, Annabelle, and it's a hell I never want to return to. I am yours, little queen, to do with as you will. My life is yours. My love is yours. My soul is yours."

Annabelle wanted to tell him that she felt the same. That her life was empty without him, but each of his thrusts had her more senseless than the last. Their skin slapped together, a sordid noise that filled the room.

Despite the fact that her last orgasm had nearly shattered her into a million pieces, Annabelle's eyes widened when she realised she was approaching another climax.

Kit seemed to know it too, gently pressing their foreheads together. The polar opposite of the savage lust their bodies engaged in. "Come for me. Clench my cock like you clenched my fingers. I want to feel you squeezing me like a vice. I can feel you, you're so nearly there. Come for me. Come for me *now*."

She detonated, screaming out his name. This climax was no less devastating than the last, with pleasure radiating out from where they were joined. Though her back tried to arch, his body pressed her downwards and forced her to take the full impact of his actions.

Kit came with a roar, curling himself around her as he did so. With each pulse of seed, he held her tighter, and Annabelle knew then that she never wanted him to let her go.

Fuck her pride. He was right.

"I love you," she choked, gripping him so tightly it hurt. "And I am yours, as you are mine. My life. My love. My soul."

14

Annabelle

It had been many a year since Annabelle had felt nervous walking up to her own front door. When she was a child, she was always getting up to mischief, but the consequences were usually her mother sighing and raising her eyebrows. Coupled with her father giving her a surreptitious grin when her mother wasn't looking.

Now, the nerves carried with them the very real consequences of Annabelle's own short-sighted, unnecessarily risky actions. For the thousandth time, she wondered how Cornelius and Eva Allenby were getting on.

Scarlett Castle, with its reddened exterior and dual crenelated towers, had always been a haven for her. Perhaps it had been a mistake to run away after Lord Linwood's ball, because now she had to find the strength to come back.

It would have been easier to telephone Emmeline and tell her where the letter was, rather than Annabelle and Kit coming here themselves.

Easier, her conscience agreed. *But it would also be the coward's way out.*

Annabelle straightened her shoulders and opened the heavy iron front door, thankful that the hinges carried most of its vast weight. Kit followed her in, the wicker basket full of sleeping, full-bellied kittens in hand, closing the door behind him.

The cavernous Atrium stood before them, topped with a glass dome that allowed the day's final sunbeams to follow them inside. Their footsteps echoed on the marble flooring as they strode between the vine-encircled columns lining the room.

The sound of voices emerged from the morning room, and so Annabelle made a beeline for it.

Upon opening the door, she found her mother, her brother Michael, and her sister-in-law Emmeline within. The conversation halted as they turned as one to stare at Annabelle, with Emmeline recovering first.

"Annabelle," Emmeline smiled and stood to encase her in a hug. For once, her wavy hair had been tamed into a neat updo—giving Annabelle a sneaking suspicion that Enid, her lady's maid, had been helping Emmeline with her hair in Annabelle's absence. "I didn't expect you to be home for weeks."

"It's only a flying visit."

Behind Emmeline, her mother and Michael were making their way over to hug her in turn.

"Even so," Emmeline shrugged and glancing politely at Kit. "And you're…?"

"This is Aylesbourne, darling," Michael answered.

Emmeline's eyes bugged, as though some hideous creature had suddenly appeared.

Ah. Yes, this would be a slight hurdle, considering Annabelle had been badmouthing Kit for years.

"How… lovely to meet you," Emmeline said, sounding almost convincing. Annabelle was tempted to congratulate her sister-in-law for her performance. "You've missed dinner, I'm afraid."

"No matter," Annabelle shrugged. "We had some on our way over."

"Oh, I have missed you, dear girl," Mama said in Annabelle's ear, giving her an extra tight squeeze that only a mother could bestow. She then turned to Kit with a fond smile. "You've certainly grown since I last saw you."

"And yet you haven't aged a day, Lady Foxcotte," Kit remarked, a flirtatious smirk playing about his lips.

Annabelle shot him a stare that promised a painful death, waiting until his mother invited the two of them to sit down to sidle over to Kit and mutter beneath her breath, "Don't flirt with my mother."

Michael caught her arm before she had the chance to sit down. "I need to speak to you."

Leaving Kit to her mother, Annabelle shadowed her brother as he trod the familiar path out of the morning room, past a solid mahogany grandfather clock, whose polished brass pendulum reflected their movements back at them, and into the ducal office.

Michael's office was a typically masculine room, dominated by a dark, dramatic desk, scarlet armchairs, and an oil painting that had been completed mere weeks before their father died. The entire family was in it—her mother and father, Theo, Michael, Annabelle herself, and a newborn Effie.

Her father's fond smile lifted her spirits for the conversation to come.

Annabelle knew why Michael had called her in here; Kit had told her that he'd read that desperate letter she'd written all those years ago.

Michael didn't speak immediately, instead pouring whiskies out for the two of them, the crystal decanter clinking against the tumblers. He passed her the second glass, leaning against the enormous desk behind him.

She took a sip. The familiar warmth of the amber nectar was a balm, and she too perched on the edge of their father's desk.

"I can't imagine how hard things must have been for you, Bels," Michael's voice was calm and contemplative. "With the child."

The unasked questions lingered between them. *Why didn't you tell me? Where is the child? How are they? Can I meet them?*

Perhaps they were only there in her mind, because all she could see in her brother's liquid silver eyes was compassion. In his position, she would feel hurt if he'd kept such a thing from her. Out of all her siblings, Michael was the one she was closest too. He was the one who understood her best.

"I wanted to tell you," she started, "but you had just left for Ceylon."

He nodded. "Aylesbourne showed me the letter. I saw the date."

The silence that materialised between them wasn't an uncomfortable one. Annabelle knew what he wanted to know. She also knew that he'd give her as much time as she needed to tell him. Regardless, it was long moments before she made her first attempt.

Only a croak came out where a name should have been.

Somehow, this was harder than telling Kit himself.

Years ago, she had stood in this very room readying her courage to tell Theo of her pregnancy. And standing there, Annabelle felt those sixteen years disintegrate into nothingness. Nerves knotted her stomach into a tangled mess, but this time the sound of Kit's honeyed laugh passing through the walls distracted her, closely followed by her mother's girlish giggle.

Annabelle almost smiled. She wasn't alone anymore, and that fact gave her the strength she needed.

"Oscar," she whispered. "His name was Oscar." A muscle in her face twitched, attempting to keep the memories at bay. "But he never even opened his eyes."

"Bels," Michael's head hung, and he shoved a hand through his thick black hair—the same colour as hers, although silver streaks were visible at his temples. "I'm sorry. I'm so sorry. No parent should have to experience such suffering. And to be without a support network…"

"Robert was there for me. And I had Theo." Annabelle's lip curved in remembrance. "I called the doctor first, and Theo second, and Theo managed to get there before the doctor—despite being ninety miles away. I dread to think of how fast he drove," she shared a laugh with Michael.

"I'm relieved to know he was there for you."

"Theo was always there for us."

Something more than grief flickered in Michael's eyes. "Always." Their mother's laughter punctured the door once more. "And Aylesbourne?"

Annabelle was going to murder him for flirting with her mother. "Is another kettle of fish entirely."

"Meaning?"

She might as well tell him. It was going to come out eventually. "I love him."

Michael lurched back, coughing on the whisky he'd been casually sipping. "*Sorry?*"

"I love him," she said again, pinning him where he was with a look.

"Bels, what he did in London—"

She cut him off with an astute look. "I know. Believe me, I know. I was there."

"And you're just going to forgive him?"

Her eyes narrowed to a dangerous degree. "Do you ever think I, of all people, would let someone off easy?"

That halted whatever it was Michael was about to say next. "And the pregnancy?"

That was easier to answer. "He didn't know."

"He *says* he didn't know."

"He rushed up to Aviemore like a madman, Michael. He looked so crazed I almost shot him when he first arrived."

Michael pinched his brow, but couldn't hide his snort of laughter. "It's a wonder any of us survived to adulthood."

"But the letter he showed you, where I told him about… about the baby, his uncle read it. He sent me a response—in Kit's name."

Michael stilled, his good humour fizzling out instantaneously. "Saying what?"

"To sod off, effectively." She pursed her lips, battling the fierce hatred that always plagued her when she thought of those words, except now they were directed at Kit's uncle instead of Kit himself. "It's upstairs in my boudoir somewhere. We're here to pick it up before we go on to Campbell House."

"To what end?"

Annabelle cast her gaze wide across the large window serving the office. The cedar trees' wide, flat branches left long shadows upon the ground beneath them. Two figures walked beneath the closest tree. "Is that Effie?"

He nodded. "And Caroline."

Her charges the night of Lord Linwood's ball. The night she had ruined herself and embarrassed all of them. Because no matter how much she wanted to place *all* the blame on Kit, there was that niggling reminder in the back of her head that she and Cornelius had been having sex in public—where anyone could have seen them.

They were asking for trouble, but the little birds she had been chaperoning had not.

God, she owed Caroline and Effie an almighty apology.

"But Lord Eric? What do you intend to do about him?"

"In terms of what he deserves…" Annabelle couldn't help the unladylike snort that left her. "Perhaps hanged, drawn, and quartered?"

"Would you like his head on a pike to go along with it?"

"Obviously," she scoffed imperiously, lifting her chin high. "Who do you think I am?"

Annabelle felt oddly queer leading Kit into her bedroom, like she was on stage at the Old Vic, wilting beneath the heated glow of the stage lights. She didn't bother to turn around to note his reaction.

The familiar scent of rosewater pervaded through the room; a gentle perfume she favoured. Her bed was perhaps the most unusual thing within. One ancestor or another had brought it back from the East more than a hundred years ago—although god knows how.

So when she heard Kit, it didn't take a genius to work out what he was referring to.

"What the devil is *that*?" he asked.

Annabelle turned, looking supremely unconcerned. "It's called a bed. It's where one sleeps at night."

He looked at her as though she'd lost her mind, bending down to open the kittens' wicker basket to reveal three sleeping balls of fluff and a selection of newly acquired toys, courtesy of her mother.

Annabelle had been pleased to discover the laughter she'd heard coming from the morning room earlier had not been because of Kit endlessly complimenting her mother; it had been because Kit had set the kittens loose—in a room that was draped in her mother's macramé creations, which the kittens had *adored*.

"That isn't a bed," Kit spluttered. "It's a fortress."

In all honesty, it probably was quite disconcerting at first glance. Even so, Annabelle had become fond of it over the years. "It's a Chinese wedding bed. From the early Qing dynasty, or so I'm told."

It was similar to a four-poster bed in that it had a poster at each of its four edges, rising up to an ornate canopy above. Perhaps Annabelle's favourite part of the bed was its canopy, which stretched out into the corners like the eaves of a pagoda.

However, where a four-poster bed had curtains on either side, Annabelle's bed had no sides at all. Instead, it was panelled in on three sides with teak wood that had been intricately carved with dragons and seed pods and strange, foreign gods. The level of detail was astounding, down to each and every scale on the dragons.

Given that the bed was boxed in on nearly every side, Annabelle would climb in from the bottom. Even this opening was elective, though. The entryway was also equipped with a pair of doors that she could close and—if she wished—lock from the inside.

Doing so would plunge her into darkness, and Annabelle loved it.

She turned on her heel, leaving Kit to gawp in her wake.

Whilst she loved her bedroom, she also loved the connecting room that came with it.

Opening the door to her boudoir, Annabelle was comforted by the familiar sight of the chandelier throwing an array of light shards across the room, hitting everything from framed illustrations by Georges Lepape to a mannequin wearing a tweed suit made by Coco Chanel herself. Indeed, the suit was toted to be an advance design for 1924.

"*Jesus!*"

Annabelle looked back to see Kit clutching the doorcase with a hand on his heart. "That thing scared the life out of me."

"That *thing* is a muslin prototype for Coco Chanel's upcoming release."

Kit grimaced at it. "Is it supposed to look like varying shades of excrement muddled together like a slice of tiffin?" Seeing the fury set in across her face, he cleared his throat. "And why do you have it, out of interest?"

"Because I was supposed to be funding its production."

"Supposed to be?"

"I made the exceedingly ill-advised decision to fornicate in public and become a social pariah, after which Mademoiselle Chanel got cold feet about the endeavour," she let out a huff.

As much as she wanted to be angry at Kit for his actions, she and Cornelius had to own up to their own stupidity at some stage. In Annabelle's case, she had been blinded by lust—and Cornelius had always gotten off on the danger of being caught.

Well, they had been caught.

All Kit had done was turn on a light.

He must have moved closer whilst she was lost in thought, because the next thing she knew his lips were pressed against her temple in a silent apology. Kit pulled back, and his dark, sorrowful eyes found hers. "I'm sorry for what I did. If I could take it back, I would."

Annabelle found herself shaking her head from side to side. "I engaged in illicit behaviour in public with a man who was not my husband."

"What's brought this on?"

"I have to take responsibility for my actions. In doing so, I also have to recognise that such actions were idiotic."

He paused for a moment. "Yours may have been idiotic, but mine were spiteful. There is a difference there, is there not? Ergo, I apologise."

Rising up onto her toes, Annabelle gave him a tender kiss. His lips softened beneath hers, before she sharply pulled away—

Remembering too late that she was wearing lipstick.

The snort that left her was more akin to a sow than a lady. "Well you do pull off that particular shade of Bésame, I must say," she managed, wiping her lip line to ensure the colour was still in place. "It does have some transferability, however."

Kit pressed his mouth against the back of his hand and grumbled when there was a clear cherry red imprint on his knuckles. "For god's sake. Where's your bathroom?" he growled.

"Back into the bedroom. The en-suite is the first door on the right."

Annabelle smiled to herself as she went over to a camphor trunk she'd received as a wedding gift from Aunt Leonora—forming part of the bottom drawer she would take to Buckford Hall. Horses had been carved into the amber wood, galloping from left to right, with their manes and tails flailing behind them in the wind.

She unclasped the latch and lifted the lid, revealing her most recent correspondence, including letters to Coco Chanel and Cornelius Allenby. There was also a letter from the local Women's Institute, whose *char-à-banc* trips Annabelle regularly sponsored and sometimes attended.

Upending the lot revealed the seemingly normal trunk base—and made a considerable mess. Ignoring it all, she reached beneath the wooden moulding decorating the base of the trunk to find a small spring catch. It took her a few seconds to remember how, but eventually she opened it to reveal the base's false bottom.

For many years, it had entombed each and every letter Kit had ever sent her. Ancient pangs of heartbreak threatened to chime at the sight of them. How long had it been since she'd last seen them, let alone read them?

Kit's approaching footsteps made her turn away from her melancholy thoughts. A moment later, he was bending down beside her, lending her the heat of his body in her time of weakness.

"You kept them all?" he whispered, reaching over to scoop up the pile of letters.

Her face was empty of emotion, despite the sediment of old hurts being kicked up. "I did."

Fury transformed his face as he shuffled to the typewritten letter that had broken her heart. "This is what my uncle sent?"

Annabelle didn't bother answering, tightly hugging her knees. It was there in black and white.

"*I will be continuing on the expedition,*" Kit spat, the paper crumpling slightly in his grip. "*You have my sympathies regarding your situation. The Duke of Aylesbourne.*" He looked over to her, his face screwed up in anger and devastation. "I'm sorry. I'm so fucking sorry."

She began to speak, to absolve him of his guilt, but his mouth was on hers before she got a word in edgeways. The force of his impassioned kiss knocked her backwards, and she landed on the mass of scattered letters.

Kit's hands were everywhere, from holding her cheeks to receive his fierce kiss to caressing every dip and crease on her body. He lingered on her hips, squeezing and kneading. "I'm sorry," he whispered when his lips finally left hers. Her eyelids lowered in parallel with his kisses, and she let out a moan as he traversed her neck, her collarbone, her chest, right down to the deep vee of her neckline—

"Pull my dress over my head," she ordered him, lifting her hips to allow him to comply.

At any other time, she would have been furious at the way he scrunched up her silvery lamé dress. The exquisitely detailed foliage portrayed on the fabric had been crafted by an expert hand—a hand that would have been horrified to see its work treated as nothing but an impediment to the wearer's baser lusts.

But the sleek dress succumbed nonetheless, slipping over Annabelle's head. It left a vengeful gift in the static electricity clinging to her hair. The short *zap* when Kit went to remove her chemise, stockings, and suspenders had her giggling.

He loomed over her newly naked body, an elbow braced on one side of her head. "Find that funny, did you?"

Annabelle lifted her head up to capture his lips in an embrace that sought to drive him to madness. Just him on top of her was sending her mind to all sorts of filthy places; the fact that he was fully clothed was the icing on the cake. The solid wall of muscle above her somehow magnified her feeling of vulnerability, coupled with the sense of security she experienced whenever she was beneath him. "Exceedingly so. Are you going to punish me for it?"

A tiny movement at the corner of his mouth promised that he would. "You'll have to wait and see."

Kit reached above her, dragging a cushion off the armchair next to them. With accomplished ease, he scooped a hand under her back to lift her before placing the macramé-laden cushion underneath her head. Its tassels mingled with her hair when he lay her back down, but Annabelle barely noticed.

Instead, her attention lay on the man above her, whose lips had returned to her skin—but this time they weren't impeded by anything so bothersome as clothing.

No, this time Kit seared kisses around her breasts, coming teasingly close to her nipples before moving away.

"Kit," she snarled, her hand digging into his overlong hair and winding it around her fingers to get a good grip. "If you don't give me what I want, I'm going to lose my mind."

"I'm in charge again tonight." His reverent words were spoken against her breast, but his harsh stubble rasped against her nipple, teasing her all the more.

Annabelle arched her back, pushing her chest towards him and clenching her thighs together, conscious of the slickness he'd evoked between them. Brazenly, she widened her legs and reached down between them, giving her clitoris less than a second of appeasement before—

Kit moved quicker than an apex predator on the hunt, slamming her hands above her head and pinning them there. "*Mine*," he growled into her ear, his hot breath summoning goosebumps down her neck. "If you *dare* touch yourself again I'll tie you to that marble column over there, do you understand?"

Oh fuck. Annabelle tried not to whimper. She wasn't the whimpering type, but even the thought of such a thing had her melting into a pool of lust.

Biting her lip, she widened her thighs.

He took the bait, sitting back on his haunches to drink her in. A whispered curse hissed out of him, and she felt herself clench around nothing.

Ever so slowly, Annabelle began to move her hand, glancing at him through lowered eyelids. He tracked every inch of her movements, watching as she crept closer and closer to her destination.

"Little queen." His voice was a dark, sinful warning.

A warning she ignored.

Annabelle moaned when her fingers brushed her clitoris, dipping down to her entrance and spreading her wetness around in blissful little circles. She had expected to be dragged over to the column, but Kit stilled. The only movement was in his eyes, watching her pleasure herself.

As time passed, she became more confident in her movements. Not because she was shy—no, in fact she was quite proud of her physique. It wasn't particularly ladylike of her, but Annabelle liked a man who knew what he wanted.

And Kit was a man who had honed in on his prey.

Rather, her confidence lay in the fact that he had become captivated by her little show, instead of immediately ripping her fingers away. Annabelle didn't miss the way the tip of his tongue darted out to lick his bottom lip.

She was nearing her climax when he finally moved, but it wasn't to stop her. Instead, he circled the rim of her entrance, coating his fingers in her wetness before sliding two of them inside her.

"*Kit!*" she gasped, quickening her pace to appease her furiously approaching climax. She panted, clenching her toes as it—

He tore her hand away, ignoring her desperate shout of disappointment. She couldn't even close her legs; his thighs were in the way, keeping her from giving herself that final burst of stimulation to drag herself over the finish line.

"Oh no, you fucking don't," he snarled into her ear, nipping at its edge before jumping up to his feet.

Annabelle shrieked as he pulled her with him, throwing her over his shoulder like a sack of grain. "What do you think you're doing?"

He forcefully thwacked her rear, pulling the button-back chaise longue with him as he walked. Its castors wheeled across the rug, until its light grey fabric came to rest against the marble column. "Don't expend all your energy protesting, little queen. We've got a long night ahead of us."

"This is so undignifi—*ooph!*" Suddenly righted, she found herself lying on the chaise longue, staring up at him. The cashmere blanket thrown over the chaise caressed her skin, but Annabelle narrowed her eyes and drew her knees together. "What exactly are you planning?"

Kit simply removed his tie with a smirk. "I'm terribly grateful that this marble column isn't as thick as the larger ones downstairs."

Her jaw dropped. "You're serious about tying me up?"

"You're damn right I am."

Residual arousal still simmered in her blood, but it ignited when she thought of being restrained. Regardless, something in her still wanted to revolt. "I'm not an obedient hound for you to shackle whenever you feel like it, Aylesbourne."

"Are you not?" Kit's eyebrow cocked as he wound the tie around his fist in a movement that almost had her panting like the dog she'd just denied being.

"No," she said simply, hiding a bold grin beneath a mask of solemnity. She trailed her foot idly up his leg, massaging his solid length through the expensive fabric of his trousers before moving up to brace against his hip. "If you want to tie me up, you'll have to do it by force."

On the final word, she gave him an almighty shove with her foot. Kit stumbled back, thrown off balance.

She didn't hang around to check whether he hit the floor. Instead, Annabelle darted to her feet and ran, aiming for the door back to her bedroom.

Did she have a clear plan for where she was going? No.

Did she want him to chase her anyway? Absolutely.

Annabelle barely got that. She'd taken three measly steps before his arms closed around her, his gruff breath in her ear, and his hard cock grinding against her hip. "You're going to regret that."

His teeth sunk into the curve of muscle at the base of her neck, but her cry of pain was impeded by the hand he'd clapped over her mouth. She kicked out at his shin, intending to send him stumbling back. Kit only latched on harder, before lapping at the hurt he'd inflicted.

Damn him, but she moaned.

And then she was thrown back on the chaise longue, her arms dragged above her head and tied together before she'd so much as blinked. True to her word, Annabelle pulled and tugged, fighting with all her strength.

He tossed her around like a rag doll, acting as though her touches were as light as air. The tinkle of a belt being released made her pause, and her arousal peaked when she realised that, between his tie and his belt, she was utterly and entirely shackled to the marble column.

Kit strode down to the foot of the chaise, crossing his arms and observing his handiwork. Ever the temptress, she spread her legs.

It was the view he wanted, and they both knew it.

"Do you think that you're going to drive me mad with lust, and I'll give you what you what?"

"I don't think," she answered, her toes digging into the soft blanket underneath her. "I know. It's only a matter of time before you resist, Aylesbourne."

Kit sat, taking the time to push her legs open further. A small noise clicked at the back of his throat; a masculine seal of approval. She raised her hips, encouraging him closer.

She hissed with pleasure at the soft scrape of his callouses against her thighs. His touch was a massage, squeezing and stroking her legs, from her toes to her hips. When he reached her feet, Annabelle was unable to stop a giggle from passing her lips, but it soon turned into a moan of pleasure as his strong thumbs caressed her skin. Any areas of soreness soon evaporated.

If this was supposed to be a punishment, she wanted to be punished all day long.

By the time Kit had massaged his way to her inner thighs, Annabelle was a puddle of contentment. She'd even forgiven him for stealing her orgasm away from her earlier—purely because the buzz of arousal was humming beneath her skin once more.

She'd expected him to stop with his soothing massage when he reached her labia, but Kit clearly had other plans. Whilst the touch had been wonderful on her muscles, it teased her clitoris to madness, his fingers slipping through the copious wetness he'd brought forth.

Within minutes she was a quivering husk of need, seconds away from coming at any given moment, if only he'd give her that final push.

"Please," she whispered finally, her voice cracking. "Let me come. Please let me come."

Annabelle's eyes rolled back in her head when he gave her what she wanted, slowly circling her clitoris. The pleasure was so intense it emptied her mind of any thought, other than one: *more*.

"It's not often I get to hear you begging, is it?" he murmured, brushing her hair from her face.

She shook her head, lost in bliss. "Kit, *oh*. I'm going to—"

He pulled away, leaning back and smirking at her outraged shriek.

"Not again," she panted. "Not again. Please, not again. Just let me come. *Please*."

Kit licked her arousal off his fingers, groaning at the taste. He ignored her pleas. "Fuck, how do you taste so good?"

"It tastes better directly from the source."

A wry smile. "I remember. How many times have I stopped you coming now?"

Annabelle gritted her jaw so hard she was surprised she didn't crack a tooth. "Two." *And when I get out of these restraints, I'm going to throttle you for it.*

The smug look on his face suggested he knew exactly what she was thinking. Manoeuvring her about on the chaise longue, he positioned her hips at the edge and knelt between her spread thighs.

Perhaps I'll spare him after all.

"I want to take you here," he whispered, his thumb wandering low enough to make her gasp. "I want to fill you until you're so desperate to come you'll scream." Kit opened her wider with his hands, delving his tongue into her entrance to swallow down her taste. She wished she could hold him where he was or, better yet, sit on his face and pin him down. It wasn't that dominating him was more pleasurable than him dominating her, but *fuck* if the latter didn't drive her mad.

If she was being truthful, there was no one else she'd entrusted with this side of her. With Kit, she could let her guard down. Her other partners were either happy with a rough fumble wherever they could get it, or surrendered control over to her.

It was only with Kit that she could be vulnerable like this.

The realisation struck her just as her climax neared, and she clenched her thighs around Kit's head to keep him steady, to keep him—

He tore free of her attempted restraints, his lips wet as he laughed at her frustration.

"I swear to god, Kit, I am going to fucking kill you."

Utterly unfazed at her threats, he stood, calmly walking over to the large drinks cabinet on the other side of the room. He perused the drinks at his leisure, as though she wasn't strung up like a butchered pig. Kit reached for a bottle of gin, but let it go after a moment's hesitation. "Do you have anything that isn't alcoholic?"

Annabelle wanted to say that he was free to drink from the toilet bowl, but something in his voice made him pause. "There's lemonade in the cupboard underneath."

He poured out a large glass and returned to sit at her feet, offering it out to her and downing it in one when she shook her head to decline. "How are you feeling?"

She decided to be honest. "Murderous."

An air of mischief softened his features. "How many times now?"

How many times had he stopped seconds before her orgasm? "Three."

How many times was she going to kill him when she was free? Also three.

Smiling, Kit pushed her legs apart once more, his thumb reanimating her arousal at the merest touch.

With her eyes closed, Annabelle gasped, "How many times are you going to do this?"

"As many times as I want," he answered, lowering his head and caressing her needy cunt with an open-mouthed kiss.

Annabelle cried out, already feeling the warmth of her climax spreading from his tongue. This time, she tried to keep her moans in. If he didn't know when she was about to come, then he couldn't stop her.

Her plan failed miserably.

His question came again. "How many?"

"Four," she growled.

There was no end in sight. Kit would build her up, letting her linger on the cusp of her orgasm again and again. Five, six, and seven came in quick succession. By ten, Annabelle was writhing desperately, fighting against her restraints to give herself relief. He had to pin her down for the rest, avoiding her thrashing limbs attempting to kick him—he barely needed to touch her, simply tapping her clitoris repeatedly was enough to have her panting and ready to explode.

On the sixteenth build-up, Annabelle was reduced to begging once more. "*Please.*"

"This is the last one," he announced, his lips moving against her slick folds.

She could have cried with relief. "Do you promise?"

He nodded, pausing to cup her cheek with an affectionate touch. "How many people have seen you like this?"

Annabelle couldn't give a shit. "Only you. Just make me come."

Instead, he crawled up her body to take her lips in a fierce embrace—perhaps finally sensing that she wouldn't bite him the first chance she got. Annabelle kissed him back, tasting the metallic tinge of her own wetness and feeling more vulnerable than she had ever been before. "Kit," she whispered, her eyes wide. "Please. I beg of you."

He nodded, his face softening as he glanced down at her protectively. "The last one," he said again.

Annabelle believed him, almost overcome with her simultaneous lack of power and utter trust in him.

She sighed when he bent down once more, his tongue lapping at her clitoris. It took seconds for the warmth to return, building for a climax it wouldn't achieve.

For the first time, Annabelle savoured it. She savoured her weakness, and the fact that she lay entirely in the power of the man between her thighs.

When Kit finally pulled away, the denial of the orgasm was almost orgasmic in itself.

"Oh *god*," she whimpered, feeling a foreign prickling behind her eyes. The squeak that left her would have been humiliating at any other time, but Kit was there for her in a heartbeat, wiping away the drop of moisture that had escaped from her eyes.

"Little queen," he choked. Kit cradled her, reaching up to release her bound hands, but she shook her head.

"Leave them," she sniffed, unable to stop more tears from running into her temple. "I love you."

"I'm sorry, Annabelle. I didn't mean to make you cry, I swear."

Annabelle gave a very wet laugh. "I don't know why I'm crying. It's ridiculous." Her gaze fixated on him, feasting on his face, the way his black hair hung around his jaw, his strong shoulders, his calloused hands. "Just tell me you love me." *And everything will be all right.*

No one else would be able to pull such a request from her, but this was Kit. And he was hers.

"I do. I love you, Annabelle. So completely and utterly that I'm a ruined man without you. Had I gotten my way, from the moment I caught you in the garden that night I would have never let you go. You're *mine*, just as I am yours. Always." Truth rang through every word, like the deafening clang of church bells.

A sigh relaxed her shoulders. "Then make me come."

"Anything for you," he responded, crawling down between her legs; his now-familiar position.

"*Oh!*" Annabelle gasped, the ecstasy so acute it cut off her windpipe. She could tell the difference immediately—the difference between the teasing nature of his past attentions and the determined adoration he was giving her now. The kind of adoration that had but one purpose: to shatter her.

Just the feel of his fingers sliding inside her nearly had her coming off the chaise. He curved them as he did so, hitting her exactly where she needed him. His lips closed over her clitoris a moment later, his groans of pleasure enhancing the bliss all the more.

Her climax charged over her in a rush of lust that laid her out flat. Annabelle screamed when it hit, barely conscious of Kit's hand over her mouth, attempting to conceal her cries. She was more concerned with the increasing difficulty of simply drawing in breath; her body was a mere slave to pleasure, no longer concerned with keeping her alive.

No, now it contracted in time with the tidal waves of ecstasy flowing through her, a sea so potent she was in danger of drowning had Kit not been keeping her afloat.

Even in the midst thereof, she knew he wouldn't let her go.

He would keep her safe.

Perhaps it was that realisation that brought her back down to earth. Her legs sagged open around his strong shoulders. The bare skin of her knees pressed against the soft cotton of his shirt, reminding her that whilst she was wholly nude, he remained fully dressed.

She looked up at her bound hands.

Well, except for his belt and tie.

Annabelle pressed the ball of her foot into his shoulder, massaging down his spine. "Aren't you stopping?" she asked, discovering that her voice was unexpectedly raspy after her climax.

He didn't pause, simply flicking his dark eyes up to her and cocking an eyebrow. There was no mistaking his meaning. *What do you think?*

Pleasure began to build once again. Was this his version of an apology for teasing her for so long?

Where her first pinnacle had struck her down like lightning, wiping the thoughts from her mind, Annabelle remained present during her second, gasping his name out like a prayer and savouring his hot groans against her skin.

But when he didn't stop afterwards, she realised what game he was playing. Two orgasms became three, and three became four, bleeding into each other until she was no longer capable of distinguishing where one ended and another began.

She had never had more than two in a row before, but soon she entered another realm entirely, where the only thing she knew was Kit's voice. Kit's tongue. Kit's touch. Kit's fingers penetrating that puckered entrance and increasing her pleasure tenfold. Soon, pleasure itself began to burn, begging for more was the norm, and she no longer had the strength to scream.

15

Kit

Kit could watch Annabelle erupt for an eternity.

He surfaced after her sixteenth orgasm, treasuring the sight of her. No one else was privileged enough to be able to witness her like this, utterly wrung out with pleasure.

She didn't stir when he released her arms from the impromptu restraints he'd bound her with. He hoisted her into his arms, her head lolling onto his shoulder. Smiling, he rubbed the tip of his nose against hers, somehow not able to believe this was real.

A thread of discontent stirred within him when he carried her back into her bedroom, stopping short at the sight of her darkened teak monstrosity of a bed.

She obviously slept in it, but Kit felt claustrophobic at the very sight of it. It was beautiful as an object, with elaborately carved designs illustrating the immense skill of the craftsmanship. He appreciated it as a piece of art, but he'd rather set it alight than sleep in it.

He clutched Annabelle closer, as if he could shield her from the danger it presented.

With four walls enclosing the sleeper—and a canopy above—it was little more than a luxurious coffin, shutting out light and air completely.

Heart thundering like the hooves of a racehorse, Kit shook his head.

He couldn't do it. He couldn't put the woman he loved in there.

Retreating back to the boudoir, he lay her down on one of the royal blue velvet loveseats, briefly returning to the bed to swipe the covers off of it for her. He wanted to get one of the pillows, but couldn't bring himself to kneel inside the bed.

Before joining Annabelle on the loveseat, Kit settled the kittens for the night, moving them into the boudoir and setting out a preprepared bowl of mashed fish and bonemeal with a side of water. The kittens stirred as he did so, leaning forward into long stretches, their claws emerging briefly, before tucking into their dinner.

Climbing onto the loveseat, Kit settled Annabelle's head on his lap, pulling his feet up on the matching royal blue pouffe.

It didn't take him long to doze off. The loveseat on which he'd settled them faced the window, and Kit was content as he gazed out into the night, knowing that he'd never let her go.

"*Excuse* me?"

Kit peeled open his bleary eyes at the furious, high-pitched voice. An oddly familiar little girl stood there wearing a hard frown. "Hello," he replied, unnerved and off balance. The boudoir was filled with the thin light of early morning, and the grittiness of his eyes told him he hadn't been asleep for anywhere near as long as he should have been.

She placed her hands on her hips. "Who are you?"

"I'm Kit." Her pale blue eyes pinned him, and Kit realised he'd seen her the day he'd charged up to Scarlett Castle to find Annabelle. Christ, she was the spitting image of Theo. This must be Dora then, judging from what Annabelle had told him.

"Why are you in Aunt Annabelle's room? And why doesn't she have any clothes on?"

Kit's head turned so fast his neck cricked. Annabelle lay underneath his right arm—thankfully curled away from them, so that all that could be seen was the bare expanse of her upper back. He tugged the covers up to protect her modesty. "Aunt Annabelle was very warm last night," he invented, glancing over his shoulder and hoping a responsible adult would come to assist. "Should you be in here?"

"I always come and say good morning to Aunt Annabelle," Dora said simply, as if it was one of the fundamental laws of nature. "Especially on the mornings we go out together. But she usually sleeps in the other room. That's her proper bedroom. Was she very upset last night?"

"Why would she be upset?"

"Aunt Effie is mad at Aunt Annabelle, did you know?"

He shook his head. "Why is she mad?"

Dora shrugged. "I don't know. I remember when Josephine was mad at me for playing with something her Great Aunt Victoria said was special, but *I* didn't realise it was special. So Mama told me that I must always look someone in the eyes when I apologise, so they know that I mean it. And I mustn't do it again, either. Because if you apologise for something and then you do it again, it means you never really meant your apology in the first place."

"Right," he said, nodding his head. He sobered as Dora chatted on about the importance of apologies, not because of anything she was saying but because he found himself wondering if this was what Oscar may have looked like had he lived.

She had the same black hair and blue eyes that Annabelle had; black hair and blue eyes that Theo had shared. Michael had the former but not the latter, his eyes settling for a stormy grey. But Dora's assertiveness was Annabelle down to a tee.

The thought lodged itself in his throat. "How old are you?" he asked.

"I'm five-and-a-half," Dora said proudly. "I'll be six in December."

Then she was born after Annabelle had returned to Scarlett Castle. Kit's hold on his little queen tightened involuntarily. She had been there throughout the entire pregnancy. She had watched Theo's wife's baby bump grow past the stage at which Annabelle's own pregnancy had ended. She would have heard the distant cries of a newborn in the castle in the days and weeks after Dora's birth.

All whilst suffering in silence.

"How old are you?" Dora asked, utterly ignorant of his newfound instincts to protect Annabelle from the world.

"Thirty-seven. And three quarters."

Dora sucked in an excited gasp, her eyes sparkling. "Are those *kittens*?"

Kit looked round to see two kittens piled on top of each other in the wicker basket. The third—the tiny boy—was making his way towards Dora with a crackly *mew*. The noise had his sleeping sisters peeling their eyes open.

"Good morning," Dora whispered, sitting cross legged on the floor. The little male climbed into her lap without invitation, rubbing his face against her clothing. Within seconds, the girls had followed, and Dora was covered in kittens. She giggled, looking up at Kit. "What are their names?"

He paused. "We haven't given them names, actually."

Another enormous gasp left Dora. "Can I name them?"

Kit didn't see why not. "Sure."

The little girl thought for a moment, clocking her jaw to the side, managing to look even more like Theo than she already did. "Well my favourite animal is a dog, so I'm going to call this one Dog." She pointed to the little male kitten.

A cat named Dog. Right.

Kit held his breath, beginning to see the flaw in telling a child she could name them.

"And Josephine's favourite animal is a dragon, so I'm going to call this one Dragon." Dora stroked the feisty little girl, who appeared to like Dora every bit as she liked Kit.

He nodded. That one was slightly better.

"And then this one can be Bumblebee. Because that's Aunt Effie's favourite animal." The sweet little female kitten purred at her new name, kneading her claws against the ruffles in Dora's dress.

"Dog, Dragon, and Bumblebee," he repeated. Well, it could have been worse.

Movement beneath his arm told him that Annabelle was stirring, and Kit made sure to keep the blanket secured around her to protect her modesty.

Annabelle sat up groggily, her black hair all skew-whiff—although her spine went as straight as a maypole when she saw they weren't alone. "Dora," she blurted, her voice raspy from sleep.

"Good morning, Aunt Annabelle," Dora chanted, a wide smile revealing a missing tooth on one side. "I named your kittens. Are we going to take Queenie and Crimson out this morning?"

Kit wondered who—or what—Queenie and Crimson were. He knew there was a family dog called Jake, though he had seen neither hide nor hair of him.

"I'm not sure if we have time for a hack this morning, Dora," Annabelle said slowly, shooting him a questioning look.

Ah. Horses, then. Kit recalled how Annabelle had been draped in injuries the night they'd met—all sustained from being thrown by a horse. He gave her a subtle nod.

"And did you say you've named the kittens?"

"Dora?" a distant voice called.

The little girl looked towards the door. "In here, Aunt Effie!"

Christ. Kit hurriedly turned to Annabelle, double checking she was all covered. He'd barely finished before a young woman poked her head through the door uncertainly, but he noted her eyes narrowed when she found Annabelle.

"Why are you in here, poppet?" Effie asked, flicking a bouncy blonde ringlet out of her face.

"I wanted to see if Aunt Annabelle and I were going on a hack. And there are *kittens!*"

Effie let her eyes roam over Annabelle, her judgement hanging thick in the air. Oh yes, there was no doubting whether Dora was correct, because Effie was *fuming.* "I think Aunt Annabelle has her hands full at the moment. Shall we walk down to the scho—?"

"Not at all, we'll go out on a hack, shan't we?" Annabelle spoke up. To anyone else, she would have looked serene, but Kit saw the hurt hidden beneath her mask. "Just give me a few moments to wash and dress and I'll be right out."

Effie had almost herded Dora away from the kittens when the little girl asked a final question. "Aunt Effie, why is there a belt tied to that column? Oh look, there's a tie too!"

If looks could kill, Effie would have burned them to a crisp.

Nevertheless, Kit stood and cleared his throat. "It's so I don't lose them."

The bedroom door slammed after Effie and Dora crossed its threshold, rattling the paintings and photographs on the wall. He didn't have to be a genius to work out which of them had been the culprit.

Annabelle leant forwards, resting her elbows on her knees. "I don't think I'll ever be able to earn her forgiveness."

"Forgiveness?"

"At Lord Linwood's ball. I ruined us all in one fell swoop. I shall regret it for the rest of my life."

Kit clenched his jaw, feeling a muscle ticking therein. Had it been Annabelle's fault, though? True, her and Allenby perhaps didn't make the wisest of decisions to dally in public, but Kit had been the one to reveal them to all and sundry.

If anyone was at fault, it was him. Annabelle and Allenby were in a secluded area, far from the ball's foot traffic.

But was there any way he could fix the damage he'd inflicted?

He bent down to kiss her forehead, giving her an encouraging smile. "You go out with Dora. And then we'll head back into London with the letter. Speaking of which, I have some letters to write before we leave."

It would be a colossal string to pull, but there was no harm in trying.

"Why did you never remarry?"

Annabelle glanced up from her perch on his chest, the afternoon sun illuminating her blue eyes into sparkling sapphires lit from within. "For much the same reason I never wanted to marry in the first place. Lack of agency being the primary factor."

With one hand propped behind his head, Kit let the other flit about Annabelle's person. From her hair to her shoulders to her naked ring finger, and occasionally down below the bedcovers to appreciate the pert curve of her rear. It had been perhaps two hours since they'd departed from Scarlett Castle, but they'd barely managed to board the *North Star* once more before tearing each other's clothes off. They'd been quickly repurposed though, because the kittens—the newly christened Dragon, Dog, and Bumblebee—had made a bed of Kit's crumpled trousers. "Was Buckford a good husband to you?"

The frown on her face had knots of worry forming in his gut. "He was unusual."

"How so?"

"Robert didn't like people. He was very set in his ways. There was an entire wing of Buckford Hall dedicated to showcasing his collection of model figurines, in addition to a host of other historical paraphernalia. In some ways, he was the coldest man I've ever met."

Kit felt a *but* coming. "But?"

"After I gave birth to Oscar," Annabelle paused, her throat jumping. "I remember him being put into my arms and I was almost… surprised at how warm he was. I don't know what I was expecting really. But once I had him in my arms, I couldn't let him go. He was the most precious thing in the world." She looked up at him, grief turning her eyes glassy.

"I know," Kit assured her.

"And then Robert came up to me with a half-finished blanket he'd been knitting for the baby, tears running down his face, saying that Oscar should be kept warm." Her voice broke on the last word. "So Robert coddled him in a homemade blanket, singing to him all the while."

Annabelle stopped, and for that Kit was grateful. His tears needed time to dry, just as the lump in his throat needed time to settle.

Out of the porthole, the last sliver of Berkshire sailed by, small streets that would soon turn into the heaving metropolitan swarm of London.

Clutching Annabelle tighter, he finally spoke. "I'm sorry I never got the chance to thank him for being there for the two of you when I couldn't be."

She nodded. "At first, I thought Robert would be one of those husbands who had no interest in children, given that he married me purely to get his heir. But he loved Oscar just as much as I did, I think. And afterwards, he was so kind and gentle it broke my heart."

"Was he kind to you… intimately?"

Her hand came up to brush through the scattering of dark hair on his chest. "The marriage was never consummated."

Kit blinked. "You were married for four *years*."

She shrugged nonchalantly. "He eschewed physical contact. Not to mention he was quite ill."

"I never realised he was ill."

She began to brush her hair out of her face, but Kit took over for her. "In the end, he had three operations whilst I was married to him."

"To what end?"

"Drain abscesses. He had appendicitis."

Kit scrunched up his face in disgust and wished he hadn't asked.

Her laughter was like a tinkling bell, clearing the residue grief had left over the room. "What about you? Why did you never marry?"

At this point, there was no point in hiding the truth from her. "For me, there was never anyone but you."

"So…" Annabelle paused, the little crease in her frown touching on something that looked like pity. "You haven't been with anyone since me?"

"I've been with courtesans," he admitted slowly. "There was one courtesan in particular I'd always visit in London."

"Was she very talented?"

Shit, this was depressing to admit. "She looks like you."

"Oh." Annabelle lifted away from him, her eyes searching his face.

"Don't look at me like that," he brushed away her pity with a kiss. "I was usually drunk and out of my mind with need."

"Need for sex?"

Kit lifted his shoulders. "Need for sex. Need for human connection. Need for you."

"Do not be ashamed," she said softly, glancing over her shoulder as Dog and Dragon scarpered around the room like a pair of drunk racehorses. "Those were my reasons too."

His chuckle was a dark sound throughout the owner's cabin. "The latter through gritted teeth I'm sure."

"Oh absolutely." Annabelle's nod was as enthusiastic as it was bold, as she lay draped across his chest. "I would sooner have been hanged at Newgate than admit it, but throughout every casual encounter I had with a man, my need for the only man I've ever loved sat at its core."

There was a word with the power to make a man—or slay him. *Love*. Kit had always tried to outrun it, the loss of Annabelle. The loss of the woman he loved. An errant strand of her hair tickled his nose, but he buried her scent deep into his lungs.

When they were young, he hadn't taken the time to savour every moment with her. His ability to recall her scent had faded in their years apart. So too had the feel of her skin and the taste of her honey. Kit had cursed himself for that, but now he was committing everything to memory. The sound of her laugh. The soft inhale as he entered her. The catch in her throat when she neared her climax. Even the warmth of her relaxing against him.

"I love you, little queen."

For the first time, Annabelle seemed almost bashful. A strange emotion on one so brazen. "And I love you."

Her words were a salve to his soul. This was one of the things he had missed most. Not the carnal satisfaction of sex, but the calmness that set over him in the aftermath, sharing sweet words with the woman who had soothed his lust.

This was what they would have been doing all along had that cursed letter never entered their lives. The lurching grief of a life lost threatened to pull him into darkness each time he thought of it. The only thing that brought him back from the brink was the woman in his arms.

Kit's chest deflated. "I wish we could have had a life together."

The hint of sorrow in her eyes suggested her feelings were much the same.

"You would have been a wonderful mother."

The compliment seemed to surprise her. "Do you think?"

The image of her getting up to mischief with their children in tow made him grin. "I do. I think we'd have to employ a herd of nannies to help corral both you and our child, but yes. You'd be firm but fair."

"Nannies?" Her eyebrow twitched. "My children wouldn't have needed a nanny. They'd be perfectly behaved little angels, thank you very much."

"With that attitude, they'd be monsters."

Annabelle's good humour withered a little. "I think my child-bearing days are over now. Bumblebee, Dragon, and Dog may be the closest thing we'll get."

Hardly. "You're thirty-two, not some enfeebled old crone. Just look at Effie."

"Effie?" she said, bewildered. "What about her?"

"She's still a child. How old would your mother have been when she had her?"

She paused to think. "Thirty… six, perhaps?"

"You see?" Kit ran his calloused palm over her cheek, smoothing away her worries. "I was born when my mother was forty-three, for heaven's sake. We may be older, but we're not dead. If you want a family, Annabelle, we have time."

"I… I don't know. I never got any answers after Oscar died. At first I counted the hours without him, and then the days, the weeks, the months. And still the only answer the doctor ever offered was that it was just *one of those things*." Her eyes narrowed. "Or that it was *god's plan*, which made me want to cave in his skull with a rounders bat." The muscles in her face twitched, her expression morphing from anger to sorrow. "But it was easier to accept that I was never meant to have children than to try again."

He pressed a kiss to her temple, clutching her close. "I understand."

"We could try, sure, but what if it happens again?"

Kit had a different view. "What if it doesn't?"

Annabelle was silent then, her focus drifting away to some unknown destination.

Kit let her ponder in peace, savouring every moment of holding her in his arms. By now, the view beyond the porthole was nothing but the London metropolis, with buildings clambering over the top of one another. They must soon be arriving at Cadogan Pier, at which point they would depart to Berkeley Square.

Nerves had begun to slip through the cracks of his determination. Kit had his uncle's journal proving that the man had been handling the post that day. He had Annabelle's letter, begging him to abandon the Nimrod expedition to Antarctica. He had the forged letter sent to Annabelle, with its cruelty on show for the world to see.

Now, he just had to confront the man who had raised him.

"After Oscar," Annabelle's voice came suddenly, "I accepted the fact that I would never have children. I'm not a particularly maternal person, so I concluded that my destiny was to be an aunt to my brothers' children—and eventually to Effie's too."

Kit nodded patiently.

"But I think I do want children, deep down," she said earnestly. "Those first few days after I told Theo of my pregnancy, before my marriage to Robert had been arranged, were the worst days of my life. I was faced with aborting a child I desperately wanted to save my own reputation—*our* child."

Her words pulled on his heartstrings like a freight train. "You should never have been forced to make that decision." *And it was all due to my uncle's actions.* "Or marry a stranger."

"Exactly. I chose the latter, but when Robert died without an heir it left Buckford Hall to me."

His brow pulled down into a frown. "I thought Eva Allenby was his niece." Saying the woman's name was a dual hit of shame and jealousy; shame over the way he'd acted at Linwood's ball, and jealousy because Cornelius Allenby had had the privilege of fucking the love of Kit's life.

"Step-niece, so there's no blood relation there."

"Oh."

"But Robert left both his fortune and Buckford Hall to me to do as I please, so..." Annabelle let loose a long, tentative breath. "I turned a wing of Buckford Hall into a mother and baby home."

Kit stared down at her. Understanding and pride washed over him in a simultaneous wave. "To help women like yourself."

The corner of her lip twitched. "I was one of the fortunate ones. It wasn't until I set up the mother and baby home that I realised what a frequent occurrence situations such as mine are."

"Do you oversee the running of it yourself?"

It was a long time before she answered. "No. I... I prefer to avoid pregnant women, if I'm honest."

Kit stroked her cheek with his knuckles, but her expression pierced his chest. "I understand."

Annabelle rolled her watery eyes, clearly angry at herself. "It's imbecilic. And I hate it. One half of me is desperate to be pregnant, to have children. The other half is terrified about the potential loss of another child and doesn't want to touch pregnancy with a barge pole. After all this time I should be *over* this but I'm not. And seeing you..."

"It brings it all back," he finished for her solemnly.

"But the desperation to be pregnant isn't even for a different child. I want to be pregnant with *Oscar* again. I want him back. I've been pining after him for sixteen years and lighting a candle every year on his birthday."

Unable to stop himself, Kit clutched her closer, rolling her onto her back and hovering over her. "We'll both light a candle, little queen. We'll both mourn him. I swear to you. You'll never be alone in your grief again."

Tears slipped from the corner of her eyes, disappearing into the blackness of her hairline. His hands stroked her face, her neck, her shoulders, offering comfort where they could. "I wanted to raise him together."

"Me too." Kit pressed their foreheads together, their breath mingling in the sliver of air between them.

The clatter of the fenders being lowered, followed by the slightest of bumps indicated that they had arrived.

The long, thin pier was one of many such piers serving the Thames, but Cadogan Pier was the most convenient for travelling to Berkeley Square. Indeed, the journey from there onwards was barely a quarter of an hour.

They bade farewell to the kittens, choosing to leave them aboard the yacht amongst all of their possessions—and, of course, the toys that the Dowager Lady Foxcotte had managed to make in a single evening. They would be back later on, and Captain Sutton was only too happy to look after Dog, Dragon, and Bumblebee in their absence.

For Kit, Annabelle's presence had provided a welcome distraction from the task that faced him.

What exactly was he going to say to his uncle?

By the time the door of Campbell House loomed before him like the door to some unknown wasteland, Kit still had no idea.

He had often thought of how life generally had a before and an after. MacGillivray had said much the same on their Everest expedition. For MacGillivray, his *after* was marrying and having children. An exciting *after*. A positive *after*.

Kit's *after* was destroying the relationship he had with the only father he'd ever known. He looked down at Annabelle, stood next to him on the pavement glancing up at Campbell House.

He pulled her close and kissed the top of her head, drawing her scent into his chest. Kit was not the one at fault for the destruction of his relationship with Uncle Eric. The man had made his choice sixteen years ago.

So Kit knocked on the door.

Ebenezer answered, the most senior of their three London footmen. "Your Grace," he blurted, astonished recognition marring his features. "We weren't expecting you today."

The footman moved aside as Kit tugged Annabelle within. "I forgot to send word of our arrival."

He hadn't, of course. Kit had intended to throw Uncle Eric off guard with his sudden appearance, giving him the perfect opportunity to pounce.

"Where is my uncle?"

"In the dining room, Your Grace," Ebenezer said promptly. "Dinner has just been served."

Kit cut a deft path through Campbell House. It was not often he visited their London home, ignoring the myriad of targes, swords, and bows lining the walls of the entrance hall. The presence of the weapons was deliberate, intended to set them apart from their London neighbours, whose *objets d'art* were typically a demonstration of the family's wealth.

Campbell House, however, was a living monument to the Aylesbourne legacy. A legacy that had started with the first Duke of Aylesbourne killing a Scotsman attempting to assassinate the Black Prince during the Hundred Years War.

It was a tad ironic, considering the dukedom married into a rich Scottish family a century later—and had remained fiercely Scottish in the six centuries since.

Kit's heart pounded with anger when he heard his uncle's booming voice coming from behind the dining room door, followed by the creak of a chair moving across wooden floorboards. He came to a halt just before opening the door and gave Annabelle's hand a squeeze. "Are you ready?"

Her eyebrow cocked. "I'm always ready."

At that, a grin broke through the red mist that had settled over his vision. "And don't I know it."

Not bothering to knock, he shoved the door open.

Neither Uncle Eric, Anthony, nor Daisy sat around the heavily-laden dining table, the plates filled with what looked like venison. Instead, all three were on their feet, Uncle Eric pulling Anthony into a crushing hug, both of them wearing beaming smiles, although they stilled at the sight of the intrusion.

"Kit!" Anthony beamed, although his smile turned into a confused expression when he saw Annabelle standing next to him. "And Lady Annabelle, I believe?" His voice tipped up at the end, as though he wasn't sure whether he was asking a question.

"Lady Buckford," Annabelle replied serenely.

Kit only just stopped himself from scoffing. *Not for long it won't be.* He looked at his family's matching expressions of joy. "Have we interrupted something?"

"Not at all," Anthony said, taking Daisy's hand and bringing it to his lips. "In fact, you're perfectly on time. Daisy and I have just announced that we're expecting our first child."

"Child?" Kit stood motionless, feeling like he'd been stunned by a blow to the back of the head.

"Isn't it wonderful?" Daisy cuddled up to Anthony, her red curls bouncing excitedly. "I'd almost lost hope of it ever happening at all."

"Wonderful," he nodded numbly, unable to stop himself from seeking out Uncle Eric's reaction. Crinkled eyes, a smile flashing beneath his heavy moustache. He was even pulling Daisy in for a celebratory hug.

He couldn't help but compare that to the cold-hearted reception Annabelle had received, to the utter *cruelty* of the letter. Lips curling into a snarl, Kit made to bite out a scathing remark at his uncle, but never got the chance.

"Congratulations," Annabelle said loudly, breaking into his thoughts. She shot him a glare that he would have been an imbecile to not understand. *Don't you dare ruin this for Daisy.* "Especially if it's such a long time coming."

Thrown off course, Kit merely stood there, watching Annabelle melt into the family celebration as though she'd been there all along. Daisy welcomed her with open arms, giving Kit a knowing glance that suggested she was glad he'd finally brought a woman home.

Their London butler, Brook, soon had Annabelle and Kit seated at the dinner table. Kit was torn between watching Annabelle nodding politely along to whatever Daisy was saying—something about their plans for a nursery—and watching his uncle's utter joy.

Kit sat there, his anger rising. He had been ready to explode with rage at the sight of his uncle, not sit down to fucking dinner with him. And Annabelle... He knew *why* she didn't want him to shout the house down, but containing his emotions was a different matter.

By the time the *bombe glacée* had been served, his patience was teetering on the edge of a cliff. He picked up the glass of feni the footman had rapidly placed in front of him, contemplating the liquid inside.

Alcohol.

When was the last time he'd had alcohol?

Since before he'd gone up to the bothy. He remembered the misery of stopping cold turkey. Since returning from his last Everest expedition alongside Brigadier-General Bruce, Kit didn't think he'd ever been entirely sober. It had become a crutch to him, growing all the more significant by the day.

The first night up at the bothy was the worst. The one he'd spent out in the rain, his body trembling constantly, as though it was furious at its lack of alcohol. He'd barely been able to sleep that night, and when he had he'd dreamt of a glass of fucking Yquem—of all things. Feni was his drink of choice, purely because it dulled his nightmares.

Kit felt his need for the alcohol begin to rise. It had been so long; surely he could have a sip.

No, you can't, his rational mind hissed. *You've told yourself that a million times before.*

That was different, he bit back. *That was before I had Annabelle.*

Annabelle...

He looked across the table to see her sitting calmly, as though Uncle Eric hadn't ruined both of their lives.

To drown his sorrows now would be the coward's way out, and after this cursed dinner was done he had some choice words to say to his uncle. Drinking now would be akin to leaving Annabelle to face his uncle alone.

At that moment, he met Uncle Eric's concerned eyes. A little divot of worry touched his brow before his gaze slunk over to Annabelle.

Kit's crystal glass shattered, spearing into the fist he'd unintentionally tightened.

Annabelle was the first to move, jumping up from her seat. Anthony and Uncle Eric weren't far behind, but Daisy simply stared at the puddle of blood creeping in her direction across the pristine white tablecloth.

"Were you trying to throttle your glass?" Annabelle whispered to him, twisting his wrist to expose the nasty wound slashed across his palm, still drenched in the sharp sting of the feni.

"It was better than the other option," he muttered wryly. He eyed Daisy, her white-knuckled hands clenching the table, looking distinctly queasy.

"Anthony," he nodded towards his cousin's wife just as Annabelle yanked the largest shard from his skin. He couldn't help a pained grunt leaving him. Was she taking them out or digging them further in? "Take Daisy out of the room."

"Strewth," Anthony whispered, rushing over to her. "Come on, sweetheart. Come and lay down for a moment."

Kit waited until the two of them had left before speaking again. "Annabelle," he said quietly. "Lock the door. And Charles—" Kit glanced to the footman hovering in the corner "—go downstairs to the servants' hall. We'll ring the bell when we need you."

Uncle Eric's moustache twitched in irritation. "We need him *now*. Call a doctor, Charles, and—"

"*No*," Kit snarled, his patience reaching its end. His hand free of glass, he plucked a clean napkin off the table and wadded it in his fist, ignoring the rivulets of blood streaming down to his elbow. And the drips that had splashed onto the tablecloth. Annabelle sat next to him, and he pulled her chair towards him with his uninjured hand, only stopping when the seats were flush against one another. "I have sat here for the last hour and played nice for Daisy's sake, but I find I have reached my limit."

With some difficulty, he reached into his inside breast pocket and drew out the three damning pieces of evidence: the two letters and the journal. "You should have seen all three of these things before, uncle, should you not?"

Bewildered, his uncle took the proffered items, casting a disapproving glance at the blood. "Is this one of my old journals?"

"Read that letter first." Kit gestured towards the letter Annabelle had sent to him, wrapping his good hand around her waist. "Aloud, if you please."

Uncle Eric's expression was seeped in worry. "Will you let me call a doctor for your hand if I do?"

"Fine."

"For god's sake," his uncle muttered, flapping the aged letter open. His focus remained on Kit's injured hand, but his eyes widened almost comically as he began to read. "*I am desperately sorry to have to send this, but I have no other option. I'm pregnant with your child, Kit—*" Uncle Eric broke off, his voice cracking. His gaze flicked to Annabelle, understanding dawning upon him before focusing back on Kit. "You have a *child*?"

"The next letter now." Kit's composure remained steadfast, his uninjured hand clenching Annabelle's waist.

"*I will be continuing on the expedition*," Uncle Eric read, a distant echo of his own voice. "*You have my sympathies regarding your situation.*" He pinned Kit with a look fragrant with undeserved disappointment. "Why would you—?"

"And now the journal. I've underlined the relevant section for you."

"*Already there is a pile of post for him, which I have sorted through and been instructed to forward on to the South Orkn…*"

Kit didn't need to cut his question off that time.

Uncle Eric deflated slightly, falling against the back of his chair. "Kit…" Uncle Eric began, brushing a hand over his mouth, smoothening down his moustache. A movement he did so often it had become automatic. Previously, Kit had always viewed it with a fond nostalgia—given that he and Anthony made a game of it as children. Whoever caught Uncle Eric smoothing down his moustache the most in a ten-minute period was the winner.

When Uncle Eric discovered their game, he had returned fire; if he caught either of them in the midst of counting, their total would be disqualified. Cue Uncle Eric purposefully tempting them into counting, and waiting until the ninth minute to declare that he'd caught them.

There was no fondness in it now, just the harrowing reminder of what had been stolen from him.

Kit clenched his jaw, squeezing the life out of the napkin in his palm and savouring the piercing pain. "Why?" he snarled. "I'd already told you I wanted to marry her."

Annabelle's head turned sharply towards him, her eyes blown wide. "*What*?"

"The first time we met you said you wanted to marry in Westminster Abbey," he said simply. "It isn't the sort of place you can hire on a whim. I asked Uncle Eric to look into booking it whilst I was in Antarctica." He vividly remembered the start of the conversation, when Uncle Eric attempted to discourage him from marrying Annabelle, as well as his grim acceptance of that fact by its end. Perhaps that was a portent of things to come. "Tell me it wasn't the dukedom, uncle."

"The dukedom?" Uncle Eric frowned.

"There is no rational explanation for why you withheld the knowledge of my *child* from me, so I've turned to the realm of the irrational. The first is that you simply didn't want me to marry at all, thus my heir would always, in the end, be Anthony. The second is that your hatred of Annabelle eclipsed the importance of my own happiness."

"You are correct in one aspect—and one aspect *only*," Uncle Eric began, resting his elbows on the table and leaning forward. "I did not like Annabelle."

"I've never spoken a single word to you!" Annabelle exclaimed in outrage, mirroring his movements. "What on earth was your hatred based on?"

"The fact that you had a reputation for being a trouble maker. You had been arrested *multiple* times. You'd attended rallies and riots—"

"They were hardly riots," she scoffed.

Uncle Eric carried on. "You attempted to storm the Houses of Parliament, for heaven's sake. The last thing a duke needs for a wife is a radical."

"Where else should we be? Imprisoned in our homes and subject to our husband's will?"

"If you must know, I recommended that Kit vote *for* women to have the vote, despite the suffragettes' actions." Uncle Eric's frown deepened. "Nor was it my only reason for disliking you. At your coming out ball, I overheard you and a friend discussing *catching* Kit like a fish."

Now it was Annabelle's turn to frown. "I don't believe I ever said anything of the sort. I had no wish to marry at that time, believe it or not."

"I distinctly remember you using the phrase *happy fishing*."

"Did you really say that?" Kit asked quietly, trying not to be hurt.

"It was sixteen years ago!" she bit back in an angry whisper. "I don't know what I said—I can barely remember what I had for dinner last night. Regardless, it was never my intention to *catch* anyone. You know full well I had no plans to marry. And if you remember rightly, I did have the opportunity to *catch* you. My mother came out into the garden that night. One word to her and we would have been up at the altar in a jiffy. Instead I told you to hide, lest we be found alone in the dark together. Are those really the actions of a woman attempting to trick you into marriage?"

God, he'd forgotten about that. "No," he said, relief flooding through his system. Kit turned back to Uncle Eric, holding Annabelle's waist to form a united front. "Was that it, then? You simply disliked Annabelle?"

"Enough to doom me to the disgraced life of an unwed mother," she finished for him.

"Even if I *had* hated you that much, I would have never willingly hidden your child from you, Kit. I would rather you be happy with a title hunter than miserable alone." Uncle Eric paused, shaking his head. "And god knows you've been miserable." He picked up the letter that Annabelle had received, purporting to come from Kit himself. "I did not send this letter. I would never commit such a heinous act of betrayal."

Kit glanced at Annabelle, whose uncertainty no doubt mirrored his own. "Swear to me. Swear to me on your honour. Swear to me on my father's grave that you did not do it, that it was not you who sent the letter."

Uncle Eric reached across the table, realising too late that Kit's hand remained locked around a blood-soaked napkin. Instead, he opted to grasp Kit's wrist with a sincere squeeze. "I swear to you on both my honour—my *life*—and your father's grave that I did not send that letter. I did not know about the child."

Relief and sorrow played in his mind, chasing everything else away. One look at Annabelle told him that she felt much the same. Relief that his uncle had not betrayed him. Relief that the last sixteen years had not been drenched in deception, but it also meant that they were no closer to identifying the culprit. "Then who did?"

"As to that, I cannot say." But Uncle Eric clearly had other things on his mind. "The child. Where is the child? Are they well?"

He held Annabelle close, sparing her from having to explain it all again. "The child was stillborn, uncle."

Shock and desolation twisted Uncle Eric's features. Tears flashed when he gazed at Kit. "Kit…" Hand shaking, he took out a handkerchief to dab at his eyes. "I'm sorry," he whispered. "I'm so, so sorry. You haven't known this entire time, have you?"

Kit shook his head. "No. I found out about the pregnancy the day I raced up to Scotland. And then when I got there, Annabelle… told me the rest."

Uncle Eric shook his head. "May I ask where the child is buried?"

How had he never thought to ask that?

Annabelle answered. "At Scarlett Castle. My brother and I buried him near an old church. He said—" Annabelle stopped suddenly, slowing her breaths before starting over. "He said we should bury him next to a meadow, so he would have somewhere to play."

Emotion burned in Kit's throat.

"It's also where we ended up putting my brother's memorial stone, so I like to think Theo is taking care of Oscar." In her lap, her hands twisted. "It's nonsense, but it's comforting."

Kit was surprised to see Uncle Eric's expression so shrouded in sorrow. "Oscar," he whispered. "Nature is never crueller than when it steals a child from its parents. It's an agony like no other."

Annabelle's head tilted to the side. "You sound as though you speak from experience."

"My wife and I lost three babes before we had Anthony."

Kit blinked. "What?"

"We struggled to conceive," Uncle Eric revealed, remembered loss weighing down his aged features. How had Kit never known? "And when we did conceive…" He trailed off, glancing out of the window's black abyss. "We buried them in the gardens here, near the willow tree. It was your aunt's favourite place."

"By the bench?" Kit and Anthony had spent so much of their childhood in the gardens here he knew it like the back of his hand. "With the stone statues of the cherubs?"

"Precisely there. We installed the bench after we lost our first, and planted the bluebells shortly afterwards; blue because the birth stone for the month we lost them was September. The white roses are for our second, because we lost them in April. The third… the third was a little girl," Uncle Eric spoke in a hushed tone, holding his hand out, palm facing upwards. "Our little Poppy was born on the 15th January." He brushed his thumb over his palm. "I had never seen something so perfect in all my life."

Kit looked away when the first tear fell down his uncle's cheek. He'd never thought there had been meaning behind the flowers around the willow tree, nor had he questioned why his uncle cared for them so attentively.

"So no, Kit," Uncle Eric began, his voice strengthening with every word. "I would have *never* concealed news of a pregnancy from you. You could have had a hundred illegitimate children by now and I would have adored every one."

The thought made him smile. "There are no illegitimate children." He caught Annabelle's eye, and hope curled in his chest, warming it from within. *But hopefully one or two legitimate ones to come.*

"May I visit?"

Kit looked at his uncle. "Visit what?"

"Oscar's grave."

It took Annabelle a moment to reply, but she nodded. "Of course."

"If it's not too much trouble," Uncle Eric continued, "I could plant some flowers in the garden here for Oscar."

"His birth month was November, so perhaps some daffodils, or primrose," Annabelle suggested.

A knot twisted in his chest. Kit had never thought to ask. Another thing he didn't know about his own son—all because of the vicious actions of whoever the letter writer had been.

At Annabelle's offer, a final tear fell down Uncle Eric's cheek, following the tracks of his smile lines. "Just so."

16

Kit

The days that followed were shrouded in the rosy glow of summer. He and Anthony had taken to sitting on the Campbell House patio of an afternoon, discussing Anthony's plans for his upcoming arrival. There would always be a sadness there for Kit, and he suspected the same sadness lay in both Annabelle and Uncle Eric. It did not take away from his joy for Anthony and Daisy, nor would he ever begrudge them their excitement. Quite the opposite, in fact. Kit was excited along with them. But that sadness was there nonetheless, hiding in the dark recesses of his mind; the sorrow of a stillbirth would never leave him. That it occurred so long ago made it harder still.

He grieved for the loss of his child. He grieved for the fact that Annabelle had had to grieve through it alone. So too did he grieve for the life he and Annabelle might have had.

And Uncle Eric had gone through this *three* times, with the fourth pregnancy resulting in the birth of a healthy child but taking the life of his wife.

It did make him see his uncle in a different light. He was far stronger than Kit had ever imagined him to be.

Yet day after day, his uncle worked on his garden. A physical representation of his capacity for love—and it was beautiful too.

The willow tree lay at the garden's centre, an ever-swaying mass of golden leaves beneath which Kit and Anthony had spent many an hour as children, and where Dog spent many an hour of late, swiping at the tree's slender branches. The garden's borders were bursting with colour at present, dominated by the yellow of the many marigolds and familiar dusky purple of the lavender. It was a scent that Kit associated with the safety of home—and the sight of his uncle working on the three circular patches that he now knew represented the children he had lost.

Uncle Eric was precise in his gardening, maintaining the three circles' sharp edging to differentiate them from the grass surrounding them. Each circle was six feet in diameter, which Uncle Eric used a measuring tape to maintain.

Only the roses and poppies were currently in bloom, but what a sight they were. So densely packed with flowers the ground was lost beneath the petals, each circle bursting with both colour and scent.

The roses—named *little white pet* roses, as his uncle so often told him—overflowed with silky white petals. At the circle's centre was a winged marble cherub, its arms spread wide as though in play. Its legs were lost beneath the roses, giving the impression that the cherub was running through them.

The vivid red of the poppies was a stark contrast to the pure white of the roses, but they too were packed in tight. The marble cherub that lay within them was sitting on a column, however, its legs curled to the side.

To the left, the circle that housed the bluebells also featured a column, but instead of sitting on top of it, the cherub lay sleeping against it, bringing its arms up to serve as a pillow. For most of the morning, Bumblebee had taken advantage of his offering, snoozing on top of the pillar alongside the little cherub.

For the first time in more than three decades, his uncle was working on a new circle. Kit had helped him dig the outline, placing a stake at the centre of their would-be circle and tying a three foot rope to it to ensure the circle did not become misshapen at any point.

Daffodils had been chosen as their flower of choice, and they had planted hundreds of bulbs over the last week, leaving a small section at the centre of the circle where the marble cherub would eventually be placed.

It had not been an entirely peaceful week for Anthony and Daisy, however. Daisy's sickness had become almost constant, and Annabelle had taught Anthony how to brew a tea infused with ginger to aid her. Dragon, their feisty little girl, had taken a particular liking to Daisy, regularly curling up over her bump.

Kit had felt a strange sense of jealousy upon watching Annabelle and Anthony together. It wasn't because he thought there was anything going on between them, but because Anthony doting upon his pregnant wife was something that Kit had missed out on.

Every time he watched his cousin taking a tray of biscuits up to their room he was envious. On the days Daisy felt well enough to leave their room, Anthony behaved like a fussing old woman, holding a parasol over her head to protect her from the sun and keeping her ginger tea topped up.

Although Daisy found Annabelle's ginger tea recipe to be somewhat unpleasant, Anthony had perfected the tea to her liking—with a healthy dose of honey.

He hoped he would have been as devoted a husband to Annabelle.

Swallowing his nerves, Kit glanced out of the window. The motor rattled along as they travelled through London's streets, bustling with cars and buses and rickshaws alike.

"I swear these bloody rickshaws have no care for their own lives," Anthony muttered next to him. He pulled out a golden pocket watch, passing his thumb over the significant dent in the hunter-case. Like Uncle Eric and his moustache, Kit suspected Anthony's movement was involuntary; a reminder of the losses he'd sustained in the war.

The difference in their respective services during the war couldn't have been more polarised. Kit had been stuck in Antarctica on a quest for personal glory, whereas Anthony had narrowly avoided death aboard HMS *Indefatigable* during the Battle of Jutland.

Kit made no answer. Even when he *had* eventually returned to Britain at the beginning of 1917, he had enlisted and been given a duty as an aide-de-camp to General Sir Henry Rawlinson.

A sorrowful pang went through him. The last time he'd seen Theo had been around that time. It pained him to think that one of his closest friends had died thinking Kit had dishonoured Annabelle.

Kit smoothed out the paper in front of him, reading the neat little letters upon the page. Most of it was fluff, taken up by titles and grand office names. The real meaning was almost buried, but its significance was enormous—at least to him. "Do you think she'll say yes?" he asked quietly.

Anthony's bewildered look was perhaps a good indication he was overthinking things. "You're asking if the woman who's spent the last week in your bed is going to want to marry you? Aren't these sort of nerves supposed to be reserved for the bride rather than the groom?"

"Were you not nervous when you asked Daisy to marry you?"

Anthony clasped his pocket watch closed, sliding it back into his jacket. "Enormously so, but I hadn't bedded her at the time. Unlike you," he tapped his chest proudly, "*I* am a gentleman and waited until after the wedding to take her to bed. In fact, I didn't even bed her on our honeymoon."

That was a detail that pulled Kit away from his nerves. Anthony's honeymoon to America hadn't been a short one. "I'm sorry, you didn't bed her until you'd been wed for more than a month?"

His cousin shrugged. "She was nervous. And I loved her."

"I didn't think you were capable of such sentiment."

That earned him a sharp kick. "Not around you I'm not," Anthony grinned, but it dissolved into a softer look of affection. "I hope she accepts you. Not just because, you know, you've already booked Westminster fucking Abbey, but because you deserve to be happy."

"If she does accept me, I hope I'm as dutiful a husband as you."

"You will be," Anthony promised him, somehow sure. "I've seen the way you've looked at Daisy recently."

Panic rounded his eyes. *Fuck*. He thought he'd been discreet. "It's not because I—"

Anthony waved his words away. "I know it's not; it's envy. I see it in your eyes. You want a family."

"I do," Kit admitted, breaking into laughter when he imagined it. "God help me, but I do. Any children of Annabelle's are going to be absolute headcases causing mischief left, right, and centre, but I want it all."

Anthony chortled along as they finally drove into Berkeley Square. "Between you and Annabelle, I don't think you've got a hope in hell of a peaceful life. I can only hope that my children get Daisy's temperament."

"When I think of the things we got up to when we were young…" Kit shook his head, remembering in horror some of their more dangerous exploits.

"Didn't we try and scale Eilean Rìgh at one point?"

"We did as well!" Kit gasped, having forgotten that particular event. As the chauffeur pulled up beside Campbell House, he leant forward, shoving his hands into his hair and resting his forehead on his palms. "God," he snorted, opening the door. "We're absolutely fucked if our kids are anything like us."

Campbell House was silent when they entered it, with the exception of Da Silva inclining his greying head respectfully as they passed in the corridor—instead of piercing Kit with a judgemental gaze.

Well, that was new.

Kit suspected the family were in the garden where he and Anthony had left them. The weather was certainly still warm enough, though he knew the colder months were fast approaching.

By the time they arrived, he hoped he'd be a married man.

The two of them made a beeline for the garden. Their hard work had paid off; the daffodil circle was nearing completion. Indeed, the only thing left to install was the marble cupid statue, although that was not yet finished. He and Annabelle had worked on its design together, a part of the process Uncle Eric had left to them.

It had been a difficult task, to create a statue to represent a child they hadn't known and never would, but he and Annabelle were pleased with the design they had settled on.

Kit relaxed when he heard her laughter coming from the garden, closely followed by his uncle's deep chuckle, and quickened his step. Just when he was about to reach the back door, he heard Brook's voice.

"Your Grace?"

He and Anthony stopped in their tracks. "Yes?" Kit said, disguising his impatience. With the letter in his pocket, Kit felt as though he was carrying a shell around with him, fearing it would explode at any moment. He wanted to ask her. He *needed* to ask her.

"Brigadier-General Bruce is waiting for you in the drawing room."

His stomach dropped, but Kit managed to draw in the breath necessary to respond. Recently, the avalanche had been at the very periphery of his mind, but suddenly the earth's furious rumble sounded in his ears, as fresh as the day he'd first heard it. "Has he been waiting long?"

"Not at all, Your Grace. He arrived a few minutes before you did. I've given him refreshments."

Kit nodded, looking at the back door and hearing Annabelle's voice once again.

"I'll tell them you'll be out in a moment," Anthony said encouragingly, disappearing through the door.

Turning away, Kit followed Brook through the house, but his mind was on the day he'd last seen Charles Bruce; the day he'd arrived back in London after their last Everest expedition, bringing John MacGillivray's body back to his family.

Brook announced Kit's arrival before he was ready. "The Duke of Aylesbourne."

Kit had no choice but to enter.

Brigadier-General Bruce was a heavy-set man approaching his sixties, but his smile belied the heart of a man half that age. He held a steaming cup in his hands, but quickly placed it on the coffee table behind him. "Aylesbourne!" Bruce shook Kit's hand, his thick black moustache tinged with grey. More greys than had been there before. "How good it is to see you."

"And you," Kit replied, attempting to look sturdier than he felt. "Sit," he said to Bruce, taking a seat on one of the teal green sofas overlooking the gardens of Berkeley Square, just underneath an oil painting completed by Anthony depicting Eilean Rìgh. "How have the meetings been coming along for the expedition next year? I fear I've missed too many whilst I've been in Scotland."

Bruce took the seat opposite him, spreading a comfortable arm along its back. "Nothing that we can't bring you up to speed on whilst we're on the ship."

"How goes the planning?"

Bruce was an honest man. It was what Kit liked about him; there was no hidden subtext beneath his words, only the truth—be it easy to digest or a meal made of disappointment. "Good and bad. We think we've got a route mapped out. It's a shame we can't go through Nepal, however."

Ah. "We haven't managed to gain access to the south side?" On their last expedition, one of the mountaineers had spied a route that looked to be a deal easier to climb. The complication being that the south side lay within Nepal, a country that did not allow outsiders within its borders.

"They've not moved an inch on the matter. Nepal is closed to us, for good or ill."

As it had when he'd first discovered it, that fact rankled at him. The access route through Nepal could potentially be significantly easier—not to mention safer—to climb. Kit shook his head. "I suppose it is their country. And what we're doing is, at its heart, a quest for glory. The ascent of Everest is neither pressing nor essential."

"Is the exploration of the world not essential?" Bruce countered.

In the grand scheme of things, no. It was not. "To you, perhaps."

"And to you, I hope."

Was it though? "It was certainly essential to Major MacGillivray."

Bruce sobered, picking up his cup of tea from the coffee table. "May he rest in peace." He watched Kit's heavy swallow with knowing eyes. "How have you been since you returned?"

"Fine."

A small noise of acknowledgement left Bruce's throat. An indication that he knew full well what Kit wasn't saying. "I see."

Keen to change the subject, Kit asked the first question that came into his head. "Have you decided the expedition's date of departure?"

"We have, actually. Our departure date is set for New Year's Eve. Start the year off with a bang and all that."

"New Year's?" he replied, his heart sinking into his empty stomach. "That's sooner than I was expecting."

"We've narrowed our window down since last we spoke. We want to arrive in Darjeeling by perhaps the end of February and spend a month hiring porters and gathering supplies, before beginning the journey proper at the end of March."

Roughly the same timing as their last attempt. "Before the monsoon season," Kit swallowed, his mind half buried in the memory of the avalanche. "Meaning we'd return by September."

"Perhaps October," Bruce agreed. "Now, I do want to discuss the financing with you. After the bankruptcy of the Bank of..."

Kit's attention drifted elsewhere. October. They'd be back in Britain by October, meaning he'd spend ten months away from Annabelle. If she accepted him, they'd be married for a mere three months before he left.

No matter how hard he tried, he couldn't blink away the image of John MacGillivray's icy body. A porter had offered to drag the travois on which MacGillivray's body lay back down Everest, but Kit had made it his sole duty.

And then there was the matter of children. MacGillivray had left two children behind; two children who would grow up without a father because of MacGillivray's desire to be part of history. Before Annabelle had crashed back into his life again, Kit would have said he understood. But now his only question was how MacGillivray could have left them.

Three months. Could Annabelle fall pregnant in three months?

All it had taken was a single night the first time.

Kit's eyes closed. With a history of stillbirth, there was no guarantee of a healthy pregnancy this time around. He could be leaving her to suffer alone once more. There was the simultaneous issue of the length of his absence. If she was pregnant by the time he left, Annabelle would give birth very much alone.

A hard clap on Kit's shoulder drove Bruce's voice through his skull with the force of a pickaxe. "Aylesbourne? Are you here with me?"

Kit managed a nod. "I'm here." *Just.*

"Will you make up the shortfall?"

"How much is it?"

Bruce gave him a sly look; a gentle chide for not paying attention. "Some £800. Likely £900, if we're bringing the oxygen equipment along too."

"Consider it done. I'll get the cheque sent over before the end of the week."

That decision was an easy one. The ascent of Everest was perhaps a frivolous endeavour, but Kit was keen to reduce the possibility of any of the men dying. If there was any chance at all the oxygen equipment could save a life, he would gladly pay it ten times over.

"Much appreciated. We're planning on meeting again next Monday. Shall I assume you'll attend?"

Kit made a non-committal noise.

Bruce took it as acceptance, getting to his feet. "Good. I'll send you over some of the correspondence with Nepal and our potential routes; I'd be interested in hearing your thoughts on the situation."

"Then you shall have them."

"Good man." He held out his hand, and Kit shook it. "I won't take up any more of your time, Aylesbourne. I'll see you next week."

Kit bade the man farewell, listening as his heavy footsteps trod the path to the front door. A few moments later, an engine fired up; no doubt Bruce's cab.

Then he sat back down and pulled out the letter he'd gone out to obtain that morning.

If he was being honest, he hadn't thought of Everest in days. Fuck, he hadn't even thought of *MacGillivray* in days. Kit wondered how MacGillivray's wife, Maria, was coping. How were their *children* coping?

Of course he'd felt sorry for MacGillivray's wife and children before. Indeed, he'd felt so strongly that he took care of their finances without question. There had been times where he would have gladly traded places with his friend; to give them back the father and husband they adored. Not that Kit would have ever admitted that to Uncle Eric.

Now he felt sorry for them in quite a different way. He read through the letter in front of him without really digesting the words.

How could John MacGillivray have risked his life when he had a family at home? A family who loved and depended on him. His face contorted when he thought of how Maria would feel. Would she wonder why her love was not enough to keep John at home, safe and sound?

If Kit was in her place, he knew he'd be wondering that very thing.

"You're leaving again."

Annabelle's voice made Kit jump so violently he almost tore the letter in two. "*Christ*," he swore. He hadn't heard her enter the room. "You made me jump out of my skin."

She didn't offer him an apology, nor did she repeat herself. Instead, Annabelle simply stood there, her face curiously empty of emotion.

Kit whipped the letter back in his pocket, but her furious reaction instantly told him this was a wrong move.

"What is that?" she asked, her brow creasing in anguish. "An itinerary for your next Everest trip? Which you conveniently forgot to mention, by the way."

"I'd forgotten about it." It was a poor defence, but it was the truth. "You've made me happy."

His response pierced her bubble of anger, but failed to deflate it entirely. "When were you planning on telling me?"

"How much did you hear?"

Annabelle rolled her eyes; a gesture that was so characteristically *her* that it was almost heart-warming. "Don't answer my question with a question. I heard enough to know that you'll be gone for almost a year. I'm *not* doing this again, Kit." This time, her anger vanished altogether, but it was replaced by vulnerability. "I'm not being left behind again. I can't do it."

Standing, Kit walked over to her. Annabelle attempted to retreat, but he pulled her close, guiding her back against the wall. He held her face in his hands, marvelling at the softness of her skin. As he always did.

"Little queen," he murmured, pressing their foreheads together.

Annabelle tried to put up an aggressive front. He *saw* it, but behind it lay who she really was. She tried to resist his touch—just as he'd tried to resist her pull.

But they were inevitable, the two of them. And they both knew it.

"I'll never leave you again," Kit promised, pulling out the slightly crumpled letter. "If you'll still have me."

Annabelle's furious defence melded into disbelief as she read the words in front of her, her lips parting.

"I have traversed the four corners of the earth," he began. "I have explored frozen oceans, deepest jungles, and the most impregnable mountain in existence, and yet there is nowhere I would rather be than standing before you, asking—nay—*begging* for your hand in marriage."

Her response remained guarded. "And Everest?"

His attention drifted to somewhere in the space between them. "I don't know how the men with families did it. How they left their wives and children when there was every chance they weren't coming back. Whenever I think of John MacGillivray, all I can think of is the family he left behind. The family I had to write to with news of his death."

Her head tilted to the side. "I didn't know you had to do that."

Kit hadn't *had* to do it. Not necessarily. But of all the men on the trip, only he had known John well enough to meet his wife and children. He'd thought that would count for something, in the grand scheme of things. "I wouldn't have wanted to learn of the death of someone I loved from a stranger. Would you?"

Annabelle looked away. "No," she said softly. "Michael was with Theo when he died, did you know that?"

Relief washed over him like a wave of cool air in a desert. "I didn't."

"Michael's telegram arrived before the official letter from the War Office, and we were thankful for that. If anyone could have been with Theo when he died, I'm glad it was Michael. We certainly found comfort in it—that he hadn't been alone."

Memories scattered across his mind. Memories of the times he had shared with Michael and Theo at Eton and Cambridge. Times on the yacht, cavorting around the seas like a pack of hooligans.

"I'm sure Lady Maria found comfort in your letter as well," she carried on.

Kit pressed his lips together. "Perhaps."

With a deep inhale, Annabelle glanced at the Archbishop's letter again, looking up at him from beneath lowered lashes. "Did you have a date in mind?"

The question sent a shiver down his spine. "You're accepting?"

Another eye roll.

Fuck, he couldn't love her more if he tried.

"Obviously I'm accepting, you utter pillock. Do you really thi—?"

Kit hoisted her into his arms, her shrieking giggle music to his ears. He spun her round, burying his face into her hair to conceal his relief. "I love you," he swore hoarsely. He couldn't get enough of her, holding her so tightly it was a wonder she could breathe. "I love you. More than anything. More than everything. You're my heart, my soul, *mo chridhe, mo bhanrigh.*"

Her hand sliding into his hair made him groan. "And I love you, Kit."

Cupping her cheeks, he kissed her, devouring her taste and savouring her touch. There was no achievement or glory that would ever exceed this. He could go on a thousand expeditions to unexplored territories and never be as happy as he was at this moment, his chest fit to burst with joy. "Marry me on the first available date."

Although she attempted to give him a stern look, it soon morphed into pink-cheeked excitement. "And children?"

"If you want to try for children, then we'll try. If you want to wait, we'll wait. And if you're never ready, then I'll spend eternity adoring you anyway."

Tight little muscles in Annabelle's face twitched, contorting her expression into one of abject worry. "And if I lose another baby?"

He pulled her into his embrace, pressing a gentle kiss to her temple. "If *we* lose another child, then I'll be there for you every step of the way, little queen. You'll never be alone again, not for a moment."

∽

Fresh from the shower, Kit stretched out on his bed, heartily enjoying the sight of Annabelle undressing in front of him. Tomorrow, the five of them would journey up to Scarlett Castle for a *dinner* Annabelle had requested. Their engagement announcement, though no one except Michael knew it. They'd no doubt be spending the night apart.

Tomorrow, Kit suspected Michael would be guarding Annabelle's bedroom door like Cerberus himself.

Tonight, he feasted.

Annabelle knew it too, teasing him in long, slow movements that emphasised her elongated legs. Kit couldn't take his eyes off them as she disrobed, his attention caught on the garters holding up her angelic white silk stockings.

"Have you been wearing those all day?" he murmured, his skin still damp from the shower. Given the heat, he lay with a towel draped over his hips, his thick erection tented beneath it, in full view of Annabelle.

She'd been watching him just as he'd been watching her, but Kit knew full well he had the better end of the bargain. "Of course."

His breathing was harsh, turning harsher by the moment when she finally began to undo the three little buttons holding up her chemise. Kit watched with rapt attention, holding his breath when she slipped the little straps off her shoulders.

His cock twitched when she let it go, revealing the tantalising lines of her body. Jaw clenched, Kit shifted his hips to reposition his length. The sight of her like this was going to drive him mad.

"Come here."

Annabelle didn't move, looking down at her stockings and garters. "You don't want me to take these off?"

"Christ no, they stay on." One arm propped behind his head, he got the barest hint of pinkness when she climbed atop him. Her legs were spread on either side of his hips, and the feel of her wet heat above his cock was mesmerising—as it would always be.

Freeing his arm, he slid his touch up and down her thighs, tilting her hips backwards to give him a better view of her cunt.

"I want to try something."

Kit looked up, blinking away the haze of lust. "What?"

"You said when we were in my boudoir that you wanted to take me."

He couldn't stop his eyebrow from popping up. "I've always wanted to *take* you."

"Not where you normally would," she replied, a devilish glare in her eye. "In my... *derrière*."

So she'd been thinking about that, had she? They'd experimented with a set of dilators he'd bought for her, but they hadn't yet worked up to his cock. "And you want to try that tonight, is that what you're saying?"

Annabelle's lips pursed, pulling to the side. "Yes and no."

He didn't say anything, merely waiting for her to explain.

"There's a significant amount of adult literature at Scarlett Castle. It's hidden, but it's there. I've read quite a lot of it."

A smile brimmed his face. "I would expect nothing less."

"And I've read that it *can* be pleasurable for women—although the authors are men so I always assumed they were lying to make themselves look good," Annabelle continued, her hand creeping up his chest. "But I've also read that men enjoy it being done *to* them."

Kit stilled. He knew *exactly* what she was talking about. He had gone to a boy's school, after all. At some point, his hands had stopped their rhythmic caressing of her thighs. "And you want to do that to me?"

Lowering her eyelids, Annabelle rocked her hips over his still-hard cock. "If that's something you're comfortable with."

It wasn't something he'd ever done before. It certainly wasn't something he would have been comfortable doing with anyone else, but whilst Kit enjoyed dominating Annabelle... he also enjoyed the reverse. And if he was wanting to do it to her, well then he may as well put them on an even playing field. "I'm comfortable with you, little queen. Anything you want to try, we'll try. I can't make any promises though. If I don't like it..."

"Then we'll stop," she assured him. Now well versed in where he kept all of his sexual paraphernalia, Annabelle lifted off of him, giving him a brief view of the mouth-watering pinkness between her thighs. She returned with a bottle of lubricant and one of the dilators he'd been using on her over the past week.

As the towel around his hips was only loosely covering him, Kit simply pulled it away, unveiling his erection before her. Immediately, Annabelle grasped it with her free hand, lazily stroking him.

"Fuck." Kit let his head fall back to expose his throat.

"I like this," she whispered, pushing one of his legs upwards. "You submitting to me like this."

A strangled noise left him when the cold touch of the slick dilator slid below his sac. He swore beneath his breath when she reached her destination, applying gentle pressure before moving away. She worked his cock with her other hand, drenched in the beginnings of his seed. The closer she came to finally penetrating him with the dilator, the more his cock wept at the prospect.

"Fuck," he said again, pulling both of his arms over his face. He began to mutter Gaelic curses he hadn't spoken in years, attempting to hold back the one word he needed to say.

"Show me your face, Aylesbourne. Don't hide it." She smirked when he pulled his arms away, her cheeks flushed pink. "The sooner you come, the sooner you get to find out how wet this is making me."

He groaned.

"To have you in my control like this. All you have to do is say one word and I'll give you what you want."

"Please," he whispered finally, his voice cracking. Her response was instant, the slick dilator penetrating him, turning his whispered plea into a groaned curse. The first stretch burned, but he wasn't proud of the whimper that left him when she began to thrust in and out, hitting him somewhere that ignited his blood. "Oh fuck, I didn't think it'd be like this."

"Like what?"

"I didn't think it would be this… *intense.*" Left to his own devices, Kit would have never explored this. Jesus, he'd only done this because it felt fair. He thought he might as well try it and see if he could learn anything from it, to ensure he didn't accidentally hurt her when he did it to her.

But this was…

Ecstasy.

Annabelle picked up the pace, caressing him somewhere that shot heat through his entire body.

"Don't stop," he groaned, catching a brief glimpse of her biting her lip. Trying to keep himself from thrashing around the bed, Kit locked his fists around the headboard so tightly he worried he was going to snap it. "Annabelle, fuck, fuck, *fuck.*"

With a trembling gasp, Kit came harder than he'd ever done in his life, roaring out his pleasure as waves of hot seed erupted from him. This was unlike any orgasm he'd had before, pulling his entire body shuddering into bliss. Before, he'd been able to maintain some awareness of his surroundings. Now, though, he couldn't have differentiated up from down.

When that ability finally returned to him, he found Annabelle gently wiping his seed off of him with the towel he'd discarded earlier.

"What the fuck did you just do to me?" he rasped. He closed his eyes, letting out a surprise noise when he felt Annabelle's lips against his own.

"Am I to understand you enjoyed that?" she asked haughtily.

"I think you know I did." He searched her gaze. "Did you enjoy it too, little queen?"

Her brow hitching, Annabelle took his hand, pulling it down between her thighs.

Kit let out a growl when he felt how slick her cunt was. Christ, she hadn't just enjoyed it. She was *drenched*. "You may have exhausted my cock, but I find I've worked up a thirst after my arduous evening."

Her vivid blue eyes blinked with an innocence he'd fucked out of her years ago. "Oh?"

"Sit on my face, Annabelle."

The moment she moved to split her thighs over him, Kit hoisted her up over his chest. His cock may have called for half time, but the rest of him was eager to get into the second half.

Although when Annabelle dug her fingers into his hair, he paused.

"I've thoroughly washed my hands," she assured him.

Relieved, Kit pulled her cunt onto his face, bathing in her scent. He moaned his approval into her wet folds, letting his tongue dart between them to gather it up and swallow it down. Annabelle rolled her hips against him, taking her pleasure where she needed it. Although he enjoyed control, when she rode his face like this…

He was content to lay back and watch the show, his hands roaming her body, plucking her nipples until she panted with need, her movements increasing in both speed and desperation.

Faster than he'd expected, Annabelle's head fell forward, her mouth opening. A rough, cracked cry escaped from her throat as she came, and her hips stuttered in their rhythm. Kit picked it up for her, licking and sucking her clitoris until she collapsed across the bed, her chest rapidly rising and falling.

The heavy exhale he expelled after he'd pulled a sleeping Annabelle into his arms was one of unutterable peace; the thing he'd been searching for for years and never found, be it on Everest's peaks or the heart of Antarctica.

Above them, the ceiling windows gave him a clear view of the night's sky. He smiled when he saw the North Star, the one he'd pointed out to her the night they'd first met. *And there it will always be.*

17

Annabelle

First kittens, now this.

There was something about watching the man she loved dote on children that had her ovaries melting into a puddle of feminine sentiment.

Scarlett Castle was a hub of familial activity these days, where every room seemed to have a discarded toy in it and the giggling of Annabelle's nieces and nephews was never far away. A decade ago, such reminders of children would have been a dagger in her heart, compounded by endless wondering of what her son would have been like.

Annabelle saw the ghost of Oscar every time her nieces trotted around the manège down in the stables. So too was she reminded of them when her twin nephews became lost in endless fits of giggles, their chubby cheeks reddening in the process—as they were now.

It had never been so difficult to separate her fantasies of what could have been from reality, however. A thick lump formed in her throat as she watched the twins laying on the picnic blanket, laughing uncontrollably. Kit knelt between them, tickling each of them in turn with a wide smile on his face.

It was a wonder the poor man wasn't exhausted.

Her nieces had capitalised on his attention first, coaxing him into playing games with them. Games that mostly involved him pretending to be a chauffeur driving them down to Weymouth for a pretend holiday. For a man who had never been around children, Kit had taken it in his stride, pulling Anthony in to act as a pretend footman.

When Dora had discovered Kit had been to places like Antarctica and India, her eyes had lit up with excitement, imploring him to tell him of every animal he had seen on his travels.

An enormous amount, as it happened.

At present, Dora and Josephine—her nieces—were currently monopolising the attentions of Lord Eric. Annabelle wondered if he struggled with the same thoughts she did. He must do. The loss of a child was a grief without end. A grief that would age with them.

They sheltered under an arbour in Scarlett Castle's sweeping grounds, the golden hues of early autumn warning them of the approaching winter. The weather had been kind to them today; a remnant of the departing summer.

Annabelle hadn't been keeping track of her family's conversation, only politely smiling whenever required. Daisy seemed to enjoy being here, asking Emmeline, Michael's wife, endless questions about pregnancy and childcare. Mama chimed in as well, although some of her advice was a tad outdated. Mrs Simpkins, Josephine's aged great-grandmother, also offered a jot of guidance here and there; her guidance was less outdated and more antediluvian, however.

When her quarry *eventually* arrived, Annabelle excused herself from the picnic, casting a long look at Kit. By now, he had little Dougie on his lap, who tugged at his overlong black hair, whilst William lounged on Anthony's knee. The men were deep in discussion with Michael and Cousin George. For the past hour, Michael and Anthony had dominated the conversation with talk of motorcycles, but now they seemed to have progressed to discussing hunting.

"When was the last time you even shot a gun?" Michael asked Kit, grinning.

"I shot at an elephant seal once."

Anthony shared a dubious glance with Michael. "Did you kill it?"

The beat of silence before Kit's reply was suspiciously long. "I may have missed it."

Michael's eyes narrowed. "How big are they again?"

"They're quite small. Easy to miss," Kit replied.

Anthony's damning answer came simultaneously. "Bigger than a Rolls Royce. He showed me a photo."

The men fell back into an easy banter, taunting one another about their hunting mishaps. Smiling, Annabelle moved away without notice. From a distance, she had seen Effie and Caroline returning from their afternoon hack, each easily differentiated on their horses. Effie, with her flowing blonde mane, favoured Dandelion. The sweetest filly Annabelle had ever known. Caroline's curvaceous figure, on the other hand, sat atop Crimson. Spirited would be one descriptor that could be applied to Crimson, but she reminded Annabelle of Olympia.

Sadness had leeched into her memories of her old horse. The last time Annabelle had seen Olympia had been the day the estate's horses were commandeered by the army to go into battle during the Great War.

A war from which Olympia had never returned.

Annabelle hoped her death had been quick.

The Foxcotte Stables was one of several businesses owned by the family, but it was the only one Annabelle found any enjoyment in. The Thoroughbred stud farm was spread across a vast network of buildings and fields, but she knew exactly in which stable the family's horses were housed.

Even if she hadn't, the presence of Jake, the family Collie, lurking outside one of the stable buildings would have led her to exactly where she wanted to go.

"Jaaaake," she sang.

Jake's ears flung back in excitement at the sound of her voice. He sprinted over, paws kicking up the dust layered over the courtyard. She bent down to fuss him up, receiving a wash of dog breath and kisses in return.

"Have you missed me?" she asked, depositing a cherry-red lipstick outline on his snout.

Tongue lolling, Jake presented her with his rear, his tail wagging uncontrollably.

With a huff, Annabelle relented, scratching the top of his hips, just above his tail. "You," she told him, scratching furiously, "are the most demanding little dog I've ever met."

Jake pinned her with his deep brown eyes. *Soulful eyes*, Mama called them, traversing the entire spectrum of brown and black, from the lightest gold to the dark of night.

Footsteps crunching across the dusty path lifted her chin. "Effie," Annabelle said quietly, the weight of her mistakes still weighing heavily on her heart.

Effie and Caroline were still in their riding gear, their faces flushed and their hair windswept. Privately, Annabelle thought Effie carried it off better. Her sister's spine was as straight as a rod, her jaw firmly set, reminding Annabelle of an Amazonian warrior.

When had her baby sister turned into a woman?

Caroline was only a year or two younger, but she was still half a child. It wasn't her fault, Annabelle knew. From what she'd discovered of Caroline's deceased parents, they were neither kind nor comforting.

The difference between Caroline and Effie was stark; Effie, who had been raised by a loving family, was strong and secure in her decisions, whilst Caroline's poor excuse of a family had turned her into a nervous wreck.

She'd improved since first arriving at Scarlett Castle the year before last, but Annabelle knew all too well that some wounds would never heal.

"My actions were selfish," Annabelle began. "Words are a poor apology for what you've endured as a result, but I apologise unreservedly to both of you. You deserved better."

Caroline looked to Effie, as though seeking guidance. Annabelle detected the slightest shake to Effie's head, but her little sister remained silent.

"Although nothing can remove my stain entirely, I'd like to financially support the two of you for next year's season to give you a proper coming out." With her father and grandfather both establishing trusts for her, Annabelle was hardly short of cash, even before adding Buckford's estate into the mix—although the latter would go directly to the mother and baby home.

"It's not about the money, Annabelle," Effie said on a deep sigh.

Annabelle thought Caroline's opinion may have differed, given the flare in her eyes.

"The offer remains open to both of you, should you want the money."

Effie's stubbornness left her all at once, her shoulders slumping. "I had a place to study at Cambridge."

Caroline's head whipped round, but Annabelle's attention was firmly focused on her younger sister. "What?"

With an apologetic look at her friend, Effie shrugged. "I was going to study Natural Sciences at Girton College." She gestured to Annabelle, utterly defeated. "And then the furore at Lord Linwood's occurred and they withdrew their offer."

Annabelle flinched, awash in guilt. "Effie, I'm so sorry. Why ever didn't you say you'd applied?"

"Because I wanted to prove I could do it on my own. If I told Michael or Mama, no doubt they'd put a word in on the sly and I'd ride in on the coattails of nepotism."

She would have liked to dispel Effie's fears, but her sister was probably right. Over the last two centuries, every man in the family had attended Cambridge, for good or ill. Even George had attended, despite being in line for the Loughborough earldom rather than the Foxcotte dukedom. *That was probably Aunt Leonora's doing.* "I'm so proud of you," Annabelle assured her.

"Have you considered Oxford?"

The question came from behind her, but Annabelle would have known Kit's velvety smooth voice anywhere. She smiled when she saw him, leaning casually against one of the newer brick buildings, arms crossed. "What are you doing here?"

He shoved himself off the wall. His stride was confident, but the wink he threw in her direction was a promise she intended to hold him to. In his hand was a letter, his name written on its face in loopy black writing. "I'm told the two of you were disinvited from Queen Charlotte's Ball."

"We were," Effie confirmed. The wind lifted her hair, tangling its long fingers through her curls. "Until the incident at the ball."

"The incident was *my* doing, Lady Effie. Annabelle may have erred in her judgement, but I am the one who revealed her to the world. I turned on the light to humiliate her. If you need someone to blame, then I am the one on whom that blame should fall."

Surprise twinkled in Effie's eyes. "You purposefully exposed her?"

"I did." Kit glanced back at Annabelle, his dark eyes undressing her. "I was jealous, and I wanted to hurt her."

Annabelle didn't miss the twist of revulsion in Effie's lips.

"Although Queen Charlotte's Ball has come and gone," Kit carried on, holding out the letter to Effie. "I did want to offer both yourself and Lady Caroline an apology."

She took it, slitting it open with her thumb. Caroline hovered at Effie's shoulder as the two of them read it. Seconds passed before Caroline's eyes blew wide and Effie choked out a shocked gasp. "An invitation to stay at Balmoral?"

"What?" Annabelle laughed, incredulous.

"I wrote to Queen Mary," Kit said, slipping his hand into hers as though it was the most natural thing in the world. "I explained the situation—one borne of my own idiocy."

"And mine."

"Perhaps. Regardless, the fault did not lie with those who were suffering most." He nodded towards the younger girls. "I asked her for a favour, and she accepted. This will be a fresh start for the two of you."

Caroline glanced at Effie. "But why would *Queen Mary* help?"

Annabelle gave a soft laugh, remembering who had found her phallic graffiti on the *North Star*. "Because she's your godmother."

"Exactly," he nodded. "To repair the damage done, Her Majesty has invited you both to stay at Balmoral Castle during the hunting season. A public demonstration of acceptance by royalty will ensure the rest of society falls into line."

"Thank you," Caroline said, her hand coming up to cover her wide smile, disappearing behind Effie's cloud of curls as the two embraced.

"And my offer of financial support still stands," Annabelle reminded them, looking more at Caroline than at Effie.

"Now…" Kit cleared his throat. "Oxford."

Effie pulled back, her attention rapt. "What about it?"

"Speaking as a Cambridge alumni, I wouldn't recommend it for you. Whilst you may have been able to study there, as a woman you're not eligible to receive a degree."

"What?" Effie blinked.

"Cambridge University doesn't allow women to graduate."

"That's outrageous!" Annabelle spat furiously.

"It is." Kit squeezed her hand. "But Oxford University does, Lady Effie. I recommend you write to a Miss Lynda Grier at Lady Margaret Hall—one of the colleges comprising Oxford University. It's an all-women college, where you'd be able to graduate with the degree of your choice."

Effie's expression was tremulous. "Are you sure?"

"There'll likely be an interview, of course," he admitted. "But if they take you, it'll be on merit, not a result of nepotism. I'll get her details sent over to you tomorrow, all right?"

Her baby sister's relieved laugh could have lit the sun itself. "Thank you." She turned to Annabelle. "I'm sorry for what I said before you left for Scotland. I'm not ashamed of you, and it wasn't better after you left. I missed you something terr—"

Effie's unnecessary apology was cut off as Annabelle swept her into a hug. "Had I been in your position, I would have said worse."

With a sheepish grin, Effie shrugged. "I couldn't think of anything worse."

"I'll teach you some better insults," Annabelle assured her, patting her cheek. "Don't you worry."

In the corner of her eye, Caroline lingered. Her hands knotted together, but the girl's eyes were firmly plastered on the ground.

Poor thing.

Annabelle strode over to engulf her in a hug. It wasn't until the last second that Caroline looked up, her eyes full of tender surprise. "I'm sorry," Annabelle told her—and she meant it. Her next words were softer, until only the two of them could hear them. "And I'll fund everything you need."

Caroline's parents had been bankrupt at their deaths, leaving their daughter penniless.

The nod Caroline gave her was subtle, but her relief was plain to see.

A hollow chime rang out across the stables, prompting Annabelle to check her wristwatch. "It's nearly time to dress for dinner."

Kit's eyes blazed with excitement. "We shouldn't miss that."

"No," she replied, standing on her tiptoes to steal a brief kiss—ignoring Caroline's scandalised look. "We absolutely should not."

Dinner, as it so often was these days, was a hectic affair. The addition of Kit's family only added more kindling to the flames. So much so, in fact, that they gathered in the formal dining room; a room that had seen little use since the Great War.

Whilst the informal dining room used by the family in their everyday life was rounded, easily distributing the conversation across itself, the formal dining room table was rectangular. Happily, this meant that she was not able to hear George and Lord Eric discussing fishing up at the other end, or Mama and Mrs Simpkin contemplating what the children would like for Christmas this year.

The formal dining room was perhaps the only room in Scarlett Castle without portraits of Fraser ancestors glaring down from the walls. The room itself was long, some forty feet, with mullioned windows traversing its length on one side and dark panels on the other. Although it was usually a pretty scene, the evening had brought with it a sudden downpour. The sound of rain pattering against the many windows was a low hum behind the night's conversation.

And soon she would be leaving this place, replacing her own ancestors for Kit's.

He was animated tonight, sitting between Effie and Emmeline. The former was chattier than the latter, drawing him into almost constant conversation.

"May I just ask," Mama's raised voice tore Annabelle away from Kit-watching, her face tightening into a pinch, "what is that?" She pointed, her finger ending in a deep burgundy nail. A polish she'd borrowed from Annabelle's collection.

"This?" Kit picked up the offending glass—his own. A garishly orange carbonated liquid fizzed around inside.

"Oh good heavens, I didn't even see that," Effie said, peering at it. "What a funny colour!"

"It's called Iron Brew. It's quite popular at home in Scotland. Have you never seen it before?"

"No," Mama shook her head, leaning forward to keep them in her line of sight. "I don't believe I have."

"It's what Papa used to give us as children when we were at Foxcotte Moor," Annabelle said. "Do you really not remember?"

Her cheeks reddening, Mama laughed, "Not at all."

"Theo and I tried putting whisky in it once," Michael chimed on, reminiscing fondly. "We must have been eleven or twelve."

Kit hissed his disgust, with Anthony not far behind. "I'm sorry, but that alone should constitute a capital offence."

"It honestly didn't taste that bad."

"May I try some?" Effie asked, angling her head towards Kit.

He offered her the glass. "Be my guest."

Her sip was tentative, but surprise flashed in her eyes. "Oh! It's sugary. I expected it to be alcoholic. But why not drink the wine instead?" Effie handed the glass back to him, picking up her own to wash the taste away.

Annabelle took note of Kit's swallow, wondering if she ought to jump in and help him. But he spoke before she could take action.

"Because I had a problem with alcohol, Lady Effie, and I want to be a better person for the people I love." Kit smiled at Annabelle unashamedly.

She could feel the stares from the table at large. On Kit's other side, Emmeline lay her hand over her chest, her expression maudlin.

"Did you know that bees can get drunk too?"

The question broke the simmering tension.

Kit dragged his head back towards Effie, blinking. "Bees?"

Effie nodded enthusiastically. "It affects them like it affects us. One time, I noticed quite a significant number of bees were missing from one of my hives, but I eventually found them scattered around an apple tree. A number of the apples had fermented, and the bees had consumed the fermenting flesh—and as a result, they were displaying some unusual behaviours, including attacking one another. They even crashed whilst flying. How fascinating is that?"

"That is actually genuinely fascinating," Kit agreed, his lip curling in amusement. Behind him, thousands of drops of rain pelted the windows. "At least humans aren't alone in their drunken indiscretions."

"Not at all. In fact, they're rather marvellous, bees. Every hive centres around the queen, and I've discovered that she seems to have a retinue of admirers who feed and groom her."

"Oho," Mama laughed, the wine turning her skin a faint pink. "If only we were all so lucky."

"Speaking of which..." Annabelle cocked her eyebrows at Kit. *It's now or never, Aylesbourne.*

His eyes were dark flames, burning brightly with excitement and adoration both. "Speaking of which," he cleared his throat and pushed his chair back. The legs scraped along the hard floor; the closest thing to a fanfare they were going to get. "I'd like to make an announcement."

In the corner of her eye, Mama snapped to attention.

"Sixteen years ago, in a darkened garden in Berkeley Square, I met the love of my life. And so it is quite frankly a *relief* to finally be able to announce my engagement to the remarkable woman sitting opposite me." Amidst Effie's excited gasp and Mama's teary sniff, Kit raised his glass of Iron Brew, an affectionate smirk tugging at the corner of his lips. "To Annabelle, the future Duchess of Aylesbourne."

The murmured toast echoed around the room. Annabelle smiled at her well-wishers, from Mama, whose joy was tinged with sadness, to Emmeline, who looked to be blinking away tears, to Anthony, whose proud, lopsided grin filled her with affection.

Mere weeks ago, the thought of marrying again would have filled her with dread. The idea that *Kit* would be the groom would have been laughable.

But then Kit winked, "My little queen."

Annabelle knew then that she would never be happier. The feeling swelled within her, her chest fit to burst with contentment—and the prospect of their shared future.

The sharp sound of a crystal wine glass shattering pierced the room's jovial atmosphere. To her right, Anthony's complexion had turned the colour of porridge. Staring at his feet, he looked as surprised as any of them to see the shattered glass. "Little queen?" he whispered, so quietly Annabelle thought she might have been the only one who caught it.

"Good heavens," Daisy said, almost knocking over her glass of ginger beer in her haste to stand. "Do sit down, darling. You're awfully pale."

Anthony shook off her attempts to corral him into the chair, mumbling apologies about the glass. His eyes darted between Kit and Annabelle.

For Kit, bewilderment was edged with concern. "Anthony?"

Unable to answer, Anthony stumbled backwards. The broken glass crunched beneath his polished Oxfords. "Excuse me," he mumbled, stepping out of the mess he'd created on the floor. "I believe I need some air."

The table watched him go as one, each diner as confused as the rest. Daisy went to follow him, concern mussing her face, but Kit waved her down. "I'll go," he reassured her, giving Lord Eric the same look as he passed.

Kit's retreating back passing through the doorway of the formal dining room marked the start of the low hum of conversation beginning anew. Those closest to Annabelle—Emmeline, Michael, Effie, and George—sent her their congratulations and Daisy their reassurances.

Annabelle's mind remained on Anthony's odd reaction throughout, not helped in the least by the shattered glass being swiftly swept up by the maids beside her.

There was no sign of either Anthony or Kit in the gloom beyond the windows opposite her, nor could she hear either of their voices out in the corridor. She offered Daisy a comforting look, leaving the real work to Emmeline.

It was a lesson she'd long since learnt in their nursing days; leave the emotional work to someone that was better equipped to deal with it. Usually Emmeline.

What the devil had set Anthony off, though? He'd been fine after the engagement announcement, smiling along with the rest of them.

Little queen?

That was what he'd asked her, shrouded in horror.

Had he not heard Kit call her that before? Surely he had. But Annabelle racked her brains, trying to think of a single example with which to confirm it—and coming up short.

So if he hadn't heard it before, then why had it evoked such a reaction in him?

It was just out of reach, the answer. But she couldn't quite grasp it.

Mama's voice interrupted her thoughts. "Have you any plans for a wedding date, darling girl?"

"Soon," Annabelle muttered, distracted. The first date they could marry was in but a fortnight, but she had neither the energy nor the inclination to answer the thousand questions her mother would have. "Effie, why don't you tell everyone your news?"

"Goodness, with the wedding announcement I almost forgot." Effie smiled excitedly, as only the young could—before life got the better of them. "Caroline and I received a letter today, Mama," Effie said across the table, narrowly avoiding dipping her blonde curls into the red wine sauce.

Whilst the rest of the table listened to Effie's news, excited by her pronouncement of an upcoming stay at Balmoral, Annabelle honed in on her target.

The letter. The pleading letter she'd sent to Kit all those years ago, only to be met with a cruel response purporting to come from Kit himself. The one she had signed, *"Little queen."*

Curiously calm, Annabelle got to her feet, excusing herself.

"Are you quite well?" Emmeline held her arm out, touching Annabelle gently. Her green eyes were tinged with concern, and sometimes she felt that Emmeline could see past her mask as well as Kit.

"Just going to spend a penny," Annabelle murmured, her heels clipping across the dining room.

As soon as she was out in the corridor, Annabelle let anger swallow her whole. The sensation raised the baby fine hairs on the back of her neck, but her feet didn't miss a beat. She stalked down the corridor, back towards the main house—the only possible destination.

But when she reached it, she knew what she had to say would break Kit's heart. Almost as broken as she'd been sixteen years ago.

18

Kit

"I fucked up." Anthony's eyes darted between Kit's own, his face bleached of colour. "Fuck. I fucked up so badly, Kit."

Kit's stomach knotted with nerves. Glancing over his shoulder, he led Anthony down a sconce-lit corridor. In a place like Scarlett Castle, filled with eyes and ears, he wanted to ensure they were not overheard—not when Anthony was in this state.

If he remembered correctly, this corridor would bring them out into the old stable courtyard. A shock of thunder rumbled by, sounding all too like the slide of an avalanche overhead. Fear rattled through him, but for once he never heard John MacGillivray's voice, nor that of Brigadier-General Bruce.

Instead, he thought of Annabelle. The silky feel of her skin. Her breathy moans when they were alone together. That impertinent eyebrow twitch he loved all too much.

Anthony opened the door out into the courtyard, depressing the handle with significantly more force than required. He flew out into the lean-to sheltering them from the heavy rain. "I fucked up," Anthony said again, shoving his hand into his hair and clenching his fist.

"That's all right," Kit replied, keen to strike a comforting tone. "Whatever's happened, we'll fix it."

"Don't be nice to me." A heavy swallow. "I don't deserve it."

He'd never seen Anthony like this, so tightly wound. "Whatever you've done can be undone, Anthony."

His cousin's focus drifted to somewhere in the space between them, and Kit was startled—and worried—to see a sheen forming in his eyes. "I was trying to protect you," he said softly, barely audible over the rain crashing down around them. "I thought someone was trying to take advantage of you, like my father had warned me."

Kit simply stood there, hoping that at some point Anthony would start to make sense.

"My father…" Anthony shook his head. "He always said I should look out for you. That being the duke came with responsibilities, that it would weigh heavy on your shoulders. He said that people would try and take advantage of you for it, to weasel their way into your lives with an endgame in mind. Be it financial or… marital."

"Marital?"

"Women would try and trap you into marriage. And they did."

Confusion narrowed his eyes. "Annabelle isn't trying to trap me into marriage, if that's what you're thinking."

"Not Annabelle. I never suspected her of such a thing. But Miss Perry tried, do you remember her?"

The name rung a bell. A very, very distant bell. "Was that the woman you were caught with in a cupboard?"

Anthony nodded sadly. "Viscount Carnford's youngest daughter. Mrs Mary Ellesmere, and others I cannot recall. They would plan to be caught in indecent circumstances with you. Mary Ellesmere—"

Kit interrupted him, another memory coming to the fore. "She was a widow, wasn't she?"

Another nod. "The one who was your mistress for a while. She planned to fake a pregnancy in a bid to force you to marry her."

There were those shivers down his spine again. "How could you possibly know that?"

"I bribed their servants most of the time. Or I'd hire a private detective to follow them. Your duty is to the dukedom, Kit. And my duty was to ensure you were able to do that without falling prey to the schemes of a charlatan."

And Kit had remained utterly ignorant of Anthony's actions. "What does this have to do with you fucking up?"

Anthony flinched, his face screwing up in a swirl of regret and disgust. "Because I was too quick to dismiss something. A letter that arrived by special messenger.

And I have only just realised that it wasn't a scheme to defraud you. Only *now*, when I am old enough to understand precisely what I took from you."

"What did you dismiss?" Unease swept in, like the sea sweeping through a hole in a boat's hull. "What did you *take*?"

Perhaps Anthony saw the panic in his eyes—or the anger. The desperate anger, pleading with him to tell Kit that it wasn't true. That his assumption was incorrect. Anthony tried to speak, stopping short before words left his mouth.

Coldness sunk into Kit, infecting his very bones and tethering his feet to the ground. His palm rasped over his jaw, catching at the stubble bleeding through his skin. Images rushed through his mind faster than he could examine them. The day the *Nimrod* had set sail from Southampton, the packed crowd waving them off. Docking in Sydney, eagerly arriving at the postmaster, only to be devastated by Uncle Eric's letter announcing that Annabelle had married Lord Buckford.

His brain filled in the blanks. Annabelle receiving the heinous reply. Annabelle marrying Buckford to ensure their child wasn't a bastard. Annabelle feeling their son kick for the first time.

Tears lined his eyes through the rest. The birth. Their tiny baby boy entering the world having already departed it.

Balling his hands, Kit's first punch was one of cold, hard fury. It landed on Anthony's cheekbone, whipping his head to the side and sending pain lancing through Kit's fist. His cousin stumbled back, leaving the cover of the shelter. Rain lashed down on them, mingling with his tears, but Kit didn't falter.

Again and again and again he struck, hitting whatever part of Anthony he could reach. The arms he'd thrown up to shield himself. His nose. His gut. The pain in his hand grew, but Kit *savoured* it like the finest wine. It centred him, a pillar in the midst of his grief around which he could cling.

He'd lost count of how many hits Anthony had taken when his cousin finally fell into the mud, crawling to lean back against the old stables. A river of blood ran from his nose, dripping onto his once-pristine white dress shirt.

A soft touch on his shoulder broke through his anger. Kit glanced back to see Annabelle standing there, her eyes wide with silent pleading.

Kit swept her into his arms, needing her touch more than anything. Her chin jerked upwards. Rage hid her emotions for now, but Kit could see them bubbling beneath the surface. The pain. The devastation. The loss. He could *feel* it in the way she clutched at him, her little fingers digging into his skin.

"Take me to see him," he choked.

Dawn was a smear of blood across the sodden sky. A meadow stretched out before them, brimming with dandelions and singing pipets. At their backs lay an ancient stone chapel, a building Theo had often talked about in their school days. It was more than a thousand years old, to hear him tell it.

Kit let his head fall back against the chapel's smooth stone wall, sat on the damp ground. To his right was Theo's headstone, its black marble soaking up the early rays of sunshine. A memorial stone, for his body was lost in the war.

On his left was a rose bush. A marker, Annabelle had told him. A stone would have been too obvious, and a small, inconspicuous trinket could have been easily moved. She and Theo had decided on a rose—her father's favourite flower. And now Kit's.

Their hands sat intertwined at the rose's base, just as intertwined as the rest of them. Kit was propped up against the church, with Annabelle sitting between his thighs, curled on her side with his morning jacket draped over her shoulder.

A robin skipped among the foliage, filling the air with its melodic calls. Kit squinted at it, remembering how Annabelle had once told him of how her father used to feed the robins at Fraser House.

How did that old saying go? *When robins appear, loved ones are near.*

Neither of them had spoken for hours—but then they didn't need to.

The three of them were together at last. And that was enough.

19

Annabelle

When Annabelle returned to Scarlett Castle, she told her family everything.

She'd had enough of Oscar being a secret, as though he was something to be ashamed of.

Her mother took it hardest, her eyes so full of heartbreak that Annabelle had to look away. "And all this time," Mama choked, tears streaming down cheeks softened with age, "I've been p-pestering you for grandchildren." She pressed her hands to her mouth, attempting to hold in her sobs. "Oh god, Annabelle. I'm sorry. I'm sorry. I'm sorry."

"It was always Theo and Michael you were pestering," Annabelle reminded her. "I was let off. I think you'd long since given up hope of me ever marrying."

Mama laughed then, a wet sound dripped in grief. "I had. Completely and utterly. My independent daughter who knew she could take on the world alone. And so you did."

Annabelle suspected that she was hugged more times in the few hours before departing for London than in the rest of her life combined.

In the days that followed, they didn't return to Campbell House, but instead stayed on the *North Star*. The kittens seemed to enjoy it, but they wouldn't remained docked on the Thames for long.

In the end, neither of them had wanted to wait.

They had chosen the first date Westminster Abbey was available.

Their wedding day was not accompanied by the fanfare Annabelle had once envisioned. There was neither a horde of guests nor a great feast. She hadn't even had time to have a proper wedding dress made.

Once, that would have horrified her. Now, she was free to choose whichever dress she found most comfortable, selecting a simple cream gown, pulling in tight at her waist and accented by flowing silk skirts.

With a deep breath, she began the long walk beneath Westminster Abbey's hammerbeam roof. The roof beneath which she'd promised her father she'd marry. In his stead, Michael held her elbow, a lock of thick black hair falling over his forehead. When she reached the Tomb of the Unknown Warrior, her steps came to a standstill on the beige stone.

"It could be Theo in here," she whispered, too low for anyone but Michael to hear. There was much to-do about the selection of the Unknown Warrior, with the end result being that there *was* a chance he may have been exhumed from Ypres. Where Theo was lost.

Michael's throat jumped. "Could be."

Annabelle glanced behind her, smiling down at her two flower girls, Dora and Josephine. The two of them wore twin necklaces of sapphire and diamond to bring out the matching colour in their eyes. A gift from Eva and Cornelius Allenby that had arrived only this morning, along with a letter congratulating Annabelle on her marriage. They had made no mention of Kit, but then she didn't blame them there.

She moved on, passing the grave of Livingstone, the man who explored Africa—and died there. A contemporary of Kit, in a way.

No more exploring, he had promised her.

If not, she feared he may have one day never returned from an expedition, lost to the wilds of a distant land.

And then the floor changed from a greyish beige to the famous checkerboard flooring. They passed beneath a gilded walkway, emerging between the choir rows. Beyond that, a small assortment of her closest family and friends had gathered.

Annabelle almost came to a standstill.

Her closest family and friends… and Queen Mary, dressed in deep blue silk satin, embroidered with floral motifs.

Oh shit. She had completely forgotten that the woman was Kit's godmother.

And that she'd found Annabelle's phallic graffiti all over the *North Star*. She hoped the Queen never discovered the culprit.

When she sighted Kit, she really *did* stop. He was not wearing a keenly styled suit, as she'd expected him to be. He was wearing a kilt of blue and green, belted at the waist and pinned over his shoulder with a silver brooch. Kit's black hair was neater than it usually was, but there was no disguising the wildness lurking beneath the noble façade.

Michael cleared his throat, whispering low in her ear. "We can still make a run for it, if you want."

Annabelle blinked, realising that she had come to a halt midway up the aisle. She smirked, her eyebrow jumping. "Do you take me for a quitter?"

This time, she didn't stop until she was at the altar, taking Kit's proffered hand. It engulfed hers, but she squeezed it tight. "You decided against the blanket at the bothy, then?"

He laughed, a rich sound that danced around the nave's vaulting. "I considered it," he admitted, before lowering to a whisper. "A bit too risqué for the Abbey, I thought."

Annabelle let her eyes rake him from head to toe. "I wouldn't have minded."

They fell silent as the reverend conducted the ceremony, solemnly reciting words she only partly heard, too busy gazing into Kit's dark eyes. She gave a little jolt of excitement when he said, "I do."

Annabelle paused when it was her turn. She didn't want to make it too easy for him, but—

"I do."

Kit didn't wait for the reverend's permission to kiss her, cutting the man off mid-sentence. She giggled into his kiss, vowing with every pass of her lips to love and to cherish him.

"*Mo chridhe*," he whispered, his chest rising and falling in great heaves. "Little queen. My wife."

"My husband." The words felt queer.

Kit tightly intertwined their fingers. "*Finally.*"

Annabelle gave a shrieking laugh as Kit carried her over the threshold of the *North Star's* owner's cabin. His bridal carry technique could use some work, in her opinion. She had been unceremoniously slung over his shoulder, giving him free access to fondle her backside.

Not that she minded.

He kicked the door shut behind him, hurling her onto the bed in a mass of skirts and sheets. "For god's sake," he hissed, climbing between her legs and taking her lips in a dominating kiss. "Why the fuck did we agree to a reception?" he groaned, delving his hands beneath her skirts. "The wedding should have been altar and then bed. I've been waiting *hours* for this."

"You invited the Queen." Annabelle sighed at his touch, the barest hint of sensation coming through the layers of her clothing. "What did you expect?"

He flipped her, an easy motion that belied his strength. The slight loosening of her dress suggested he was making quick work of its soft white buttons. "She's my godmother, I had to invite her." After undoing each button, he pressed a kiss to the skin beneath. "And her attendance is a seal of approval for society."

Annabelle's eyes went from lowered with arousal to fully rounded in less than the blink of an eye. "Wait, what?"

Kit pushed her loosened dress off her shoulder, running the tip of his nose over her skin. "You won't be shunned anymore. Our spat at Linwood's will likely not be forgotten, but if you wish to re-enter society… you can do so. It won't cause any further difficulty for your family either. Queen Mary has invited herself to stay at Scarlett Castle and Allenby's estate in Bristol. Plus, she's invited us to pop into Balmoral on our honeymoon."

"What?" Annabelle turned, hindered by Kit nuzzling into her neck. "Why?"

"Because I asked her to—as a wedding gift. It'll make life easier for you. After what I did."

And then he was peeling her dress off her. Annabelle waited, biting her plump bottom lip in anticipation. With her wedding dress being an afterthought, what to wear beneath it hadn't even crossed her mind.

So she chose—

"Have you seriously been naked underneath your clothes all day?" Kit's shocked voice came.

Annabelle rolled onto her back lazily, smirking up at him. "Is one not *always* naked beneath their clothes?" She bent her knees, lifting them up to put them in his line of sight. "Besides, I'm wearing socks."

He barked out a laugh at the sight of them—knitted socks in the same tartan as his kilt. "The Aylesbourne tartan? Where did you get these?"

"Daisy smuggled a pair over for me when she visited the yacht for tea last week," she said, twitching her ankle. "We both wore them today. I got a photographer to take a photo of us with our matching ankles on show."

Kit rested the soles of her feet on his broad shoulders. "How scandalous," he said in an exaggerated tone, drifting light touches up and down the bare skin of her leg, bringing goosebumps to the surface.

"I'm afraid Eric caught us," Annabelle's lip twitched to the side. "But thankfully he was wearing Aylesbourne tartan socks too, so he could join in."

It had been quite the sight, with Annabelle and Daisy lifting their skirts two or three inches above the ground to proudly show off their socks… and then Lord Eric mock-lifting his knee-length kilt to match their pose.

Kit's laugh was a hacking snort, his torso shaking against her legs. "I can't wait to see those photos. He's never going to live that down. Those are going to take pride of place in our apartments at Eilean Rìgh."

She let out a moan when his touch moved to her feet, his strong thumbs making quick work of the residual soreness inflicted by her heels. A hum escaped her, and she let her head fall back in pleasure. "Is that where we're going to live? Eilean Rìgh?"

"We'll live wherever you wish to live. Eilean Rìgh. Campbell House. Or even permanent residents on the *North Star*."

His hands moved again, focusing on the ball of her feet. The long, repetitive rolls of his thumbs rendered her wordless, and another of her moans filled the room.

"I expected our wedding night to be full of such sounds, but I didn't quite envision it like this," Kit admitted, the corner of his lips tugging upwards in a grin.

Reluctantly, Annabelle pulled her legs free of his grasp and let them fall apart. "What else did you have in mind, husband?"

Kit's eyes darkened until they were almost black, his nostrils flaring as he beheld what she was offering. A purr rumbled in his throat, surveying his new wife.

Pouncing, he grabbed her, flipping her onto her front and pulling her up onto her knees. "Fuck, little queen," he cursed, his voice harsh with reverence.

Taking back control of her body, she spread her knees, feeling the cool rush of air hitting her exposed folds as she rocked her hips towards him. She wanted to tease him, to tempt him into letting loose, to give her everything he had.

Arousal lit like a fuse from within when he slapped a hand on either side of her rear, pulling her cheeks apart until there was nowhere to hide.

But she let out a yelp when the heat of his tongue met her slick flesh, delving into the well of arousal collecting at her entrance and groaning his approval at her taste. She whimpered into the bedcovers when he found her clitoris, sucking in rhythmic bursts until she was a trembling mess murmuring incoherent pleas for more.

Her fingers disappeared into the sheets, the only thing keeping her steady against Kit's wet onslaught. "Yes," she panted desperately, rolling her hips against his face. Every move brought her closer to the ecstasy lying at the end.

A sharp pinch at her nipple brought forth a cry from her lungs just as her cunt clenched around nothing. She had been so lost to pleasure she hadn't noticed his hand creeping along her underside to play with her swaying breast.

"Again," she commanded, lifting her torso to give him better access.

To her dismay, it didn't come.

"Kit, ple—"

He rose to his full height. "You'll get what you're given." She let out a sigh when one of his hands coursed down her spine, whilst the other circled the delicate, sensitive skin at her entrance. Slick arousal made his movements audible, a filthy melody to accompany their joining. Another finger joined the first, stretching her wider still.

"More, Kit. Please. I need you inside me."

Casting an impatient look over her shoulder, she saw him reaching over to the bedside table, to the drawer in which the condoms were stored.

"Wait," she gasped, her heart thundering in her chest.

His hand stilled in mid-air.

A thick lump formed in her throat, impervious to her attempts to swallow it down. "I'm… I'm not saying I want to try."

"But?" he asked, his voice hushed.

"But I'm not saying I want to avoid it," she admitted.

His hand disappeared from her line of vision, reappearing in a gentle touch at her hips. "You want fate to choose."

"No," Annabelle took his hand, rising onto her knees until she felt his bare chest at her back. He must have removed his shirt at some point, but his kilt remained on. Kit nuzzled into her neck, his lips quickly finding purchase. "I want *you*."

"*Mo chridhe*," he whispered, his voice throaty with arousal—or emotion. She couldn't quite tell.

Behind her, his kilt's heavy wool rustled. And then there was no mistaking the thick length pressing at her back.

"Yes," she whispered, canting her hips ready to receive him. "I want you inside me. I *need* you inside me."

Kit swiped his cock between her thighs, coating it in her arousal. The blunt head pressed against her entrance, and she let out a mewl of need at his heat.

"There, there, *there*."

His first intrusion was a slow, blissful slide that had them gasping as one. He stilled for a moment, and Annabelle was glad of the chance to savour it, whispering his name in wonder.

One of his muscled arms came to rest across her torso like a sash, his fingers curling around her shoulder. His other hand stretched out in front of them to grasp the thick bedpost, supporting them both.

Holding her in place, Kit began to move. He rolled his hips slowly at first, each teasing movement promising more pleasure than it offered, stirring his cock inside her.

"Faster," she begged.

The next thrust pushed a solitary moan out from her.

"Kit, for god's sake."

His breathing was hot and harsh in her ear. "Shut the fuck up and take my cock."

It was the last coherent word either of them spoke for quite some time.

His next thrust was punishingly hard, but he held her in place to take it, his fingers digging into her shoulder. Annabelle gasped, but the noise had barely escaped her before his cock slammed into her again, setting a rhythm that soon had both of them slick with sweat and mindless with pleasure.

Their passion was a storm of emotion, an endless current of lust that had their bodies locked together. She adored every groan in her ear, every squeeze of his hand, every roll of his hips, every thud of the bed. Every sound, every movement, every thought was wild and lustful and needy, until she balanced on the precipice of her climax.

The next thrust sent her skywards, her orgasm clenching his cock so tightly her legs shook with the force of it. Within seconds of her broken cry reverberating across the room, a bellow joined it—Kit's, smothered in the sensitive skin beneath her ear. He pulsed inside her, a hot gush of seed bathing her insides.

When he collapsed, so did she.

Even then, Kit pulled her close. His breaths were great heaves of exhaustion, his chest damp with sweat. Annabelle wasn't far behind, boneless and satiated. With her last ounce of energy, she draped a sock-clad leg over him, needing to be closer.

"Little queen," he rasped, his chest finally slowing.

Annabelle looked up, her eyebrow twitching. "Oh no. I believe I'm quite content with *duchess*, actually."

"Are we ready to leave for the bothy?" Annabelle said, walking through Eilean Rìgh's cloisters to find an array of suitcases and an empty wicker basket. Dog the cat trotted up to her, closely followed by his sister Bumblebee.

Apparently not, then.

Kit sat on the low stone wall, his brow furrowed in concentration as he read a letter. Dragon sat next to him, purring in contentment as he idly scratched her head.

"Kit?" she asked, paying the cats their dues. "Are we ready to leave?"

He looked up, blinking in surprise. "You're ready."

She nodded. They'd stopped at Eilean Rìgh for the weekend after their wedding. Today was the beginning of their honeymoon proper, the first stop of which would be the bothy up at Foxcotte Moor.

Kit had surprised her with that particular detail, and she loved him for it.

"Quite." Annabelle offered him a small smile. "Are you quite well? You're very pale." She went to press her palm to his forehead, but he caught it, kissing her knuckles.

"I'm fine," he assured her, waving the letter in his hand. "I simply received this from my uncle... and Anthony."

The smile slid off her face. "Oh."

Kit's head nodded. "My uncle says the stone cupid has arrived."

"Oh," she said again, her face softening.

"And Anthony..." Kit sighed. "He apologises. For the thousandth time. But he's painted something for us." He patted a small rectangular parcel leaning against the stone wall, thickly wrapped in beige fabric. "He didn't want it to be a surprise if we weren't ready to see it."

Annabelle frowned at the parcel as though it was about to jump out and bite her. "What is it a painting of?"

Kit took her hand, calming her with the comforting abrasion of his calluses across her palm. "The three of us." He applied a light pressure, pulling her towards him to sit across his muscled thigh.

"Do you want to open it?" she asked him.

He didn't give her an answer. "Do *you*?"

"I think I just might."

Kit levelled a fond stare at her, the edge of his lip curling. "Me too."

Trepidation rose in her chest as he picked up the tightly wrapped portrait. It wasn't large—perhaps slightly larger than the letter that accompanied it. Whilst Kit held it steady, Annabelle unwrapped its many layers, never knowing which would be the last before the portrait's subject was revealed.

Her heart skipped a beat when she saw it, Kit's fingers suddenly biting into her waist.

The painting was a sampling of their everyday life, as though the painter had caught a glimpse of the three of them in a moment of peace.

The delicate brushstrokes swirled together to depict Annabelle and Kit sat on a picnic blanket together, beneath the towering Highland mountains surrounding Eilean Rìgh. Annabelle cradled a dark-haired baby in her arms, his face hidden from view. Both she and Kit were glancing down at the child, utterly content in their idyll.

Annabelle blew out a long breath, her gaze going to Kit—only to find he was already looking at her.

The painting was a slice of the life they may have once had—or perhaps the one they were going to have.

"It's perfect," she whispered.

Kit's chest expanded on a deep inhale, and he smiled. "I know."

Want to read a bonus epilogue for Annabelle and Kit? Yes, there's another sex scene. Who do you think I am? **It's available to read at steviesparks.com**

Do you fancy something a little bit more modern, but just as steamy? Fear not, I have a contemporary dark billionaire romance, Heart of Stone, available to read on Kindle Unlimited.

Also By Stevie Sparks

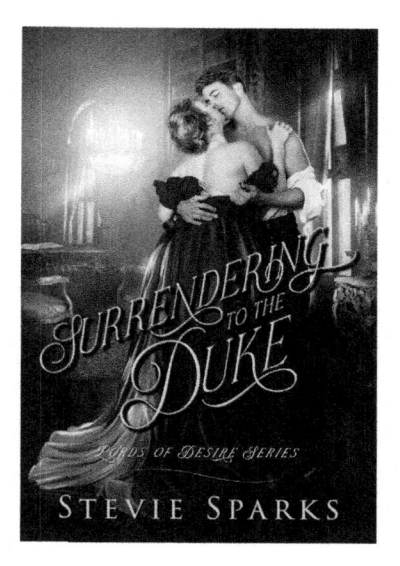

His brother's wife. He loved his brother's wife.

After losing his heart to Emmeline, the one woman he could never have, Michael committed himself to a life in the army, fighting for King and country in the Great War.

...Until his brother died, and Michael returned to Scarlett Castle as the Duke of Foxcotte.

Fed up with her lack of grandchildren, Michael's mother hatches a plan to bring Michael and Emmeline together in a marriage of convenience. However, whilst Michael agrees to court Emmeline, they both secretly long for something more passionate than a business arrangement. But Michael could have never imagined that hidden trauma lurked beneath Emmeline's emerald eyes.

Michael and Emmeline soon ignite a flame that threatens to consume them both as they learn that all relationships come with risks both wanted and unwanted. *Will their marriage of convenience be successful? Or will Emmeline's traumatic past catch up to her and sweep her away?*
Surrendering to the Duke is available to read on Amazon

Emmeline

"Are you quite, *quite* ready for your surprise?" Emmeline Fraser, the Duchess of Foxcotte, asked her daughter Dora, unable to stop a beam of excitement spreading across her face. The two of them approached the stables, following the long shadows that Scarlett Castle's many turrets had cast upon the ground. "Because I can *always* take it back if you don't want it."

"No, Mama!" Dora giggled thickly, her shoulder-length black hair shining in the hot, oppressive sunshine.

"Very well, if you're sure," Emmeline gave a great gusty sigh of faux reluctance. The gravel crunched under their feet as they made their way towards the complex of buildings comprising the Foxcotte Stables. They'd dedicated much of the space to the Thoroughbred stud farm, one of the commercial enterprises attached to the dukedom's estate. Her late husband, Theo, the 9th Duke of Foxcotte, had been particularly proud of its success.

"Why am I wearing trousers, Mama?"

She quirked a brow. "If I tell you, it shan't be a surprise anymore. Do you like them?"

"They feel strange to walk in."

"You can take them off when we get back home to the castle. Don't worry."

"Is Uncle Michael home? Is that my surprise?" Dora asked hopefully, clutching her stubby hands to her chest.

Emmeline bent down to her daughter's level. "Uncle Michael will be home tomorrow. Grandmama had a telegram at luncheon saying he'd arrived at Liverpool, so he's travelling down to Hampshire as we speak." Her mother-in-law had almost combusted with happiness at the news her only remaining son was back in England.

"Right now?"

She nodded. "Right now." In truth, her brother-in-law Michael, the 10th Duke of Foxcotte, would likely spend the day in a hotel after over-imbibing with his unit the night before. "I know he can't wait to see you. At bedtime, shall I read you the last letter he sent again?"

"Yes, please," Dora answered. "Do you think he'll bring me sweets?"

"I *know* he'll bring you sweets," she laughed. "Now come—your present is this way."

Emmeline directed Dora towards the family's personal stables. Recently, the worn grey stone had become dusty with the long drought, and she and Dora had regularly seen the stable hands taking the horses down to the River Blackwater to cool off in. "This one, sweetheart."

The cool air rushed over them as they entered, a welcome reprieve from the sticky heat of the day. The stable manager, a short, barrel-chested man called McNally, approached them as Emmeline's eyes adjusted to the indoors. "Lady Foxcotte," he took his flat cap off. "Lady Dora. Right on time."

"Lady Dora's present has arrived, then?" Emmeline asked.

McNally nodded, the lines in his weathered face creasing as he smiled. "Follow me."

Dora glanced hopefully up at the stable doors they walked past. "Where are all the horses?"

"Out in the fields, Lady Dora," McNally answered, coming to rest at the last stall. Movement came from within. "Here we are."

A moment later, a dappled grey horse poked its head out over the stable door. Dora cooed with delight. "Can I say hello?"

"Course you can," McNally replied, his voice gruff.

It was Emmeline's second time meeting the mare. She'd enlisted the help of her widowed sister-in-law, Annabelle, to find Dora the right horse. "Technically," Annabelle had said immediately, "what you want is a pony." A day later, Annabelle came back with the name and number of a breeder of Welsh Ponies. They had gone together to Merthyr Tydfil to visit the breeder, who'd looked vaguely familiar. Annabelle selected Queenie on account of Emmeline having just enough knowledge of horses to tell the front end from the back and call it a day.

Emmeline bent down to pick up her daughter. "Do you remember I said I'd buy you your own horse once you were big enough to learn to ride?"

Dora nodded ferociously, her pale blue eyes flicking between Emmeline and the new horse. The same colour as Theo's had been.

Smiling, Emmeline gave the horse a gentle, slightly uncertain pat. "This is your new horse. Her name is Queenie."

The news sent Dora into fits of infantile elation, flashing her milk teeth in a wide grin. "Can I ride her today?" she said excitedly.

The stable master paused, presumably to untangle Dora's speech. It was getting better, but only close family members could understand her all the time. "Just around the manège today," McNally answered finally, opening both the door behind him and Queenie's stable door. The path outside led to one of the fenced enclosures on the site. "Come on then, Queenie. I've already saddled her, Lady Foxcotte." He gave her a surreptitious look. "Not side saddle?"

"Absolutely not," Emmeline replied, strapping Dora's new helmet for her. *That* had been a decision she'd made by herself, though Annabelle had fully supported it—unsurprisingly, given her sister-in-law was the one who fell off riding side saddle and nearly cracked her head open.

When they emerged out into the enclosure, Emmeline blinked in surprise. A willowy figure stood against the fence, clearly waiting for their arrival. Mary. She swallowed. Her mother-in-law.

...who Emmeline had avoided telling about the visit because of Dora's new trousers.

Helping her daughter onto the horse, Emmeline held Dora's hand as McNally walked Queenie towards the fence.

"Grandmama, look! Look! Look!" Dora squealed, waving her free arm madly. "I'm on a horse."

Mary returned the wave with a touch more dignity. "So I see," she said heartily, watching as they approached the fence. In the background, Jake, the family Collie, cocked his leg against a building. "Do you like her?"

Dora's burbling laugh was a delight. "Yes, she's called Queenie."

"Queenie? I say! In that case, she outranks us all."

The grizzled McNally brought Queenie to a stop. "If you hold this little strap here, Lady Dora," he tapped the leather handhold attached to Queenie's saddle, "I'll walk you around the manège to allow you to get used to sitting on the pony. What do you think of that?"

Dora looked to Emmeline at once, her black hair swishing at her chin. "Am I allowed to, Mama?"

Emmeline made a noise of false indecision. "I don't know. That sort of thing is only for big girls. You'd have to hold it tight the entire time. Can you do that?"

"I can," Dora exclaimed, sitting taller in the saddle. "I'm a big girl, Mama."

Emmeline kissed her daughter on the forehead and tucked Dora's hair behind her ears. "All right then, off you go. I'll stand here with Grandmama and watch."

True to her word, Dora clutched the little handhold like her life depended on it, chattering away to McNally. Emmeline's heart thundered with anxiety, and she pressed a hand over her chest as though to calm it. Out of the corner of her eye, she glanced at Mary. "Who gave me away?"

Mary pursed her lips, though Emmeline could see a tinge of amusement in her eyes. "I saw the pony being unloaded this morning, and then noticed the helmet hanging up in the stables."

"Ah. And there was only one person in the house it could fit?"

"Quite." Mary looked round at Jake. Their slightly defective, sheep-phobic Collie. "Although I suppose it could fit the dog. With the things the shepherds have them doing, I wouldn't be surprised if they could ride a pony."

"Wouldn't that be a sight?" Taking Mary's lead and not mentioning the trousers, she cleared her throat. "I think it went well." Jake trotted over to her, leaning against her legs. She bent down to stroke his head as he gazed at her, giving him a kiss on the snout for good measure.

"I think it's the happiest I've ever seen her," said Mary, watching Dora with a melancholic look in her eyes. Her mother-in-law's grey hair flowed in waves against her scalp; the sole concession that she gave to modern style. Perhaps because it suited her naturally curly hair. On the other hand, Mary's richly embroidered navy day dress fell in ripples from her neck to her feet like a true Victorian. Emmeline felt rather shabby by comparison, wearing a serviceable grey frock. "She's Theodore in miniature, is she not?"

"She is," Emmeline agreed readily. It was what Mary wanted to hear. An awkward feeling came over her whenever Mary discussed Emmeline's deceased husband. They had been married for almost two years, but the Great War had meant that, all in all, she hadn't known her husband that well. It was an odd thing to know her husband—the father of her child—more from photographs and family anecdotes than anything else. At the funeral, she had felt like an intruder upon the family's grief, even as she waddled between the pews, heavy with his child.

Her daughter's squeal was ecstatic as Queenie sped up slightly. It made Emmeline feel guiltier than ever. The last thing she wanted was for Dora to grow up in an environment resembling her own childhood; an orphan in a cold and empty home. No, she wanted Dora to grow up as one of many adored children; to have a home that always echoed with laughter and was full to the brim with toys and books and family.

As a widow, the best Emmeline could give her daughter was a horse.

She swallowed, recalling the years of silence she endured as a girl. Giving Dora a horse was at least better than nothing… wasn't it?

It was late afternoon by the time they left the stables. Emmeline thanked McNally profusely, warning him that Dora would probably be back first thing in the morning. Dora said goodbye to Queenie with a peck on the nose before hurrying back into Emmeline's arms. With surprising strength, she squeezed Emmeline's neck. "Thank you, Mama. I love her *this* much." She spread her arms wide, almost taking Emmeline's nose off.

"I'm glad, darling. You did so well riding her. If you work really hard, I'm sure you'll be riding out with Aunt Annabelle in no time." Preferably not on any of the jumps Annabelle loved, however. "For now, let's get you back. It's almost time for your dinner."

Judging by the fact that Dora fell asleep in the middle of her meal, she had worked quite hard enough for one day.

After putting Dora to bed, Emmeline sighed as she walked down Scarlett Castle's Grand Staircase into the Atrium. The glass dome at its peak revealed the sun's downward course, setting the sky alight in dazzling shades of fiery bronze. The evenings were her favourite thing about summer. She would often take a book up to the Eastern Tower and watch the sun slowly descend below the horizon.

"Emmeline?"

She whipped around, fighting to remember how to breathe. Michael stood in front of her in his officers uniform, creased and dusty from his travels. His black hair had become speckled with the odd grey at his temples, whilst the sudden appearance of a short beard transformed his looks from traditional nobleman to rugged explorer. "You're supposed to be arriving tomorrow."

"Forgive me, how rude," Michael said, leaning against a column with the air of a schoolboy up to no good. He crossed his arms over his chest and fingered the leather webbing of his uniform. "Would you like me to come back in the morning?"

"If you wouldn't mind," she said stiffly, fighting to keep a smile off her face. "And I'll have to make a complaint to the War Office, you know. This is dreadfully inconvenient. They can't just be dropping officers all over England willy nilly."

"I don't see why not." His polished boot tapped against the marble flooring lightly, although his liquid silver eyes were fixed upon her. "The ladies seem to be thrilled whenever officers drop in unexpectedly. I tell you, the reception we receive is simply *marvellous*."

Emmeline could imagine. She'd heard rumours of both Michael and Theo's exploits in their youths, of flings with courtesans and young women in the village. "Your mother has succumbed to this madness, I hear."

Michael's eyes narrowed, though his face still sparkled with amusement. "If I hear some scoundrel has been casing the place in my absence, I shall be forced to take action."

She had only meant Mary's love for her only remaining son, but she was quite content to play along. "Will you fight with sword or pistol?" Emmeline wondered cheerfully.

"Pistol," he replied immediately, as sure of himself as he always was. "I'm not best keen on sharp edges."

And no wonder.

She and Annabelle, both of whom trained as nurses during the war, cared for him when he was sent back to Yateley Military Hospital in the village. Purportedly with a *bayonet wound*, according to his notes. It was a crime to describe his injuries as such. Annabelle had summarised it succinctly on the day he'd arrived: Michael had been butchered, with angry, jagged gashes across his torso that branched out like furious lightning bolts weeping blood with every movement.

Mary had nearly fainted when the telegram arrived, almost a year to the day after the telegram notifying them of Theo's death had darkened their doorstep. Annabelle had been the one to wrench it from her mother's shaking hands, unable to bear Mary's fearful hesitation. Emmeline and Effie—her younger sister-in-law—had all but propped Mary up as Annabelle read out the letter, afraid she would drop like a stone.

"As one of the nurses who helped to stitch you back together, I'm glad you learnt your lesson," she said kindly, feeling their playful banter fall by the wayside. Emmeline walked forwards and pulled him into a hug. "And I'm ever so glad you're back."

His grin was roguishly low as he leant in, as though the slow, pained weeks of recovery had been nothing at all. The hug was quick, with him releasing her almost immediately. "As am I."

"We didn't expect you until tomorrow. I thought you would be recovering from your crossing."

A cavalier shrug lifted his shoulders. The spattering of silver at his temple gleamed in the dappled sunlight falling through the Atrium, simultaneously making his dark hair even darker. "I got lucky. The sea was calm, and I didn't drink too—" Michael cleared his throat. His focus shot away suddenly, before a beaming smile split his face. "Evening, Mama."

It was Emmeline's only warning before Mary's cry filled the Atrium. Her heels clipped against the floor as she ran to greet her son, clasping his cheeks and yanking him into a desperate hug that pulled at Emmeline's heartstrings. "Oh my darling, darling, *darling* boy," Mary choked, smothering him with her motherly embrace. Jake, her black-and-white shadow, slunk around them, barking excitedly. "Thank heavens you're home. You're back. You're safe."

"I'm here, Mama," Michael grinned. He bent down to give Jake a thorough scratch. "Sitting in on hearings and court martials in Ireland is not particularly dangerous." His smile faded. "It's... many things, but not that."

Emmeline sympathised. She knew how hard the past few years had been for him. He had served in the Great War from its beginning to its end. But then he had gone straight over to Ireland, working, as he put it in his letters, *for a cause I do not believe in*.

Up on the first floor, Emmeline paused at the tinkling of a bell. The nursery bell. Excusing herself from Mary's audible adorations over Michael, Emmeline ascended the staircase in time to see Dora walking down the corridor barefoot.

"Why is Jake barking, Mama?" she asked innocently, a wide-eyed excuse.

Hefting Dora onto her hip, she brushed the hair out of her daughter's eyes. "Shall we go downstairs and see?"

Descending the Grand Staircase for the second time in five minutes, Dora's delighted squeal at finding Michael standing in the Atrium deafened Emmeline.

Michael's long legs bridged the gap between them with ease. He beamed as he met them halfway. "Hello, poppet."

Dora threw herself into her uncle's arms, her face scrunching into a tear-stained mess of excitement. "I missed you," she wept into his neck. "Mama said you wouldn't b-be here until tomorrow."

"I wanted to surprise you all."

Dora's bottom lip wobbled dangerously, but she sniffed. "Did you bring me sweets?" she said piteously, her weeping disappearing.

Mary ushered them into her morning room as Michael laughed.

Emmeline winced, catching Mary's eye. "Dora, that isn't polite."

But neither Michael nor Dora took any notice. "I may have done," Michael said. He caught Emmeline's eye. "Although I can't remember where I left them," he said unconvincingly. "You may have to wait until tomorrow."

Her lips tilted softly. In so many ways, she was so lucky to have him. Not just because he was kind and he loved Dora, but because he didn't bulldoze his way over her authority as Dora's mother. Still, not even she would try to get Dora back to sleep now. A Sisyphean task if ever there was one. Adding a packet of sweets would be as inconsequential as adding a single match to a blazing inferno. "I'm sure we can find them this evening, Dora. Don't worry."

Michael tapped his breast pocket, sending a telltale rustle through the room. "Ah. I think I may have found them."

Dora dived in like a gannet, pulling out a packet of toffees.

"How have you been doing whilst I've been away, sweetheart?" Michael asked Dora, helping her to open the packet.

"Mama gave me a pony today," Dora said thickly, her speech slowed by the toffee.

"A pony, you say? As in, a real one?"

"A real one. Her name is Queenie. And—and—and—and I rode her today. Mama said I was a big girl, and I waved to her and Grandmama. Will you take me to ride her in the morning?"

Emmeline spoke up. "Uncle Michael has had a long journey, Dora. He might want to have a rest tomorrow." She knew she certainly would.

Dora changed topic at the drop of a hat. "Last week at the nursery we went to see the King." Dora offered no further information, digging further into her sweet packet.

Michael blinked before looking up at Emmeline, a devious smirk hiding behind his eyes. "I say. The King?"

"We took the children attending the charity school to Windsor to see Windsor Castle," she explained. They'd walked along the Thames, seen the Changing of the Guard, and taken a photograph of the children in front of the castle itself. "Ten children are now official pupils, all aged 14 and up." Ten children who would receive a proper secondary education, allowing them to go on to university or get an apprenticeship. The village school provided free education for children between ages five and 14, but there was scant help for children outside those ages. "The nursery is now bigger than ever as well. We moved into a new building in April—the converted mews on the estate. We've two nursery teachers too. Dora loves going there, don't you, Dora?"

Dora nodded, entering into a tirade about her partner-in-crime, a little girl called Josephine, whose cantankerous great-aunt ran the tearoom in the village.

It had been one of the most painful things about her widowhood. The slow, begrudging acceptance of the fact that she would have but a single child. Not that Dora was lacking in *any* sense of the word. Rather, it was the environment that Dora would have to grow up in that pained Emmeline, given its haunting similarity to her own childhood.

The silver lining was that whilst Dora may be an only child, she was loved and adored to within an inch of her life.

Emmeline had not been so lucky.

Perhaps it was because her uncle filled her own childhood with isolation and horrors that Emmeline felt the need to provide the exact opposite to her own child.

Child. Not children.

After Theo died, Emmeline had decided that if she could not provide love and stability for a horde of her own children, then the least she could do was to provide that for the children around her.

And so her idea of a charity school had come about. Although her parents had failed in their duty to select a safe guardian for her, they had at least been generous financially. Theo had left her a trust that was more than ample to cover her needs as well, meaning she had a sizeable sum to start her off.

Within six months, she'd converted the estate's old mews into schoolrooms. Within a year, she'd had four secondary students and nine children in the nursery, not including Dora, who went several times a week.

After Michael put Dora down on the rug to feast on the sweets, Mary tugged him to the sofa, clinging to him like a burr. She reached over to the bellpull and gave it a sharp yank. "How are you, darling boy?" she asked him, rapturous happiness in her eyes. "You look like you've lost weight. Have the army not been feeding you? Honestly, you've been good enough to stay on for years after the war. It's the least they can do. We'll get Mrs Kirkpatrick to rustle up some dainties for you. And send Jayaweera up with a razor. Clearly you've lost yours. He'll be able to shave off that horrid beard for you."

"It's not a beard, Mama. It's just facial hair. And I'd be quite happy to never shave again now that I'm out of the army."

Mary looked unconvinced, but smiled as Dora's laughter drifted over the drawing room. "You look so much better without the beard, dear."

Michael sighed good-naturedly.

Ignoring him, Mary carried on. "We heard about that awful business at the Custom House when you were in Dublin. I was so worried I could hardly sleep, wasn't I, Emmeline? They said it burnt for five days in the paper."

Mary wasn't lying. Emmeline had found her in the library one evening, weeping into her sherry. It had taken an hour for her to calm Mary down enough to get her to go to bed. The next night had been easier, for her sisters-in-law, Effie and Annabelle, had returned from their trip to London and were better able to offer their mother comfort, but Mary had still been a terrified shell until she managed to get in touch with Michael, in danger of exploding into tears wherever she stood. Emmeline could not judge her; her mother-in-law had never been the same after the telegram announcing Theo's death had arrived.

"Mama, I was nowhere near the Custom House."

"A mother will always worry."

"You can stop now," Michael soothed her. "I'm home. But what of here?"

Emmeline wracked her brains. "One of the new tractors has broken down—something to do with the priming rod, although don't ask me what—but they should fix it in time for the harvest in August. But the remaining tractors are making the fertilising ten times easier than using the Shires and our old equipment. Lambing season is well underway too—albeit slightly later than usual this year. There were some issues with getting a ram in. We've set up the lambing rooms in one of the spare barns by the River Blackwater. There's been nearly two hundred already and they're adorable, even if we are just going to eat them eventually. The watermill is also running well; we've just signed a new contract with a distributor in Southampton. The drought is seriously starting to bite with the crops, though."

She chewed her lip, trying to think of what else had happened since they last saw Michael on leave.

Mary took over for her. "Oh! Cousin Ruth visited with her new baby. Born on Empire Day. Isn't he sweet, Emmeline?" Her eyes never left Michael. "And currently the only heir to the dukedom," she muttered.

"His name is Arthur," Emmeline cut in sharply. "Arthur Frederick."

"I'll have to pay them a visit." Michael leant forward, dodging his mother's stare. "What about the extension at the back of the East Wing? Have the maintenance workers fixed the leak in the roof yet? You wrote about it in your letters a while back, but haven't mentioned it since."

"Yes, that's all sorted," Emmeline replied, relieved that *that* debacle was over and done with. "Cost a pretty penny, but it's sorted. It had leaked right through to the floorboards and rotted everything away."

He nodded. "On my way in, I noticed some of the trees along the driveway had been cut down."

"There were signs they were diseased. They're going to check the rest of the estate later in the year."

To the side of them, the door opened, and Granville entered the room. A decade older than Michael, the man cut an imperial figure in his butler's morning coat and striped trousers—compared to the footmen's simple liveries.

"Ah, Granville," Mary turned in her seat. "Would we be able to have tea brought up now, please? And can you ask Mrs Kirkpatrick to send up some extra cakes for His Grace?"

"Of course, Your Grace."

"Is George here?" Michael looked from Mary to Emmeline.

Mary opened her mouth to speak, but Emmeline interrupted. George, a maternal cousin of Michael's, was rather a sensitive topic at present. "George is living in one of the cottages near the pond."

A broad smile lit up Michael's face. "Ah, excellent. Is he coming to dinner?"

Emmeline didn't think George was in any condition to be attending dinner parties, never mind the fact that Mary had banned him from the house.

"I'm not sure George is up to it at the moment, Michael," Emmeline said delicately, hoping Mary wouldn't shove her opinion into the conversation. When she had visited George that afternoon, he was barely conscious and lying next to a pile of his own vomit. With all his trouble sleeping, she didn't have it in her to rouse him from what little peace he could find, and so she had mopped up and left him sandwiches wrapped in brown paper.

Michael tensed, rubbing his thumb along his dark whiskers. "What do you mean 'not up to it?'"

"He's not well," she said kindly, shooting her mother-in-law a polite but firm look. "I'll tell you about it *later*."

Michael's expression told her she didn't even have to try. He knew what some of the men were like, and shell-shock had been all too common after the Great War. Mary had tried to insist on sending George for inpatient treatment at Netley Hospital in Southampton, but Emmeline overruled her. She had taken the time to research the treatments such hospitals offered, ranging from solitary confinement and electric shocks to lobotomies. But George did not need a cure, he just needed care. *Much like me, I suppose.*

"When did you last see him, Emmeline?"

"Luncheon," she explained, jumping as Dora slapped her hand on the floor whilst playing with Jake. She scolded her body's reaction and carried on. "I visit him to make sure he's eaten and whatnot. Annabelle and Effie often come with me as well, but they're both out today."

Michael looked around as though the thought had suddenly occurred to him. "Come to think of it, where are my wonderful sisters?"

"Annabelle's off on a char-à-banc trip with the Women's Institute. She'll be gone for the night," Emmeline offered helpfully. "And Effie is visiting Cousin Ruth in London. The Entomological Society was holding a lecture at the Natural History Museum and she wanted to attend."

Her mother-in-law's smile was banal. "And meet little Arthur."

Granville bustled back in with two pots of tea, followed by a footman carrying a tray of cakes. As they were setting up, Michael cleared his throat. "After tea, I'd like to visit Theo's memorial." He stopped at Mary's sharp intake of breath, but carried on regardless. "And then I want to see George. I'll be back before the dinner gong."

Emmeline stood to pour milk into her tea. "Very well, but I'll come with you. And you must change out of your uniform before you go. You're awfully dusty." George would no doubt have one of his episodes if he saw an army officer at his front door, regardless of whether it was his own cousin.

If Emmeline had more than a passing interest in history, she would be very interested indeed in the Chapel of St Mary Magdalene. Little more than a single-roomed stone barn, the church was said to be built on the estate lands back in the seventh century. It was nestled amongst rolling hills and buzzing meadows; a manmade jewel in a woodland crown.

On her first proper tour of Scarlett Castle's estate, Theo, ever the historian, had been particularly proud to show the chapel off to her. With its teeny tiny windows and ancient beams, even Emmeline could appreciate the historical value of such a place.

Her husband had spread his arms wide in the middle of the single-roomed chapel, smiling at the wooden beams above their heads. "This is *by far* my favourite building on the estate. One Bishop Cedd, who had been sent by the King of the Saxons to spread Christianity through the land, built it back in 660. This was one of many such chapels he built before succumbing to the plague in 664."

Emmeline nodded politely. They were alone out here. The nearest building was a tenant farmer's cottage a mile back, with its wonky gate and garden full of fat clucking chickens. She had been introduced to the tenants in question not long after the wedding. Mr and Mrs McLaurin. Or something. They had seemed kind, but out here she was beyond their help. She looked at her new husband with suspicious eyes.

For all his kindness, she and Theo had never been truly alone until this moment.

"It's quite remarkable, in fact," he carried on, oblivious to her nerves. "It's burnt down several times over the years and fallen into disuse here and there. But it's been properly maintained and repaired since the estate came into the hands of the Frasers—ceiling tiles and whatnot, although it's been quite a job finding ones that are in-keeping with the structure," he took her hand and gave her an encouraging smile as she stood in the empty church like a spectre; one of those ancient souls who had haunted this building for more than a millennium. "I know I may not be the typical husband, Emmeline, but I will do right by you. I can see you're scared, but you're safe here, I promise. None at Scarlett Castle would harm you." He frowned, the first sign of displeasure she'd seen from him. "From what I've been able to ascertain, the same could not be said of Holyhead. Of Edinburgh."

Emmeline sucked in a deep breath, panic roiling through her. It was silly. She *was* Scottish, but the mere mention of it sent fear deep into her heart. Memories of her uncle's wandering hands and explosive temper echoed in her mind. Uncle Murray—Lord Cambury—knew how to threaten her with little more than a frenzied look. Because with him, it was never just a look. It was a promise.

"How old were you when your parents died?" Theo continued.

"Three."

"And your mother's twin sister took you in?"

"Yes," Emmeline answered.

Theo nodded solemnly. "They have two children, Caroline and Oliver?"

"They do now. My Aunt and Uncle were childless when I first arrived."

Last night cast a pall over her—consummating their marriage, Theo's weight on top of her, the overwhelming smell of alcohol on his breath. She had initially feared the worst, but his touch had been kinder than she had any right to expect. Perfunctory, but kind. She was thankful for that.

After he had left, she had assumed her usual job of watching her bedroom door in the night. She ached to roll over, to close her eyes and try to sleep peacefully. But she could not. Emmeline lay like a sentinel guarding her bedroom door until exhaustion took her unawares in the early hours.

Even at Scarlett Castle, every shadow seemed to hide her uncle in its clutches.

"My Mama visited Holyhead earlier this year," Theodore explained gently. "Do you remember her? Mary?"

"Somewhat." Uncle Murray had rarely permitted Aunt Hilda's friends to visit.

Theo smiled encouragingly. "My mama and yours were the closest of friends at finishing school, did you know? Along with your aunt, of course."

Emmeline shook her head, wondering where this was going.

"The last time my mother visited, she was... *displeased* with your care—or lack thereof."

"Oh?"

Crossing his arms, he sighed. "I questioned some of the staff working at Holyhead."

A sharp, choking inhale whistled down her throat, just as quickly as a shiver ran along her spine. *Oh god.*

"Was it just your uncle that was cruel to you, or your aunt as well?" Theo asked her, anger prickling his tone.

"Only he was cruel physically." Terror filled her at the fury flaring on her husband's face. "Did I displease you last night? Are you sending me back to him?"

Whispering something under his breath, Theodore wrapped her in the first hug she could ever remember receiving. One kind touch was all it took for her to break, to hug him back, to make herself vulnerable, to leave herself open to further pain.

But Theodore didn't take the opportunity to do so. He simply stood there, offering nothing but comfort, murmuring words of safety. A good man. A good husband. "I'll not lie to you, Emmeline." He pulled back, staring into her eyes. "I cannot give you love," he told her apologetically. "But I will always keep you safe, and I hope in time we can be friends."

She had simply nodded, still too wary to believe her apparent good luck. A kindly duke proposing out of nowhere and lifting her from abuse? "Friends."

Michael's voice dragged her back to the sweltering evening and the overgrown hedges surrounding the church, a robin hopping from branch to branch. He was looking at her expectantly as they stood in front of Theo's tombstone. The grave itself was empty, for Theo's body had never left Passchendaele.

She wiped a tear from her eye at the memory of her husband's kindness. "Did you say something, Michael?"

"Would you like to put the flowers down, or should I?"

"You do it," Emmeline reassured him. "Mary and I come here every week. You haven't been home since last year." For perhaps the thousandth time, she read the inscription they'd commissioned on the dark grey stone.

In ever loving memory of a dearest son, husband, and father
Theodore Phillip Fraser, 9th Duke of Foxcotte
Died 10th November, 1917
Aged 32 Years

After a long silence, Michael's shoulders heaved. "Strange to be older than him," he mumbled, running a hand through his perpetually messy black hair. "*They shall not grow old, as we that are left grow old,*" he recited. "*Age shall not weary them, nor the years condemn.* Knowing that whilst I'll continue to age and wither, he'll be eternally young in my memories. Getting further away every year."

"Or closer, depending on your perspective."

The corners of Michael's mouth twitched as his eyes roved over her. "That's a nice way of looking at it."

Was it? She wasn't sure that the promise of ever-approaching death was all that pleasant. Perhaps that was death's consolation; to be with one's family again. She shuddered, hoping death could distinguish between *which* family would wait for her when the time came. Emmeline watched as the robin landed on the church roof, flitting around with a bundle of dried grass in its beak. The church had once been a hive of activity; now only the robin reigned here. Death had come for each of them.

"Dora looks more like him each time I see her," Michael said.

She looked up, noticing that he had even more grey hairs around his temple than he did the last time he was on leave. Back at the beginning of the Great War, his hair had been as black as the night's sky. And then Theodore had died, and the grey crept in. "Your mother says the same thing."

"I never thanked you," he said quietly, crossing his arms over his chest. The movement stretched his jacket across his arms, outlining the muscles built by years of competitive rowing and rugby.

"For what?"

"For caring for him. When Theo first told me he'd found a wife, I was... hesitant. You could have made his life miserable. Instead, you were devoted to him, gave him a daughter, managed the estate to keep it afloat after his death, looked after the family in our grief, and even four years later, you still put flowers on Theodore's grave each week."

Emmeline half winced, half grimaced. Theo had provided her with the first home she'd ever known. He was *kind* to her. He'd taken her under his wing and taught her how to be human, instead of just existing. He'd given her so much—how could she not do everything she could in return?

"You don't have to thank me, Michael." For the first time in her life, she had someone to care for. It had come as a surprise to realise she had needed someone to tend to just as much as she'd needed someone to tend to her in return.

But then that was one disadvantage of her childhood. Being raised in isolation with a monster meant she had no clue what she was missing until it was planted in her lap.

The months after she had moved to Scarlett Castle had been the hardest. She had learnt what it was like to have a genuine, loving family around her. The Frasers cared for her like she was their own. Every day had been a reminder of what she'd been missing her entire life, like parading an emaciated child in front of a ceremonial banquet. *Here, see what everyone else has been feasting on whilst you've starved. Isn't it wonderful?*

It had taken her time to heal. But she had grown stronger every year. Her memories would never leave her; even now, her wounds were ragged scars instead of open sores. She still had her little foibles; things that would plunge her back in time, though these days they came few and far between. Emmeline didn't think the pain would ever leave her entirely.

It did, however, seem to shrink a little more each year with the passing of time, like a storm blowing itself out in the night. It would erupt occasionally. A scar would split open, revealing feelings long since buried and exposing them to the cold bite of the open air. As time had proven, though, these would always heal. Eventually.

And she would carry on, as she had always done, facilitated by the love of the family she had found.

Michael took out his battered pocket watch. A 17th Century Fraser family heirloom passed from father to son—and from Theo to Michael. "We should visit George before it gets too late," he offered her his arm for the uneven walk back to the car. "And incidentally, what weren't you saying about him earlier?"

Emmeline let Michael guide her along the path. "I need your help with him. All he consumes is cocaine and alcohol, Michael. Opium too. Anything he can get his hands on. Mary flew into a rage and banned him from the house on New Year's Day. She wants to put him in hospital—or a lunatic asylum."

Michael swore, running a weary hand over his thick black hair.

"He seemed like he was doing fine, but then your aunt passed and… I don't know whether he was just hiding it well all along or if her death tipped him over the edge. Mary moved him to the Pond Cottage so the villagers wouldn't see what a state he's in and gossip. And I can warn you of one thing: she wants you to marry. Desperately."

"Christ," he mumbled.

"How was it you scared off the one that had you ensnared last summer when you were on leave? Lord Crackfleet's daughter."

Michael barked out a laugh as they reached the car. "I belched in front of her and called her the wrong name. In my defence, she was awful."

"There we are then. Just use that approach with all of them."

"Did you know," Michael leant in conspiratorially, "that at Eton, Theo and I devoted a not insignificant number of hours learning to belch the alphabet?"

"An excellent use of the fortune your parents paid in tuition fees," Emmeline smiled.

Darkness had fallen by the time the wheels of the motor had rasped to a stop on the shingle sprinkled outside the pretty cottage behind Scarlett Castle. Emmeline felt a certain trepidation. George was not expecting her again today. What was she going to find?

"Perhaps you should wait outside," Emmeline suggested as they walked to George's front door, hoping Michael would hang back. "Then I can let him know you're here too."

"Whatever you think best."

Emmeline fished the key from under the neglected flowerpot and let herself in, knowing how much George hated sudden knocks at his front door. The smell of stagnant air and stale smoke hit her. There were no lights on in the house, despite all the curtains being closed. "George?" she called into the shadowy hallway. "Are you awake? It's just me."

"Mmm?" came a voice from the drawing room.

Reaching around for the doorknob in the dark, Emmeline finally pushed the door open, finding George in much the same position he had been in earlier: reclining his lanky form on the couch surrounded by a mass of pillows and blankets, his feet hanging over its arm by some margin. The faint smell of sick pervaded through the room like an unwanted guest.

Noting the sandwiches she'd set down on the table earlier had not been touched, she sighed. Emmeline crouched down next to him and lay a hand on his arm. "Michael is here. He'd like to see you. Can he come in?"

"Michael?" George croaked, rubbing his eyes and wiping his nose. She tried not to react to his acrid breath, but did not fail to notice that his pupils were enormous. "He's in Ireland."

"No, he returned late this afternoon. He's demobbed—discharged—from the army. He's quite eager to see you."

George dragged his gaze around the room as though he were seeing it for the first time. A whisper of shame crept into his demeanour. "I can't let him in here."

"Why don't we go to the music room? You cleaned it yesterday when you were in one of your… moods. It's quite spotless."

"How do I look?" he sniffed.

Emmeline paused, taking him in as objectively as she could, as opposed to comparing his current appearance to what he'd look like yesterday or last week. Messy hair. Creased shirt. Bloodshot eyes. Greasy face. Unpleasant scent. There was certainly room to improve.

"Perhaps you might have a quick wash," she suggested kindly. "With soap."

"As opposed to washing with what, faeces?"

She smirked, looking fondly upon the troubled man in front of her, despite his faults. "Don't backchat me, George, or I'll scrub you with lye myself."

"I know a place in London where people would pay good money for that."

"Perhaps you should visit."

When the three of them sat down in the pristine music room to exchange niceties, George resembled a bloodshot picture of respectability. He soon began fidgeting in the chaise longue, tapping his fingers on the seat.

"You look like you're drinking more than is good for you, George," Michael said quietly. His dark blue day suit camouflaged against the navy armchair, although his leather Oxfords differed slightly from the chair's gold gilding. Emmeline privately thought Michael could pull it off, and Jayaweera would be thrilled to drape Michael in gold trimmings. "Mind you, I'm willing to bet what you've got here is better than the rum rations I received in the trenches."

George's only response was a huff.

"What did you get in Gallipoli, then?"

His cheeks drained of blood. "Don't."

Michael held his hands up in apology. "Emmeline tells me my mother has been making things difficult for you. She forced you to leave your old cottage for this one, is that right?"

"She forced nothing. Aunt Mary mentioned it and I agreed." George looked out of the window, which Emmeline had opened to let in some much-needed light and air. The explosion of carnations threw pink light into the room. "It's quieter here. In the village, there are horses and motors and children shrieking enough to shake the foundations."

"What about Scarlett Castle? How often do you walk over?" Michael reclined in the seat, looking at Emmeline quickly.

"I visited at Christmas."

Michael knew this, for Emmeline had brought him up to date on the happenings around George on their drive over, but he continued. "It's July. The walk is all of thirty seconds. I could probably hold my breath and reach the back door before I keeled over."

"I'm no longer welcome." The dark circles under his eyes were almost as dark as his hair. "Nor do I deserve to be."

"It's my house, ergo you are always welcome. So welcome, in fact, that Emmeline and I think you should move in."

"Excuse me?" George hissed, his eyes darting between the two of them.

"You're moving into Scarlett Castle, George," Emmeline said in a tone that brokered no argument; it was the one she used when completing her duties on the estate. At first, some of the men she dealt with had not taken kindly to her authority. George had helped her with that, she remembered. He had encouraged her when she wanted to tuck tail and run whenever a man raised his voice, lending her his calm presence whenever she doubted herself. "You're isolated and damaging yourself further, and family is literally a stone's throw away."

"I don't want to go anywhere. I'm perfectly happy here."

"Yes, you're the picture of health," Michael quipped. "I want you to move into Scarlett Castle willingly."

George shook his head like a dog ridding its ears of water. "I wish to be here, Michael. Aunt Mary—"

"If you don't move into Scarlett Castle willingly, however," Michael continued as though George had not commented, his voice strengthening with every syllable, steel layer upon steel layer, "then I will have you placed under my guardianship on account of your behaviour, in which case you will be *forced* to live at Scarlett Castle. Make your choice."

"And you agree with this?" George looked askance at Emmeline.

"Yes," she said simply, deciding not to mention that the plan had been hers. Emmeline had gone to the point of fetching the family solicitor from London to ensure it was possible. Not that she had mentioned her intentions to Mary. Her mother-in-law was going to be furious.

George lurched to his feet, unsteady with outrage and alcohol. His eyes were cold. "Even after *everything* I told you," his voice was low. "Everything I trusted you with. You would have me around your daughter."

She stepped forward, slow and delicate. Her heart broke for the broken man before her. Shortly after his mother's death, George had wept in her arms one night, telling her of horrors she had never imagined. Had she once thought she had experienced the depravities of man? She had never even come close. "You reacted as a good man would, George," choosing her words carefully, wary of Michael's presence.

"A cold-blooded murderer," George replied, teary-eyed.

"Just because a man begs for mercy does not mean they are worth saving," Emmeline declared fiercely.

A heavy breath seemed to deflate George, leaving him shrunken and exhausted. "Why can you not leave me be, Emmeline?"

"Because one day I am going to come into this house and find nothing but a corpse lying on the sofa," Emmeline stood calmly. "Or Annabelle. Or Effie. I worry every time I put the key into the lock, wondering *is this the day I'm going to find him dead?*"

George stared at her hatefully, looking more like an island than ever; isolated among the raging sea. "I trusted you with *everything*."

She stood and stepped forward, unflinching. "Then you will trust me to do what is best for you." If George thought he could hurt her with something as trivial as *words*, then Emmeline doubted he really knew her at all.

Michael

It was a fine day for a run. Michael had risen with the sun, eager to get out of the house, to rid himself of the fussing and the pampering he'd experienced in the fortnight since he'd arrived back home—a fortnight of dinner parties and family visits.

Michael knew he was being ungrateful, and that his mother was just happy to have him back in one piece at last, but he felt claustrophobic. The sprawling buildings comprising Scarlett Castle felt more confining than shoddily constructed dugouts ever had. He had taken to squirrelling himself away in the deserted East Wing.

The only time he'd really enjoyed himself had been the family picnic. Mama had assumed a dignified pose with her macrame on a bench, whilst Effie read the latest edition of *Nature*. Michael, Annabelle, Emmeline, and Dora, on the other hand, collected pebbles in the stream and raced hobbyhorses, with Emmeline offering to wave an imaginary flag at the finish line. Unsurprisingly, Michael had tripped over a soaking wet Jake, snapping the hobbyhorse's head off, and lying flat on his back on the grass. It was at that moment that the very muddy Jake decided to jump on his face.

Even the memory of Dora's uncontrollable giggling could not lift his spirits.

Mary had cornered him that night. She must have followed him to the billiards room in the East Wing, for he had barely finished pouring himself a whisky before the thick oak door opened once again. Warm light had spilled into the room, illuminating the billiards table, a wall of bookshelves, and two Monarch stag heads glaring at each other on opposite walls. He had purposefully left himself in darkness, hoping to remain undisturbed.

It had not worked.

Mama considered him, still dressed for dinner in a cerulean evening dress that matched her eyes. Shadows covered her face, but he could tell she was glaring at him like an angry governess. "You should not be sitting whilst I am standing, Michael."

"And yet," Michael spread his arms wide, accompanying the movement with a humourless smile. He took several unconcerned sips of whisky. "I need to be sitting and in arm's reach of alcohol if we are to have this conversation. Emmeline has already apprised me of your wishes."

"Do you recall Theo's wake?"

"Parts of it," he admitted. He'd drunk slightly too much slightly too quickly. Given the circumstances of Theo's death, no one had blamed him. He wondered what they would think if they knew the truth.

She sat on the sofa underneath one of the stag heads and raised a regal eyebrow. "Then you won't complain or back out of your promise."

A promise he had made whilst inebriated and grief-stricken over losing his brother. A promise she should never have requested if she had a heart. A promise he had hoped she'd forgotten in the years since.

He didn't respond.

Mama leant forward, the tip of her nose catching the dull light. "I need to hear you say it, Michael."

"Now that I have demobbed from the army, I promise to take a wife and sire an heir," he recited hatefully. "Like you requested when I was drunk and wracked by guilt over not being able to save Theo. Is that what you wanted to hear?"

"It is." In a single graceful movement that sent swirls of her perfume fluttering through the air, Mary stood and walked towards the door, only looking back at the last moment. "I know you think I'm being cruel, Michael, but I am simply doing what needs to be done for the good of the dukedom. For the good of the estate and, frankly, the good of the family."

He had thought of little else in the week since.

Nearing the end of his run, he crested a steep hill. Scarlett Castle rose proudly in the distance, parting the immaculate gardens lined by majestic cedar trees; his mother was fond of boasting that Capability Brown himself had landscaped the gardens. The original castle dated back to the twelfth century, but had fallen into disrepair by the sixteenth. The current Restoration era additions swallowed the remains thereof. Two enormous crenelated towers dominated the landscape, rising six storeys into the air, soaring high over the surrounding hills and countryside. Michael had spent many an hour savouring the view, feeling like he was on top of the world. The East Wing housed only the vast marble ballroom, the billiards room, and the formal dining room, whilst the West Wing comprised enough parlours, bedrooms, and boudoirs to keep even their meticulous housekeeper, Mrs Evans, on her toes.

Michael had a simple word for it: home.

Bright sunlight flashed off the arched windows as he set off once more, averting his gaze lest the early morning sun blind him.

The wind blew through his hair as he set an energetic pace across the ridge. He would be sore tomorrow, he knew. He had not run like this in years, and his muscles were unused to the movements. Still, he ran on, parting a mass of oak trees as the dawn chorus cheered him on.

This is what I need, he thought, slowing to a jog through the village. Though it was still early, there were people about. He nodded to those he knew by sight. The rag and bone man, ringing his bell to collect old metal, empty glass bottles and jars, even unwanted animal skins. Outside the White Lion Inn, his local pub, Michael saw the ice man making a delivery, slinging a lethal hook into the blocks. On one side of the pub sat Gadd's, a combined greengrocers and post office. Mr Gadd, who had run the greengrocers for many a year, had died only a few months ago, according to his mother. Michael had been sad to hear it; Mr Gadd had always been kind to him, despite him being a little oik in his youth.

Outside Simpkin's Tearoom, Michael greeted the milkman, a jovial Mr Haroldson, who he'd run into at the Somme by chance. A rare slice of sanity in the trenches. He'd been pleased to buy him a drink in a French *estaminet* and reminisce about home before they went their separate ways.

"Through here, Mr Haroldson," came the acrid tone of the tearoom's white-haired owner. "I don't have all—"

Michael braced himself for disapproval. "Good morning, Mrs Simpkin."

Mrs Simpkin, a bad-mannered old crone whose age was approaching triple digits, let out a huff of displeasure through her beaky nose. She rapped her walking stick on the door with a sharpened glance at Mr Haroldson. "In there." As Mr Haroldson dutifully obeyed, carrying a stack of milk churns into the tearoom, Mrs Simpkin pursed her deeply wrinkled lips. "I see you've returned. *Lord Foxcotte*." His title was a curse upon her lips.

"I have." Michael remained a respectable distance away, given he had been running for the better part of an hour. "I haven't had a chance to offer my condolences on the loss of your granddaughter Honoria." It had been years, but Michael knew how his grief for Theo lingered. Losing her only child's only child, though… A cruel error of nature. His own mother would never be the same after Theo's loss. No doubt Mrs Simpkin was the same.

The venom in Mrs Simpkin's expression made him wary. "I need no sympathy from you." The door slammed in his face with a dangerous wobble.

Very well. Michael resumed his running. Mrs Simpkin had hated her brother as well. He wondered if she'd hated his father too? Or his grandfather? The woman was old enough to remember.

There was a rightness to the burn in his chest from physical exertion. Even as a young man, Michael had never cared for bloodsport. Instead, he'd found a passion for rugby at Eton, and a natural talent for rowing at Oxford. He'd won the Boat Race during his time at university, and the Grand Challenge Cup at Henley Royal Regatta—three years in a row.

True, Michael was good at rowing, but his real sporting love was rugby. When they'd relegated him to a wing position in his first year at Eton, he'd been devastated. As one of the biggest lads in his year, he'd wanted to be a prop forward, driving the scrums, in there with the best of them.

The coach had taken one look at his speed and crushed his dream, sending him to the back.

Twenty years later, Michael was quite glad of the coach's decision—for it meant he'd avoided the dreaded cauliflower ear that plagued some of his teammates.

As he neared home, Michael patted down his right thigh; a habit long since ingrained in him over the past few years. It felt strange not to feel the crinkle of the letter he had written to Emmeline hidden there. It was like he was naked without it. If he were to crack his head open or have his heart give out, he would carry his secrets to the grave. On the days when his death felt all but guaranteed, like the first day of the Battle of Albert, the letter had given him peace when nothing surrounded him but slaughter. Even if he died, his last words—written ones, admittedly—would be a true reflection of himself; something he could never voice when he was alive.

Michael stared into the distance, brooding. He hated this. It had been easier when he was in the army, be it Ceylon or France or Belgium or even Ireland. There was always something needing to be done, action needing to be taken, words needing to be said. And Michael had been happy to oblige.

Now that he was back at Scarlett Castle, the pain in his chest was stronger than ever. He clung to it and cursed it at the same time. It was a part of him now, as permanent as any limb.

Sometimes he wondered what his life would be like without it. A few years ago, he would have laughed at the idea of falling in love with someone at first sight. How could such a deep, complex emotion be instant without knowing a single thing about the other person? Love at first sight was a fiction. A tall tale told to hopeful young girls. He had been certain of it. In fact, Michael would have happily bet every penny he owned that there was no such thing.

He would have lost.

But he had found Emmeline.

The first time they'd met, her pale green eyes had hit him like a shell blast, tearing through his chest without a thought for the damage it left behind. He had not realised who she was at first. Michael had torn up the ballroom to reach her, to pull her onto the dancefloor and find out everything about her, this woman who had stolen his heart without so much as a smile. In a single moment, his world had changed. She had become as central to his continued existence as the very air he breathed. Had it changed for her too? Could she feel this connection between them? He had been so eager to reach her that it wasn't until he was six feet away that he realised Theo's arm was around her waist.

His life had never been the same since.

By the time he returned to the castle, it was high noon and his stomach was groaning for food. The smells coming from inside the informal dining room did little to improve its rumblings. Showering and dressing in clean clothes as quickly as possible, he flew back down the Grand Staircase.

Upon entering the deserted dining room, he made for the side table and piled his plate high with shredded chicken positively drowning in chive vinaigrette, in addition to lobster salad. The side table was to allow the family to serve themselves when they pleased. Michael only wished all their meals could be like this, rather than having to go through the rigmarole of formal dinners.

Just as Michael was thinking he was glad for the lack of company, Annabelle and Effie trailed in, chatting amiably about—as far as Michael could tell—dukes. An audible panting told Michael that Jake was not far behind them.

Agitation needled him, his body alight with an irritation he neither wanted nor needed. His sisters were perfectly entitled to join him for luncheon. But something in him wanted to be alone after *so* many years of war. One after another, lost in a sea of soldiers, all waiting for the next attack—be it at the front or in Ireland.

Annabelle stopped in her tracks as she saw him. "And where the chuffing hell have you been all morning? Mama has been unbearable."

Well accustomed to his sister's language, Michael did not bat an eyelid. "Running. I needed the fresh air."

"She's had all the staff up in arms searching the house for you. She even had a telegram sent to Berkeley Square in case you'd gone there—presumably in search of, shall we say, *company*." Her voice hardened, despite the close relationship the two of them had always shared. "You could have left a note."

"Then she'd know where to find me." Michael leant back in his seat, the wood creaking as he did. "Are you not going to scuttle off to report on my whereabouts?"

Spearing him with a look, Annabelle made no move towards the door. Instead, she began filling a plate and joined him at the table. "I'm busy."

"So I see."

Effie sat down on his left, all grace and innocence; her blonde curls fluttering as she flicked them over her shoulder. Effie fed Jake bits of sausage, whilst Michael smiled at his baby sister. "Leave him alone, Annabelle," she chastised. "Michael is entitled to a bit of peace and quiet out on *his* estate."

"I have had years of Mama *hounding* me about marrying again." Annabelle griped, leaning her chair back on two legs. With practised efficiency, she swiped a copy of The Times from the sideboard behind her and let her chair regain its proper footing with a heavy *thud*. "The least he can do is take her off our hands now he's back."

Michael winced. It was bad enough his mother had been on at him since he'd returned; Annabelle did not need to add her voice to the marital cacophony. "It's barely luncheon, Bels. Do show a chap some mercy."

Effie stepped in. "How are you feeling otherwise, Michael? You've been up to Theo's tombstone quite a lot."

His heart pounded as he remembered Passchendaele, the clinging, consuming mud, the feeling of hopelessness as his heart was ripped out of his chest, as he watched one of the people he loved most in the world sink just out of his reach.

It was the moment everything in his life had changed. The moment his life had gone from his career in the army, supporting his unit in the field and his brother at home, to stepping into his brother's shoes as the head of the family.

Until that point, he had effectively been in the reserve, supporting Theo as he led the charge. Michael had never resented his brother's inheritance. It was true; Theo had received the dukedom, the estate, the family fortune. But so too had Theo inherited the responsibilities attached with that good fortune. He had shouldered them as though he'd been born to them—which, of course, he had.

But the change in Michael's own fortunes had not been the biggest change of the day.

He had lost his brother. And his brother had lost his life.

I died in hell. They called it Passchendaele.

"I'm feeling much improved," he croaked over the dinner table. "Why were you talking about dukes?"

Annabelle muttered something under her breath before returning to a normal volume. "Effie wishes to marry one."

His lips twisted in revulsion. They were not straying far from marriage then. The notion of Effie marrying made him feel ill. She was still a child, for heaven's sake. Admittedly, she was turning 18 this year, but in his mind she was little more than a babe in arms, as she had been when their father died.

"I have tried to explain that the notion is ridiculous," Annabelle said sternly, sounding all too much like an overly concerned maiden aunt.

Effie frowned, clearly taking offence. "It is *not* ridiculous. As far as I am concerned, it is eminently achievable. I am the sister of the Duke of Foxcotte." On his next mouthful of sausage, Jake inadvertently sunk his teeth into Effie's fingers. "Ouch! *Gentle,* sweetling."

"Except it isn't *eminently achievable*. The only thing less achievable would be if you wanted to marry royalty." Annabelle jabbed her fork towards Effie as she spoke. "Do you know how many dukes there are in this country?"

Effie stroked Jake's feathery ears. "I suspect you're about to tell me."

"There's thirty-six dukedoms held by thirty dukes. If we're excluding royal dukes, it's thirty-two dukedoms and twenty-seven dukes."

"Is that *it*?" Effie's mouth fell open.

"Yes, *that's it*. Now, do you know how many of them are under fifty?"

"Half, I would hope?"

Michael prodded a bit of lobster in silence, utterly uninterested in the subject of dukes and marriage—especially marriage. His mother had been dropping hints as subtle as shells since the day he'd arrived home. In fact, he wouldn't be surprised if she started importing debs in from London.

As the duke, he had a duty to marry. He knew that. His mother knew that.

It was the realities of marriage that Michael was struggling with. He'd have to bed this hypothetical wife. And when had he last bedded a woman? Michael wracked his brain. It had been before he'd laid eyes on Emmeline. The thought made him miserable. Five years. He'd lived as a monk for five fucking years because his love for one woman had eclipsed his desire for any other.

Suddenly, he wanted to be alone again.

Annabelle carried on, ignorant of his inner turmoil. "Wrong. Dukes only become dukes when their father dies, meaning most of them are well into middle age by the time such a title is bestowed upon them. At present, less than a third of the original twenty-five are under half a century old, judging by their appearances, which brings us to an approximate nine. Of that nine, I estimate two are in their thirties. I wouldn't want to go any older than that."

Michael rankled at the cut-off point. "People don't just become shrivelled husks as soon as they reach forty."

"Well, obviously," Annabelle answered, rolling her eyes as if he was a simpleton. "But for Effie, if she goes any higher then they're old enough to be her father."

The thought was an uncomfortable one. Annabelle had a point. "I don't see why Effie needs to marry at all." Michael stretched his legs out, eager to relieve his already-sore muscles from a hard morning's work. He'd run a scorching hot bath for himself as soon as he finished luncheon.

"No one asked for your opinion, Michael." She turned away from him. "The two that *are* in their thirties." Annabelle poked a lobster-laden fork at Effie. Jake's dark eyes followed it with rapt interest. "The issue is quite simple, really. One is your brother. The other is a bastard. And so your search for dukes dies before it begins. Your best bet is to marry a duke's heir. Their fathers will die eventually."

"What do you mean about the younger duke being a *you-know*? How can he have inherited the title?" Effie asked.

"He's not literally a bastard…" Bels quirked her lips with a hard glint in her eye. "Just figuratively."

Effie hesitated, her fingers dancing along Jake's soft fur. "How do you know?"

Click here to read Surrendering to the Duke on Kindle Unlimited!

About the Author

Stevie Sparks is a British author and long-time copy editor. She suffers from a terrible medical condition that has left her incapable of reading books without smut. She can be found on Goodreads, TikTok, Instagram, Facebook, and Twitter.

Printed in Great Britain
by Amazon